Katie MacAlister

Suffragette
in the City

AUTHOR'S NOTE

This book has its origins in the very first novel I wrote ten years ago, and resembles its original form only in the sense that the basic storyline is the same. A few years after it was written, I revised it into its current form, and being busy with meeting what seemed like a gazillion deadlines, promptly forgot about it. Thus, there are parts that may seem very familiar to those folks who read the original book.

Although I have gone on to write more than thirty other novels since that first book, I have held it back from publication because I felt it didn't quite have the same tone as my other historical romances.

Since many of my readers have been clamoring for a new historical—but I'm still trying to squeeze one into my publishing schedule—I've decided to release this as a special edition for a limited amount of time.

For more information about this and other books, feel free to visit my website at www.katiemacalister.com

~Katie MacAlister

CHAPTER ONE

"Votes for women!" Above the jeering of the crowd, a suffragette waved her banner, her voice piercing the air high over the rumble of motorcars and rattle of carriages. "Support the cause! Votes for women!"

In one of those odd moments of silence that sometimes occur in a crowd, peace descended along my little stretch of the fence just long enough for the following to be heard with crystal clarity: "Bloody, buggery hell!"

Several heads swiveled in my direction. The suffragette nearest me stared, her eyes wide in shock. The steady stream of people passing us seemed to freeze for several seconds, the faces of the men and women headed inside the magnificent building behind me all reflecting the same astonishment.

There was nothing else to do. I turned and glared into the bushes, saying loudly, "Merciful heavens! What is the world coming to when people hide in shrubberies and yell out profanities?"

The suffragette looked suspicious as the people once again moved past.

"Is there a problem, sister?" she asked when I cleared my throat and shook the chain that was giving me so much grief.

"Problem? Me? Whatever gives you that idea?"

She pursed her lips and gestured to her right. All along the massive, wrought iron fence that bounded the grounds of Wentworth House, women were arranged with their backs pressed firmly against the cold metal railing, chains holding them into place.

"It's just my chain," I told my neighbor, shaking it at her. "It's defective."

"Your chain is *defective*?"

"Yes. It refuses to cooperate, and if there's anything I demand in a chain, it's cooperation. I don't suppose you have an extra one?"

5

She gave me a look that by rights should have been accompanied by a thick clout upside the head. As it was I took a step or two back from her, relieved to see that her chain bound her firmly to the fence. "Chains are not defective. Why did you volunteer for this protest if you have no intention of participating fully?"

I ignored the rumbles of a particularly deep-voiced old gentlemen as he passed by, giving my chain a firm shake and making another attempt to wind it through the fence. "I am wholly devoted to the cause. But I fail to see how I am expected to make a stand when the equipment I am given simply will not function."

"Are there problems?" One of the Women's Suffrage Union officers moved down along the line, pausing when she got to me at the end of the fence.

"Yes, there are problems," I muttered, catching my fingers painfully on the shrub that poked through the railing.

"She *claims* her chain is defective," my tattle-tale neighbor said with irritating smugness.

I gave her a stern look. She returned it with narrowed eyes.

"Defective?" the officer asked, looking puzzled. "In what way?"

"It won't go through the fence," I explained. "I think there's something wrong with it."

"Or something wrong with you," my neighbor murmured. Beyond her, two women giggled.

I glared over her head to them. They quickly averted their gazes and stared out defiantly at the passing crowd.

"Well...do the best you can," the officer said, looking a bit peevish. I knew just how she felt. "We were promised coverage by the newspapers tonight, and it is vital that we present a unified front."

"I think *someone* simply doesn't wish to ruin her fancy gown," my neighbor commented in a waspish voice.

"What you want to be wearing something like that to a protest?" the woman beyond her asked, craning her head to look at me.

Irritated, I jerked my coat closed, cursing the fact that I had forgotten to have Annie repair the buttons I'd torn off earlier while practicing chaining myself to a tree in the park. "I really don't see that my choice of garment has anything to do with my devotion to the cause. One might just as well ask why she—" I pointed to my irksome neighbor. "—feels the need to cause dissention in the ranks."

"Dissention! Me? You...you..."

I smiled and took a step toward her, just out of her reach. "A unified front, remember?"

She sputtered some words that were unknown to me, and I made a mental note to add them to my repertoire of oaths and profanities before taking my chain once again with a firm hand.

"You will behave," I told it as I jabbed it through the fence, ignoring the pain of the shrub's branches as it poked into my flesh.

"Ignore the crowds, sisters, and stand tall!" the officer cried as she faced the line of women. "Remember, you are fighting for a glorious cause!"

"It'll all be for naught if we don't show solidarity," the woman next to me said with a glint in her eyes that I felt was most unwarranted.

The heads of women all down the fence turned to look at me.

"I am doing the best I can! But how I am expected to work with a defective chain is beyond me—" A shove at my back had me spinning around to confront my assailant. "Sir!"

"I'd apologize for bumping into you if you were a decent woman, but it's clear that you're not." The rotund, top-hatted gentleman who had plowed into me scornfully considered the women on the fence before returning his attention to me. "Simply appalling! Such displays are most unwomanly! Ought to be stopped! Interfering besoms!"

I jerked my coat closed again. "You leave my bosom out of this!"

The man snorted and clutched the arm of a thin, pinched-faced woman, escorting her down the sidewalk to the gate. Due to the crush of carriages and motor cars inside the short drive, many people had opted to disembark from their vehicles down the block, and walk the rest of the way in to the charity ball. The change from light drizzle to rain had lessened their numbers, but a few brave souls ventured forth bearing large, glistening black umbrellas.

"Oh, this is ridiculous," I snapped, so frustrated I could scream. "I'll just stand here and pretend I'm chained to the fence."

"I knew you would give up. You're afraid of getting your pretty frock dirty."

"If you keep using that nasty tone of voice, you'll be stuck with it forever," I answered with a sniff. "I assure you that it would take a lot more than a little rain to disconcert me. I do not frighten easily. I am all steadiness in the face of mice. I can watch animals copulate in the fields without the slightest hint of a blush. In fact, I find it all rather fascinating, and just as soon as I get myself set up properly, I shall emulate the animals and take a lover."

The woman's jaw sagged slightly.

"Yes," I said, nodding, pleased that my dashing audacity had left her speechless. "I am a New Woman, you see. Such things do not bother me in the least. Any day now I will take up smoking cigarettes."

A motorcar hooted its annoyance at a stoppage in traffic, part of the steady stream of carriages and automobiles stopped outside of the gates to Wentworth House. Shiny dark umbrellas bobbed by, their everyday appearance in sharp contrast to the finery displayed below them. Although the night was dark and damp, the parade of ladies in brilliant colors, flashing jewels, and exotic perfumes was almost overwhelming to the senses. Midnight blues, pigeon's blood reds, and greens the color of the sea passed by. By contrast, our group was a somber gathering; I was clad in the sole exception to the dark dresses the suffrage workers wore. Each member had a swath of white across her bosom proclaiming *Votes For Women*. Pride filled me as I read the sashes. Pride that quickly crumbled to dust as I stared down at my sash-less coat.

"Damn. I forgot to get a sash. I don't suppose…"

"No!" my neighbor snarled as I looked at hers.

"Charity begins at home," I reminded her, but to no avail. "Fine. You keep your sash; I'll do my part regardless."

"You're not even chained," my unpleasant neighbor scoffed. "You have no sash, and you aren't chained. No one will know you're with us. Why don't you just go home?"

I took a deep, calming breath. "If appearances are all that concern you, perhaps I will simply drape the chain over one shoulder..."

"There. This is the best I can do. How does it look?" I turned to my testy neighbor, one cold, damp length of chain hanging over my shoulder, wrapped around to the opposite hip, hopefully giving the appearance of binding me to the fence.

It was another voice that answered.

"You should be ashamed of yourself!" A very bulky shape rose up before me, her spiteful face thrust into mine. "Don't you have any humility? What would your parents think of you now, Cassandra Jane Whitney? Making a fool of yourself in public!"

I identified the face as belonging to Eloise McGregor, one of my late mother's oldest friends. She grabbed my arm and pulled me down the street a few yards.

"Eloise, what a surprise to see you. I'm afraid I'm a bit busy at the moment. Perhaps we can talk later?"

She jerked me down another few yards, ignoring my polite hint, puffing obnoxious peppermint-scented breath in my face as she blocked the entire sidewalk in order to chastise me. "What can you be thinking, girl? Have you no shame? No dignity? How can you stand there like a common trollop and make such a spectacle of yourself?"

A hasty glance down the fence confirmed my fear that the demonstration was proceeding without me. My neighbor chanted "Votes for women!" with a particularly obnoxious vigor, accompanied by frequent triumphant glances sent my way.

I ground my teeth.

"Your mother would be disgraced to see you here, as would all your family," Eloise continued, snatching my chain off my shoulder and throwing it to the ground before taking my arm again.

I winched at the strength of her grip. "Such folly! Such insolence! I shall be sure to inform your sister of your unwomanly conduct when she returns."

"Damnation! You're bruising me!"

"Profanity! Blasphemer!" Eloise's voice carried extremely well over the noise of the crowd. A number of heads turned our way in what appeared to be hopeful interest. "Your presence here just goes to show how low into depravity you have sunk."

Over her shoulder I could see a small clutch of people. As she berated me, a tall man with a pale woman on his arm scowled and tried to get Eloise's attention, asking to pass. Dismay filled his companion's face as she glanced at the stream of muddy water that flowed down the nearest edge of the pavement. Although the rain had slowed again, the gutters gurgled with the recent downfall.

Eloise ignored the man and continued to harangue me. "You always were a headstrong, obstinate girl. Obstinate and bad tempered! You'll end up no better than you should, if you don't take care. When I think of the pain your sainted mother went through. . . ."

I ignored Eloise's rants and looked down the fence to where my sisters in suffrage attracted considerable attention, including that of the beat constable who was pleading with them to release themselves. The crowd shouted suggestions to the constable, many of them offering in unpleasant terms to help "take care of the troublemakers."

"Madam, would you allow us to pass?"

". . . let alone the fact that you never gave her a moment's comfort. . . ."

"People wish to pass, Eloise. You really should go now."

A deep male voice rose over that of the surrounding cacophony. "You are blocking the pavement, madam. Please allow us by."

"You may think nothing of breaking your mother's heart, but I will not fail her, my dearest friend! You will come with me at once." She pulled hard on my arm, jerking me forward.

"I will not! Go away!" I struggled back to the fence. "I may not be chained, but by god, I will do my duty!"

Another policeman arrived, his whistle piercing the discord.

"Madam, please let us by!" the deep voice roared over the growing clamor. I turned my head just enough to witness the tall man behind Eloise try gently to move her aside. She tightened her grip on my arm in response, her fingers digging painfully into my flesh.

"As will I do my duty and save you from the depths of degradation with which you are so intent upon besmirching yourself!" She pulled me toward her.

I clutched the fence in desperation.

"Votes for women! Votes for women!" chanted the suffragettes.

More constables arrived, their whistles shrill over the calls of the crowd.

". . . sinful and degraded. . . ."

"We wish to pass, blast you!"

"This is ridiculous—please go away!" I yelled at Eloise. "Leave me be!"

"...willful and proud..."

"This is a public street, madam! I insist you allow us to pass!"

Snarling to myself in aggravation, I used both hands to grip the fence.

". . . nothing but grief, always thinking of yourself and never of your poor mother. . . ."

The bystanders were frenzied now, keyed up by the arrival of several policemen on horseback. To the left, a small cluster of partygoers was backed up, still blocked by Eloise, loudly expressing their desire to move by us. To the right, the demonstrators, all successfully chained to the fence save me, chanted and sang in unison.

"I will not let you ruin my demonstration!" I shouted over the noise to Eloise, just as she heaved her ample bulk and succeeded in prying me off the fence. At the same moment, the man behind her gave her a shove forward, sending me hurtling towards him, rather than her.

The force of my not-insubstantial weight thrown off balance and directly onto him resulted in our crashing to the pavement in an awkward display of petticoats, umbrellas, chain, and limbs.

CHAPTER TWO

I lay stunned for a moment, staring stupidly down into the diamond studs in his shirt. Before I could think to move, hands lifted me to my feet.

"Good heavens," I gasped as soon as I could gather my breath, "I do apologize! Eloise—my mother's friend—she was much stronger than I imagined. Are you injured?"

The man swore into his chest as he bent down to assess the damage. He was muddied and wet down the left side, and, I feared, extremely damp on the back. His top hat had been ruined, and his white gloves were black with mud. Although my coat was buttonless, its heavy material, and the fact that I fell on top of the gentleman, left me relatively unaffected by the mishap.

"Just you wait and see, Cassandra Whitney!" Eloise screeched as she was carried forward by the momentum of the crowd. "You'll come to a bad end!"

Two ladies and a short, bald gentleman had stopped near us, inquiring anxiously as to the muddied man's state. The pale woman handed me a jeweled comb that had flown from my hair.

"Please forgive me," I stammered, ignoring the man's frown to dab at him ineffectually with my handkerchief. "I am mortified. Eloise is clearly a danger to the public. Let me help clean you off. I am very capable in the removal of mud, having lived in the country all my life. If we just wipe it off carefully like so—"

I patted a spot of dirt, but pulled away my handkerchief only to find I had left a long diagonal smear of mud across the snowy white expanse of his shirt front.

"Oh, dear."

He looked at his chest in disbelief.

The bald man in formal apparel leaned forward and muttered to my unfortunate victim, then turned to me and said in a loud, piercing voice, "Young woman, you have done quite enough damage for the night with your savage excuse for manners. Kindly stand away from my brother and allow us to pass."

A sudden swelling of enthusiastic noise washed over us. The short man's eyes widened at the vocal output of the protesters.

"Good Gad!" he barked. "Why aren't the police arresting those anarchists? What has this country come to when such displays are tolerated? Those harlots should be horsewhipped!"

"This is very embarrassing," I murmured as I gazed at the mud on the tall man's chest. "I don't make it a habit of flinging myself on gentlemen, I can assure you, and am mortified despite the fact...erm...never mind."

"Despite what?" he asked.

"It's not important. I do apologize."

"I accept your apology. What is not important?"

He had amber eyes, very disconcerting amber eyes. So disconcerting, I spoke without thinking. "It's just that I should take such things as falling on a strange man in stride. Naturally, common good manners make me regret the damage to your clothing, but for the rest...well, I am a New Woman, you see. Falling on men is nothing to us. In fact, I am shortly to take a lover, and smoke cigarettes."

His lips twitched. "At the same time?"

"Of course not. That would be unhygienic." I paused, considering what he suggested. "I don't believe it would be possible, either, but that really is neither here nor there."

"No, it isn't. Are you all right?"

As I nodded, a thin woman in a dress that was a bilious shade of green brushed his arm and said, "Come, Griffin, we're late. You can repair the damage this creature did to you inside." She paused to toss a hateful stare at me before taking the arm of the sputtering bald man, the pair of them moving down the sidewalk with stately arrogance.

The tall man named Griffin muttered a few words to the other woman, who quickly followed the first pair.

"Despite my New Womanhood, I feel terrible. I wish I could make Eloise apologize as well, but as you may have noticed, she's quite deranged."

He gazed at me for a moment then unexpectedly tipped his head back and laughed. "Don't look so distressed. I didn't particularly wish to attend this ball. In fact, I'm grateful to you for offering me an excuse to avoid it, although," he looked at his shirt front ruefully, "I wish you could have managed it in some other fashion."

I dabbed unhappily at the mud on his arm, removing a wet leaf from his lapel. "I fear your companions are less understanding. I can't blame them for being angry at the unfortunate accident."

He turned and waved at someone behind him. "My brother and his wife find these functions enjoyable; I do not."

"But the lady with you, surely—" I indicated the distant figures of his party and covertly picked off a small snail making its way up his shoulder when he glanced the other way.

"My sister. She will have no difficulty enjoying herself without me."

He handed me the bag and umbrella that had been knocked from my hands earlier. Looking at it rather curiously, he picked up the chain in his ungloved hand. As I reached out to take it, a fawn-colored motor car pulled up alongside him. The driver leaped out and opened the door.

"Will you be going inside," Griffin nodded toward the ball, "or can I offer you a ride somewhere else?"

I looked right to where street children, passing citizens, partygoers, and now a sizable number of constables surrounded the women protestors. The noise was almost deafening. My heart sank as I nodded at the nearest suffragette. "I am with them. At least, I was supposed to be with them. I have a defective chain, however."

His eyebrows rose.

"Why does everyone act like it's impossible for a chain to cease working?" I told his eyebrows. "I defy you to bind yourself to the rail using that chain."

The eyebrows lowered again, and once more, the corners of his mouth twitched. It had the unfortunate result of making me stare at his mouth, an act that had me thinking of the animals in the field, and my determination to take a lover.

"I see. If it's defective, then you won't be wanting it back." He held up the chain, making no move to return it to me.

"Not particularly. I will admit that at this moment, I feel nothing but animosity for the horrid thing." Why was his mouth holding such fascination for me? Was he married? Did he like tall women of overly abundant upper quarters, and red hair?

"A just feeling, I suspect." A frown creased his forehead as he considered me, his eyes narrowing into two amber slits as they raked me from head to foot. "Why would a woman like yourself want to be a part of such a spectacle?"

A sudden jarring note interrupted the pleasant contemplation of what his bare derriere might look like. I frowned in turn. "Spectacle?"

"Spectacle," he said firmly. "A display of bad behavior."

"I know what the word means!"

"Surely a woman like you should be inside waltzing with a suitor rather than chaining yourself to a fence in a manner that does nothing but amuse the general population."

Those fascinating amber eyes flashed in the night, but they were no match for mine. My tendency to plumpness I inherited from my mother, my temper from my father. Anger and my chin rose in response to his arrogant and condescending attitude. "You are very opinionated on the subject for someone who does not have a uterus!"

Surprise flickered in his eyes. "What the hell does that have to do with anything?"

"You are a man," I pointed out, waving toward his groin. I had the worst urge to walk around behind him to see if his wet trousers were plastered to his rear parts, but managed to squelch that desire and focus on what was important. "You do not understand at all what it is to be a woman."

"I assure you, madam, that one does not need a uterus to think," he retorted.

"No, but it helps," I answered, smiling a little to myself as the barb drove home. "As for your accusation, I do not consider the pursuit of emancipation a spectacle. Quite the contrary! I consider it my Christian duty to chain myself to this fence in order to strike a blow for the rights of women everywhere. And I would do so if I wasn't cursed with a chain that was clearly forged in hell."

He eyed my low décolletage speculatively. "You certainly are dressed for the event."

"Why is everyone obsessed with my gown? I had a dinner engagement! I could hardly dress in something more suited for gardening!" I clutched my button-less coat tight across my bosom.

"Dinner with one of your lovers?"

"I don't have any yet, not that it is any of your business. My dinner engagement was with a man I was considering for the position, but he dribbled soup, and one cannot have a lover who dribbles soup."

He stared at my breasts, now hidden beneath my coat. "Give the amount of cleavage you were showing, I'm surprised soup is all he dribbled."

"My dress is the very latest fashion!" I snapped. "And it is not any concern of yours."

"Except when I find it lying on top of me in the mud," he said quickly, suddenly grinning.

My legs felt suddenly wobbly under the influence of that grin. I stiffened them. "I have apologized for the unfortunate accident. If you are not gracious enough to accept that apology, perhaps you will allow me to get on with my business."

"By all means. Would you like me to round up a few men so you might consider them for the position?"

"I do not need your help to find a lover!"

Given the cacophony of sound generated by the demonstration to my right, I had felt it necessary to raise my voice to a volume at which I could be heard without undue strain, but once again, a strange hush fell over the crowd, creating the perfect setting for my words to echo off the buildings that lined the street. For the third time that night, heads swiveled in unison to look in my direction.

Griffin leaned back against his motor and folded his arms across his chest. "Temper, Cassandra Whitney. First swearing and now bellowing like a stevedore—you wouldn't want people to think that your disposition is as fiery as your hair."

Momentarily confused by his use of my name, I remembered Eloise's mean, and regrettably public, comments earlier. I was in the middle of formulating an exceedingly clever and biting retort when a great cheer from the crowd distracted me. Several police vans had arrived with reinforcements. A large number of constables emerged and swarmed along the protest line, arguing with the bound women and trying to forcibly remove the chains. "Bloody hell!"

"I *beg* your pardon?"

I glared at the irritating man opposite me. He was laughing at me, his eyes all but mocking me. "My first demonstration for the rights of women, and I am going to miss everything!"

"And what a tragedy that would be."

"You who do not have uteruses…uteri…collectively more than one uterus may think so, but I assure you that we brave New Women will win out the day!" I snatched the chain from his hand and ran back to the fence, muttering under my breath that I would not allow myself to be distracted by such an infuriating, if incredibly charismatic, and very well built man.

"Do you need help with your defective chain?" his bemused voice followed me. "I would be happy to assist if you find you can't manage such a highly technical feat by yourself."

A visit to the dentist was going to be in order if I continued to grind my teeth as I had wont to do several times that evening. "I do not need your help. I think you will find that women can do most anything without the assistance of a man."

"Surely not everything," he drawled. "Else you would have no need for a lover."

I struggled for a few minutes with the uncooperative chain, then flung it down in a pique. Biting back an oath, I glared again at Griffin. Still smiling, he politely tipped his muddied hat, and got into the motor car.

"Of all the insolent, infuriating, rude—" I grumbled to myself, watching his motor drive off. "And I didn't even get a good look at his derriere. Damn."

Screams, jeers, yells, and a variety of oaths washed out into the damp night as several newly arrived constables pushed past me and began yanking at the nearby protesters, forcibly dragging my sisters in suffrage from their positions.

I didn't hesitate in the least in making my presence known.

"Stop that immediately," I yelled over the noise, hitting the nearest constable on the head with my umbrella as he struggled with my unpleasant neighbor. "She may be annoying, but she is devoted to the cause. Leave her alone!"

Without looking, he shoved me back into the gathering crowd, which closed tightly around me. Crushed by the mass of people surrounding me, I was unable to move forward as the constable tried to squeeze the suffragette out of the chains that bound her.

Hastily I apologized for my rudeness to the gentleman upon whose toes I had inadvertently trod, and found myself gently but persistently pushed to the back of the crowd. "No, you don't understand, I'm with them! Please allow me forward, I am one of them."

Struggling, I tried to force my way to the front of the sizable group with every intention of doing what I could to help the women, but I was impeded from behind, and just then the crowd swelled backwards. I was flung up against a man behind me. I righted myself with an apology.

"No harm done, miss." A gold tooth winked as he gave me an amiable smile, then he touched his bowler and melted into the crowd.

A horrible noise rent the air. The crowd's mood had changed abruptly from that content with simple jeers and verbal abuses, to an active participation in removing the women from their chains. Horror crawled up my spine two constables held my recent neighbor while a third man cut off the chains with a heavy bolt cutter. As the woman was freed, the constables seized her and dragged her off to the Black Mariah, much to the delight of the crowd. Cheers rose over the noise as one by one, the constables swarmed the struggling women, cutting them from the fence.

"Damnation!" I swore again, utterly defeated. My chain hung limply from the fence, abandoned and ignored as the last of the protesters were bundled into the Black Marias. I had failed my sisters in suffrage, failed my cause, and failed myself.

The police quickly disbanded the crowd of bystanders, waved off the urchins, and broke up the groups of onlookers. In a short amount of time there were no protesters left other than me. I stood alone, disheveled and damp on a wet, empty pavement. A sudden gust of wind caused an object to flutter across my feet. I reached down to pick up a torn *Votes For Women* sash and stared at it.

"Maybe Eloise is right. What am I doing here?" I asked the sash. "Why did I think I could help?"

I could almost hear my father's voice sneering at me. What gentleman would want me, with my runaway tongue, my odd interests, and an wholly unconventional nature? My actions this evening had left me open to contempt and ridicule of my friends and family—worse than that, the experience was all for nothing. I had failed to complete my one assigned task, fulfilling my father's dying curse.

"No. I will not fail this," I swore to myself, then raised my fist and shook it at the ghost of my father. "I will not let you win! I have chosen my path, and I will see it out come what may! Think about that while you roast in hell for an eternity!"

There was no answer on the wind but a sudden chill that left me shivering. I looked about for a hansom cab, but none were in sight. Mentally shrugging my shoulders, I gathered up my accessories, chain included, and made my way home.

CHAPTER THREE

"Women's Suffrage Union Members Arrested. Several women were arrested last evening for causing an obstruction outside Wentworth House in Holland Park, where Their Royal Highnesses, the Prince and Princess of Wales, attended the annual charity Hospital Ball," Freddy read aloud from a fainting couch, his booted feet resting carelessly on several lovely tapestry pillows. The mauve shawl draped across one end would no doubt be irrevocably stained with his hair oil. "Good Lord, Cassandra, don't tell me you were mixed up with that crowd?"

"Freddy, read to yourself. Aunt Caroline is not interested." I turned back to my aunt and accepted the cup she held out. "I hope you don't mind Emma taking tea with us. She's been such a dear friend to me, but I don't think she knows a great many people in town."

"I don't mind you bringing her at all," my aunt replied in her usual dulcet tones. A faint frown wrinkled her brow. "However, I feel that I owe it to your dear mama to mention...well, you know."

I frowned over the cup of tea. "No, I don't know."

"It says here that several women were fined half a guinea for assaulting police officers," Freddy continued. "Dearest cousin, I must protest. I understand your desire to take part in this ridiculous cause—"

My gaze narrowed upon him.

"—at what is no doubt a very worthy cause, but surely you can appreciate that those of us who love you are concerned when the organization you have bound yourself to is involved in such escapades."

I looked away from Freddy's pale blue eyes to consider my aunt, avoiding, as best I could, the result of her latest redecorating scheme. Deep mauve walls filled the room with a heated glow, while fine lace hung at the windows, shaded on either side by heavy wine-colored draperies. It was an altogether ghastly combination.

"It is so difficult to explain," Caroline said faintly, glancing toward the door. Emma, my oldest friend, had excused herself to use the water closet. "You do know, of course, that she has...leanings."

"Leanings? What do you mean?"

She glanced toward Freddy, who was watching us over the top of the newspaper. He choked and quickly hid behind it.

"Leanings," Caroline repeated, her hand making a vague gesture that confused me even more. She appeared to think for a moment before saying, "You have heard of Sappho, have you not?"

I searched the rather dusty hallways of my memory. "A poet? A woman poet? Greek, I think?"

"Yes, she was, amongst other things, a poet." Caroline smiled gently at me. "Your friend is a follower, I believe."

"Oh, I have no doubt about that," I said, sitting back. At last it had dawned on me what Caroline was so carefully alluding to. "You need not fear that I am offended by that."

"You're not?" Her eyebrows rose a smidgen.

"No, not in the least."

"You're not...like her, are you?" Freddy asked, still peering over the newspaper.

"You know full well I'm not," I answered.

His eyes widened, and I could swear he blushed as he stammered a protestation to our aunt. "I know nothing of the sort!"

"Yes, you do. I've never been to university, while Emma spent several years there. Frankly, given Father's opinion on education for women, I'm lucky I can read and write. I will never be a great scholar as she is."

"Who is a great scholar?" the woman in question asked as she reentered the room and accepted a cup of tea.

"You are," I answered.

Emma Debenham, whom I had known for some twenty years, looked surprised by the word, but made no comment.

"I was explaining that you are my oldest friend," I added.

"It has been many a year since I saw the little red-headed girl peeping out at me from behind the hedgerow. I used to see Cassandra when I walked to the village," she told my aunt.

"Emma was the only one who defied Father's order that no one speak to me," I said, a lump in my throat when I thought of all she had gone through to befriend me. "I believed that earned her more than one whipping from her father."

She shrugged. "I was forever getting into trouble because of one interest or another. I wasn't about to let your despotic father rule my life, as well. Besides," she touched my hair with a gentle hand. "I've always had a weakness for redheads. There's no way I could resist you."

Freddy choked on the sip of tea he'd taken, spewing it all over the newspaper.

"Freddy, really!" I gave him a stern look. "If you're going to behave like an animal, you may take your tea outside!"

He coughed in an attempt to get the tea out of his lungs, glaring first at me, then at Emma.

"I just wish I could convince you to stay with me while you're in London, Emma."

"You know how much I appreciate that offer, but I am quite comfortable in my rooms, I assure you."

"I've sworn that I wouldn't interfere in your studies. Emma has recently taken up sketching," I told my aunt. "Right now she's focusing on the human form."

"Female?" Freddy asked in a peculiar choked voice.

"Yes," I said, frowning at him. "She's done some lovely drawings. I only hope that one day, she'll find me worthy to be a subject."

Caroline, still not moving, looked at Emma.

Emma beamed me. "Perhaps some day. I'm still...er...experimenting. With my style, that is."

I nodded. My father had felt art was too godless a subject to be taught to his daughters, so I contented myself to admiring those who had skills in that area.

"It's been some weeks since you've been here," Caroline said, clearly feeling a change of conversation was needed. "I've redecorated."

"Yes, indeed you have!" I caught Emma's eye, and had to dab at my lips with a napkin to keep from giggling.

Her shoulders shook as she, too, held in her laughter.

"I can't say when I've seen mauve and wine put to such an interesting use," I added.

"And the puce touches? Do they soothe your eye?" my aunt asked.

Puce, wine, and mauve, the unholy trinity of colors. I smiled. "So much so that I hesitate to look at them for very long, lest my eyes be soothed into a stupor. Now, tell me, how was Boston? Did Uncle Henry enjoy the visit to his brother?"

Caroline's pale blue eyes—almost identical to Freddy's—sparkled with obvious amusement. "It was a lovely visit, Cassandra. Christmas was a most enjoyable holiday, and Henry's family was very. . ." She paused, considering her words. ". . . interesting. Americans always are, I find. While we were in Boston, we met a fascinating young man. I'm sure he would—"

I raised my hand in warning. "Although I appreciate your motives, I am not in the least bit interested in hearing about the latest in a regrettably long line of men you have selected to share my life."

"Do I have any say in this matter?" Freddy asked, peering over the sodden, tea-splattered newspaper.

"No," we both told him.

"But my dear," Caroline continued on, "Mr. Teller has a delightful character—"

"I'm sure he does," I said amiably. "But you fail to take into consideration *my* character. And as you are married to the only man who combines those qualities of intelligence, wit, and strength of mind which make a man superior, I shall have to bear the lack of a husband as best I can."

"I have intelligence, wit, and strength of mind, and I *have* proposed, dearest. Several times. Seven, to be exact."

"Nine in the last six weeks," I told Freddy, softening the words with a smile. "And I appreciate your desire to save me from the horrors of spinsterhood, but you know perfectly well we wouldn't suit. Besides, there is that other matter to which I alluded last week."

His gaze moved to Emma, rife with speculation. "Not...er..."

I sighed, not wanting to upset my aunt, but feeling the need to take charge of my life. "What I am about to say will shock you."

"Do you think so, dear? How fascinating." She, too, glanced at Emma, who gave her a little shake of the head. "Whatever can this shocking subject be?"

"My future with regards to men." I cleared my throat and sat up a bit straighter. "Since the long overdue death of my father, I have become a New Woman."

"Indeed. Although I am not sure it is kind to refer to your father's death as overdue, I would agree that I would have been much easier in my mind about you had Henry and I been able to persuade him to let us have you."

"That's all in the past," I said, waving away a lifetime of abuse and torment, both mental and physical. "What matters now is the present, and as a New Woman, I have taken a stand on several causes. One of which Freddy alluded to in the newspaper article. The other is my attitude toward men."

"What attitude would that be?" Caroline asked.

Emma smiled into her cup.

"I will, at some point in my life, probably twenty or thirty years from now, marry. Until then—" I took another deep breath. "I shall take a lover."

Silence filled the overstuffed, overheated room.

"Dearest, might I offer myself—"

"No," I said quickly, keeping my eyes on my aunt. To my surprise, she didn't look shocked or scandalized, or even unduly impressed. She merely hummed a little song to herself and sipped her tea.

"You're not angry with me, are you?" I couldn't help but ask.

"Why would I be angry? Cassandra, my dear, you are thirty years old."

"Twenty-nine!" I said quickly. "Only twenty-nine!"

"That is certainly old enough to know what you want. If you wish to flaunt convention, then far be it from me to stop you."

"Oh." I glanced at Emma. She winked. "I see. Well...good. I am much relieved. I was concerned that my decision to take charge of my life and send it in a new direction would cause you some concern."

"No," she said, lifting the tea pot. "None at all."

"Good." I felt deflated for some absurd reason.

Caroline waved towards Freddy's paper. "Tell me more about your involvement with this organization."

"Yes, do, dearest," Freddy pushed the paper aside and got to his feet. "Perhaps Caroline can talk some sense into you."

I gave him a mean look.

"Don't ruffle your adorable feathers at me," Freddy said as he strolled over to me to press a kiss to the back of my hand. "I mean no criticism of the suffrage movement on the whole, but I can and will express concern about the welfare of a dearly beloved cousin who involves herself with a group of female roughnecks and hooligans."

"Odious man," I said fondly, pulling my hand from his. "The members of the Women's Suffrage Union are neither roughnecks nor hooligans."

"No?" Freddy accepted another cup of tea and several almond biscuits. "I've heard that the organization is just bursting with women who want to wear trousers, smoke pipes, and run the government. I am told it is common knowledge they have failed in all the feminine arts, and live unnatural and disappointed lives."

Emma made a little noise of distress.

"No insult intended, I'm sure," Freddy said quickly.

"Poppycock," I said sharply, frowning at my cousin. "That will teach you to listen to such ill-informed sources of information. There is nothing at all unnatural about wearing trousers, although we prefer to call them bloomers. They are most healthful and hygienic when bicycling. I have a pair myself, although I haven't had the opportunity to wear them, so I suppose you could say I'm disappointed in that sense, but that is not what you mean."

"No," Freddy answered, stuffing a biscuit into his mouth. "That's not at all what I mean."

"You must admit that there does seem to be a certain amount of danger involved," Caroline said, sending an oddly reproachful glance at Freddy. "If the newspaper is at all accurate, each instance of this group's demonstration has ended in some form of violence. I question the wisdom of involvement in that sort of protest."

"There has been violence only because people fear what the Union represents."

"But it *is* dangerous," Freddy said, agreeing with Caroline.

The memory of the violent slurs and attacks against the suffragettes rose with stark clarity in my mind. "No more so than any other cause I might involve myself in, so about this let us please agree to differ."

Caroline continued to look worried. Emma gave me a small, supportive smile.

"With regards to your original question, Aunt Caroline, the Union has pledged itself to obtain the right for women to vote. That is their sole purpose, and one to which I have wholly devoted myself."

Freddy sat in a puce-accessorized, wine-colored chair and waved at the still soggy newspaper with an almond biscuit. "Suffragettes, that's what they're calling you, dearest one. Suffragettes! I ask you, how can any man take seriously a woman who calls herself a suffragette? You simply must urge your group to come up with a less humorous label."

Caroline frowned and shook her head at Freddy before asking me, "And how do they intend to achieve that noble goal?"

"Through non-violent protest and every constitutional means. Our plan is to attract attention to the cause via protests, meetings, and parades."

"But demonstrating in public, my dear. Is it prudent?"

"You don't mind at all the fact that I intend to take a lover, but you object to me participating in a support parade?" I asked in surprise.

"One can be discreet with a lover," she said, shocking me to the very tips of my toes. She and Henry had always seemed so devoted that I couldn't help but wonder if she was speaking from experience. "The same cannot be said of marching about with signs, and chaining yourself to a railing."

"I don't believe Cassandra is looking for attention, if that is what concerns you," Emma said in my defense. "I stopped by briefly to see her last night, before the demonstration had taken place, and she had chosen a spot furthest from those who organized the event, no doubt in due respect for the finer feelings of her relatives."

That, or I was simply late from my dinner out with the soup dribbler. I cleared my throat and nodded, trying to look considerate of her fine feelings.

"Naturally, we respect and appreciate that. But I worry that there may come a time when you will be absorbed, if you will, by the danger, and not be able to escape it."

"That is what I have been telling her, Aunt. I have pleaded with her to take heed of my warnings, but you see before you a man whose every word is discounted and ignored." Freddy slipped from the chair to his knees before me, taking my hand in his. "Beloved one, you know how I feel about you—"

"Oh Freddy, for heaven's sake, not again!" I struggled to pull my hand from his. Caroline watched in surprise as Freddy, strengthening his hold on my hand, attempted to pull me down into his embrace.

Emma laughed outright as we had a regrettable little struggle which I won just as Hargreaves, Caroline's butler, opened the sitting room door to announce visitors. Freddy rose quickly from where he had tumbled when I yanked my hand away.

"They're here early," I murmured to Emma as Caroline went forward to greet her guests.

"Who's expected today, do you know?" Emma asked in a whisper, looking vaguely worried.

I patted her hand. She was a naturally shy person, quite timid around men she didn't know. "A very tame group, just a countess whose husband had become an important political acquaintance of Uncle Henry's, and an opera singer who will make her debut next week in Covent Garden."

"Ah. That is tame."

Freddy said from his chair, "I expected at least an Arctic explorer or the reigning pugilistic champion."

Emma stood beside me a short while later as we greeted the opera singer. The pleasantries over, I was in the process of taking a cup of tea to Senora Monteneros, who I was delighted to see took immediately to Emma despite the obvious barriers of language and background, when Hargreaves announced the entrance of the countess, Lady Sherringham.

"Do you take cream, Senora Monteneros?" I inquired as I glanced over to the door. "Oh, good god!"

Despite unjust and inaccurate claims to the contrary, I am not by nature a clumsy person. However, upon viewing the newest arrivals, I will admit to a slight lack of adroitness when I spilled an entire jug of cream down the front of the Senora's ruby-colored velvet and lace tea gown.

The countess was none other than the thin-faced woman in bilious green from the past evening, and she had brought with her the pale, shy looking girl that I had last seen on the infuriatingly smug, equally infuriatingly attractive Griffin's arm...who was three paces behind her, his amber eyes immediately seeking mine, his gaze just as disconcerting as I remembered it.

"Bloody hell," I whispered to myself. This was *not* going to be a pleasant afternoon.

CHAPTER FOUR

"Senora, I am so sorry, I can't think how—I've never spilled dairy products on anyone before—I'm sure my aunt's maid will assist you," I stammered, trying to mop up the mess as Senora Monteneros expressed her opinion of me loudly and vehemently in Spanish.

"It's all right, Cassandra. I'll help her," Emma said, taking the opera singer's arm and deftly guiding her through the maze of incidental tables full of bric-a-brac that cluttered my aunt's sitting room.

The newcomers were still across the room, greeting Caroline and Freddy. I looked quickly for an escape, and had just opened the door at the opposite end of the long room when my aunt's light, piping voice reached me. "Cassandra, dear, I'd like you to meet Lady Sherringham."

I stopped in the doorway and looked through it wistfully to freedom, briefly contemplating bolting down the hallway before reminding myself that I was not a coward. I had faced much worse things than three people invited to tea. I turned to smile at my aunt's guests.

The three pairs of eyes boring into me drove the smile from my lips.

"Hargreaves, send Grangly to attend Senora Monteneros and Miss Debenham," my aunt directed, eyeing the front of the opera singer's gown with interest.

I moved slowly, gritting my teeth and forcing the smile back upon my lips, all the while studiously avoiding tall figure beside my aunt.

"Lady Sherringham, may I introduce my niece, Cassandra Whitney? My dear, this is Lady Helena St. John, the earl's sister."

I am nothing if not well trained in the standard pleasantries, and thus I duly murmured polite phrases as we all shook hands. The countess's hand felt cold even through her gloves. Lady Helena, the tall, willowy young woman with hair the color of burnished gold, smiled a genuine smile, and greeted me with obvious pleasure. I liked her at once, and pitied her for having such a cold sister-in-law.

"And this is Mr. Griffin St. John, the earl's younger brother."

I dreaded looking up into those mocking amber eyes. "Miss Whitney, it is a pleasure."

Raising my gaze to his, I offered a firm hand. He took it gravely and bowed over it with only the slightest hint of a smile on his lips. I used the opportunity of daylight to examine his face. He was not handsome by conventional standards, but I decided his features were pleasing overall. The tanned cheeks bespoke time outdoors, while the firm set of his chin, and direct gaze gave him an unmistakable air of a man who was comfortable with himself.

His eyes, those glittering amber eyes, held an intense regard that challenged, however, and I recognized that he was a man who was not used to having his authority questioned. I found myself lifting my chin in answer to the look.

With a disarming grin he dropped my hand, and suddenly I noticed the way the corners of his eyes crinkled when he smiled, and how charming he could be when he wasn't spouting nonsense or being generally obnoxious. Then there was the consideration of just what he might look like without his clothes…

"You are in town long, Miss Whitney?"

The glacial tones of his sister-in-law ended such enjoyable thoughts.

"I am. I have lived my life in the country, and thought a change would be pleasant."

"Indeed," she said with frosty grandeur, accepting a cup of tea from Caroline.

"Lady Helena, would you care to sit on the wine and puce settee? I assure you it is better to have it beneath you than in a position to catch your eye," I said in a quiet tone, steering her toward the piece of furniture in question.

Helena giggled, and I chewed over the question of whether or not any of her party was going to mention the fracas of the previous evening to my aunt. Although I was not ashamed of my actions, I had not known at the time that Griffin's brother was of political importance to my uncle.

"It wouldn't have stopped me from speaking to him as I did, though," I murmured to myself as I took my seat.

"Pardon?" Helena asked.

"Oh, nothing. I spent a good deal of my time alone, and thus I have a bad habit of talking to myself. Did you enjoy the Hospital Ball?"

She chatted merrily away about the ball while I indulged in a bit of subtle interrogation. By the time Emma and the Senora returned, the latter still glaring, I felt it safe to excuse myself and leave Helena to Freddy, who had just wandered over to join us.

"I'm so sorry that you had to take care of that odious opera singer," I told Emma, pulling her aside. "Was she too horrid?"

"Not at all," Emma answered with a smile that was sent to the Spaniard. "I find her charming, to be honest."

"You two seemed to be getting along quite amiably. I had no idea you spoke Spanish."

"I don't," she said simply, then laughed at my look of confusion, and nodded toward Freddy and Helena. "She's lovely. Is that the important countess?"

"Her sister. Her name is Helena, and she's twenty-one years old."

"Mmm, a bit young, but still delectable, with a delicate complexion that gives her the appearance of a fragile china doll, all sweetness and no vices. Pity. I'd give anything for that hair, though. And the widow's peak. Are her eyes brown or hazel?"

"Brown. Her brother's are amber."

"Are they."

My gaze went to where he stood leaning casually against the fireplace, turned toward my aunt, but to my surprise, it was us he was watching. "He really is...well, there's just no other word for it but magnificent, don't you think?"

"Very," she said, without looking his way.

I nudged her with my elbow. "Not Freddy, Griffin. That is, Mr. St. John. It's just a shame his personality doesn't match his external appearance."

She spared him a glance, but then urged me over to the sofa where Helena sat. "Yes, quite."

I made the introductions, taking my seat in chair upon whose arm Freddy lounged while Emma sat next to Helena.

"Have you lived long in London?" Emma asked Helena.

"Oh yes, for some time. I live with my brother."

"Indeed," I glanced toward that person. His unblinking gaze met mine.

"We all live together, although Griffin frequently travels. He has only just returned from Arabia."

Emma smiled and pressed her hand. "You must be delighted to have him home again."

"Yes," Helena hesitated. A faint frown creased her lovely brow as her gaze wandered over to the topic of our conversation. "Although of late it almost seems . . . ." She paused and turned a brilliant smile on me. "I worry so when he travels to dangerous locations."

"I have no doubt you do," I said. "Do you go with him?"

"Unfortunately, no. I stay at home with Letitia and Harold. I would like to travel, but Griffin refuses to take me, so I have to content myself with reading about his journeys instead."

"Ah, you enjoy reading?" I gave Emma a smile. "Emma is quite the scholar."

"Yes, indeed she is," Freddy said in a slow, lazy voice. "She's exceptionally well versed in the art of Sapphistry, aren't you, Miss Debenham?"

Helena looked dubiously at Emma.

"Don't worry," I told her, shoving Freddy just hard enough that he tottered off the arm of the chair. "Emma may be a great scholar of all things Greek, but she's no bluestocking. You needn't feel you need to brush up on the classics to talk with her."

"Quite the contrary, I would say," Freddy said as he dusted himself off and wandered over to where Griffin stood.

Emma shot him a sharp look and murmured an excuse before moving over to sit next to the Senora.

"I'm afraid the only thing I ever read are the most frivolous of novels," I said, moving over to the sofa. "Do you enjoy them, too, by chance?"

"Oh yes, whenever I get the chance. My sister-in-law," she cast a fearful glance towards the countess, "doesn't approve of popular novels, but I am lucky in that my brother has such a large library."

Full of sermons and political treatises on the superiority of men, I thought sourly as I remembered the venomous stout man's comments.

"My brother Griffin, I should say," she smiled.

I amended the thought to include those books deemed convivial by pig-headed males. "How lucky you are. And what types of books does your brother read?"

"He enjoys many types of books, but spends much of his time writing rather than reading. Perhaps you have read his books? They are very popular and are full of the most exciting adventures. He has received a great deal of acclaim," she added with pride.

"St. John," I said slowly. "No, the only book by a St. John that I am aware of is a horrible little volume pontificating the superiority of men over women explorers—something about the Englishmen abroad . . . ."

I stopped as an appalling thought crossed my mind.

"*The Englishman's Role Abroad* was the title," she said, smiling to my great discomfort. "It is a very popular book, although I don't agree with all Griffin says in it."

I stammered an apology for my rude comments. Helena waved it away and continued. "He has written other books as well, ones about his travels which I'm certain you would enjoy."

"I shall certainly look for them. I have always wanted to travel, but have been obligated to stay at home with my parents in the country."

"I would be happy to lend you my copies, if you would really like to read them. He's written seven books—the last is my favorite. It's a journal of his travels in Africa last year."

Her voice faltered as she looked over my shoulder, then she leaned forward conspiratorially. "Miss Whitney, might I ask you a personal question?"

"Yes, certainly."

"Last night," she began, making me flush with remembrance, "last night you were—*demonstrating* with a group of women."

I nodded.

"Can you tell me—" She threw another worried glance toward Lady Sherringham, then hurried ahead in a rushed whisper." Would you be kind enough to tell me about the suffrage movement? I am so interested, but my brother will not let the subject be spoken of, and I do not often have the opportunity of talking about such things."

"I would be delighted to tell you about it. The goal of the Women's Suffrage Union is to obtain the right for women to vote."

"Yes," she said intently, "but *why* do you want to vote? Women don't have the experience that men have in politics. I don't wish to be rude, but I don't see what there is to gain by being able to vote."

I beamed at her, happy to be able to clear up her obvious misconceptions. "You must be aware of how much women have gained in the last thirty years. We may now fill a number of important positions previously denied to our sex. We can be churchwardens, sextons, members of school boards, and even members of parish councils. Unfortunately, there are many avenues still closed to us: men refuse to allow women the right to serve on a county council, stand for Member of Parliament, or to vote on the subject of imperial matters."

"I agree with you, of course, but I cannot help but feel that my brother is partially right when he says women don't have the experience needed to vote with intelligence."

I wondered to which brother she was referring, then decided it was probably both. "That's utter codswallop."

A faint blush stained her cheeks. "I agree that it sounds silly, but I suppose I can see some reason in it. Only, why do *you* support women's suffrage?"

"Oh, well, there are many reasons."

"Please enlighten us, Miss Whitney," a deep voice spoke behind me. I tensed as Griffin moved to sit across from his sister. "I am always delighted to hear of charitable causes, and yours seems a most needy one."

A blush heated its way up my neck. "Charitable cause? We are not a charity, Mr. St. John. The Women's Suffrage Union represents women everywhere who have been denied their rights too long. Needy, I will grant you, but a charity? No."

His smile mocked me. "Perhaps you will explain to us the difference?"

I raised my chin and gave him the loftiest of looks. "We are needy because throughout history women have been the backbone that has held the family together. No, you cannot deny it." I shook my finger at him as he opened his mouth to protest. "For centuries women have had the responsibility of raising children; if we have the right to mold children into upstanding, moral adults, why should we not have the right to influence public morals as well? Why should women be allowed to sit on a parish council, but not a county council?"

"Your question is based on the assumption that women have the ability to form a correct opinion on matters outside their expertise: their homes, children, education—" Griffin scowled as he spoke.

"And *your* opinion is based on the idea that women are unable to do almost everything a man can do. Given the experience, a woman can hold any job—"

"Bah!" he rumbled, pounding his fist on his leg for emphasis. "Women solicitors, women overseers, even lady doctors are now a common sight! Why your sex feels it necessary to join every profession they can, rather than do what they are most suited for, is beyond me—"

It was my turn to interrupt. I sent a reassuring smile to my aunt, who was beginning to look concerned at the heated manner of our discussion, then turned my attention with pleasure to my opponent. "Why is it that men call women weak and inferior, and yet when we want to have an occupation or acquire an education, you deny us those rights?"

"The issue is moot—women *are* allowed to vote, but on matters they are familiar with, such as health, education, and welfare." His voice was angry, but his attitude was one of studied indifference.

I put down my teacup firmly upon the round table in front of me.

"We are allowed to vote in municipal and county elections, yes. If, according to you and other misguided males of your ilk, women are incapable of making lucid decisions regarding anything outside of the home, why are we allowed to vote at all? I will tell you why! Because we have proven that, given access to education and free citizenship, women make decisions that are just as informed as their male counterparts."

He snorted indignantly. "Women are free to become educated—attend Cambridge and Oxford. What more do you want?"

"Free to attend Cambridge and Oxford, certainly, but not free to acquire a degree. My dearest friend Emma is by common consent a noted scholar in Greek works. And yet why should she not be recognized for her detailed and meticulous research into the works of the poet Sappho, while men are free to do so?"

Griffin looked startled for a moment, and shot Emma a quick glance. She murmured something to the Senora and rose, heading for us, no doubt to caution me against further argument.

"Why is it right that the female students such as her, who do work as good, or better, than the male students, should not be given the same reward?" I asked before she could reach us.

Griffin's amber eyes turned dark with emotion. If I didn't know better, I would think he was enjoying the argument as much as I was. "I have seen a great deal of the world, Miss Whitney, and can tell you one result of educating women and releasing them upon the unwitting public. Not content to inflict themselves upon their own countrymen, hordes of *educated* British women trample every spot dear to man. From the ancient Greek ruins to the jungles of the Amazon you'll find them, waving their nationality and gender as a passport that will open every door. Even in the wilds of Katmandu are not sacred, for there your educated sisters can be seen, clutching their cups of tea and shoving their idea of civility down the throats of the natives."

Emma reached me, a cautioning hand on my arm as I stood up and gripped the table. "Why are men allowed to force their political ideas upon citizens of other countries, but when women try to bring much needed education and welfare to those who need the aid, we are damned for meddling in native affairs?"

"Cassandra, perhaps you wish to moderate your voice," Emma murmured.

"I will not be silenced! This is the very thing we are fighting, Emma! Misinformation is our enemy. It is our duty to educate where we can." Griffin ignored her and frowned at me in an intimidating manner, opening his mouth to refute my questions, but I would not be stopped. "Do you think your sex is the only one that has the right to experience the wonders and splendor the world has to offer? Women do not want to be pandered to, nor do we intend to be pacified with token examples of freedom such as you have mentioned. We expect, nay, *demand* the same rights as men!"

My aunt desperately tried to catch my eye, but I was too infuriated to care. To think that this wretched man, whom I had briefly thought so charming, so attractive, so interesting that I was considering offering him the position of my lover, should turn out to be just as stodgy and backwards-thinking as others of his sex.

"The only reason the average Englishwoman wants to travel is to show the world that she is capable of doing so." Griffin stood to face me across the table. "She cares nothing about seeing the 'wonders and splendor' of the world, as you put it, except to tick them off on her Baedeker's list of sights to see."

Helena made a squeak of distress, and rose to stand beside him. "Griffin, there is no need to yell—"

"I am delighted to know you are such an expert on women's feelings and thoughts. Perhaps you will write a book about *that*, as well!"

The retort made him tighten his lips. We glared at each other across the table, and despite my anger, I found myself enjoying the confrontation. He was so maddening, so frustrating, and I just knew in my bones that his derriere would be such that it would hold my interest for many years, and yet...

"Perhaps I will. I've found that it doesn't take much to understand the minds of women."

"No doubt because our minds are beyond your level of understanding."

"If that's true," he growled, "it's because there's no sense or logic in the feminine mind. Women are not able to discuss subjects of importance in any reasonable manner without bringing emotions into the issue."

"You are the most insulting, insufferable, misinformed man I have ever met!" I pounded the table in front of me.

"Cassandra!" Emma grabbed my arm and pulled me back a few steps. Caroline stared at me in stark horror.

"You are the most obstinate, stubborn, *emotional* woman I have met, and I've met several of your kind!" he roared back at me.

"Griffin!" Helena's face was as shocked as my aunt's.

Emma's tone was level, but the restraining hand she placed on my arm gripped firmly. "I urge you to moderate your voice. I understand your wish to educate, but there is no need to yell at Mr. St. John." She turned to him, and smiled endearingly. "I'm sure you will forgive my friend her passion; she feels things so strongly that sometimes she forgets herself."

"You need not make excuses for me," I said stiffly, rubbing hands that were stiff with strain.

Griffin stepped back as well. "As a matter of fact, I believe passion is an admirable quality in a woman. However, I am to blame for being the cause of the argument. My apologies."

He smiled at Emma, and turned to his sister. In the heat of our argument I had forgotten her. Stood next to Griffin, as flushed as if she had been in battle. Her eyes sparkled with a strong emotion as she gazed at us. Griffin held out his hand to her, but she ignored it; instead she leaped forward to grasp my hand, pressing it dramatically as he turned away.

"I so admire you! You have such fire! Such spirit! Does she not, Miss Debenham?"

"Very much," Emma agreed, and with another little smile, returned to the Spanish opera singer.

I was taken aback by Helena's candor, but thanked her regardless.

"You are very brave to talk so to Griffin. No one speaks to him like that!"

"I rather wonder he allows women to speak in his august presence at all, given his attitude towards our gender," I said, loud enough to ensure he heard. His back twitched under the tweed cloth of his coat as he spoke to my aunt.

"Oh, it's not that at all. You see—"

"Helena!" A shrill voice cut through her comments. "You will stop your discussion with Miss Whitney this instant. We are leaving."

Caroline flustered her way over to where Lady Sherringham maintained a regal and disdaining attitude by the door, a subdued Freddy next to her. Lady Sherringham glared at me for several seconds, then took her leave of my aunt. I felt wholly ashamed of myself. Caroline had particularly asked that Freddy and I be pleasant to the countess for our uncle's sake, and what must I do but enter into a screaming match with his infuriating, arousing brother. No doubt I ruined any chance of the earl's offering to sponsor to the bill Uncle Henry supported.

"I meant what I said, you know. Passion is a trait I believe should be nurtured rather than stifled."

I lifted my gaze to the wary amber one waiting for me. His expression was somber, and in the depths of those incredible eyes, I beheld mingled exasperation and anger. But as I held his gaze and refused to look away, the anger faded and he gave me a long, questioning look.

"But not, perhaps, as cherished as restraint?" I couldn't help but ask.

He bowed slightly and, as he walked past me towards the door, paused briefly to slip a heavy white object into my hand. He shook hands with my aunt and the others, then left with his ladies.

I looked dully at the square white object resting against my palm, then tucked it away in my pocket. With one hand on my burning cheek, I shut my eyes as my aunt, in passing, asked softly, "What were you thinking, Cassandra?"

CHAPTER FIVE

"Clearly the man suffers from poor reasoning and a lack of self control. Is that my blue shirtwaist?"

"No, miss, it's your old flannel petticoat."

"Oh. Put it on the governess stack. I am more than a bit at a loss why I should be so...oh, well, let us be honest and use the word...*captivated* by such a thoroughly exasperating, frustrating man. What on earth is that?"

"I think it's your old bicycle suit."

I sat back on my heels and wrinkled my nose at the blue worsted suit Annie held up. "Into the governess stack. I much prefer the bloomers. Where was I?"

"You were saying that you were captivated by Mr. St. John."

"Yes, but it's an *understandable* captivation. You can add those boots, too, they make my feet look huge. After all, I have had a very quiet upbringing, excluding my father's rages, of course, but I am quite sure it was my sedate life in the country rather than any *personal* attraction that has made Mr. St. John seem so invigorating. A fine derriere notwithstanding, there is much to be said for a man who holds the same beliefs as you."

"What about this dressing gown?"

"Is it the one with the gold braid?" I asked, my head in the lower part of the wardrobe where I was trying to extract a recalcitrant dancing slipper.

"Yes."

"Governess stack." I pulled my head out and frowned at the dancing slipper. "What on earth would possess me to purchase slippers with pink fairies painted on the toes?"

"Whimsy?"

"Do I strike you as a pink fairy sort of person?"

Annie giggled. "No, miss."

"Hmm." I handed the horrible things to her. "I must have been deranged or intoxicated when I bought them. As for yesterday, I honestly believe that a good part of the enjoyment I experienced was due to the utter disregard Mr. St. John felt toward societal norms. No polite gentleman would allow himself to enter into a public shouting match with a woman. After the innuendoes and polite manners common to London society, I have to admit I found it refreshing to converse with someone who spoke as he thought."

"I suppose that makes sense."

"Of course it does. I am an imminently sensible person. And then there is the matter of the padlock."

"What padlock?"

"The one I had dropped with that repulsive chain. He returned the padlock to me. Good god, what was I thinking buying mustard-colored stockings? Governess them! What is it, Mullin?"

My sister's butler, a stately if somewhat diminutive man, looked horrified at the clothing strew with wanton disregard around the room. "Lady Helena St. John to see you, miss."

"Really? How curious. You know what I don't wear, Annie—separate those things out and pack them up for the unemployed governesses."

I brushed off my knees and hurried down to the drawing room. Helena sat on a particularly slippery horsehair loveseat, clad in a lovely peach-colored watered silk day dress cut in the latest fashion. My mouth watered at the sight of it.

As I entered the room, she twisted matching peach-colored gloves, too distracted to notice the destruction she inflicted, jumping up when she saw me.

"Lady Helena, how delightful to see you again. Is Lady Sherringham with you?"

"Oh no," she gasped, horrified. "Letitia thinks I'm at a fitting. She would not be—that is, she would not approve—" She stopped, blushed, and started again. "Forgive me for visiting you this way, Miss Whitney, but I simply must speak with you."

I smiled encouragingly, and waved her back towards the couch. "In what way may I help you?"

"It is I who wish to help," she declared dramatically, one hand to her bosom, the other outstretched. "Miss Whitney, I would very much like to join the Women's Suffrage Union, and to fight for the rights of women everywhere. I applaud the way you stood up to Griffin yesterday—it was magnificent! You are the very epitome of the New Woman, and oh, how I wish I could be as well. I would never dare to speak in such a manner to Griffin as you did. He gets so angry about those sorts of things."

"Indeed," I said dryly. I liked her; she was rather shy and prone to dramatic attitudes and phrases, but it was clear that she harbored a strong desire to get out from under her family's stifling control. "It is not my place to advise you how to speak with your brother, but I will admit that it's my heartfelt belief that one should be free to express one's opinion in one's own home."

"Oh, I agree, I absolutely agree. Tell me what I must do, I beg of you. I look to you for advice, for I have no one else to whom I can turn."

Another dramatic speech, I smiled to myself. "You understand that I am in an awkward position with regards to your family. I cannot tell you what to do, nor is it my wish to cause friction at home."

"But you spoke so bravely to Griffin yesterday! You stood up to him and made him respect you!" She looked down at her hands for a moment. "I would like to be able to speak so openly and make him respect me as well."

"You are his sister—of course he respects you!"

"Not in the manner he does you," she replied with a faint smile.

"Oh, come now, Lady Helena, I don't believe in false compliments. Although you believe I spoke with bravery yesterday, it was, in hindsight, an error to speak so rudely at a polite gathering, and for my part, I am ashamed of how things got out of hand."

"But you shouldn't be! Ashamed, that is. Griffin admires you very much, he told me so."

I blinked at her in disbelief.

"You have to understand, Miss Whitney, he is a very strong man, and despite his protests, he has the greatest respect for a woman who can stand up to him."

"He has an extremely odd manner of showing his respect."

She caught the tone of sarcasm in my voice and let a slight smile play across her lips. "I believe you are similarly minded, Miss Whitney. I doubt if you tolerate well those of weak intellect."

There being no need to deny to that, I rose and pressed the bell. "Would you care for coffee? Or perhaps you would prefer tea?"

"Yes, thank you." She looked at her gloves for a moment, then spoke again. "You were so eloquent about the Women's Suffrage Union last night; I wonder...would it be possible—would you take me to one of their meetings? I would like to join their cause, but I would be afraid to go on my own. If I could attend with you, I would feel much more comfortable about participating."

I admit I was surprised, but equally delighted. Here was a woman who was very much under the thumb of a pair of tyrannical brothers and a cold sister-in-law, and yet she was willing to fight to have her own voice. A pleasurable picture arose in my mind of the two of us, side-by-side, marching in sisterhood for women's rights, waving our banners and breaking down the wall of male domination. There was only one blot in such a heartwarming image.

Her family.

"There is a meeting tonight at the home of one of the officers, Mrs. Knox," I mused out loud. "Although not strictly a membership meeting, I don't see what objections they could have to your attending it. What of your family? Surely they will pose objections? I am afraid that I have not made the . . . er . . . very best of impressions with them, and we both know how Mr. St. John feels about women's suffrage."

"Your introduction may have been slightly unorthodox, but you have made quite an impression with Griffin." She paused. "I will admit that he does not support women's rights, but I have determined to not let that stand in my way. I don't believe Griffin will have any objections to my attending meetings in your company."

"That astonishes me greatly, I must confess. While I have known your brother only a short time, I'm afraid the impression he has left upon me is one of boorishness and a closed mind." Wrapped up in an incredibly attractive package, but I needn't tell her of the more lustful of my thoughts. "I fear you are in for more dissension than you are allowing."

Helena looked shocked, and made an exclamation. I halted her by saying, "Forgive me for speaking so rudely, but Mr. St. John's opinions are exactly those against which we are struggling! If you wish to take a part in this glorious battle, you must be prepared to face such beliefs, and to do your best to educate those ignorant minds, as I have strived to do."

"But," she stammered, "that is not at all what he was saying last night, at home—he is not at all like that—"

I cut short her protestations. "I will give you some literature that states the Women's Suffrage Union views, which you may use as a verbal sword when attacked by those of weaker intellect."

"I suppose that would help..."

I rose and gathered a collection of pamphlets from the desk. The tea arrived, and as I handed Helena a cup, I motioned towards the pamphlets.

"Take these home with you. I feel firmly that your family will oppose you attending the Union's meetings, but since you are determined . . . ." My eyebrows rose questioningly.

She nodded. "There is one thing I should tell you, Miss Whitney. It is about my brother."

"Something more?"

"No, it is about my older brother, Lord Sherringham." She paused, and clasped her hands in distress. "He has very different opinions than ours, as you might have noticed."

I remembered with clarity his rude comments outside of the Hospital Ball.

"I should warn you that he has taken a stand against suffrage in the House of Lords, and is considered one of the leading proponents against our noble cause."

I mentally groaned. Oh, I had put myself in a fine position—mentor to the only sister of the enemy camp's leading supporter. Swallowing my concern, I smiled grimly at her. "We certainly have our work cut out for us, do we not?"

"I look forward to joining the Women's Union tonight, and declaring myself in the war against men."

"It's not quite a war," I cautioned, disliking her to believe that violence was a part of Union work. "Nor is it really a Union meeting tonight. I don't want you to be disappointed—the recording secretary is ill, and I will be taking notes of a meeting between a few of the officers only. They will be discussing the roster of active suffragists, and beginning to plan the demonstrations that we will hold in the coming months. It's bound to be a bit tedious. Are you sure you want to come?"

"Very much so. We are to go to dinner at a distant cousin's, but I am sure I can get out of it." She looked up at me with sudden humor. "I believe I shall have a headache, and retire early to my bed."

We agreed that Helena would meet me at my sister's home, and from here we would drive to the meeting at Mrs. Knox's house near the British Museum. After a few more pleasantries and another cup of tea, Helena departed. I went back to the task of sorting out clothes for charity, and spent the rest of the day in fittings for several new dresses.

As I tried on the garments, I reveled in the feminine pleasure of purchasing an entirely new wardrobe. Prior to my father's death some two months past, I was allowed little scope with regards to anything but the most mundane of fashions. Once I arrived in London, however, I was driven by the desire to appear, if not in the latest fashions, at the least somewhat fashionably dressed. I could only conclude that the giddy joy of ordering as many clothes as I desired had led me to the regrettable purchase of the pink fairy dancing slippers.

"I'll take three of the lawn shirtwaists, and two of the tweed walking skirts—one navy, one brown—and I'd like to look at walking suits. Those are the ones with narrower skirts and the cunning matching jackets, yes? Those should be perfect for any marches I participate in."

"Yes, indeed they would be perfect," Madame Renoir the modiste simpered at me, taking down my order with a flurry of her hands as she directed her girls into parading the latest models before me.

I had a short argument with Madame Renoir about the Healthy and Artistic Dress Union, which denounced as unnatural and unhealthy the current fad of forcing women's figures into an unnatural S-shape. Emma felt as I did, but I could tell by the willowy form that Helena presented that she was on the other side so far as corsets went. Perhaps one day I would convince her as to the wisdom of throwing away her corset. Another verbal scuffle broke out when I demanded the new "combinations" as they were called, but after a sizeable order that consisted of several pieces of fine lawn knickers and chemises, relations turned amiable again.

Riding high on the crest of my success of dismissing the need for a corset, in a moment of pure indulgence I commissioned the creation of four evening gowns of the new Empire style, each with a high waist and short sleeves. "You're sure it's not too revealing," I said, eyeing with concern the model as she turned and pirouetted in front of me.

"But *non*! It is the very latest style. Your corset, it will keep you all that is modest."

"But we just—"

"If you wish to wear these gowns, you must have the corsets," Madame insisted.

I was half tempted to walk out, but the lovely silks and gauzes as displayed by the models swayed my concerns of healthfulness.

"Fine," I told her after ordering the new gowns. "I will get a corset, but it will be one of my choosing."

There was nothing she could say to that, so I left, and accordingly went shopping for a Rational corset that was not constricting or binding.

The day passed quickly, and I was still dressing for the Union meeting when Helena arrived. As Annie buttoned me into a cream colored linen skirt with thin blue stripes and matching pale blue shirtwaist, I hunted for my small leather notebook. "Have you seen it, Annie?"

A short, stout woman with charming dimples, Annie was the one person I was happy to bring with me from my old home. Despite a disfigurement to her face, she normally maintained a sunny disposition and never failed to cheer me up. "I thought it was in your stocking drawer."

"Why would I put it...well, for heaven's sake, so it is. I won't be home until late, Annie, so you may have the evening off."

"Thank you, miss."

I eyed her before I left the room. Annie was a favorite with my sister Mabel's household, and I sometimes worried that her attachment to Jackson, the coachman, was not reciprocated and would end in disaster. Tonight she seemed moody and distracted, although she denied any ailment or personal problems. "Is anything amiss?"

"No, miss. I'm fine, thank you."

Hmm. She didn't look fine. Still, I hated to pry. I told her to enjoy herself and hurried down to Helena. She was wearing a stunning pale pink dress—a sheer tunic covered the dark silk underskirt, very narrow and elegant, with a matching coat. A pink hat decorated with feathers and dried flowers completed her ensemble.

"Good heavens, Lady Helena," I said in stark admiration, "That dress is absolutely mouth-watering. It's like spun sugar."

She waved her hand depreciatingly and asked, "Please call me Helena. I don't use the title, and even though we've known each other only a short while, I feel as if you are an old and dear friend."

I consented, and sent Theodore, the footman, in search of a cab.

"Is your friend Miss Debenham not joining us?"

"Emma? No, she's not at all interested in the cause. Well, I should correct that—she is interested, but she has her studies to attend to. Her insights are very much in demand at Sappho's Circle."

"Is that a literary salon?" Helena asked.

"I believe it's some sort of club for Greek scholars. She mentioned something about occasionally staying overnight when she was engaged in late-night study sessions."

Helena, no more a scholar than I was, murmured something noncommittal.

"Did you manage your headache with success?" I asked with a smile.

"Oh yes—well, I think I did."

I looked at her questioningly. "I'm afraid Griffin suspects something. He told me, just as he and my brother and sister-in-law were leaving, to please be careful with whatever it was I was planning."

"Oh, dear. That does sound rather ominous." I chewed my lip in thought as we entered the cab.

"I never could hide anything from Griffin."

"I'm surprised he let you stay home alone, if he suspected you. I had thought his opinion of women would demand that he play watchdog."

"You are mistaken about Griffin, truly you are. You must give him credit for having suffered a broken heart."

"A broken heart? Mr. St. John?" I asked incredulously.

"It happened a long time ago, when I was a girl, but I know Griffin still feels it a great deal." She looked at me sideways. "Rather, I thought he did."

I said nothing, but looked at her inquiringly.

"When Griffin was eighteen, he fell madly in love with Grace Perry, the cousin of my sister-in-law, Letitia. I was living with Harold and Letitia then, my parents having died some years earlier, and Griffin had just returned from his Grand Tour. Grace was staying with us, and Griffin—well, you know how these things can happen."

I nodded, absorbed in a variety of mental images, many of which concerned just what Griffin looked like underneath all those clothes.

"Grace was a very outspoken woman, rather rough and common I think now, although she impressed me at the time. She was a little older than Griffin, and had done a lot of traveling by herself. Although she was fond of him, I don't believe that she ever loved him in return."

"Were they engaged?"

"No, not formally, although I believe he had been pressing her. She left shortly thereafter."

"Why did she leave?"

"She and Griffin had an argument one night. My sister-in-law was having a dinner and Griffin tried to press Grace into a commitment so they could announce their engagement that night." She glanced at me, her lips curling slightly. "I was supposed to be upstairs since I was too young to attend the dinner, but I had hidden in my brother's library and was reading a book of fairy tales. Griffin and Grace did not know I was curled up on a chair when they had their argument."

"Ah. So the lady jilted your brother?" This was delicious gossip, and as ashamed as I was for participating in it, I reveled in every moment.

"Yes. She told Griffin that she had no intention of marrying him, that he was not the type of man any sane woman would spend the rest of her life with, and she did not intend to waste the best years of her life adapting her lifestyle to his."

"That was rather blunt of her."

"Griffin was furious. He spoke quietly, but I knew he was mad—his voice drops when he gets very angry. Grace made rather a common scene, and stormed out of the room. She refused to appear at dinner, and left shortly thereafter. Griffin would not speak of her, but I knew he must have been terribly hurt."

I suspected that a good part of the hurt was due to wounded pride, but did not voice that opinion.

"That is why, dear Cassandra, you must make allowance for Griffin's attitude towards outspoken women. Should the right woman come along," she dropped her gaze to her hands, "she might find that she could heal his wounded heart."

"More likely she would have her head snapped off for trying," I said dryly, and spent the remainder of the ride in contemplation of him nonetheless.

CHAPTER SIX

Mrs. Knox lived in a small, white stone building on the quiet edge of Russell Square. Climbing the steps to the house, I cautioned Helena about detailing her relationship with Lord Sherringham. "It is not that they would refuse you admittance into the Union, but they might feel hesitant to discuss topics of a sensitive nature, such as the plans for our next demonstration and protests, before they know you well."

She nodded, but had no time to say anything before we were admitted. The women welcomed her, and without much delay, the meeting commenced. Each member contributed many ideas and opinions as to the Union's planned activism, so many that although I wrote quickly, I was hard put to keep up with the pace of the ideas that flowed forth. Petitions were organized, deputations were planned, marches plotted, demonstrations ordered, and processions detailed. I tucked a list of volunteers assigned to each event into my notebook, to be typed up later.

"I cannot see what good these plans will be when we will not be taken seriously by the press and the public until they see we are committed body and soul to the cause," a petite red-haired Irish woman named Maggie interrupted the speaker as she reviewed the final list of activities for the next month.

"We do not condone violent acts—" one of the other Union officials started to say.

"I say we strike, and strike hard!" Maggie cried, rising to her feet. Several other members nodded. "You talk about marches and protests and petitions—we have tried them all, and they have failed. This is the time for action, and without it, our cause is doomed."

"Maggie Greene, you are out of order," Mrs. Heywood, the head of the Union said.

"I have a voice just as does any other member in the Union!"

"A voice, yes, but the National Women's Union has never condoned violence, and we will not start now. *We will not start now*," Mrs. Heywood repeated over the grumbling of a handful of women who favored such extreme forms of protest.

I held my breath, worried that the militant faction would continue to press the issue, but although they demanded a vote to determine the type of future actions, they were outvoted by a clear majority. The NSU would continue its policy of non-violent protest. I breathed a sigh of relief, and promised to type up the report on my new typewriting machine. As the meeting ended, Helena and I walked down the steps to the street with several of the other ladies.

"We can take you home, if you don't mind being crowded," one woman offered, indicating her motor.

"Thank you, but the evening is fine, and I need a good walk. But perhaps Miss St. John..."

"I'll walk with you," she said quickly, with a bright smile.

"You are welcome to take a cab home," I said as we set off. "I really don't mind walking by myself." I stopped to allow her to catch up to me.

"I never thought of the problems of walking any distance when I bought this terrible gown," she said, vexed.

I surveyed the narrow skirt with some skepticism. "Why men want to hobble women in the name of fashion is beyond me."

"It *is* pretty."

"Very." I took her arm and slowed my steps to hers. "And we have a lovely evening for a leisurely stroll. Since we are closer to my house, I suggest we head there first. I will have my sister's coachman drive you home from there."

As we walked, I was surprised and, I confess, dismayed to find that the woman I thought so frail and gentle had a spirit that more than matched my own.

"But surely you must agree that the public will never take us seriously unless we make them do so," she demanded after ten minutes of debate.

I was silent a moment, considering how best to calm her impassioned and rather bloodthirsty heart while not dampening her spirit for the cause. "I can't say I agree with you, Helena. I understand the reasoning behind Maggie Greene's desire to advance the Union to a more militant stand, but the thought of using violence to further our cause is abhorrent to me. I don't believe it is needed."

"But consider the past twenty years! If, according to the pamphlet you gave me, women have been trying by constitutional means to get the vote and failing, then the time has come to make the public aware of our cause. What better way can we prove that we are serious?"

I opened my mouth to argue the point, but all that came out was a loud "Ooof!"

A sharp blow to the middle of my back sent me sprawling into a nearby lamppost. I slumped against it, dazed and stunned. Shaking my head to clear it, I attempted to stand up. On the third try I was successful, and looked around for my attacker.

"Next time ye'll think twice afore ye go meddlin' in matters that don't concern ye," a thick voice growled from the shadows of the building. A dark shape moved in the shadows, clearly retreating down a darkened alley. I rubbed my head and limped over to the street.

Helena had been dumped unceremoniously about thirty feet away, directly into a large mound of horse droppings. "Cassandra, I can't...and it's all over...it's oozing on my leg!" she wailed as she tried to get up.

I helped her to her feet and surveyed the result. Her lovely pink coat now covered in muck.

"What am I going to do?" Helena held her arms out stiffly, and promptly burst into tears.

"Are you hurt?" I asked, looking for signs of injury.

She shook her head.

"Thank heavens for that. Take off your coat, let me give you my handkerchief. You are certainly a mess. Damnation! My bag has been stolen."

She shivered in her thin gown.

"Here." I removed my own coat and handed it to her. "Wrap this around you. You'll have to have your coat cleaned before you can wear it again."

She protested, but I was in no mood to argue with her. I buttoned her into my coat and picked up her soiled garment with two fingers.

"This is covered in filth. Luckily, it's long enough to prevent most of your skirt from coming in contact with the refuse." I set the coat down again and considered our situation. "We are less than a mile from my home, further from yours. I suppose we could go back to Mrs. Knox's and beg for assistance."

"No!" Helena wailed. "I could not face that, I could not!"

"Then we shan't go there," I said soothingly, knowing full well that she would not be able to stand up to ridicule, however politely spoken. I looked at her critically. "Oh, dear, you *are* a mess."

Muck was smeared up to the ankles of her lovely boots, her hemline was soiled, and her face was tearstained and grubby. Her chin quivered ominously, and her eyes shined with tears on the verge of falling again. Clearly, I could not leave her to her own devices. I gave a mental shrug and looked around for a cab. "Do you still have your bag, Helena?"

She nodded.

"Do you have any money?"

"A little. Not much, though." Tears began to course down her cheeks again as she peered forlornly into her bag. She handed me a few coins.

A hansom cab loitered far down the street at an intersection. Indicating it, I grabbed the spoiled coat in one hand, Helena's arm in another, and pulled her towards it.

Her tears had stopped by the time we were settled in the cab, although she was still sniffling in an unladylike manner. I pointed this out to her, and waited until she had composed herself. "Did you see the thug who attacked us, Helena?"

"It was so quick, I didn't see him at all."

"Oh, dear. I didn't see him either, I was too busy seeing stars from my collision with the lamppost. All I saw was his shadow, but I did think his voice was quite rough and common."

"Oh, Cassandra," she gasped, turning to me with concern. "Were you injured?"

"Just my pride," I said grimly. "I shall ring the police from home and report the attack."

Helena looked scared and turned pale, her cold hand gripping mine with surprising strength.

"Don't worry, I won't mention your name." The grip relaxed. "The last thing I want is for your family to find out you were attacked because I wished to walk home rather than take a cab. We will drop you off first, then I will go home and telephone the authorities."

Helena was very quiet during the ride to her brother's house, and a quick peek at her strained, white face told me she was nervous about her reception.

"Your family is away this evening, you said?" I asked cautiously.

"Yes, they are at the Edward Smythe's tonight." She had found one of my best Irish linen handkerchiefs in my coat pocket, and unconsciously twisted it into a knot.

"Good. You should be able to smuggle your coat in and have your maid attend to it before they return home." The coat currently resided on the outer seat next to the cabby. "You might tell her that you slipped and fell."

Helena surprised me by bursting into laughter. "I certainly won't tell her I was assaulted by a strange man as I walked home from a secret suffrage meeting, when I was supposed to be in bed with a headache."

There is nothing more infectious than laughter at an inappropriate time, and before long the cab pulled up outside Lord Sherringham's house in Balmour Street with the pair of us mopping our streaming eyes, trying to control our outbursts.

We were still giggling like schoolgirls when, telling the cabby to wait, I accompanied her and her coat to the door. Hushing both of us to be quiet, she let herself in with a latchkey and waved me across the threshold.

"Let me take the coat directly to Mariah," she said quietly.

I held the repulsive garment out to her at arm's length. We looked at it in disbelief for a moment, then catching each other's eyes, dissolved once more into a silly display.

"Really," I gasped through the tears of hilarity, "it is a horrible thing to behold."

Helena clutched her sides, not doing any better than me at retaining control. She pointed at the coat, and opened her mouth to make a further comment. Looking past me, her face suddenly froze. The transformation was so quick, the expression on her face so awful that I stopped laughing and looked over my shoulder to see what grisly sight had such a terrible effect on her.

Lady Sherringham came out of a nearby door. Swift on her heels was the stout, bald man I remembered from the scene outside of the Hospital Ball. Across the hall, another door opened and the tall figure that had taken to haunting my thoughts stepped out.

I closed my mouth, and with a swift move scooped up the coat from where it had fallen and turned to stand in front of Helena. She gripped my arm from behind, her hand shaking as she moved to my side.

"Helena, my dear sister. How is it you come to be here and not in your bed?" her sister-in-law inquired in an acid tone, looking not at Helena, but at me. "We rushed home to tend you, and now we find that you are not in bed, but instead sneaking into our home in the company of this...*this woman!*"

Before I could think up a reasonable explanation, the earl spoke directly to me.

"Who are you, madam, that you feel it appropriate to wrench my sister out of the safety and security of her family at this time of night? Have you no feelings of decency? What are your morals that you would secretly spirit away a young girl from those who are responsible for her welfare?"

Lady Sherringham saved me the effort of answering the question.

"Surely you recognize her, Harold," she crowed. "This is Cassandra Whitney, Sir Henry Benson's niece. She is the woman we saw outside of the Hospital Ball—the one who threw herself upon Griffin in that repulsive attempt to attract our notice."

"I did no such thing," I retorted, finding my voice at last. "It was an unfortunate accident. I had no intention of throwing myself on anyone, least of all Mr. St. John. And as for your sister, my lord, I did not wrench her from your house—she willingly attended a meeting with me. Furthermore, I find your insinuations offensive and boorish."

I would have continued along similar lines, but a consideration of my less than blameless role in the evening's events, not to mention Helena's strained, pale face, caused me to bite back anything else I might say.

"Isn't it clear, Harold?" The countess's voice had a barbed quality that made me flinch. "She has taken our dear Helena to one of those anarchistic suffrage gatherings! I knew this would happen—I could tell at once what sort of person she was. This is what comes from allowing women of her low morals to mingle with decent people. Helena, dear, are you hurt in any way? Those women are so rough, there is no telling what they might have done to you. Come, child, let me look at you."

Griffin stood outside of the circle of light with his arms folded across his chest, a shadow on his face leaving his expression unreadable. He watched us, saying nothing until Helena turned to him with her hands held wide in a gesture of distress. Walking forward, he put one arm around her shoulders and pulled her toward him. He faced his brother and sister-in-law, the symbolism of his stance clear—he would support Helena against any further attack. Relieved and warmed at the example of brotherly love, I felt it an opportune time for my withdrawal. Excusing myself in a low voice, I turned to leave.

"Young woman," a voice trumpeted across the hallway, stopping me in mid-step.

I turned slowly at the earl's harsh voice. His face was red with fury.

"Let there be no misunderstanding whatsoever concerning my feelings in this matter. I forbid you to see Helena again. I forbid you to meet her. I forbid you to have any further contact with her. She is young and innocent, and I will not have you dragging her down to the level your type inhabits. Women such as you ought to be flogged and placed in prison with the whores, where you belong."

I stood still, my gaze on Griffin as he comforted his sister. His head was bent close to hers as she clung to him, sobbing quietly into his chest, and in a most inexplicable burst of emotion, I wanted to be in those arms, I wanted to be the one who was comforted. Instead, I stood alone and unprotected against the earl's attack.

"I have no qualms in consulting with the police over your behavior. It is shameless and godless, and if I had my way—"

A low growl broke in. "That's enough, Sherry."

"I have a great deal more to say, and I'll thank you to stay out of this, Griffin." Lord Sherringham's voice cut through me like a knife. "You may not be aware, madam, but I am currently very much taken up with the foolish topic of suffrage at the House of Lords. Your offensive and reprehensible behavior is more proof of just how dangerous is the idea of giving women the vote. You may be assured I will remember your actions when discussing the issue with my fellow peers."

"I see no reason why you should," I said, stung into a response. "It is quite apparent from your rude and insulting comments that you have already made up your mind against women's suffrage."

"Of course I have," he snapped. "It is a ridiculous subject, one no decent man would even consider."

"Stop it!" Griffin roared.

The volume and tone of his voice were surprising in their intensity. He turned to me and said in a voice thick with fatigue, "My apologies for my brother's rudeness, Miss Whitney. Thank you for accompanying Helena home." He looked down at her tenderly, then up at me with a faint smile.

Silence filled the hall as I turned towards the door, the familiar numbness that I associated with the aftermath of one of my father's rages leaving me silent as I left the house. I gave the cabby my address automatically, and rode in an unthinking state until I arrived at home.

CHAPTER SEVEN

A restless night dawned into an equally restless morning. Exhausted, I lay in bed and watched the sky lighten from indigo to a soft blue-grey as I considered the matter that consumed my thoughts.

"Let us look at it from a strictly analytical point of view," I told Annie when she brought me my morning tea.

"If you like, miss, although I've often found that affairs of the heart can't often be analyzed."

"Hmm. Well, we shall try. You will admit that I have been unusually sheltered during my years with Father."

"That is true, miss."

"With no one who could even remotely be considered a suitor."

"Very true."

"Thus it's perfectly reasonable that this attraction I feel for Mr. St. John is simply my mind reacting to the pleasures to be found in the company of a man who you have to admit is devastatingly handsome."

"Mr. St. John?" Annie appeared to consider it. "I haven't seen him, but if you say so, then he must be."

"It is merely a brief and mild infatuation, no more," I said as I slipped on my dressing gown.

Annie made a noise somewhat resembling a stifled laugh.

"And everyone knows that an infatuation of the brief and mild variety is best treated as if it is any other minor physical affliction—I will ignore it and it will go away on its own."

"Is that so?" she asked, handing me my brush.

"Yes." I was tired but resolute. I would forget about Griffin and concentrate on more important things.

Following that plan, I tended to some correspondence, then settled down with my typewriting machine, and prepared to transcribe my notes from the prior evening. I looked around the desk, but could not find my notebook. Frowning, I tried to remember what I had done with it. The horribly memory of the night before returned with a sick feeling in my stomach. "Oh, blast! The attack. I forgot all about it."

Due to my emotional state after returning home from the Sherringham's, I had neglected to report the assault to the police. Annoyed at the distraction, I dutifully placed a telephone call to the local police station and explained the situation. While waiting for a constable to stop by and take my report, I went upstairs to locate the notebook.

"Annie, have you seen my notebook? The one with the brown leather cover?"

"No, miss, I haven't. Would it be in your bag?"

I pulled my head out from where I had been peering under the bed and sat back on my heels. "No, it's too big for that. I thought it might have fallen out of my skirt, but I can't find it. You didn't take it out of my skirt pocket, by any chance?"

"No, I haven't."

"Hmmm." I chewed my lip again in thought. "It must be in my coat. Have you seen . . . oh, good heavens!"

The sudden, horrible thought came to me that I was no longer in possession of my coat—I had given it to Helena the night before when her own had been ruined. I raced downstairs to locate the coat I had brought home. I had a vague memory of throwing it into the corner of the hall because of its stench.

My sister's household staff is nothing if not efficient...no coat was lying anywhere in the hall. I went through the green baize door, hoping Mullin would know of its whereabouts. "Mullin, did you find a coat I left in the hall last night?"

He looked up from polishing a particularly ugly silver fish knife. "Yes, miss, I did. It seemed to be soiled, so I sent it to Smith. I hope I have not acted expeditiously."

"No, not at all," I said over my shoulder as I flew down the stairs to the basement. Smith was the laundress who came in three days a week to do our laundry. Luckily today was not one of her days. With a muted groan, I lifted Helena's pink coat from the pile of garments.

"Oh—damn!" I swore out loud as I surveyed the offensive item, checking to be sure the notebook had not magically appeared in its pockets.

Every moment the notebook resided in Lord Sherringham's house, the more opportunity he would have to stumble across it and read the notes I had so thoroughly taken. Sick at the thought of him becoming privy to the Union's plans, I hurried up the stairs, leaving the coat behind.

"The constable is here," Mullin told me, interrupting my unhappy meditation.

I met him in the sitting room and succinctly gave him details of the assault, keeping Helena's participation in the events out of the narrative.

"You ought to know better than to walk about by yourself at night, miss. It's not like you was still in the country," he lectured me.

"Am I correct in understanding, Constable Merrywhite," I asked politely as we strolled out to the front steps to enjoy the sunny morning, "that it is unsafe for anyone to walk through this area of London at night?"

I gestured at the pleasant scene in front of us. Across from the house was a small square presently inhabited by a nanny whose two charges skipped alongside a pram, and an elderly gentleman who hobbled before them, waving his stick in greeting to a passing motor. On a bench facing the house sat a man in a brown checked suit and bowler. It was peaceful, serene, and utterly lacking in any threatening elements.

"It's not wise for you to be walking anywhere at night by yourself, miss."

The man on the bench looked vaguely familiar, but I couldn't place him. After a few moments he stretched, stood, and with a disinterested air, sauntered off down the block.

"How very odd..." I murmured.

"Not odd so much as unwise," the constable corrected.

"No, I meant...never mind." I thanked him for his advice and time, and returned to the house to consider the problem of the missing notebook. I had just settled down to write a note to Helena when I was summoned to the telephone.

"Cassandra, my dearest, I was hoping you would be home so I might call on you around tea time. I have an important subject to discuss with you."

"Freddy, you are incorrigible. Your important subject wouldn't happen to be one of a matrimonial nature?"

"My dear, your suspicious mind! Can a dearly loved cousin not visit without being expected to propose?"

I smiled. "In your case, I sincerely doubt it. I am engaged this afternoon, Freddy, so you won't find me at home. What, if it wasn't marriage, did you wish to discuss?"

"Your happiness, dearest cousin," he sighed dramatically.

"Freddy—"

"You know how devoted I am to you! It is not my own passionate feelings that I am considering. No, it is your welfare that is uppermost in my mind. I want to save you from the grief your life as a spinster must give—unloved, unwanted, moving from relation to relation in the fruitless quest for a home…"

"In other words, you want to save me from a life like yours," I interrupted, laughing. "Thank you for the tenth proposal. Consider it denied."

"My dearest, my own, think of what I offer! Position, a husband who worships you, protection—"

I wondered idly if I had told Cook to prepare chicken for dinner.

"Protection," he repeated, his voice silky, "from all sorts of evils. With myself at your side, you would never need worry about your personal safety."

"I don't worry about my personal safety now, Freddy."

"But you should, Cassandra. If you continue your connection with the suffragists, you must surely expose yourself to all sorts of violent elements, and I know how you abhor violence."

"Freddy—" I protested, growing uncomfortable with the turn the conversation had taken. Beside Emma, Freddy was the only other person who knew what extreme lengths my father's fury had often taken.

"Fairest one, I do not wish to cause you pain by reminding you of the unpleasantness of the past, indeed, it is my intention to shield you from ever having to experience such atrocities again. You must see, however, if you continue to pursue your work with the Union you run the risk of becoming involved in unwholesome situations."

"Unwholesome? Freddy, you exaggerate."

"Have you read the morning papers? There was a demonstration in Manchester last night. Three women were hospitalized with broken bones after the crowd assaulted them."

I was silent, unsure of what to say.

"Cassandra, I have seen you beaten and bruised time after time, and was unable to do anything about it. I will not allow you to put yourself in such a position again."

It was on the tip of my tongue to point out that I had no choice in the matter of my father's abuse, but I knew he hadn't really meant to imply that I had *allowed* myself to be beaten. "Thank you for your concern. I can only promise you that I am using the utmost caution, and have every intention of continuing to do so. Now if there is nothing else, I really must go."

"Cousin—"

"Good bye, Freddy," I said firmly, and gently rang off.

It was noon when I sat down again to write Helena. I was not altogether sure if the note would reach its intended recipient. Lady Sherringham seemed the type of person who would feel no qualms about interfering with Helena's mail. I was in the library, chewing on the end of a pen and staring at a blank sheet of writing paper, wondering what to say to Helena, when visitors were announced.

"I will never get this blasted note finished at this rate. Who is it now—"

I took the card Theodore the footman offered, and leaped up with an exclamation of joy. I almost trampled the poor lad so quick was I to run down the stairs, flinging open the door to the drawing room, and saying, "Helena! I am so glad you brought my coat. I was about to write to you to request it. You will never guess—"

Griffin stood by the window. My heart jumped unreasonably, and suddenly there was no air in my lungs. He turned and looked at me curiously.

Helena held out her hands as she approached, kissing me cheek as she said, "Please forgive us, dear Cassandra, for calling without notice. I hope we haven't disturbed you."

I looked at her elegant tweed walking suit with cream satin waistcoat, then down at my new dark green day dress with black corded piping and sighed to myself. No matter how new my clothes, Helena always succeeded in putting me to shame.

"Not at all," I said weakly. I offered my hand to Griffin; he took it and looked at it as if it were something faintly unsavory, then released it and turned away.

I wondered what it was about him that had caught my unwilling fancy. Once I had thought him pleasant in appearance, but nothing more. But now I looked on his features—his nose a shade too pronounced, his jaw set with a firmness that belied obstinacy, his eyes perhaps a little too far apart—and my heart beat with a rhythm it had never adopted for anyone else. If only I could shake myself of this unreasonable interest in the man. Perhaps if I was to indulge myself in a carnal relationship with him, my ardor would cool.

I was considering just what form a carnal relationship might take when I realized that Helena was looking at me expectantly. "Where are my manners? Please, sit down."

Helena stood her ground. "I must first unburden myself and beg your forgiveness."

"Beg my forgiveness?" I asked with confusion, amused by her dramatic air. "What on earth have you done to me that you need to be forgiven?"

Her eyes filled with tears, and she seemed to be having a hard time speaking. I looked at Griffin helplessly. He stood with his hands clasped behind his back, sunlight from a nearby window casting a halo over his hair. His face was inscrutable as he watched his sister.

"Helena?" I asked her gently. "Whatever can be the matter?"

Two fat tears spilled over her lashes as she grabbed for her handkerchief. She clutched my arm and sobbed onto my shoulder, weeping as if her heart were broken

"For heaven's sake, Helena, you are the weepingest woman I know. Wipe your eyes and tell me what the problem is."

Griffin, suddenly grinning, seated himself on a nearby couch. His left hand was heavily bandaged, although the bandage appeared a big ragged, as if he had been worrying it.

"I'm so sorry, Cassandra. I would never have asked you to take me with you last night if I had known Letitia would return home early."

I noted absently that she had begun the process of ruining yet another pair of gloves, and wondered if the destruction of hand wear was an inherited trait in the St. John family.

"Can you ever forgive me for exposing you to such abuse?"

"Don't be silly, Helena. It wasn't your fault at all. I knew full well the feelings of your family, and can't blame them for being upset at your unexplained disappearance."

I looked over at her brother, who was being unusually (and to my mind suspiciously) quiet.

"You are so good, so understanding," she sniffled into her handkerchief. "Harold and Letitia have been particularly . . . unhappy since Rosewood burned down."

"Rosewood?"

Griffin spoke. "Rosewood was our family home in Devonshire. The house burned down a few years ago."

"I'm sorry to hear that. I take it Rosewood was the earl's country seat?"

He gave an odd bark of laughter. "You could say that."

Gripping my hand, Helena gave me a strange, impassioned look. "I can't tell you how I cherish your friendship. It means a great deal to me, and I wouldn't want anything to destroy it. You are so good, so kind—"

"Hardly either," I interrupted, uncomfortable with her fervent gaze. "No harm has been done other than a little damage to my pride, and that, I can assure you, will repair itself in no time. I admit that I was concerned about what sort of reception you would meet after I left."

"I'm not afraid of Harold when Griffin is home."

Griffin fidgeted uncomfortably, scratching at his collar. "My sister has told me of the evening's activities."

"Did she?" I glanced at Helena, surprised that she would mention the exact details of our outing.

With an air of martyrdom, he continued, although he averted his gaze from mine. "I attach no blame to her or you for the events that transpired. I was glad she had you as a companion."

Clearly she didn't tell him about the purse thief. "I appreciate your support in this matter. I am just sorry that your brother and sister-in-law do not share your opinion."

"This is not easy for me to say. You . . . er . . . know my feelings upon the subject of women's suffrage."

I started to make a face, then remembered he was a guest in my home and nodded instead.

He cleared his throat and glanced at his sister. "My feelings have not changed about the appropriateness of women's participation in politics; however, I have discussed the issue with Helena, and have agreed to allow her to attend meetings as long as she is in your presence."

Helena leaned slightly to the left and prodded at him.

"Despite my better feelings, I have also . . . er . . . agreed to let her become a member of that women's club you belong to."

"The Women's Suffrage Union." I spoke absently, suddenly wondering about his bandaged hand.

As his words sunk in, I looked up in surprise. Given the feelings that the earl had so vehemently expressed the night before, I had no doubt that Helena's foray into political activism would be swiftly and irrevocably nipped in the bud.

"However," he said loudly and with some force, "that does not mean I authorize her to participate in any demonstrations or public displays. I cannot control *your* actions... "

My eyebrows rose at the very idea.

". . . but I would recommend you stop your campaigning as well. I've heard from Sherry that the new head of Scotland Yard is proceeding with a strict policy of non-tolerance against suffrage demonstrators. If you don't want to be arrested, I'd advise you to stay clear of any further public scenes."

His speech over, he sat back down on the couch and looked at me belligerently, as if challenging me to make a defense. I wondered briefly if he had an ulterior motive in allowing Helena to join in the union, but was unable to think of any benefit her participation would have for him or his brother.

I surprised both of us by saying simply, "I agree with you. It would be unwise for Helena to expose herself to any danger by becoming involved in a suffrage protest, and I am sure she will agree to such a reasonable request."

Helena looked at me with open-mouthed surprise. "I don't agree all!" she cried. "How can you say that—you who feel so strongly, and know how strongly I feel about the cause?"

I spread my hands in a placatory gesture. "I know you hold the cause very tightly to your bosom, but you must see that about this, your brother is right. There is no reason to risk your personal safety."

"I see no such thing. I *will* be at the rally tomorrow!"

"Rally tomorrow?" Griffin repeated suspiciously. He turned to me. "What rally tomorrow?"

I waved my hand in a dismissive fashion. "A small rally in Hyde Park. It's a minor gathering, no demonstrations, no protests, just an attempt to raise funds and public awareness for the Union."

"Helena will not be attending the rally, Miss Whitney." He tugged at the bandage on his hand as he spoke. "And I strongly urge you to reconsider your attendance at such a public spectacle."

"Mr. St. John, I took umbrage with you when you used that particular word before, and I take umbrage at it now. How you can interpret a peaceful, organized rally at Speaker's Corner as a *spectacle* is beyond me!"

He looked surprised by the vehemence in my voice and absently continued to pick at the bandage. "You may consider your cause one that is peaceful and organized, but I would be willing to wager that the public does not see it that way. Helena will not attend."

"Griffin!"

We both turned to look at Helena, who had risen and was standing with fists clenched. "I am twenty-one years old and of legal age. If I choose to participate in a peaceful rally in Hyde Park with my dear friend Cassandra, then I shall do so."

I gave her a mental pat on the back for standing up for her beliefs, and smiled smugly at her brother, who looked stunned at her vehemence. A dull red color flooded his face as he started to answer, but I interrupted, unable, any longer, to stand him tearing away at the remaining bits of bandage. "What did you do to your hand?"

"Eh? Oh, my hand. I had an accident—some damned fool knocked me down with his motor car."

"Good heavens! You were lucky to escape with only a minor injury."

"Lucky?" he snorted, tearing off a shred of bandage and placing it absentmindedly into his pocket. "I would be a good deal luckier if people would learn to handle their motors before they took to the public streets with them."

Helena, reminded of her brother's recent accident, lost her belligerent look. A glimmer could be seen in her eyes, and I hoped we wouldn't have a repeat of her tears. "You are having too many accidents since you have been home, Griffin. First, there was the ruffian in Limehouse—"

"A common navvy under the influence of a local opium den. It was not a personal attack against me," Griffin interrupted.

"And then there was the incident a few weeks ago when you fell down the back stairs—"

"A loose carpet rod."

"And just last week you had that terrible bilious attack that Doctor Treadway called suspicious."

Griffin groaned as he glanced at me, obviously embarrassed by his sister's candor. "I doubt if Miss Whitney wants to hear about my internal complaints, Helena. We are boring her. And I'm not through discussing this rally tomorrow—"

"On the contrary, you are not boring me at all. In fact, it sounds like you are a character out of a novel I am at present reading."

He grunted and looked out the window as Helena asked, "A novel?"

"Your brother's recent escapades strike me as the melodramatic stuff that makes up popular novels. The type with the dark, brooding hero who someone is trying to do away with. I picked up just such a novel the other day."

Griffin muttered a rude comment under his breath, but loud enough for me to hear. "About that rally you plan to go to tomorrow . . . ." he started to say, then fell silent as the butler stepped into the room.

"Miss Debenham."

"Emma! How delightful to see you. You will remember Mr. and Miss St. John." I rose to greet my old friend.

"Of course. It's a pleasure to see you both again. Cassandra, I'm sorry to interrupt. I had no idea you had visitors. I can come back another time—"

"Don't be silly. I'm always happy to see you. Mullin, bring tea." I escorted Emma to a chair and sat beside her, giving her hand a little pat of support. Despite our success the other day at my aunt's tea, I knew Emma still felt awkward in the company of anyone but her oldest friends.

Griffin looked with much speculation first at Emma, then at my hand on hers, then to me.

"You look flushed, Cassandra. Are you feeling well?" Emma asked as silence descended in the room.

"Quite well. I had a busy morning. Helena—"

The slight young woman jumped as I spoke her name. Emma and I looked in surprise at her reaction.

"What's the matter?" I asked.

"I'm sorry. It's just..." Helena knelt next to me, taking my arm. "You mentioned...you don't think...oh, surely it can't be true! Griffin, say it is not true!"

"It's not true," he obediently said.

"What's not true?" Emma asked me.

"I have no idea. Mr. St. John?"

He shrugged. "Helena has a vivid imagination. No doubt that is giving her grief right now."

"Helena, what—" I started to ask, but she gripped my hands then, her fingers digging into mine with unexpected strength.

"Griffin," she whispered hoarsely, her face a bloodless mask. "Do you really think someone is...someone want to...someone plans to do away with him?"

CHAPTER EIGHT

We all looked at Griffin: Helena in horror, full of concern for a beloved brother, Emma with thoughtful surprise, and me with more than a little amusement.

Griffin rolled his eyes at Helena's question. "No one is trying to kill me. That suggestion was a figment of Miss Whitney's mind, which she herself just admitted is overheated with the inane ramblings of women's novels."

"I admitted nothing of the kind! I can think of several reasons that someone might wish to murder your brother. I, myself . . .but we will not go into that. Doubtless, he has made many enemies with his abrasive manners and misguided beliefs." A low growl emitted from the vicinity of the window. I continued at a louder volume. "And certainly there must be a vast number of women travelers who would be delighted to see him in the hereafter, but I must admit that his recent accidents seem more a result of his own clumsiness than a planned assault by an unknown person." I thought for a moment. "Or persons, perhaps even an organized group with an international membership—"

"Blast you, woman," he roared. "I am the mildest of men! I have no enemies other than the ever-increasing hordes of women who insist on getting in my way!"

Helena bleated at him in a distressed manner, while Emma stifled her laugher. Griffin, eyes alight and nostrils flaring, glared at me in a magnificent example of a righteously enraged Englishman.

As a dedicated New Woman, I could not resist toying with him a little longer.

"Do you mean to say that women who travel abroad do so with the sole purpose of placing themselves in your way? It seems a rather conceited idea, but if it pleases you to believe that the world revolves around you..." I ignored Griffin's enraged bellow as Mullin brought in the tea, followed by Theodore with assorted teacakes. "Tea, Helena? Emma, you must try the seed cake. Cook does it particularly well."

"Cassandra, I must know—do you really feel that Griffin is in any danger?"

I looked up from pouring tea and sighed. It wasn't fair to torment Helena because I wanted to tease her brother. "Unfortunately for the future of women travelers, no, I don't feel he is in danger. I think he is just clumsy—or accident-prone."

"Typical female attitude," he muttered as he accepted a cup of tea and plate of cake. "I'm fine as am I. If you women weren't so determined to meddle in a man's affairs . . . and speaking of that, this rally tomorrow—"

Wishing to avoid another argument, and to keep his mind from the subject of the Hyde Park gathering, I interrupted him. "Emma, did you know that Mr. St. John was recently in Arabia?"

"Really?" Interest lit her dark eyes. She looked at him. "Did you enjoy yourself?"

"Yes," he said gruffly, stuffing half of the seed cake into his mouth.

"Why don't you tell us about the trip?" I asked, smiling. "I'm sure Emma would like to hear about it, and I would be most interested. When exactly did you return home?"

"Three weeks ago." He glared at me with a decidedly suspicious glint in his cat-like amber eyes.

"Arabia . . . it sounds so exotic," I mused, my mind a thousand miles away. "Minarets."

"Camels," Helena said, a similar faraway look in her eyes.

"Rugs and tiny little cups of coffee," I added.

"Harems," Emma said, her voice breathy with pleasure.

Griffin snorted. "There is a lot more to the country than rugs, camels, and harems."

"Tell us about it," I invited.

He gave me a long look, then, grudgingly at first, told us about his latest journey. As he spoke, animation crept over his face, passion for a topic near to his heart softening his features and giving him a vitality that took him beyond merely handsome, to breathtakingly gorgeous.

My admiration grew as he spoke; here was a man who was not content to live in a settled, safe life. Not for him, the routine, the humdrum; instead he walked a path that few Englishmen had walked before. Brave, heroic, adventurous, he faced life and death on a daily basis, and relished every minute of it.

"How I wish I could have such adventures!" I cried, envious and rapt with admiration at the same time. "Oh, Emma, don't you wish we could do the same?"

She raised her eyebrows, nibbling on a lemon tart. "It sounds very exotic, but I believe I prefer familiar surroundings to those of a more daring nature."

"I would love to have adventures," Helena declared, sitting forward on the chair. "Life here is so boring!"

"Can you imagine meeting a sheikh, Helena? Eating a meal of sheep's eyes? Riding a camel across the desert? And the men, how dashing and handsome they sound, how brave and daring." A sudden thought occurred to me, and I asked hopefully, "Did you see the sheikh's harem?"

"Good lord, no!" Griffin looked at me askance. "No man is allowed to see a sheikh's harem and live to tell about it."

"Oh," I said, disappointed. "Why?"

His shocked look was answer enough.

Emma coughed. I patted her on the back as I murmured, glancing at Helena, "Perhaps another time. Now, you were saying something about a nomad tribe?"

I fell silent and let him continue his narrative. Although he was a fascinating orator, and told his spine-chilling tales well, I slowly found my concentration waning.

Instead of thrilling to his adventure with a camel thief in Baghdad, I found myself gazing appreciatively at his broad shoulders. He told of a narrow escape through a bazaar while I admired the way his hair curled back from his brow, my fingers itching to touch the silky curls. When he took off his coat and rolled up his sleeve to show us a tattoo received at the hands of a Zulu warrior, I noticed the way the fine, golden brown hairs grew on his arms. The ease with which he strode about captivated me, his deep, resonant voice rolled around the small room, sweeping me up in its warmth, and making me tingle in places I had never known to tingle before.

This is no soup dribbler, I told myself. *He is prime lover material, a virile man who thinks nothing of staring fear in the face.* And I was determined to have him.

My mind wandered pathways that involved his bare flesh under my hands, my breasts growing heavy as the overwhelming desire to be pressed up against him washed over me. Having grown up with a father whose religious beliefs were borderline fanatical, I had no experience of the carnal acts, but I could not deny that there were parts of me, personal parts, *tingly* parts that had developed an intense interest in learning all about them with Griffin. I recalled every Greek statue I had ever seen, and wondered how he would compare. Would his fig leaf bulge in as enticingly a manner as the statue of Apollo I had once seen?

With a start, I realized he had stopped speaking. Both Emma and Helena watched me with evident concern.

"Fig leaf," I said, then realized my mouth had spoken without my thinking, and cleared my throat. I picked up the cold teapot. "More tea, anyone?"

Helena and Griffin took their leave not long after that. As I was seeing them out, Helena stopped suddenly in the hallway.

"I have forgotten!" She darted forward and snatched up a package. "Your coat. Griffin returned it to me this morning. I had foolishly left it in the hall."

She smiled warmly as our eyes met. There was no sign of trepidation about her countenance—I doubt if it had occurred to her to look in the coat pockets.

"Thank you for thinking of it," I said weakly, relief flooding me.

She gave me a shy smile and turned to leave. As she did, Griffin leaned towards me and withdrew a familiar leather notebook from his coat and spoke quietly. "In the future, I would advise you to keep such information safe, and not make it available to people who could use it to your detriment."

"Thank you," I said in a small voice, too horrified by the thoughts running through my head to congratulate myself on keeping the topic of tomorrow's rally from discussion. I watched silently as they entered their motorcar, then ran back to the sanctuary of the library.

"They seem like pleasant people," Emma commented as I stood panting at the door. "Without the odious sister-in-law. I like Helena very much. I think she'll be good friend for you. Her brother is—what on earth is the matter with you?"

I caught my breath and staggered into the room, collapsing on the sofa next to her. Quickly I explained about the events the previous evening. "The question is, will he tell his brother? Familial duty would require it, but would he betray Helena and me in such a manner?"

"I don't know," Emma said thoughtfully. "Men are such curious creatures. So unpredictable."

"Was that why he had warned me against any further demonstrations? Was he trying to tell me the Union's secrets were no longer safe? Can I trust him, or not?"

"I'm afraid I don't know any of those answers. Cassandra..." Emma gave me a curious look.

"Hmm?"

"You like him, don't you?"

"Griffin? Er...Mr. St. John?"

She laughed. "I can see you do."

I set down the notebook and did my best to look like a worldly New Woman. "I am considering him for the position of lover, yes."

"Considering him for—" She came to an abrupt stop, her lips pressed together tightly for a few seconds. "Have you told him of this opportunity?"

"No, I thought it best to wait until I had made a final decision," I said, idly rubbing a spot on the knee of my gown. "Men, I have found, are often inflexible when it comes to such matters. It is best if I don't mention anything until I've narrowed down the candidates to just him."

"That would seem eminently wise," she said with a suspicious tremor in her voice. "Would you think me rude if I asked about the other candidates?"

"Well, there's Freddy of course, although I don't really consider him a candidate. He's my cousin, after all, and I although I have much affection for him, it is impossible for me to consider him in the light of a lover."

"Very insightful of you," she agreed.

"And then there was the dribbler."

She looked somewhat startled. "Who?"

"Soup dribbler."

"Ah."

"I could never have carnal relations with a man who dribbled soup. Griffin doesn't look in the least like he'd dribble, does he?"

"Not soup, no," she said.

I narrowed my gaze on her. She seemed to be developing some sort of a facial tic.

"Any other candidates?" she asked.

"Not really, no. There's Theodore the footman, but I caught him once picking his ear." I shuddered.

She made a face. "Definitely not. I would say, then, that Mr. St. John stands a fair chance of being suitable for the position."

I beamed at her, pleased with her approval of my choice. We chatted for a few minutes about her latest events—her literary circle was having some sort of reenactment of a historical event, and she wanted to get her costume just right—but my mind was consumed with worry, and I fear she noticed.

"The interpretive dance sounds lovely, Emma, although I don't quite understand why you need to apply oil to the dancers. Does it have some historical importance?"

"You could say that. You have something on your mind, don't you?"

I sighed. "I'm sorry, I haven't been a good friend at all."

"You've been the truest friend I have, but you know that. Tell me what's bothering you. Is it the business with this notebook?"

"Yes." Tracing idly around the notebook's leather cover, I let my mind play with suppositions.

"All right." She set down my sister's orange cat Marmalade who seemed to prefer the library to any other room of the house. "Let's take this in an orderly fashion. You believe that Mr. St. John has read the notebook, and might have told his brother about it. What if Lord Sherringham saw the information? What possible damage could he do with it? It is not as if he could use it to stop the campaign."

Marmalade wandered over and begged a piece of seed cake from me before settling down on my lap. I stroked him absently as I thought. "I'm not so sure about that, Emma. There's the arrest of the ten women protesting at the Hospital Ball, not to mention the three women injured in Manchester that Griffin mentioned. If the police are losing their tolerance of suffrage protests, the information from my notebook could allow them to halt the demonstrations before they began."

"That does sound rather ominous. What are you going to do?"

I sighed. "I don't know, that's just the problem. I will, of course, tell Mrs. Heywood about the mishap with the notebook. She will certainly see the potential for damage, and may go so far as to censure me. As for the other matter, I can see no way to find out whether or not Griffin has revealed the information to his brother without compromising myself."

"Have you thought of simply asking him about it?"

"I couldn't do that!"

"Why not?"

"He's a potential lover. The question would be tantamount to accusing him, and I could not possibly treat a lover in such a cavalier manner."

Her facial tic returned. "As I see it, you don't have many options open to you. I suppose you considered asking his sister for help?"

"Yes, and dismissed her for similar reasons as her brother, although without the carnal implications, naturally."

"Naturally."

I could have sworn I heard laughter in her voice, but when I glanced at her, her expression was somber. "It is a difficult situation, to be true, but I feel sure that whatever course you choose will be the appropriate one."

I nodded my head glumly. Emma exclaimed at the time and dashed off for her historical reenactment costume fitting. I retired to my typewriting machine and transcribed my notes, my heart heavy and my spirits dulled.

CHAPTER NINE

It was with great relief a few hours later that I sat down next to my aunt in her plaid boudoir, a tribute to the late Queen Victoria's love of the Scottish.

"I'm so glad we're alone. I just don't think I could cope with any more of Freddy's proposals," I said, accepting a cup of China tea. "I have had a very trying day, and I much need a few moments of respite."

"Trying how, dear?" she asked.

"It's…it's a rather delicate situation."

"Really?" Aunt Caroline looked at me with undisguised interest. "You're not going to tell me to change this room again, are you? If so, you know your uncle won't let me—his mother was a distant cousin of the late Queen."

"No," I replied with a wry smile. I looked around the room and tried not to wince at the abundant, and somewhat garish, collection of plaid furnishings. "Although I'm sure by now he would let you change the décor—but we'll go into that another time. What I was referring to is of a personal nature."

She sat back on a Black Watch plaid chaise and looked at me eagerly. "How very intriguing. It wouldn't have anything to do with—"

"Ah, good, tea time!" Cousin Freddy popped into the room rubbing his hands.

"Hellfire and damnation!" I exclaimed.

He stopped upon seeing me and clasped his hand over his heart in a fashion that would be perfectly at home on the music hall stage. "Dearest cousin, beloved Cassandra. I knew you could not refuse me for long." He perched himself on the arm of my Stuart plaid chair, and clutched my hand in his. "You see, Aunt—she has come to her senses at last and has decided to accept me. Happy day!"

"You are the most ridiculous man I have ever met," I said, irritability overriding the fondness I normally felt for him. "What are you doing here? I thought rakes like yourself spent your days pursuing young ladies of fortune."

"There's only one lady of fortune I wish to pursue," he said with a waggle of his brows. "I was at my club, but it's too tedious for words so I thought I would return home. Since Aunt and Uncle have asked me to stay here while I recover from my broken heart, I think it only polite to be available when my presence might be wanted."

"Your broken heart," I muttered in disbelief.

"A heart, dearest one, that only *you* can mend." He leaned forward and leered at me in a suggestive manner.

I was a little taken aback by the wolfish smile, and looked at my aunt. She watched us with a smile hovering around the corners of her lips. "You really are beyond the limit, Freddy. I wish to have a private talk with Aunt Caroline, so please take yourself elsewhere."

"Have some good gossip, eh?" He looked interested. "Perhaps I should stay."

"If you don't go now," I warned, sending him a look brimming with portent, "I will tell Uncle Henry what you did your last year at Cambridge when—"

There was no need to finish. Freddy made a polite bow and wished us well.

"I can't tell you how grateful I am that blackmail always works on those of weak character," I said as he left.

Aunt Caroline asked curiously, "What *did* Freddy do at Cambridge?"

"I'll tell you another time. How are you doing with him constantly underfoot?"

"He's not so bad, and he has nowhere else to go. Henry feels it is important to support the family, so Freddy visits us when we are in town—though I admit that sometimes he is rather trying. But tell me about your problem. Does it concern the handsome Mr. St. John?"

I looked at her in surprise. "How did you know that?"

She smiled and ignored the question. "I like him very much. And his sister, of course."

"Sometimes I think you're a witch. The problem does concern the St. Johns, but not in the manner you think."

"I was not thinking of him in any particular manner, my dear," she said gently as she poured me another cup of tea. "Were you?"

I thought about my curiosity regarding Griffin stripped naked, and blushed. "Well...possibly. He's on my list of candidates, you see."

"Candidates? Oh, for a lover?" She considered that idea for a moment before shaking her head. "No, I think not. He wouldn't be suitable in the least."

My stomach dropped. "He wouldn't?"

"Definitely not. He is not the lover type of man. Some men are, you know. They may appear interested in one, and quite devoted, but after a certain length of time, their interest wanes. That is the type of man you should have for a lover."

"I see." I felt deflated again, as if someone had let all the wind out of my balloon.

She adjusted a pillow behind her back, giving me a gentle smile as she continued. "Mr. St. John is not at all that sort of a man—he is the type who, once his affections have been engaged, will be steadfast. His interest will not wane. You would find yourself with a permanent partner, not a lover whom you will eventually grow tired of and replace."

The thought of having Griffin as a permanent lover didn't sound at all unappealing. Quite the opposite.

"There is that, of course," I said slowly. "But I admit that I've always had an admiration for constancy in a man. You and Uncle Henry, for instance, have been most devoted to you."

"Yes, Henry is the same sort of man as Mr. St. John," she said complacently, smoothing out the lace at her wrists. "He is the ideal husband, but as a lover...no. He would not have done."

I made a little face as I thought over what she said, feeling as if the rug had been pulled from beneath me. Griffin had seemed so idea for the role of lover. What if, knowing I wished to remain unmarried for many years, he refused me? Would I ever be able to suffer the mortification of that? "Thank you for your candid advice," I finally said, my mind full of miserable speculation.

"Not at all. Before I forget, dear, Henry and I would like you to attend the opening of that new opera tomorrow night. What is the name of it—the one where everyone dresses as peasants and drinks wine and the woman dies? Henry has taken a box for the season, and we both would like for you to use it."

Almost as amused by her description of the opera as I was touched by her thoughtfulness, I thanked her and accepted. We chatted for a few minutes more, then I took my leave. As I stepped out into the hall, I was startled to find Freddy holding my russet wool coat.

"What on earth are you doing?" I asked curiously.

Freddy jumped. "I was just going to help you on with your coat," he said with a smile.

A faint sense of unease rippled through my mind. Freddy had always been so warm, so charming, and yet for the first time, I thought I saw something other than fond affection in his eyes.

"Might I take this opportunity, dearest—"

"Thank you, Freddy, I would prefer you not."

He sighed and placed a hand over his chest. "My poor heart will never heal at this rate."

I smiled and patted him on his cheek. "I have every confidence that your heart will make a miraculous recovery just as soon as you meet a woman with a larger fortune than mine."

"Cousin, you wound me!"

I laughed and allowed him to help me into the carriage, directing the coachman to Mrs. Heywood's house in Islington. When I arrived, I was shown into a small study on the ground floor. I paced the room, worried about Mrs. Heywood's reaction to my careless actions, biting my lip as I tried to formulate an explanation that didn't sound too cowardly or weak.

Loud voices interrupted my pacing. I would have ignored them had one not caught my interest. The Irish brogue strongly resembled that of Maggie Greene, one of the Union officials.

Although I am not one for eavesdropping, curiosity got the better of me. I opened the study door a crack and held my breath as I listened.

". . . take it to a vote of the full membership. I'm sure the members won't consider any such actions, Maggie. They are dangerous, unnecessary, and deliberately inflammatory. Such a plan would alienate us from the very people we are striving to reach."

"Unnecessary, is it? Inflammatory, is it? Shame on you, Lenore Heywood, for turning your back on danger! Where our glorious cause is concerned, the end is worth any means. No action is too extreme, no sacrifice too great. We must strike now, while the House of Lords is still debating, to show them that we will not go quietly!"

Mrs. Heywood murmured a soft answer.

"I warn you, Lenore, I'll not be pushed aside as you have the others. There are many women both in the union and outside of it who are behind me on this. We are gaining strength, and have more support than you can conceive. The time is coming when you will find your precious non-violent Union disabled and ineffective. You have one last chance to achieve success. Will you take it?"

"I have told you that we will not adopt a militant policy—"

Maggie spat out an invective as she strode to the front door, pausing to point her finger dramatically as she said, "You have been warned. If necessary, we will bring the Union to its knees to attain our goal. We could survive such a division—could you?"

She turned and stalked through the doorway before Mrs. Heywood could answer.

I returned to my chair, and prepared to interest myself in the stuffed hedgehog that resided on a table next to it, and was examining its curious snout when, a few moments later, the butler entered and informed me that Mrs. Heywood would see me. Though it was early evening, she greeted me in a lovely morning room filled with flowers and tapestries.

"You must forgive me for having you brought here, but it is my favorite room. Please be seated. What can I do for you?"

I explained the situation with the notebook as quickly as possible.

"And so the *brother* of Lord Sherringham returned the notebook to you?" Mrs. Heywood asked quietly when I was finished.

"Yes." I felt sick thinking of the consequences of my carelessness.

"I see." She contemplated the typed notes that I had given her. "You are aware of Lord Sherringham's position in the House of Lords, aren't you?"

"Yes, I am. I cannot tell you how badly I feel about this terrible, terrible calamity—" I stopped myself abruptly. I was beginning to sound like Helena.

"I don't believe it is as terrible a calamity as that," she said with a faint smile. "You have no indication that the information was disseminated, although I believe it would be prudent to change the dates and locations of those demonstrations to be held a few weeks hence. We cannot do anything about the events in the next few days, but we will trust that there is too little time for action to be taken against us."

"The rally tomorrow?" I asked, still miserable.

"That is public knowledge, so we have no fear for the integrity of that gathering." Mrs. Heywood walked down the stairs with me and placed her hand on my arm as I prepared to take my leave. "Don't worry. I have a feeling that in the large picture of life, this incident will matter little."

She turned to go when I was finally unable to hold my tongue any longer. "Mrs. Heywood?"

"Yes, my dear?"

I glanced at the footman who was standing at attention next to the front door in preparation for my departure. I moved closer to her and dropped my voice. "I couldn't help but overhear Maggie Greene earlier."

She sighed, and passed a long pale hand over her brow as if fatigued.

"Is there a problem with the Union? I am concerned that Maggie is trying to divide the membership. Is there anything I can do to help stop such a tragedy?"

She smiled wearily at me and patted my hand. "Thank you, I appreciate your concern. There is nothing you can do now, although there may be a time when you are called upon to stand behind the Union. As for Maggie...well, we won't discuss her now. She is so very emotional, and is often overly excited about imagined slights. Good night, Miss Whitney, and thank you for bringing the situation with your notebook to my attention."

I could not ignore that gentle but pointed hint, and so departed for home. When we arrived at my sister's house, Jackson silently handed me down and prepared to leave.

"I'd like a word with you for a moment, Jackson—gracious!"

I turned to look at the man who swayed into me as he walked past. He smelled of strong spirits and I would have thought nothing more about it except I saw a glint of gold when he begged my pardon. He moved off down the street in rather a serpentine fashion, pausing now and again as if lost in thought.

"Yes, miss?" Jackson reminded me he was still waiting.

I dragged my attention back to Jackson. A wiry man of about thirty-five, Jackson had shifty gray eyes, and hair that was so blond it was almost white. A short upper lip, combined with the inability to look me in the eye, gave me suspicions as to his moral character.

"It's about Annie. . . ." I paused, still disturbed by the encounter with the drunkard. "Have you ever seen that man before?"

"No, miss. You mentioned Annie?"

"Hmm. Yes. Annie. Oh, I understand you have been walking out with her."

Jackson dipped his head, and mumbled that he had once or twice, but had not seen her lately.

I ignored his excuse and took a deep breath. "I realize that, as I am not your employer, it is not my place to question you about so personal a matter, but Annie *is* my maid, and I value her a great deal. I would not like to see her hurt in any manner."

He looked in the vicinity of my left shoulder, and said, "No, miss. Nor would I want to see Annie hurt."

"What, if you don't mind my asking, are your intentions towards her?"

He shifted his focus to a spot some inches from the top of my head. "Intentions, miss?"

"Yes, intentions," I said firmly. "Do you plan to marry?"

Evidently I startled him with my directness, for his gaze dropped to my right hip. "It's not that I wouldn't want to—I'm not the marrying type, miss."

"I see. Thank you, Jackson, you have told me what I want to know."

I went into the house, more concerned than ever about Annie.

The next morning dawned with a clear sky, and as the sun rose, so did my spirits despite my concern over Griffin. A wire announcing my sister's imminent return came, requiring a discussion with the household staff, but that was soon taken care of. I avoided thinking about Mabel's reaction to my New Womanhood, and more specifically my support of women's rights, by borrowing my aunt's horse Marianne for a solitary ride in Rotten Row.

The Row was busy that Saturday, with couples and families out riding in the unusual spell of warm spring weather. I saw one or two acquaintances as I rode, but kept my conversations short.

A sudden, bellowed, "Good morning, Miss Whitney," from immediately behind startled me into a precarious lurch, forcing me to jerk back on the reins to retain my seat. Marianne stopped abruptly, directly in the path of the horse behind, which responded to the sudden obstacle by giving her a sharp nip on the rump. She bucked in protest at the assault, and I slid out of the saddle and onto the ground with a solid thump.

I looked up from where I was sprawled in the dirt and commented, "I should have known it was you. What other man would find it necessary to knock me to the ground to greet me?"

Griffin, for it was he who rode the horse behind me, roared with laughter, slapping at his leg in a most common manner. He wiped his eyes, then leaped down and helped me to my feet.

"On the contrary, my dear Miss Cassandra, experience has shown that you are just as likely as I am to be the catalyst for such a greeting."

I ignored the jibe. Brushing myself off, I went to retrieve my horse. I checked the bite; it was minor and did not require attention.

"Help me up," was my only comment as I tried unsuccessfully to remount.

"Certainly," he replied cheerfully. "Always glad to be of service. Put your foot here." He made a step with his hands. Placing one hand on his strong shoulder and the other on the saddle, I stepped onto his hands. He heaved me up and almost over the other side of the horse.

Clutching the sidesaddle and arranging my skirt as best I could, I gathered the reins and reached for the offered riding crop. My hand closed on his, and I looked down on him for a moment.

"Are you riding alone?" I asked, flooded with the by-now-familiar conflicting emotions and various tingling body parts that seemed to accompany his presence.

"I am." He jumped into his saddle from a standing position (something I have always wanted to learn, but have never been able to convince anyone to teach me), and walked his horse over to me. "May I join you?"

"It would certainly be better to have you where I can keep an eye out for you, in case your horse decides to take another bite out of Marianne." I tapped at the mare with the whip, and we set off at a brisk trot.

Griffin eyed my tenuous riding posture with some concern. "Are you sure you're not going to fall off again?"

"I never would have fallen off if you hadn't startled me, and your horse brutally attacked mine."

He grinned at me and my heart melted into a puddle. "Winston wouldn't attack a lady unless provoked. He's as gentle as a baby."

"Oh really?" I questioned, noting the firm hand he used to control the gray stallion. "Then I am sure you wouldn't have any qualms about letting me try him."

"No."

"But if he's so gentle—"

"No!"

"He is lovely." I reached over to pat the stallion's neck. "I don't suppose you'd be willing to part with him?"

"I'd sooner cut off my left...er...no, I am not selling him."

"I notice your hand is better," I said conversationally.

"Yes."

"It is curious, your having so many accidents since your return home. You don't think—"

"No!" he snapped.

I glanced at him out of the corner of my eye. He seemed to be somewhat moody now, yet he made no move to part company. Deciding any further comments about his accidents would be poorly received, I broached a subject about which I was curious.

"Tell me about Rosewood."

He looked startled by my request. "Rosewood? Why do you want to know about Rosewood?"

"It burned down, did it not?"

"Yes," he said warily.

"Why?"

He gave me a considering look, then sent Winston into an easy canter. Marianne followed suit without my urging.

"Well?"

"Why do you want to know?"

"It's part of my theory of why someone would want to do away with you."

He frowned in response to my smile. "You've been reading too many novels. There's nothing suspicious about my run of bad luck lately, and for the fire at Rosewood, it was caused by a faulty gas pipe."

"Ah. So there is not a tribe in Africa that has condemned you to death for the sacrilegious act you committed upon the chief's eldest daughter?"

"Not his *eldest* daughter." He grinned suddenly, sending my heart soaring. "No, no angry African tribe. You'll have to look closer to home for your murderous theories."

"So, you admit it is more than one person," I teased him gently.

"What about you?" he asked, changing the subject abruptly. His grin had evaporated, the familiar frown having returned.

"Me? I am not the one who is having suspicious accidents."

"That's not what Helena says." He pulled the horse up, his voice suddenly grim. "Evidently you ran into trouble the night you both went to that blasted meeting."

"Oh that," I waved a hand, thinking for some reason of the man with the gold tooth. "He was a simple thief who saw an opportunity and took it. He was obviously intimidated by there being two of us, or else he would have asked for our jewelry as well."

"Even you can hardly dismiss such an attack. Why were you walking home?"

"I like walking," I said airily. "I find it beneficial to the constitution. You are making too much out of a little incident— nothing happened other than the loss of a bag and a few shillings."

"Both of you could have been hurt."

"But we weren't."

We glared at each other until a passing rider distracted us.

"You haven't finished telling me about Rosewood," I pointed out as our horses walked on.

"I wasn't aware that I had *begun* telling you about it."

I stopped Marianne. He rode on a few paces, staring ahead until he noticed we were not at his side. He turned back when I spoke. "Tell me, Mr. St. John, is it women in general, or is there something specific about my person that forces you into rude and belligerent behavior?"

He glowered at me for a minute, then a slow smile spread across his face. All those tingly parts of me began to cheer as he walked Winston over to me. "What do you want to know about Rosewood?"

Caught once again in the snare of his amber eyes, I felt a blush creeping up over my neck and face as he looked at me steadily. I stifled the sudden clamoring of my mind as it urged me to throw myself into his arm, and tried to remember what we had been discussing. "Why did it burn down?"

"I told you—it burned because of a gas pipe."

"Gas pipes seldom burst suddenly into flames and burn down houses. There must have been a reason for it to do so."

He looked away for a moment. Tension was written into every muscle, so much so that his fingers were positively white with strain, and his voice, when he spoke, was flat and devoid of emotion. "One of the gas jets was left open in my mother's room."

I gasped, horrified at the thought of a woman trapped in a fire.

"My mother has been dead since I was fifteen," he said quickly. "The room was unoccupied."

I knew by the pain in his eyes that there was more to the situation than a simple fire, and touched his hand, wanting to ease the pain. "I'm sorry. It must have been horrible for your family to lose your home in such a manner."

He looked down at my hand for a moment, then met my eyes. I flushed with his nearness, with the sudden flare of heat in his eyes as he leaned toward me. I was suddenly aware that we were alone on a shaded bend of the Row, just the two of us, a man and a woman, and he was about to kiss me.

His saddle creaked as his lips brushed mine, heat from the contact bursting into life deep in the untouched parts of me. *Ask him now*, my brain demanded. *Tell him the position is his if he wants it.*

"Why are you doing this to me?" he asked, his breath fanning across my mouth, his eyes burning into mine.

"I don't seem to be able to stop," I admitted, filled with conflicting emotions. Every sensation seemed to be *right* with Griffin, and yet I knew that no proper lady acted this way.

"Good," he answered, just before his lips fully claimed mine. The kiss was hard at first, hard and aggressive and demanding, then all of a sudden his lips softened. I gasped with surprise at such a marvelous feeling, moaning when he surged into my mouth. It was sinful, it was wrong, it was shameful…it was heaven and I didn't want it to stop.

He pulled his mouth from mine as a group of people cantered around the bend, turning his horse. I put pressed my heels against Marianne, and we walked on without speaking.

"You're sure you would not consider selling Winston?" I broke the silence a few minutes later.

"What? No, I wouldn't." He seemed distracted and looked at me curiously, as if appraising me. I licked my lips, hoping he wouldn't think I was a brazen hussy. His gaze shot to my mouth.

My whole body was tingling now, but I firmly gave it the order to cease, so I could focus on what was important, like asking him if he'd like to fill the duties of a lover. "What will you do with him when you go on your next trip?"

"It depends."

"When do you plan to leave?"

He frowned briefly. "I'm not sure. Do you desire me gone?"

"Not at all," I said brightly, trying desperately to rein in an unreasonable giddy feeling that suddenly filled me. Without my permission, my breasts tightened as I wondered if he would try to kiss me again.

He didn't, but his face lightened at my words.

"I asked because—" I paused as he stared at my mouth. He was thinking about that kiss, I was sure he was. *Now is the time*, my brain screamed. *Ask him!*

I opened my mouth to speak, suddenly nervous. What if he refused me? "I simply wanted to know—"

"Yes?" he asked quickly, turning in his saddle to look me full in the face.

"I wondered if you would be interested...that is, if you would like to...er..."

"What is it you're trying to say, Cassandra?"

I stared at him in frustration and desire, mingled together in a confusion of emotion. "I wanted to know if..." I took a deep breath, telling my jangled nerves to just say the words. *Be my lover*, my brain coached me. *I want to know if you'd like to be my lover.*

"Well?"

The words came out in a rush. Unfortunately, they weren't the ones either of us were expecting. "I wondered if you might not let me borrow Winston when you are gone. I am sure the exercise would be good for him, and—" I halted in faux surprise at his roar of anger. "Is there something wrong?"

He seemed choked for words and had difficulty speaking.

"Women!" he sputtered at last.

CHAPTER TEN

"Oh no. Not another one of those African artifacts from Joshua," I said when, arriving home, Theodore presented me with a package. "They're certainly interesting, but some of them are not suitable for mixed company. There was a male one that had an enormous...ahem."

Theodore grinned as I closed the library door. Luckily for the peace of minds of the maids who were called upon to dust such things, the package did not contain yet another fertility god, but a collection of books. I lifted the top one off the stack and was surprised to see *From Sultan to Sahara* by G. H. M. St. John. An inscription inside read: *To Cassandra Whitney, May you wander the paths you seek.*

Touched by Griffin's generosity in sending me the books, I smiled when I noticed that he did not include the volume tirading against women travelers.

"He does show wisdom in some things," I told Annie when I was dressing for the rally.

"That's good, miss."

As I was about to don my blue serge suit, I noticed something amiss in the hem. "Annie, you haven't removed all of the trimming!"

"Oh. I...er...it must have slipped my mind." She looked guilty at my observation.

I frowned at the black braid trim that was too elaborate for my taste. "This is not like you, Annie. Are you unwell? Is something bothering you? Have you been crying!"

She avoided my eye and looked down at the garment. "No, miss. I'm sorry about the skirt."

"Annie..." I pulled her to a chair, concerned now by her attitude. She looked flushed and close to tears. "If you have a problem, you know I am happy to help. Would you like some time off? Is your mother ailing again?"

"No, thank you, my mother is well."

I patted her on the arm sympathetically, but did not press her any further. We had been together through hard times, the two of us, and I knew when she was ready to tell me what was bothering her, she would.

The sun was hiding behind several ominous-looking dark clouds, making me glad of my wool dress as I met Helena near the entrance to Hyde Park.

"You're here early," I told her as we strolled into the park.

"For a reason," she answered, linking her arm through mine. "You give me such support—I would never dare arrive without you!"

"Ridiculous," I said, oddly touched by her warmth. "There's nothing to be ashamed about attending a rally for women's rights. There will be no demonstrations, no protests, only speeches. What possible objection could anyone have to you simply listening to speeches?"

"Harold forbade me to attend." She looked at me from the corner of her eye as she spoke. "Griffin asked me if I was going to attend the rally with you."

"Did he?" I asked brightly. "I take it he successfully voiced the objections he had begun yesterday?"

"Can you doubt that? But I am being unfair. Griffin didn't voice an objection, he just asked me if I was attending."

We passed one of the many groundskeepers' sheds as I mused over this strange behavior. "Hmmm. That's odd. I wonder—"

My only excuse for what followed is that my thoughts were focused on thoughts of Griffin, and not our surroundings. Thus when a dark shadow loomed up from a nearby shrub, it didn't register until after I found myself in his foul embrace. A musty black cloth was jammed down over my head and torso, effectively pinning my arms to my sides. Without any warning, I was picked up and carried a short distance, the entire episode so quick, I had neither time to warn Helena or call for help.

Deposited abruptly on a wooden floor, I struggled to a sitting position. Distressed noises nearby indicated a second person next to me.

"It's an easy job, picking off ladies what go out without the protection of a man," an odious voice crowed as the door slammed.

"Helena?" I cried, trying to make my escape from the damnable black cloth.

"Cassandra?" came the answering wail.

"Thank heavens you're not hurt." I rose to my knees and divested myself of the bag before turning my attention to the figure that lay struggling next to me. "Here, let me help you get that off. You're just tangling yourself up more."

Once freed, we sat on the floor, flustered and mussed, and looked around us.

"This appears to be a gardener's shed judging by the tools and tea things," I said, noting a sagging basket chair, filthy windows, and gardening implements.

"What...what happened?" Helena's voice quavered, but she was obviously made of sterner material than I had previously thought.

"For some reason that I am not yet able to explain, we have been abducted." I rose and went to the door. It was locked.

"But why should we be abducted?"

"I have no idea," I replied, bending down to look through the keyhole. No key was in evidence.

"Cassandra, what are we going to do?" Her voice rose at the end of the sentence, indicating a corresponding rise in panic.

I picked up my hat from where it had been knocked onto the floor. "Never fear, Helena. I have the greatest confidence that we shall make our escape."

She rose to her feet slowly, watching as I tidied up my tangled hair as best I could before pulling a couple of hatpins from my modest chapeau. "Although I don't wear the large hats bedecked with dead birds and other such unsavory items that so many women seem to favor, I do need several long, sturdy hatpins to secure a hat to my head. Ah, these will do, I think."

I pulled two hat pins free and bent over the lock.

"What are you doing?" she asked, craning over my shoulder.

"Rory, the blacksmith in the village where I lived, showed me this trick when I was a girl. My father had a tendency to lock me in the coal room as punishment."

Helena made a horrified noise.

"Later it was the linen closet, and once, a trunk he kept stored in the stables. I haven't had to do this in some time, but I believe...ah, there it goes." The lock clicked. I opened the door with a triumphant gesture. "Shall we go on to the rally, or would you prefer to go home and recover from this experience?"

Helena stood open-mouthed, staring at me with astonishment. I must admit I relished the look of admiration that came over her face as she ran over and hugged me fiercely. "You're amazing!"

"My dear, you embarrass me. It is a simple lock—a child could have made his way out of the shed. Besides," I said with honesty, uncomfortable with her effusive praise, "a groundskeeper was soon to arrive. They are always busy about the area and make, I have noticed, frequent visits to the sheds. I'm sure that we were in no danger at all."

We walked quickly across the green, discussing the possible reasons someone might want to abduct us in such a manner.

"Should we contact the police, do you think?" Helena asked.

"It must surely have been a prank," I said hesitantly. "What sane abductor would choose such a public place to enact a nefarious plot? No, I feel confident it was a simple prank . . . that or—"

I paused as an insidious thought struck me.

Helena caught my arm, her face pale and distressed. "What?"

"It could be..." I dropped my voice and whispered my suspicion.

"White slavery?" Helena repeated, a look of disbelief crossing her face.

"If not a prank, that's really the only other explanation that makes sense. You are lovely, and I don't make people retch when they see me, so what other reason would someone have to abduct us? No doubt the kidnappers left us to fetch a carriage by which they would take us to their headquarters."

"But—*white slavery?*"

"Can you think of any other reasonable explanation given the words that the villain flung at us as he left?"

"Well...no." Helena fell silent, but I suspected I had not convinced her.

Fortunately, we neared Speaker's Corner, and our abduction was forgotten in the excitement of the moment.

"I have been considering what you said before we were diverted from our way," I said as we waited patiently for the other members to gather.

"What is that?"

"Oh...perhaps it is nothing, but doesn't it seem strange to you that your brother was so calm about your attending the rally today? He was very angry about it yesterday, and I cannot imagine what has made him so unconcerned now, unless he plans to keep an eye on you himself."

"You mean he would follow me?" She looked around nervously.

"No, I doubt if he would follow you, and surely if he did he would have seen us detained by the white slavers, and affected our release before I had a chance to do so. No, it seems to me more likely that as he knows exactly where and when the rally is, he will simply show up."

"He wouldn't! Oh!" We both cast suspicious glances about us.

There was a sizable gathering of Union members present, but as yet only a handful of onlookers. While a few women set up a large *Votes For Women* banner, others were donning their sashes. Two women in suffragette suits were passing through the crowd with a basket, accepting donations for the cause. Mrs. Heywood was present, as was the fiery Maggie Greene, the latter holding court with a dozen women from the militant clique. I pointed them out to Helena. She seemed fascinated with their plans.

"Honestly, Helena, you don't want to involve yourself with them," I cautioned, remembering my surprise and dismay at her enthusiasm for the militant's brutal tactics. "Surely, you don't wish to become involved with setting fire to post boxes and throwing stones at officials?"

"No, of course not," Helena said slowly, watching them enviously. "But I do admire their spirit. They seem…so alive! Not content to just sit and let things happen, they *make* things happen. Doesn't that stir you?"

"All it stirs is a feeling of unease and dread," I replied grimly, watching her eager expression with a profound sense of dismay. "I know the result of violence, Helena. It ends in fear and subjugation and stirs the embers of bitterness and hatred. I believe their radical policy will do us more harm than good."

Our argument was brought to an end when, glancing around casually, my attention was caught by a large, bulky shape half-hidden behind a nearby tree.

"My cup runneth over," I muttered.

"In what way?"

I smiled at Helena. "Nothing. I am just pleased to be proven right."

We devoted the next quarter of an hour to handing out pamphlets advocating the Union's stand on suffrage while several speakers addressed the small crowd of about forty people. When Maggie Greene took the makeshift podium, there was considerable agitation in the officials' ranks.

"I wager they were not expecting her to speak," I whispered to Helena, who shushed me so she could listen with a rapt expression to Maggie. I had to admit that the little Irishwoman was an excellent speaker, electrifying the crowd and drawing cheers of support from the public, but I soon found my attention wandering from her rhetoric.

In the excitement of the invigorating speeches, I had forgotten about the shape seen lurking behind a nearby tree. It was brought again to my attention when I turned to Helena, about to suggest that we leave, and saw Griffin striding our way in a determined manner. It was at that point that the crowd attacked.

Perhaps the word *attacked* is too harsh for the situation; looking back over the event, I can pinpoint the change in the crowd's mood to the time of Maggie's speech. Regardless of whether the attackers came prepared to wreak havoc (and, given their ammunition, there can be no doubt that they did), or whether Maggie was responsible for inciting the less controlled members of the audience, the fact remains that suddenly Union members were subjected to a volley of ripe tomatoes.

"Cassandra!" Helena shrieked as a particularly offensive tomato sailed past my head and struck a woman standing beside me.

"Damnation!" I shouted, infuriated. "How dare they throw tomatoes at us? We are peaceably gathered, not doing anyone any harm, promoting a cause that would benefit everyone in the United Kingdom. It is an insult, and I will not stand for it. Take cover, Helena!"

The situation degenerated into a free-for-all as audience members threw themselves into the fray. Fights broke out around us, men fighting men, women fighting women, and, in a few cases, suffragettes fighting one or two of the men armed with a seemingly never-ending supply of tomatoes.

"Stay back," I shouted to Helena over my shoulder as I hefted a slimy, but intact, tomato. "Run to your brother; he will take care of you."

As I turned my head back toward the attackers, I was struck by a wet, stinging object.

"Oh!" I cried, fury filling me. A roar echoed behind me that I assumed was Griffin protecting Helena in the resulting melee. I weighed the tomato in my hand as I considered the best target, and remembering the lessons learn from my youth in the art of throwing hard, green apples, I took careful aim and let the tomato fly.

It hit one of the men in the eye, and I had the satisfaction of seeing him go to the ground before a strong arm grabbed me roughly around the waist and jerked me back.

"Ooof! What the devil?" The arm squeezed the breath out of me, so tightly bound around me that I was left unable to draw another. My hat slid down over my left eye in a rakish manner as I was lifted from my feet and carried outside the fringe of the confrontation. Police whistles blew, people screamed, and hoarse voices shouted unmentionable observations as I struggled against the arm, desperate to catch my breath.

"Show me a riot and I know who's in the bloody middle of it," a familiar voice grumbled from above.

I was set down roughly, and stood clutching my sides, gasping for air. As soon as my eyes cleared, they landed on the sight of a furious Griffin. He was arguing with Helena, ordering her to leave, but she refused to go until I was able to walk.

He turned back to me with a look that almost made me flinch. "Of all the foolish … have you no brain in that pretty head?"

I blinked at him as I held my ribs, still trying to catch my breath.

"Is that all you can do, stand there and gape at me like a fish out of water?"

The insult stung me into proper posture. Candidate for the position of lover or not, no one tells me I gape like a fish. I straightened up, closed my mouth, and glared out at him from under the angle of my hat. "You might better ask if I can still breathe after my ribs have been broken by your manhandling!"

He grabbed my arm and dragged me to where Helena stood. "Walk," he ordered in a tone that I chose not to challenge. He pushed us forward. We walked.

"May I inquire as to why you saw fit to remove me, without my permission, from the rally?" I asked as the ache in my ribs faded.

He kept a hand on my elbow, pushing me forward, the touch starting a wave of sensation that rippled over my torso, pooling in deep, intimate parts that had taken to making themselves known whenever he was around.

"I thought that would be obvious even to you. A common brawl is no place for a lady." He stopped suddenly and turned. "Or was it your intention to fight each one of those men?"

"I fail to see how you can interpret the throwing of one tomato as the desire to brawl. Why you must misjudge everything I do—"

A muscle in his cheek twitched, stopping me from finishing the sentence. It took him a moment, but at last, with his jaw held tight, he said simply, "Go home. Helena, come with me."

He strode off in an arrogant manner, not looking back at us.

"Well," I said to myself. "He might be exceeding gifted when it comes to kissing, but he is a *very* illogical man." She choked, and I hastened to cover up my comment. "I think, Helena, that you should go to your brother. I would not, however, mention our earlier adventure—he seems to be a little belligerent at the moment and is positively shaking with anger."

"I don't believe you have to worry about him being angry," she said slowly, then kissed my cheek and ran after her brother.

I pondered her comment for a moment, concluded her senses were still overcome with emotion from the abduction and rally, and since the rally had broken up, made my way home without further incident.

CHAPTER ELEVEN

I had planned a quiet evening at home reviewing the household accounts so that they might be ready for Mabel's return, but, as I have had occasion to note, things often do not work out as I plan. Annie burst into tears upon seeing me, and hurried toward the back stairs when I called after her.

The evening post brought with it a large, stiff envelope with a prominent coronet. It turned out to be an invitation to the Duchess of St. Alban's annual masquerade ball a few days hence. I was surprised at the invitation since I do not move in that circle of society, but a moment of thought cleared up the situation.

"Helena," I told Marmalade the cat. "She's a friend of one of the daughters of the duke. No doubt she asked the duchess to add me to the invitation list, thinking I would enjoy the opportunity to parade around in an extravagant costume with the cream of society. The question is whether I should send my regrets, or indulge in the sheer waste of time and money that being costumed would require?"

Marmalade, a wise cat, made no comment other than to purr and rub his teeth on my hand as we sat before the fire.

"I agree. It would be an insult to Helena were I to refuse. That just means I must come up quickly with an idea for a costume. Something simple and plain, I think, like a toga. Oh! Emma will be able to help me! Surely with her knowledge of the ancient Greeks she can help me design a Greek costume, elegant and graceful, draped in a flattering fashion."

I ousted Marmalade from my lap and left a message for Emma, asking for her assistance. As I entered the hall, Mullin stopped me with a note from Helena.

"Has there been any trouble below stairs," I said as I took it. "Annie seems to be upset about something."

Mullin was an admirable butler, but he had one failing—he loved to gossip. I could almost see his ears prick up when I mentioned Annie's behavior. "No, miss. Nothing that I am aware of. Would you like me to make inquiries?"

"I'm sure it's nothing." I thanked him and opened Helena's note. My stomach tightened with dismay as I read the words. *Maggie Green has invited me to participate in a protest tomorrow morning outside of Bosworth's club. I feel I must go, and would be delighted if you were free to join us.*

"Of all the idiotic..." I muttered to myself as I marched back to the library. "Now I'm going to have to go with her just to see that she is kept out of trouble."

I wrote another note accepting her invitation, and was eyeing the account book when Theodore returned with the intelligence that Emma was not at home. "Her landlady says she's likely down at her club," he intoned in a slightly adenoidal voice.

"That's perfect," I said, brushing the cat hair off my lap as I gathered up my hat and bag. "I'll go there and see all of the excellent costumes her club members have made up for their historical reenactments. Perhaps they will provide me with inspiration."

As I was about to leave, Mullin materialized at my side. I could tell something was wrong because his face was pink with excitement.

"Yes? What is it?" I asked wearily, wondering what catastrophe had befallen us now.

"Excuse me for interrupting you, Miss Cassandra, but you asked earlier about Annie, and now it appears that she has locked herself in her room. We have tried to speak with her, but she won't answer. Mrs. Mullin is concerned that she might have done some harm to herself."

"I see. Theodore, give the cabby a few pennies for his trouble and send him away. I'll have to go to the Sapphist's Club later." Removing my hat, I ran up the three flights of stairs to the room that Annie shared with another maid, and spoke loudly outside of her door. "Annie, let me in. I want to talk with you."

"She won't answer, miss," one of the housemaids said from behind me. "I've tried and tried, but she just won't answer me."

Most of the household staff was gathered with her, waiting to see what would happen. I heard noises from inside Annie's room, and turned to the staff and shooed them away. "Go on, back to your work. I will take care of this."

Mullin's face dropped, but he herded everyone downstairs.

"Annie?" I tapped at her door. "Everyone is gone except me. Will you please let me in?"

There was a scuffling noise, then the lock turned and the door opened to reveal a haggard Annie, her face swollen and red from crying. She looked so miserable it almost broke my heart.

"Oh, dear," I said, closing the door behind me. "Whatever is the matter?"

She wiped at her face with a scrap of handkerchief and mumbled something incomprehensible.

A firm approach was clearly called for. I shook her gently. "This sobbing will do you no good. Now dry your tears and tell me what the problem is."

"Oh, miss, I can't, I just can't," she wailed, squinting her eyes with the effort of crying. No tears came, indicating that she had been sobbing for some time.

"I will not leave this room until you do so. Annie, look at me," I softened my voice. "There is nothing you can't tell me. I'm your friend, you know that, don't you?"

The words must have penetrated her misery, for she made an effort to collect herself. "Yes, miss, you are a friend. And I know you won't think the less of me for my fall."

"You fell?" I asked, looking her over for signs of injury. "Are you hurt?"

"No, miss, not that kind of fall." She took a deep breath. "I have been ruined."

"Ruined," I repeated stupidly, not comprehending at first. My eyes widened. "Oh, *ruined!*"

Annie nodded, and a few weak tears straggled down her face. "What will I do?"

I sat down abruptly in an old rocking chair in the corner. "Oh, my goodness. Ruined. Are you—is there—will there be a baby?"

She nodded, her face puckered as two thin lines of tears stole down her cheeks.

"Oh, Annie, how?" I blushed as I heard my own inane question. "That is to say, how did you come to this? Is it...is Jackson responsible?"

She shook her head miserably. "Mrs. Garner will dismiss me as soon as she comes home. Oh, miss! Please don't let them send me to the workhouse. I can't go home, the shame would kill my mum. Don't let them send me away."

"You are my maid, not Mrs. Garner's, so she cannot dismiss you. And I am not likely to," I said in response to her panicked look. "Who is it who has led you to this situation?"

"Mr. Jones," she snuffled into my skirt.

"I don't think I know him. Has he offered to make an honest woman out of you?"

She shook her head.

"Have you had a discussion at all about marriage?"

"No, miss."

"If he was agreeable, would you wish to marry him?"

"No, miss."

I was surprised by her answer; I was sure she would feel the situation was serious enough to make her desire marriage over an illegitimate baby. "Oh, dear," I sighed to myself, at a rare loss for words.

Annie looked up with a wretched expression. "You won't turn me out, will you?"

"I've already said I wouldn't, and I mean it. Let's get you into bed. You've had a terrible day, but don't worry. We'll work things out somehow."

I spent another ten minutes reassuring her and getting her tucked into bed before I pressed her for details about the father.

"William Jones, his name is. I met him when we first came to London. He was ever so smart, and I was the envy of all the housemaids for having such a beau." She smiled with the memory of her domestic coup. "He took me to the Music Hall on my evenings off. We had such larks, you would laugh to see the way he went on."

"Do you know where he is employed?"

"Self-employed, he said. He was on a very important job that he couldn't tell me about, but he was never mean with his money, not like some I could say."

"When did you last see him?"

Tears pooled in her eyes again. "It's been over four days, now. He used to call for me every day, faithful like, but now he's stopped calling for me, and won't answer any of my letters."

"Four days isn't very long. Don't worry, we'll find him," I said, wondering how one went about finding a recalcitrant suitor. "What does he look like?"

"He's ever so good looking," she said, sniffling. "Brown hair and eyes, not too tall, and dresses sharp. And he's got a lovely gold tooth."

Blood pounded in my ears as I swayed against the door. There must be hundreds of people in London with gold teeth. Perhaps thousands. "A gold tooth? Where?"

"In the front. It shines when he smiles."

Mullin was lurking around the stairs as I descended, my knees unusually wobbly, and my brain whirling with speculation.

"Everything is fine, Mullin. No need to worry," I repeated the platitudes. "Tell Mrs. Mullin that Annie will do herself no harm. She is just a little upset over a bit of trouble in her family."

Since I had yet to deal with the neglected household accounts, I was up early the next morning. After a few mundane tasks, I set off to meet Helena. Other than casting a suspicious glance up and down the street for a man with a gold tooth as I left, I did not spend much time musing over Annie's dilemma. I would support whatever choice she made, either finding her a small cottage on my late father's estate, or keeping her in service if that was her desire.

"I only wish I could so easily resolve the worry about Helena," I said with a sigh as the carriage rolled along. While it was true she was an adult woman and ultimately responsible for her own behavior, I felt a distinct unease when I considered her unbridled enthusiasm. She was putty in the hands of the manipulative Maggie Greene. "It's very clear that I'm going to have to keep an eye on her, no matter what my feelings about the militants."

"What's that, miss?" Jackson asked as he opened the door for Helena.

"Nothing. Oh, my, Helena, that is an incredibly lovely walking suit. That amethyst is absolutely gorgeous."

"Thank you, dear Cassandra." She beamed as she sat beside me, the color from her dress casting a brilliant hue over my ivory gown. I looked critically at her dress, trying to find a fault or flaw in it. There were none.

"How do you do it?" I asked in defeat. "Every time I meet you I pick out a dress I think is particularly smart, but on each occasion you put me to shame."

"I put you to shame? Cassandra, you have it reversed. I try my best to keep up with your fashions but cannot come close. Look at your lovely ivory gown—those crossed panels of black velvet ribbon are simple, and yet entirely elegant."

"You are a true friend to fib to me like that. I appreciate the compliment, but I think we both know that your figure is the one favored by fashion. But come," I said quickly to forestall her protests, "tell me about the Duchess of St. Alban's masquerade ball."

"I hope you don't think it forward of me to suggest that you be invited to the ball. Lady Alice particularly asked me who I might like to have come, and there was no one I would rather see there than you."

I took the compliment with the grain of salt I felt it deserved, but thanked her anyway. "Will your *entire* family be attending?" I asked with studied nonchalance.

"Harold and Letitia will," she said pulling a face. "Griffin is invited, but he said . . . well, he said some rather rude things about the ball."

"Ah. I can understand his reticence—I am not fond of such events either."

"Oh, but you'll come, won't you? I *had* thought you might like to have your cousin as your escort," she smiled, "but perhaps now you would prefer someone else."

I sighed. "I'm afraid I don't have that many male relations who would be able to accompany me, so even if I did want to attend—and I must admit I have thought of an excessively cunning costume—my lack of an escort will keep me home."

"Oh, but surely there must be someone...I beg your pardon, Cassandra, that was rude of me. Of course, if you would rather not go I can understand your desire to stay home. But dear, dear friend," she grasped my hand and pressed it between her lovely amethyst-colored gloves, "if it is simply for the lack of an escort, your problem is solved. I'm sure Griffin would be delighted—"

I pulled my hand back quickly. "No, thank you, Helena. It will not be necessary to foist me upon your brother. Besides, a bachelor escort who is not a relative would never be acceptable in the eyes of society."

"Why, Cassandra," Helena said, clearly amused. "I never thought you would be a slave to society's rules."

I squirmed a bit at her gentle teasing. "I'm not, for my sake. But there are my aunt and uncle to consider...oh! That might be the answer to my problem. I wonder if they have been invited?"

"I'm sure they must be, your uncle is such a prominent man. What an excellent solution! You could attend with them, and we could stand together and make wicked comments about the couples dancing."

"I doubt that you will do much standing," I said with a smile.

She smiled back happily, and we indulged in a cheerful gossip for the remainder of the trip. I was just about to ask her a few subtle questions about Griffin when we arrived at our destination. I put my hand on her arm as she started out of the carriage. "Helena, please . . . let me caution you about becoming too involved with Maggie Greene's group. I know you are excited and determined to do your part, but please allow your good sense to guide your actions."

She flashed a smile. "I won't do anything that I think you wouldn't do."

I followed behind her, far from reassured.

Maggie stood in a cluster of about twenty women. She was a little perturbed to see me, but took my appearance in stride. "Ladies, this is an important protest that we will make today. Has everyone a sign?"

Helena held up her hand, and one of Maggie's minions brought over two signs. Helena's read *Women Demand Equality*, while mine mysteriously proclaimed to one and all that I was *Ignorant No More*.

The bulk of the women, including Helena, were gathered in a cluster at the front of the club entrance. Maggie sent me down the street about half a block with the instruction to wave my sign at every passing vehicle. I was rather hesitant to leave Helena, but her assurance that she would not act foolishly still rang in my ears. Giving her one last uncertain look, I took my assigned position.

The club steward came out and wrung his hands anxiously as he spoke with Maggie, but she soon sent him packing. A few minutes later, a pair of constables arrived and proceeded to shoo away Maggie and the others.

I moved closer, expecting the worse, but she surprised me with her acceptance of the inevitable. Gathering the group together, she herded us across the street. "The club clearly has the local police in their pocket," she informed us with a determination that filled me with foreboding. "We are forbidden to demonstrate directly in front of the entrance. They said nothing about demonstrating across the street, however, so this is where we will make our stand!"

As we took our new positions, vehicles poured into the street from the far end. I peered into a few of the carriages and motorcars as they stopped alongside the curb, but they were all empty. A suspicion began to take form when the first group of men exited the club.

Maggie and her contingent were in a knot directly across from the club exit; as the first gentleman stepped out onto the pavement, the militants increased the volume of their chants and waved their signs vigorously. The man ignored them and marched down the street to where his motorcar was waiting.

Uneasy, I started for Helena; as I dodged one of the protestors who was shaking her sign vigorously, I saw Maggie's hand flash and heard the impact as a stone smashed the window of the motorcar parked opposite.

"I knew it!" Horrified, I dropped my sign and ran forward as the women began flinging stones with abandon. Torn as I was with the desire to haul Helena away, I was more concerned about Maggie harming someone. I launched myself at her from the side, hoping that the others would stop if I could down her. We fell together, hitting the pavement with a force that made my teeth rattle. Hats flying, we startled a few of the women closest, but the rest seemed to think nothing as we rolled in the street, Maggie screaming curses and trying to gouge my face with her fingernails.

Rocks and debris dug painfully into my back as I did what I could to wrest a large stone from Maggie's right hand, and at the same time keep out of reach of the talon-like left. A sharp elbow to my jaw made me see stars but had the benefit of reminding me I wasn't a helpless victim. Gritting my teeth against the pain of Maggie's knee in my ribs, I made a fist and punch out blindly. Luckily, I connected with her face, snapping her head back into the curbstone. I hauled myself upright, breathing heavily, my lip swollen and wet from where she had landed a blow. I licked off the blood as I got to my feet, bending over to examine Maggie. She was dazed but not seriously hurt.

"Helena!" I yelled, trying to get her attention. She seemed oblivious to me.

Several other women in the street yelled oaths and profanities at the men as I pried the stone from Maggie's fingers. They continued to stone the club members, most of whom had taken refuge within the safety of the building. Two of the men stormed out into the street with the intent of stopping the attack. As I straightened painfully, a stone whistled past my ear and struck a man as he approached.

Maggie kicked out at my leg just then, and I went down painfully on top of her. My fall seemed to knock the wind out of her for she stopped struggling and lay inert, gasping for air. As soon as I was able to stand, I ran forward to help the injured man up off the street.

"Are you all right, sir? Let me help you—" my voice died as the man looked up. "Oh, my…Lord Sherringham."

A shadow fell over me as I tried, despite his incoherent sputtering, to help him up. I stepped back and bumped into a large, hard object.

"I beg your pardon," I said automatically, stepping around the object. A hand descended upon my shoulder and spun me around to face Griffin.

"Is this the sort of activity you champion, Miss Whitney? The stoning of men has a biblical quality, I grant you, but it is not one I would've believed you to condone."

"No—of course not—" I stammered, at a loss for an explanation. "I do not condone it…in fact, I was trying to stop the women from throwing any more—"

Griffin looked down at my hand which still held the stone I had wrestled from Maggie, then up at me with an eyebrow raised quizzically. "Do you often find it necessary to carry a large rock with you?"

I flushed, knowing full well I would never be able to explain the events. The thought crossed my mind that someone, somewhere was having a good deal of fun at my expense. "Yes, Mr. St. John, I often do carry a large rock around with me. I find it comes in handy when I am called upon to knock someone silly with it. Perhaps another time I can demonstrate the technique for you."

A flash of blue to the left caught my eye. I groaned and turned on my heel as two constables rushed up. Having executed their plan with brutal success, the militants had scattered when they'd heard the sound of the bobbies' whistles. I walked rapidly across the street to where Helena was standing, her arms limp at her sides, her mouth forming an "Oh!" as she watched Lord Sherringham assisted back into the club.

"Helena? Don't worry, I'm sure your brother is all right. I suggest you go home and wait for him there."

She didn't move, but went a shade paler. I put a gentle hand on her shoulder.

"Helena?"

"Oh, Cassandra," she wailed suddenly, flinging herself on me. "What have I done? Why didn't I heed your warning? I could have killed Harold with that stone! How could I have done it?"

I felt Griffin's presence behind me. I was confident he would shield Helena from the wrath of the police, but knew he wouldn't go to any trouble to keep me from being arrested. Not even the fact that we had shared a very pleasing kiss would be enough to excuse what he believed to be my latest folly.

Helena suddenly noticed the policemen arriving in large numbers. She gave a gigantic gulp and looked like a scared rabbit. "What—what will they do with me?"

"Nothing, if you leave now. I'm sure your brother will tell them you had nothing to do with any of it."

Helena was plainly terrified at the results of her violent actions. I was pleased by that for a moment, and then without warning, I was furious. I spun around and faced Griffin, angry at the circumstance that I found myself in, angry that he would never believe my innocence given the evidence against me, and angrier still that I had not been able to keep Helena out of trouble and shield her from the baser side of life.

"Just so you know—what Helena did was not her fault. She was under the influence of an extremely persuasive person, and if you say one word of criticism to this poor girl, I will take great pleasure in doing you a bodily harm, no matter what effect it might have regarding your candidacy for position of lover."

One of the bobbies, seeing me wave the stone at Griffin, ran over to where we were standing and placed a restraining hand on my arm. "Now then, no more of that, miss. You'll have to come with me, you and the other lady."

"I will do nothing of the kind," I said primly, ignoring the stunned look on Griffin's face. "I have committed no crime, and do not have the time to spend discussing the issue with you."

He tightened his grip and would, I believe, have forced me to accompany him had Griffin not regained his wits and stepped in.

"You are mistaken, Constable," he said. "This lady and the other were simply passing down the street and attempted to stop the attacks."

Helena and I looked at one another, she with terror written plainly on her face, and me with astonishment at Griffin's action.

"Is that so?" the constable asked, clearing harboring some suspicion.

He looked from my stone to Helena's sign.

"Er...she just picked that up," I said, pointing to the sign.

She squeaked and dropped it.

"And that?" the constable asked, nodding at the rock in my hand.

"She took it from one of the women," Griffin said. "I saw her do so."

"Did she now. And yet this lady looks as if she's been fighting," the policemen told him, eying me dubiously.

"You can't take a rock from a woman bent on stoning people without some sort of a struggle," I said a righteous snort.

It took another five minutes of Griffin waxing eloquent before the policemen finally accepted our stories.

"I'll be taking your names as witnesses," the bobbie warned, doing just that. "I'd advise you to be on your way, and stay away from any such disturbances in the future."

He moved off to join his colleague, and we were left staring at one another. Feeling there was nothing more to be said, I squeezed Helena's arm reassuringly as Griffin handed her into his motorcar.

"I will take you home," he said to me. "I can come back for Sherry afterward."

"That's not at all necessary. Your brother should probably see a doctor as soon as possible. I'll take a cab."

"Stay here," he told Helena, and escorted me down the street to the nearest available cab.

The silence hung heavily over me for a good two minutes before I broke it. "Thank you for what you did back there. I know it must have gone against your wishes to protect me as well as Helena, but I do appreciate it."

"I just hope you both learned something from it," he muttered, seemingly distracted. It wasn't until another few minutes passed that he found a cab, and handed me into it. He leaned in, the oddest expression on his face. "Er...what you said a few minutes ago—"

"That I was sorry you had to protect me?"

"No, not that."

Chagrin flashed across his face as he ran a distracted hand through his hair

"What then?" I asked, desperately fighting the urge to kiss him.

"What you said after that. You said something about being your lover." His eyes were softly luminescent, warm pools of amber that snared me with no difficulty at all.

"Oh. That."Beneath my chemise, my nipples hardened. They'd never done that before, not in response to a man's look, but it certainly was Griffin leaning in the cab that had them behaving in such a distracting manner. No doubt it was also his presence that left me short of breath, my heart pounding uncomfortably, my skin suddenly extremely sensitive. I licked the small cut on the corner of my lip. Griffin's gaze pounced on the movement. "Yes. I...I feel that we have a certain....affinity despite our differences, and wondered...er..."

He dragged his gaze back to my eyes. Oddly enough, he looked as bemused as I felt. I decided it was the lack of oxygen to my brain that was making him appear so. Men of the world like Griffin did not bemuse easily. "Yes?"

"Well...it was an idea I had..." I said, distracted by his nearness. "I wondered if you had ever thought about the idea...if you'd ever considered the possibility...you seemed to like kissing me, you see, and I enjoyed it very much, and I thought..."

"What did you think, Cassandra?" he asked, brushing his thumb along my lower lip.

"I thought you might want to do it again," I said, my mind giving up the battle.

He leaned forward and gently caressed my lips with his. Heat pooled inside me, deep within me, radiating outward in waves of anticipation. "Say it."

"Would you consider filling the position of my lover?" I asked.

"No, say what you really want."

"Oh, I *really* want that," I said earnestly.

He laughed, and kissed me again. "Tell me what you want."

"You. I want you."

His tongue touched the bruised corner of my mouth before sliding between my lips. I was shocked and surprised and thrilled all at once, my brain and body reeling at the intimate touch of his tongue against mine.

"Yes," he said finally, after he stole away my breath.

"Yes?" I asked, befuddled to the point of incomprehension.

"Yes, I will become your lover."

"Oh, thank you." I couldn't keep from smiling, relief filling me. "I was so worried about asking you, but it really wasn't as bad as I thought. And I believe having you as a lover will be very nice."

He gave me a look that sent my entire body tingling, his amber eyes filled with a passionate promise that had my heart speeding up. "It will be much, much more than nice, Cassandra."

The door to the cab closed, and I sank back against the cushions, whooshing out a breath that I didn't remember holding. It was only when I arrived at home that I noticed I still carried the stone.

CHAPTER TWELVE

"Only foolish women pout," I told Annie that night as I was dressing for the opera. She artfully twisted my hair into a semblance of the latest fashion. "Just because he didn't say when things will commence doesn't mean I should feel abused. Right?"

"I'm not sure what you're talking about," Annie mumbled, her mouth full of hairpins as she tucked a recalcitrant curl back into place.

I lifted my chin and gave her a serene look. "As you know, I am an independent, modern New Woman. I have thus chosen a man to be my lover."

Annie's jaw dropped, the hairpins scattering all over the carpet. "You, miss?"

"Yes." I tried to look nonchalant about the whole thing, as if taking a lover was a trivial act, one I did every day.

"Would that be Mr. St. John?" she asked, her eyes round as she hurriedly gathered up the hairpins.

"As a matter of fact, yes, he is the man I have chosen for that position."

Her shoulders sagged in relief. "Oh, well, then, if he's the one, that's all right."

I frowned. "What do you mean if he's the one?"

"Well, he's a gentleman, isn't he?" She finished with my hair and gestured for me to stand.

I did so, and she eyed my dress, looking for anything that needed adjustment. "Yes, but any man I chose to be my lover would be a gentleman."

"There's gentlemen, and then there's *gentlemen*," she said sagely, tugging at a sleeve. "Mr. St. John is a proper gentleman. He won't see you hurt."

"I am a grown woman, Annie. You are feeling vulnerable at the moment because of your situation, but I assure you that I will not allow myself to be so burdened unless I desire it."

"You won't?" She looked like she wanted to smile but didn't dare.

"No. I have it on the best authority that there are ways to prevent such things. I will no doubt discuss the matter with Mr. St. John, and we will come to an understanding."

A slight noise escaped her, something sounding remarkably like a titter. "I'm sure you will. That's done, I think."

I looked into the mirror and was pleased by the dress and Annie's skill. I have no pretensions to any beauty, but the sapphire blue satin gown, with its accompanying midnight blue gauze tunic studded with crystals, set off my red hair well, and made my skin look paler than it really was.

Grimacing only slightly at my freckles, I took one last unsure look at the low neckline of the dress, gathered up my bag and velvet coat, thanked Annie for her work and ordered her to bed before departing for my aunt's house.

Uncle Henry was in the sitting room when I arrived, and since he had the skill of making one feel specially chosen to receive his undivided attention, a conversation with him was always an enjoyable event.

"Cassandra, my dear," he stood to greet me, his shock of white hair as unruly as ever. He held out his hands. "How lovely you look in that blue gown. Could it be that you've grown even prettier since we last met?"

"None of that, Uncle Henry," I said, kissing him on his freshly-shaven cheek. "You are looking particularly handsome this evening. Tell me, how did you find Boston?"

He huffed into his mustache, as white as his hair. "Your hands are like ice, my dear. Sit here, next to the fire. Boston was the same as it always is—full of Americans. Speaking of visitors, when do you expect your sister and her family?"

"I had a letter from them yesterday—they were leaving Cape Town the following day, so I expect they should arrive at the end of the week."

"Ah, good."

"Uncle Henry, have you been invited to the St. Alban's masquerade ball?"

He stood as my aunt came into the room, regal in rose velvet and lace. She touched the diamond dog collar at her throat and murmured, "My dear, the gown is lovely, but that neckline—are you sure it isn't too low?"

I assured her it was the latest fashion, but remained very conscious of my exposed bosom for the rest of the evening. It was not an *entirely* unpleasant feeling.

"Yes, my dear, we have, but Caroline was not sure she wanted to attend."

"Attend what, my dear? Oh, Consuelo's costume ball. I thought we had quite decided against it. Why do you ask, Cassandra—have you been invited as well?"

"Yes," I said slowly, not wanting my aunt to see my eagerness. "But without Mabel and Joshua, I have no one to act as escort. Freddy is…well, I would prefer not to attend with him. He would just propose every five minutes. I thought I would go with you, but if you do not plan to attend—"

"Nonsense. We'd be delighted to take you!" Henry took my arm. "I can't think of anything we would enjoy more, can you Caroline?"

"Quite a few things, my dear, but I am content to escort Cassandra."

"There, that's all decided," Henry said. "I warn you though, I shall embarrass you both by refusing to wear a costume."

"A costume," my aunt said dreamily. "I see something in lace…but three days doesn't give me much time."

Henry sighed in an exaggerated manner, winking at me as he did so. "Later, Caroline. First I must get you both to the opera on time, where I shall be the envy of all who see me with two such lovely belles on my arms."

The opera house was dazzling with flashing jewels, the shiny silks and satins of the ladies' gowns, and the brilliance of starched white against the black of the gentlemen's evening clothes. I was halfway up the grand staircase, speaking with an old friend of my father's, when my aunt jostled my arm. "Isn't that Lord and Lady Sherringham by the door?"

I turned quickly and scanned the crowd. Just coming in the door, Lord Sherringham was laughing jovially with a white-haired man in a military uniform.

"Yes, I believe it is." Watching out of the corner of my eye, my entire body felt electrified when I saw the entire family was present—Lady Sherringham in a horrible orange chiffon gown, Helena appearing worried in pale mauve, and Griffin looking devastatingly handsome in evening clothes.

Pressure from behind forced me to continue the slow ascent to the top of the stairs. Fighting my way to my aunt's side, I asked quietly, "Did you know they were attending tonight? Is that why you invited me?"

"My dear, of course not! Henry thought you would enjoy the opera since you are alone and Mabel is not due home for a few more days. I had no idea the Sherringhams would be in attendance." Her eyes wandered over the crowd as she spoke. I could never detect my aunt in a lie, so I cannot say for certain that she was telling an untruth, but I suspected some duplicity in the matter.

My uncle's box was situated next to the last on the left side of the theater, offering a good view of both the stage and audience. I turned my chair away slightly from the stage so as to have a view of the audience, pretending to read the program, all the while trying to calm myself so I felt less like I was being eaten alive by fire ants. Caroline ignored me as I continued my subtle scan of the people streaming in. Before long, the opening refrains of the overture quieted conversation somewhat, and resignedly I turned to face the stage.

Directly to my left were the Sherringhams. Helena sat closest to me, talking to someone over her left shoulder. Lady Sherringham sat next to her in the front, and I could see the stout form of Lord Sherringham behind her, in muffled conversation. Etiquette would not allow me to turn around and stare into their box, although I desperately wanted to.

The opera was lost on me; I spent the time in impure thoughts so scandalous that when the intermission brought the house lights up, I was left suddenly feeling exposed and turned toward my aunt for security.

Henry stood just outside of the box talking to two of his colleagues. Caroline patted my hand sympathetically, then leaned toward the other side of the box to speak with her neighbor on the right.

"My dear," Henry said just as I was going to greet Helena, "I believe you know this gentleman. He was most desirous of having a few words with you."

Griffin stepped forward and offered his hand. My body cheered in response.

"How nice to see you again, Mr. St. John," I stood and shook his hand, my breath caught in throat as his fingers lingered a moment on mine. "Are you enjoying the opera?"

"Not particularly. Helena wanted me to attend. She thought it would be good for my uncivilized soul. I'm glad to see you have suffered no ill effects from this morning's trial."

His eyes laughed at me, and I felt giddy with happiness. It was too public a place for me to discuss the subject nearest to my heart, so I confined myself to speaking with obtuseness. "I had imagined it would be good deal more trying than it was."

"Perhaps you anticipated it too long? I've found that once I make up my mind on a subject, it's best dealt with immediately."

"That is certainly wise, although sometimes there are situations where one has to consider the feelings of others."

"I would have thought those were apparent." His gaze dropped to my lips, and my entire body tightened.

"Sometimes innocent acts can be misinterpreted," I said somewhat breathlessly. "I feel it's best to ascertain the true state of the situation before acting."

He took a step closer to me, his voice dropping to an intimate level. "I can assure you that any action I take is most heartfelt."

I found myself leaning toward him until my uncle turned to speak with someone who just arrived at the box. Griffin took a step back, and I changed the subject to one that was less charged. "How is Helena?"

He lowered his voice. "Fine, now. I gather from what she said that you warned her against this Greene female. I apologize for my hasty conclusion earlier. Helena informed me that you were against the protest from the beginning."

I accepted his apology, basking in the warm glow of admiration in his eyes as I asked after his brother. Griffin scratched at his collar as he answered. "Sherry's all right. Nothing more than a cut to the forehead, although he isn't aware of who threw the stone."

He looked at me meaningfully.

"And I'm sure he never shall be."

"Yes. Well." An awkward silence fell. Griffin waved in the general direction of my torso. "That's attractive."

"Thank you," I said, amused by the bluntness of the compliment. "You look very nice as well."

He put a finger in his collar. "It's damned uncomfortable."

"Is it? Perhaps next time you should get a larger collar."

"What do you mean by that?" he asked, frowning.

"Nothing other than that your collar might be too small."

"Is that a criticism, or an attempt at humor?" he asked.

"Neither. It was merely an observation. It really is too bad that you and I cannot converse with ending in an argument. You should make an effort to be less critical."

He opened his eyes wide with indignation. "I am the most tolerant of men. You insist on arguing every point."

Receiving a warning glance from my aunt at Griffin's loud protestation, I quickly changed the topic. "Will you go away soon?"

A fleeting look crossed his face, one that so resembled pain that my heart constricted at the sight of it.

"That is," I corrected myself, ignoring the pounding of blood in my ears, "will you be going abroad soon? I asked you earlier but did not hear plans of your further travels."

"I haven't made up my mind yet. There are certain obligations I have recently undertaken." His eyes were molten with sudden heat.

My knees wobbled. "I imagine you would be anxious to be on your way—after you attend to your obligations, of course."

"Do you really believe they will be over so quickly?"

I realized with some surprise he was teasing me. "Well, I know how men are," I said, making a vague gesture.

"I don't think you do," he said dryly.

I glanced at my aunt. She was still in conversation. "Actually, I was thinking of taking a trip abroad myself. Where would you recommend I visit?"

He grinned. "Really, Miss Whitney, you surprise me. Can it be you are willing to abandon the cause that means so much to you? Have you lost such faith in the suffrage movement already that you are considering leaving it?"

It was impossible to be angry with him when he look so roguish.

"On the contrary," I bantered in faux seriousness. "I plan to take the word of women's emancipation abroad, and spread it as I travel. Your own excellent commentary on foreign cultures has made it clear that enlightenment with regards to women's rights is needed in most lands, and as an Englishwoman, it is, according to your definition, my duty to meddle where I may."

He laughed at that, and said with mock gravity, "I would be happy to consult with you as to the best itinerary for your plans. I can think of several places I would like to see meddling Englishwomen visit."

His eyes held mine as he as he spoke, the intent in them causing a blush to creep up from my exposed bosom. He brushed my fingers lightly with his lips. The touch was electrifying, and set my heart racing yet again. What it did to my intimate parts was unmentionable.

The third act began, and with much regret I tucked away the lurid seduction scenes playing in my head, and turned my attention to the stage, avoiding the box to my left. During the fourth act I was indulging in a pleasant daydream of just exactly how Griffin would respond to my seduction with a ravishment of his own, when a sudden shout from below broke my reverie. I peered over the edge of the box and gasped with horror at the sight.

Six suffragettes with *Votes For Women* sashes draped over their fronts marched down the two side aisles, shouting slogans and hurling vegetables at the stage. The audience sat shocked for a moment, then a handful of men ran forward and grappled with the women in an attempt to remove them. Ushers raced down the aisle to assist as two protesters gained the stage and began shouting at the audience. Speechless with horror, I turned to my aunt. She watched the proceedings with some interest, pausing now and again to glance questioningly at me.

"I'm sure we have you to thank for this travesty," Lord Sherringham's loud voice echoed off the balconies. I turned, surprised at his comment. He stood at the front of his box and leaned forward to address my uncle. "If my niece exhibited such dangerous tendencies, Benson, I would take a horse whip to her. She does you much discredit."

I was frozen with horror at his words, unable to move or protest, a statue on display for all to see and judge. The thought of what Griffin must think made me sick.

"My niece would not have anything to do with a party that takes action in such a disruptive manner," Uncle Henry said mildly. "I have implicit faith in her good judgment and sensibility."

"As for you, miss," Lord Sherringham continued, his eyes narrowing on me, "I shall take steps to ensure you and your foul organization do no further damage."

"I know nothing about this," I said in a small voice to his retreating figure. My eyes sought those of Griffin, but when I found them, but they gave me no pleasure. It was quite clear from his scornful look that he, too, evidently believed I had a part in the spectacle below.

The shock was wearing off of the audience as the suffragettes were forcibly removed. Voices rose expressing their astonishment, amusement, and disapproval. Wishing I knew how to swoon properly, I turned to my aunt. "You know I had nothing to do with this."

"Of course I do, my dear. I fear, however, that you will have a difficult time persuading other people of your innocence."

"I have a horrible headache," I said truthfully. "Would you mind if I left now?"

"Not at all. Let me tell Henry we're going."

"It's not necessary for you to leave early. I'd feel terrible if you had to miss the rest of the opera."

It took some persuading, but at last I secured my early release. I slipped out of the box, my cheeks hot with embarrassment as I ran down the stairs. There were a few people about, mostly ushers who were clustered together in excited groups, but the atmosphere was close and stifling, I couldn't bear it. I gathered up my coat and bolted for the exit.

Outside the night air was cool and soft, washing over my heated cheeks like cold water. Brushing away a few rogue tears, I glanced up and down the line for my uncle's carriage. Unable to find it, and desperate to get away from the site of my humiliation, I decided to walk the distance to my sister's house. Clutching my coat against the chill night, I set out.

CHAPTER THIRTEEN

I love Covent Garden in the evening, after the night has settled and the tradesmen have rolled away their carts. Although wary after my experiences with the purse thief and the men in Hyde Park, embarrassment over the debacle at the opera house made walking through the empty streets seem like a frolic in comparison. My spirits sank as I strode along, miserably contemplating the evidence. "The sad truth is that you've gone and fallen in love with him, and now you're paying the price of such folly."

My voice echoed off the closed shops, making an eerie counterpoint to the sound of my shoes on the cobblestones. I stopped. Frowning with concentration, I held my breath and listened. From somewhere came the unmistakable sounds of pursuit: strong footsteps moving quickly. A vision of the man with the bowler and gold tooth rose before my eyes, followed by a sharp bite of fear. I slipped into a dark doorway and peered out into the blackness.

"I'm being silly," I whispered to myself with far more bravado than I felt as the footsteps grew louder. "It could be anyone. And even if it is Mr. Jones, I have no reason to fear him."

The footsteps paused for a moment, giving me hope that whoever it was had nothing to do with me. But a minute later a figured loomed up in a pool of light from a distant lamppost, passing quickly and silently into the darkness.

Stepping out of my doorway when the man was almost upon me, I said amiably, "Out for an evening stroll, Mr. St. John?"

He let out a startled exclamation of surprise, and grasped my arm with a ferocity that surprised me. "You damned fool woman! Don't you have any better sense than to leap out at a man unexpectedly?"

"I thought it better to see who you were, first." He looked so indignant, I couldn't help but smile, which, of course, is the wrong way to greet a freshly startled man.

"What the hell what are you doing out here by yourself? It's not safe for a female to march through the city after dark by herself. I thought you had learned that lesson."

I raised my chin and sent him a quelling glare down my nose. Lover or no lover, I refuse to be browbeaten. "We've had this conversation before. I am quite capable of taking care of myself, thank you."

I turned and tried to leave, but he still had a hold of my arm. Spinning me around to face him, he said, "I've no doubt about that; it was the unwary marauders I was worried about."

I made an unladylike face at him and tried to free my arm.

"Did you have anything to do with that display back there?" he asked quietly, his eyes dark with suspicion.

"Certainly not!" I raised my chin another notch, then realized how ridiculous I must look and lowered it again. "I knew nothing about it, Griffin. I was as appalled as everyone else."

I pulled my arm again. Instead of letting go, he took my other arm in his free hand. Peering intently into my eyes, he leaned forward and kissed me. His lips were gentle on mine at first, caressing, persuasive, yet demanding. I breathed in his scent, waves of excitement buzzing down my body. My vision blurred as I looked into those deep, endless pools of amber, eyes that glowed from within as he touched the back of my neck lightly, caressing, stroking my skin. It electrified me; I felt his touch all the way down to my toes. He nipped my lip until I gave him what he wanted, allowing him to sink into my mouth, his groan of pleasure matching my own. My fingers curled through hair soft as silk, tugging him closer when my body clamored to feel him. He pulled me tighter, one hand on my behind, the other tangled in my hair as he thoroughly, leisurely, wantonly explored my mouth.

Just when I thought I would swoon with the delight of it all, he ended the kiss, his mouth shifting to caress my neck, my hair, and my ears.

"Why, oh why, didn't I think of taking a lover before?" I murmured to myself.

He laughed, breaking the mood of the moment. I pulled away, desperately trying to catch my breath.

"I believe, madam, that we have an appointment?"

His raised eyebrow sent little shivers of delight down my back as I understood what he was asking. "Yes, we certainly do."

He held out his arm. I took it, and we walked in silence to the nearest cab.

I waited until the cab had set off for my house before turning to him. To my surprise, he held me off. "No."

"I'm sorry," I said, suddenly flushed with shame. I'd thrown myself at him and he was repulsed! "I shouldn't have—"

"Yes, you should, but not here in the cab. It's going to be difficult enough to walk without you making it worse."

"Are you injured in some way?" I asked, concerned.

"I hurt, if that's what you mean. Cassandra..." His words trailed off.

Now I really was concerned. "If you are in pain, I can summon a doctor."

"I can just imagine what he'd say. You have no idea what I'm talking about, do you?"

"No, but if you've had another accident—"

"I suspected that was the case." He took my hand and placed it on his lap, pressing my fingers into his groin.

I froze for a moment. "Oh. I see."

"You don't, but you will. It's painful for a man to be so aroused, and if you were to kiss me like you obviously wish to, you might push me over the edge."

I felt strangely proud of myself, enough so that I took to the liberty to explore the apparently vast lengths his arousal rose to. So to speak.

"And that will definitely do the job if kissing you didn't," he said in a tight voice, prying my hand off his groin.

"I'm sorry. I won't do it again."

"I pray fervently that you will, but not in a cab. Have you considered the ramifications of what this will mean to your home?"

"The servants, you mean?" I smiled and held up my bag. "I told Mullin that I would let myself in. My maid will be discreet, of that you have no fear."

"I have no fear of servants, but I don't want you to be made to feel uncomfortable."

"Leave that to me," I said with confidence.

The ride home seemed interminable since I couldn't spend it kissing Griffin, but at long last I closed the door to the library, and sighed in relief. Then I hiccupped.

"Are you all right?" Griffin asked, eyeing me carefully.

"Yes, perfectly. I always have the hiccups when I laugh too hard."

"You have picked a strange time to be laughing," he murmured, his head bent so he could feather a kiss to my bare collarbone.

"I can't help it," I breathed, arching my back so my breasts were pressed against him. "The shocked expression on Mullin's face when you followed me in here made me laugh, and when I do that, I get the hiccups."

He pressed me against the library wall, his eyes steaming with desire, his hands stroking down my bare arms to my waist. "You dragged me in here, madam. *That* is what he was staring at."

I smiled and brushed his lips with mine, feeling terribly wanton, but knowing that this was right. I was meant to be with Griffin, meant to do all of the things I wanted to do with him. "I wish I could yell at him for waiting up for me, but he looked so concerned. Until he saw you, that is."

"We could go elsewhere," he murmured, his mouth closing on mine. The wood was cool against my back, but Griffin was fire against my front. I slipped my hands up his waistcoat and over his shoulders, pushing his evening jacket off.

"No. It'll be all right. We'll stay here."

His tongue was bossy, pushing mine around until I suckled it, then he moaned into my mouth. My fingers danced down the line of buttons on his waistcoat, pushing it off after his jacket.

His hands slid around to my front, and finally closed around breasts that had been screaming for his attention. I leaned into his palms, leaned into all of him, reveling in the hardness of his body as he plundered my mouth again.

I plundered back.

"No corset?" he asked when we came up for breath, the wicked glint in his beautiful eyes lighting all sorts of fires around various parts of my body. I pulled his tie off as he nibbled at a sweet spot just behind my ear.

"Too confining," I murmured, tugging on his hair until I could suck his lower lip into my mouth. I wrapped my arms around him, releasing button after button on the back of his shirt.

"I like women who don't wear corsets," he groaned as I spread my fingers wide on the smooth bare skin of his back.

With a move that was so quick it was over before I was aware it began, he whisked my sapphire gown over my head and tossed it in the direction of a chair. There wasn't much more of me to be exposed in my underfrillies, but it felt scandalously naughty to stand there in front of him in nothing but my chemise and combinations.

I reveled in every moment of it.

"I like a man who likes a woman who doesn't wear a corset." I kissed him with every ounce of desire I possessed, my fingers tugging and twisting until I had his cufflinks off.

His hands fumbled on the hooks that ran down the back of my chemise, pausing just long enough to shed his shirt. I stared hungrily at his chest, his magnificent chest, his wonderful, fabulous, breathtakingly beautiful chest, a veritable wonderland of muscle and sinews and dark, curly hair that suddenly made my legs go boneless.

"Chest," I squeaked, spreading my fingers across it, tracing all the contours that swooped and bulged in amazingly wonderful curves.

"Yes, it is," he answered, having unhooked enough of my chemise that he could tug it down over my hips, until it fell with a soft whisper of silk and lace at my feet. "And it's the most beautiful chest I've ever seen."

I arched my back when his hands closed on my bare breasts, my eyes closing as I gave myself up to the wonderful fires his fingers started. His breath was hot on my skin as he kissed a trail from my neck down to where my breasts tightened and grew heavy. His kisses were warm, steaming me as his lips caressed the sensitive flesh. I wanted to move, wanted to touch him, but with every brush of his lips against me, I lost more of myself to him.

"You're so beautiful. You taste of fire." His mouth closed around one aching nipple and I groaned my pleasure, my nails digging into his shoulders. "You're soft and silky and I want to taste all of you."

I clung to him as his mouth moved over to my other breast, too overwhelmed with the sensations he was stirring to speak.

"You make me mad with desire. I've wanted you since that first day, wanted to touch you and fill my senses with you."

I whimpered my pleasure at both his words and actions, unable to pull enough coherent thoughts together to speak. With a murmur against my breast, he scooped me up in his arms and set me down carefully on the rug before the fire, propping himself up on his elbows, his chest pressed against mine as he kissed me again.

"Griffin?" I breathed against his shoulder, squirming delightedly against him, kissing the tanned column of his throat as he divested me of the remainder of my garments. I knew I should remind him to lock the door, but all thoughts left my mind when his mouth followed his fingers as he kissed a path down my belly. His hands traced serpentine designs on the flesh of my thighs until I parted them for him, then suddenly he was down there, in the tingliest of all my tingly spots, his fingers dancing a seductive waltz that left me aching for more.

"My beautiful Cassandra," he rumbled, his eyes alight with passion so hot it scorched my skin. I traced the line of his jaw until he looked up, his gaze holding mine.

"The door," I said, aware of nothing but the magic in his fingers as they caressed and teased, tension coiling inside me, winding tighter and tighter with each stroke.

"The door," he said, his mouth closing over my breast, suckling hard at my nipple until I almost came off the floor.

"Yes, yes! The door, oh, Griffin, the door!"

"The door is beautiful," he murmured against my other breast, teasing it with sweet nips that turned all the fires within me to raging infernos. One long finger sank within me, causing my hips to arch beneath his hand. "I have never seen such a beautiful, luscious door in all my life. It is soft as silk, and so hot it burns me. I want the door. I crave the door. Let me have the door, Cassandra."

"It's all yours," I shrieked as something inside me exploded into chaos, a wondrous chaos of joy and ecstasy that had its beginning and ending in Griffin.

His fingers slid from my body as I lay panting on the rug before the fire, one side of me warmed by the flames, the other scorched by Griffin. I heard the rustle of cloth against skin, and then he was over me, nudging my legs wider, his chest hair teasing my aching nipples.

"Tell me you want it, too," he said, his eyes molten with passion. "Tell me you want it as much as I do."

"I do," I promised, kissing his beautiful throat. "I want it more than anything I've ever wanted. Give it to me, Griffin."

He groaned as my fingers sculpted the contours of his back, then he was pressing against me, nudging his way into my body, entering me in a way that suddenly had me worried.

"Um. Griffin?"

His head sank to my shoulder as he kissed my neck, nibbling on me while the surprisingly solid length of him pressed slowly inside. He was hot and hard and filled me, stretching me until I squirmed beneath him. He groaned again, mumbling something about me not moving until he caught his breath.

"Griffin, I think I've changed my mind. I think that there's something not quite right with this situation. You must be built too large or perhaps I'm too small or maybe I just over-anticipated this actual event, but you're beginning to hurt me and I think I'd like you to—"

He plunged forward, a burst of pain flaring to life deep within me. I bit his shoulder in protest and tried to push him off me, but he was too heavy. He surrounded me, filled me, he was everywhere, leaving me no escape. Panic swamped me, the familiar flame of fear licking the edges of my mind, and I was just about to start screaming for help when he lifted his head and kissed me.

"I'm sorry, sweetheart. I know I hurt you, but it will be better in a moment. Just don't move."

Somehow, just the sight of his eyes, full of concern, full of desire and yearning calmed me. The panic and fear faded as I kissed him in return, and suddenly, the pressure of him filling me took on a new dimension, one of pleasure, one of need that only he could satisfy. I moved my hips just a little to experiment with this new sensation, capturing his groan in my mouth. "Cassandra, no, for the love of God, don't move—"

I shifted my hips again, and he slid deeper into me.

He moved then, a beautiful rhythm that sent me soaring, thrusting in with long, deep strokes that joined his body fully with mine until there was no way to separate us. His movements quickened, his kisses becoming harder, more demanding as his body pounded into mine. I wrapped my legs around his hips and matched his kisses, taking his heat and returning it with a fire of my own. We burner hot, hotter than I thought possible, our flesh bound together until in one brilliant moment, we slipped past mere mortal pleasure and entered the realm of heaven.

Griffin's back arched as his shouted my name, his voice mingling with mine as I gave myself over to the beauty of the moment.

A long time later, after our hearts had stopped pounding, after our breathing had changed from ragged gasps to a more regular pattern, after the fire we had created burned down to deep, satisfying embers, Griffin lifted his head from my neck and looked down on me.

"Did you say something about the door?"

I smiled and kissed the tip of his nose. Men were such amusing creatures. "Don't be silly, why would I choose such a moment to talk about architecture?"

I suppose I ought to have felt some shame or regret for the loss of my innocence, or at least embarrassment that I all but seduced Griffin, but in truth, all I felt as we assisted each other into our respective garments was the sadness that I would not be able to spend the night lying in his arms.

Oh, there was satisfaction that I had chosen my lover well, and there was the knowledge that our time together would be pleasurable beyond what I had believed possible, but still, there was a faint sense of loss that lingered.

When he had adjusted the last button on my gown, and I had slipped his cufflinks back into place, we faced each other silently.

"May I see you tomorrow?"

I looked at him solemnly, slowing regaining control of myself. I wondered if I would ever be the same. "I will be participating in a march to the Houses of Parliament tomorrow at noon."

His jaw tightened as he dropped my hand. "After tonight's episode at the opera, you still intend on joining that group of misguided women?"

"I do indeed," I said, anger slowly blotting out the warmer feelings that had remained. How could I feel so close to him, be so intimate with him, and yet so distant at the same time? "I've told you that I knew nothing about the demonstration tonight, and I had no part in the terrible attack this morning. I *do* know that the Women's Suffrage Union does not condone violence. The women who acted tonight were a small faction, a minority. The rest of the Union is not like them."

He snorted indignant. "Whether their actions are sanctioned by your group or not, can't you see how foolish they look, what a mockery they make of your cause? Is that how you want to appear to your family and friends?"

His amber eyes flashed with anger, but I did not quail before them. "I admit they were wrong in disrupting the opera, but frankly, I applaud their efforts. What they did took nerve and bravery."

"Bravery! Bravery? What that pack of screeching she-wolves displayed was nothing more than cowardice, attacking a group of unarmed musicians and singers."

I was annoyed with his deliberate attempt to shift the focus of the argument. I opened my mouth to say more, then thought better of it. This was not a battle I would win standing in the library while the taste of him still lingered on my lips.

"Thank you for escorting me home," I said primly. "And for everything else. It was enlightening."

His hands closed around my shoulders, stopping me, his voice low and urgent. "So you understand, I will spell it out for you. What you are doing is dangerous to yourself and others. You are playing a game with adversaries who will show you no mercy. Do not doubt that they will win, no matter what the cost."

My cheeks burned with indignation and the after-effects of our lovemaking; for a time I didn't know which emotion had the upper hand, anger or love. The anger won out. I turned just enough to let him see the resolve in my eyes. "Thank you for your warning, it's much appreciated, but I have no fear about any danger befalling us."

"I...would be...*pleased* if you did not participate in the march."

Disappointment that nothing had changed between us deafened my ears to the pleading undertone in his voice.

"I am sure you would be, just as I am sure you would be pleased if every woman in Britain gave up the right to think for herself. But that, Griffin St. John, is not going happen. I will attend the march tomorrow, with my head held high, proud to be a part of such a noble cause."

His jaw twitched dangerously as he stuffed his fists into his pockets. "Do whatever you want, you aggravating woman!" he roared as he threw open the door and stalked out of it.

I closed it and stood with my back to the cool wood, the pounding of my heart drowning out every other sounds as I closed my eyes and relived every exquisite moment of our lovemaking.

Could it be that everything I believed in was wrong? As long as there were men like my Uncle Henry, who treated women with respect and dignity, was it right for women to demand the same of all men? And Griffin—would he ever change his opinion of women's suffrage? Was my love doomed even before it was requited? Were a few stolen moments together between arguments all we were to have?

"Enough of this." I shook myself, and went upstairs to bed.

CHAPTER FOURTEEN

The sun was out the next morning, reminding me how lovely the sky could be when freshly washed with blue. Feeling the need for exercise to clear my head after the events of the past evening, I set out to walk the scant mile to the rendezvous point near the Houses of Parliament. I had plenty of time as I walked to recall again, for what seemed to be the one hundredth time, the words Griffin and I had hurled at each other, but I was sad to note that in this instance, familiarity did not bring resolution.

Helena was waiting for me in a mouth-watering Kingfisher Blue walking skirt and matching coat that once again put my own ensemble to shame. Her radiant smile greeted me as we clasped each other's hands like excited schoolgirls.

"What a fine day for a march," she exclaimed happily. "And what a lovely skirt! The color matches your eyes."

"Thank you." I hesitated. "I notice your brother is not glowering behind you. Are you sure you are willing to go through with this? After last night's display, I doubt if your family would be pleased with your participation. You may be opening yourself up to a great deal of trouble at home."

She waved off my warning. "Wasn't that exciting last night? I couldn't believe the bravery of those women, to march into the middle of the opera!"

"Yes, they were brave, but I believe they could have chosen a different event to protest. I am sure Maggie Greene was behind it, which would explain the choice of targets."

Helena looked down at her hands for a moment, her lovely face clouded. "Cassandra, I owe you an apology about yesterday morning. I acted foolishly, and ignored your warnings. I don't know what came over me, but I do know I won't do it again. Thank you for being there with me."

"I have to ask you one question, and then we will let the subject drop. Did you know that your brothers would be at the club?"

She nodded her head, worrying her gloves. "Maggie asked when Harold would be at his club, and I mentioned that they were having a vote about a troublesome member. She thought that would be a good time to have our protest. Griffin seldom visits it, but because of the vote—" Her voice trailed off.

"I see. Never mind." I took her arm as we walked towards the gathering women. "It is a sorry person who cannot learn from her mistakes. Now, as for last night, while I applaud the intentions and bravery it took to demonstrate at the opera, I am opposed to disruptive methods such as the militants used. It was very embarrassing."

"You poor dear; it must have been beastly for you with Harold being so rude. Were your aunt and uncle offended?"

"Shocked more than offended, I believe."

"I hope they paid no heed to what Harold said." She looked at me from the corner of her eye. "Griffin left shortly after you did...you didn't see him, by any chance?"

"Helena, you need not be coy with me. I am sure your brother told you that he accompanied me home."

"Oh, no, Cassandra, I wasn't being coy, I assure you. Griffin told me nothing last night, except—" She smiled. "He was throwing things around his study and muttering something about you when I went in to say goodnight."

It was inevitable. I blushed. The feeling of being held in his arms, our bodies joined together, wrapped in ecstasy had quickly become my most cherished memory.

"I apologize for the accusation, Helena. There is nothing really I can tell you. I left early after the disgraceful scene, Griffin met me outside, and he kindly accompanied me home."

"Ah," she said, still smiling. "I wonder that he was in such a curious mood then, one moment elated, the next frustrated. You didn't argue with him?"

I cleared my throat and watched a clutch of children skip by. "We had a discussion, yes. You know how unreasonable he is about the cause. He may have interpreted the discussion as an argument."

"I'm sure that's it." She frowned briefly as she watched the Union leaders consult one another. "The oddest thing happened this morning. I was passing the telephone room and I thought I heard Harold mention something about the march today..." Her voice trailed off as we were beckoned forward. "Look, I believe they are starting."

A short, energetic woman in her thirties passed among us, distributing *Votes For Women* sashes to those who did not possess one. Helena and I each obtained a sash, and I could not help but notice that the excitement of the march brought color and animation to her usually pale cheeks.

"This is a truly a glorious moment. I am so glad you are with me, dear Cassandra. To be here with our sisters in bondage, marching down Parliament Street side by side, proud to be women, proud to striking a blow against tyranny, proud to be a part of this great cause."

I watched her dramatics with a jaded eye, then said softly, "You are a bit of a romantic."

She smiled at me tolerantly, and squeezed my arm. "We both are. After all, that's what makes our friendship so strong! With you as my sister—" She choked briefly. I patted her on the back and she continued. "—without you as my sister in suffrage, I would be lost. It is you I have to thank for unshackling me from the bonds of my slavery!"

"Good lord, you *have* been reading the pamphlets." I laughed at her impassioned speech.

"My dear friends," Mrs. Heywood said, drawing our attention. "We are about to undertake a great protest. Our march today to the Houses of Parliament will go down in history as one of the greatest demonstrations against male tyranny."

Helena nudged me, almost dancing with excitement.

"You will be able to tell your daughters of your courageous fight for your freedom, for *their* freedom. Do not give in, no matter how dangerous or difficult the battle. Stand tall! Stand strong! Stand firm for your rights!"

The inspiring words enthralled me until it struck me to wonder if Helena had heard correctly. Since it was obvious that my notebook hadn't reached Lord Sherringham's hands, if he really *had* said something about today's march, there could be only one person from whom he could have acquired the details—Griffin.

"We are women of the twentieth century. No longer are we bound to the rules and laws of our grandmothers—our future can be one of equality, but to obtain that future, we must be willing to work."

My heart sank. What had happened last night was not as profoundly important to Griffin as it was to me—men being what they are—but somehow, I had thought of him as being different from other men, superior to them, trustworthy where others were not.

"No," I said softly to myself. "He *is* different. He wouldn't do this to us."

"Our path will not be easy, it may not even seem to be going anywhere, but along it we must trod if we are to secure for ourselves and our children those basic rights denied our sex for so long."

The women around me cheered and applauded Mrs. Heywood, but I ceased to hear them or her as conflicting emotions swelled within me. Had our intimacy indicated Griffin had deep feelings for me, or was I just a pleasant diversion to be used and discarded when he tired of me? I found it impossible to believe he would betray us, but if his brother had the information about the march, where else could it have come from?

"Today we will present before the House of Lords a petition containing ten thousand, two hundred signatures. As we march, you will, under no circumstances, respond to any comments or jeers from the crowd, nor will you commit any acts of violence, such as throwing stones. Stay in formation until the deputation to the House of Lords has returned, at which time we shall continue the march to Westminster Abbey, where we will hold a brief rally and disband."

"I won't believe it," I told myself. "There has to be another explanation."

"Sorry?" Helena said, leaning in to whisper. "I didn't hear what you said."

"Nothing important. They're forming up. Shall we take our places?"

"I wish we had a sign," she answered as we took up a position on the right flank.

"That would be nice, but we can be just as proud wearing only our sashes," I answered, pushing the worry over Griffin from my mind. I wouldn't be able to resolve anything on that front until I had proof either way, and the march was an important act, my first true protest. I was determined to enjoy every moment of it.

Horses, carriages, and motorcars moved out of our way when we marched as a group down the middle of the street. The usual taunting and slurs were tossed at us as we passed, but we ignored them. Several women were singing a new suffrage song, and although I did not know the lyrics, I kept a smile on my face as I hummed along with the others. In no time we were stopped in front of Parliament.

Unfortunately, so were the local police.

Several ranks of constables had formed a blockade across the front of Parliament. When the deputation of three women approached the constables, showing them the petitions and asking for admission, they were rudely pushed back and summarily refused.

"Oh, dear. This looks somewhat ominous," I told Helena as we exchanged glances, our hearts sinking. "This many policemen...perhaps I was a little hasty in dismissing Griffin's warning. These men looked as if they would have little mercy."

"What warning?"

"You know Griffin, he's always warning us away from protests." It was a feeble explanation at best, but Helena was too distracted to examine it closely. We stood together, watching silently as the deputation continued to plead with the police. My thoughts were dark as a crowd began to gather.

"Surely they cannot arrest us for simply marching down the street?" I asked Helena. "We have committed no violent acts, nor performed any illegal act."

Her face was pale as she watched the Union officers arguing with the constables. "I can't see how they could arrest us. We are being peaceable and orderly."

"Oh, no!" Suddenly a cheer went up from the gathering crowd. Their arms pinned behind them, the three members of the deputation were pushed through the crowd toward a row of police conveyances. Cries of concern and distress broke out in our group, and several members rushed forward to help. Without warning, Helena and I found ourselves pushed from behind up against the wall of constables.

Details about the brutal treatment we suffered that day at the hands of the police are common knowledge, but I am ashamed and sickened to say that I saw English policemen attacking English gentlewomen in a manner more suitable to common thugs. Although we used no violence, and were peaceable and open to reason, we were treated to savage and inhuman acts of violence.

A constable grabbed me as the pressure from behind flung me up against him. He wrenched my arms backwards, and hauled me toward the police vans. Helena struggled with another constable, and although I tried to tell her to not fight him, the shrieks and screams from the other women were too great to allow me to be heard.

To my great horror, we were placed in the police vans. I was rather proud to see the way some women fought, although I knew they were the ones who would suffer the most. Other women, such as Mrs. Heywood and the petition deputation, retained their natural dignity and allowed themselves to be led away without a struggle.

"Are you all right?" I asked as I crawled over a woman's legs to get to where Helena had been thrown into my van. Her hair was tumbled down about her shoulders, her gown torn. She sobbed my name and scrambled over two other suffragettes to reach me. "Are you hurt? Did he do anything to harm you?"

"No," she sobbed, her face streaked and dirty. "I'm fine. Are you well?"

I had the ridiculous urge to laugh at her question, but fought down both it and the hysteria that threatened to follow. "I'm not hurt either. I tried to tell you not to fight, but I don't think you heard me."

She shook her head, her frail body trembling violently against me as two more women were hurled into the van. The doors slammed shut and we were left in darkness, the only sounds audible were that of gentle sobbing.

"Cassandra, what are we going to do?" Helena asked me softly.

"I wish I knew," I answered. "We'll just have to see what we are charged with."

We were driven to the local police station where our pitiful group was herded into a room. Helena held fast to me as we were escorted into the police station, then brought forward to be interviewed.

"Name?" A burly constable asked.

"Cassandra Whitney."

"Address?"

I gave him Mabel's address.

"Husband's name?"

"I'm not married."

The constable dismissed me without a second glance and turned his attention to Helena. I was herded off before she was interviewed, but was surprised by her unexpected inner strength. When she rejoined our group, she was not in tears as I had assumed she would be, and in fact, did her best to reassure me.

The police facility was overwhelmed with our numbers, and I later found out that many women had been sent to other districts. Our group of ten was sent to share a hideous room with six wooden cots, no blankets, and I suspect a great many vermin. After the noise of the march and subsequent arrest, the women in our cell were quiet—stunned, like myself, by the unexpected and unwarranted treatment. Most of the women had scratches and bruises but were not hurt seriously. A few shared a bed; others sat on the floor, the very pictures of dejection.

Two hours after the march began, Helena and I sat on a bed together, comforting one another as best we could. I had fully expected that she would become hysterical under such tortuous treatment, but once again she surprised me.

"Don't worry, dearest Cassandra," she said, attempting to comfort me. "Griffin will have us out in no time. I told that police constable who interviewed us who I was, and to contact Griffin for our release."

The woman in the bed next to ours lifted her head. Helena gasped in surprise at her face, the bruised jaw and a small trickle of dried blood gave the appearance of a battle-weary warrior. I recognized the woman as Maureen Worrit, a particularly devoted suffragette who had been arrested a year ago for attacking a policeman.

"Release you?" Maureen's voice pierced the room. "You can't ask for release—it's our duty to serve the sentence, for it is only through our martyrdom that we will achieve our goal. This is our chance to protest through deed, not through mere words! Imprisonment is a fact that cannot be disputed or wiped from the record!"

I will admit that my spirits dropped even lower at those words. We could not, in good faith, abandon our sisters now and expect to be welcomed back at our convenience. I slid a glance toward Helena, convinced she would never hold up under such a strain as prison would afford, and also worried about what my family would say. Mabel was due to arrive home the following day…how would she take the news that her sister had been sent to prison for participation in a suffrage march? My stomach lurched at the thought of it.

There was very little talking during the day and night that followed; when there was talk, it was mainly by the women who had first-hand knowledge of imprisonment.

"Your sisters before you have all committed themselves to a hunger strike. They have sworn a solemn oath that they will not eat until they are released from their unjust imprisonment."

"I've heard a rumor that hunger strikers are horribly abused," Helena whispered to me, her face as pale as ivory.

I heard the fear in her voice, and felt it echoed in my heart.

"The Union is fighting to have our sisters labeled as political prisoners rather than common criminals, but the government refuses to listen to reason," Maureen added. "You see now why it is so important that we continue our protests whether jailed or free."

The warders brought in the evening meal, a repulsive gray stew that we all refused. Even if I had not adopted the policy of a hunger strike, I would have never eaten such unhealthy food.

How Helena and I made it through that long night, I can't honestly say. We cried, hugged each other for support, and slept very little. The other women were in similar situations, worried about their families and friends who would in turn be horrified at their imprisonment. Uppermost in our minds, however, was what would happen when we were brought before the magistrate.

Morning came at last, and we were taken, unwashed and bedraggled, before the Thames Police Court, where we were charged with the crime of assault upon a policeman. I stared around the court as suffragette after suffragette was brought before the bench, charged, interviewed briefly, then sentenced.

"Courage," I whispered to Helena as she held my hand tightly. She squeezed my fingers in response.

When my turn before the magistrate came, I stood with dignity and pled not guilty, but was not allowed to make any statement or ask any questions. I received the standard fine of half a crown. Acting in accordance with my fellow suffrage workers, I refused to pay the fine, and was sentenced to three days in jail. The jailers took me away before I could see Helena brought up, but later she told me her experience had been similar.

Those of us who had not been arrested before were sent back to the foul cell from which we had emerged, while the other women—the ones who had been arrested before in the service of the cause—were sent on to prison for longer sentences.

"If you behave yourselves, I'll let you keep your clothing," the wardress told our motley group. Two of the women struggled and refused to comply with her demand we return to our cell—they were taken to separate cells where they were stripped of their dresses and left to sit in their chemises.

"We can be devoted to the cause and still maintain our dignity," I told Helena when she looked at me with wild eyes as the two were dragged away screaming and kicking. "We will cooperate with the officials."

And we did. The wardress allowed us to stay together in our cell, where we were later joined by two other women who were also scared, worried, and did not wish to precipitate any further trouble.

Our thoughts that day were understandably dark. Mine were particularly so, for I carried the additional burden of having involved an innocent girl in a situation with grave ramifications. Sick with worry as to what my family and Helena's would go through when they learned we were imprisoned, I'm not ashamed to admit my fleeting doubts about involvement with the cause rose.

"It looks fine on paper," I said quietly to Helena. "But when you find yourself sitting on a filthy wooden plank, sharing a chamber pot with three other women, with no hope of release for two more days, no food, and no water to wash yourself, your perspective changes."

Helena was curled up at the bottom of my cot, trying to comb her disheveled hair with her fingers. She glanced at the other two women, but they appeared to be sleeping. "Do you think we should give up the cause?"

"I don't know," I answered, aware of the lines of strain around her mouth. I had the feeling Helena was maintaining a very tight control of herself, and only just keeping from indulging in a fit of hysterics. "I still believe in the right of women to vote, I still believe in the Women's Suffrage Union, but this...well, I just cannot see how being dirty and miserable for three days is going to further the cause. The police and public won't respect us any more for it, will they?"

"I think they might. If they knew how we were abused, that is. Perhaps we could interest a newspaper in our experiences?"

I shook my head, too tired, confused, and scared to try to reason it out.

By afternoon, I was also exceedingly hungry, and bored with my own dark thoughts. Helena and one of the other women were sleeping, and conversation with our remaining cellmate had proved disappointing. I was mentally writing a strongly worded letter to *The Times* about our treatment at the hands of the police when the wardress opened our cell.

"St. John and Whitney, you are to come with me to the Inspector's office."

Surprised and worried, we followed her through a maze of corridors to the Inspector's room, Helena in front of me as the wardress stepped aside. She paused in the doorway briefly before flinging herself forward with a glad cry. My vision was blocked by the wardress who entered after her, but I assumed the cause of Helena's joy to be her brother.

I wondered briefly how Griffin had affected our freedom, and toyed with the idea of refusing to leave before my time was served, but that thought vanished quickly. I had enough of imprisonment and looked forward to going home, even if it meant having to listen to Griffin's lecture about the folly of ignoring his advice.

Relief flooded me as I peered around the wardress into the room. It *was* Griffin that Helena was holding so fiercely. I am ashamed to admit that, even in that horrible place, under such excruciating circumstances, I was filled with jealousy as I watched Helena cling to him. I knew just how strong his arms were, and how safe I felt in them. I envied Helena her protector.

"You there!" Blinking back a few tears, I turned toward the strident voice only to see Lady Sherringham being escorted down the hallway. "Who is that woman standing there? She looks familiar."

I quickly spun around in the other direction and scurried in a most cowardly fashion to a chair a little way down the hall. I had little hope she didn't recognize me, but at least I could keep out of her way. After a day of imprisonment with little sleep, and suffering the results of a horrible assault, I was in no shape to withstand Lady Sherringham's venomous attack.

I put my head in my hands, and watched through my fingers as she entered the Inspector's office, only to reemerge a few seconds later with a reluctant Helena in tow. Helena looked for me, offered a weak smile over her shoulder, and allowed herself to be walked briskly away.

I closed my fingers around my eyes with the thought of what she would have to endure from her sister-in-law, and wondered idly if she would not be better off in prison. My musings were brought to a quick end by the feeling of strong fingers on mine. I took my hands from my eyes and looked up, trying to gauge his mood.

"Hello, Griffin." He stood like that for a moment, holding my hands in his, looking down at me from what seemed a very distant height. "We thought you might come. Helena was sure of it. I thought perhaps you might like to let us stew for a bit."

He said nothing, just heaved a big sigh and pulled me to my feet and into his arms. I would like to say I pushed away from this unseemly position in such a public place, but instead I did the opposite. I buried my face into his collar, and clung to him tightly, kissing his neck and his jaw, turning my head until I found his mouth. His lips were gentle, almost tentative as if seeking reassurance. I slid my hands into his hair and opened my mouth to him, my heart beating wildly as he stroked my tongue, building the familiar fire of passion deep within me. His hands were gentle on me, touching my hair, my back, my face. I wanted to stay like that forever—loved, protected, wanted. Instead, he pulled away from me and, with an unreadable expression, marched me out of the building and into a cab.

I sat next to him in the confined space of the cab, his arm around me keeping me pressed firmly up against his side. I tried to think of something to say, but for once I was speechless. I peeked out of the corner of my eye at him. He looked straight ahead with no expression on his face.

As I watched, a muscle in his jaw twitched.

Not a good sign.

I opened my mouth to say something, anything, but he must have heard me inhale in preparation to speaking. His head snapped around. On his face was a look that I did not care to investigate.

I closed my mouth and looked out the window.

It was in this manner that we arrived at my sister's house. I expected him to blow up at any moment, but in silence he handed me down.

I turned back to thank him, assuming he would get back into the cab, only to find him paying the cabby.

I felt that this, too, was not a good sign.

Not looking at me, Griffin rang the bell. Mullin opened the door and stared at me in surprise. "Miss Cassandra! It is you! We were worried when you did not return home yesterday—" His words were abruptly cut short when Griffin pushed me past him.

"It's all right, Mullin," I said reassuringly, watching Griffin carefully. "It was just a little misunderstanding. Has Mrs. Garner arrived yet?"

"No, miss. There was a wire saying they had docked at Southampton this morning and would arrive this afternoon."

Griffin pushed me into the library.

"That's fine," I said as he closed the doors behind him. "Thank you."

This last was said to the door, Griffin not waiting until I finished speaking to close them.

Feeling like a guilty schoolchild, I watch with concern as he turned and faced me, his arms crossed over his chest, the expression on his face one of a man struggling to keep control. He continued to look at me, saying nothing. His eyes held mine in a gaze I was unable to break.

Nervously, I spoke. "I would like to thank you for having us released. I don't know how you accomplished it, but I am sure it must have cost you dearly..."

I watched closely for any change in expression. I watched in vain.

"I offer you my humblest and most grateful thanks."

He shifted his weight and continued to regard me silently. Only the tension in his jaw gave me a clue to his feelings. It was at that point that I began to babble. "I realize now that you had a valid point when you warned me against participation in this march."

His amber eyes blazed at me. I decided he had been quiet long enough. "It is a point I shall certainly remember when I next attend such a protest."

I won't reproduce his response here except to say that he knew quite a few more oaths than my father's coachman, who had been my previous source of information on that subject. I badly wanted to make note of a few of the more creative ones, but felt that would have to wait for a more auspicious time. "Ah," I said once he had worn himself out. "I thought that would encourage you to speak."

He choked back another oath and walked towards me, a dangerous look on his face. I watched him approach with some trepidation; if he was violent in his anger, it was better I learn the worst now. He grasped my arm in a strong grip and pulled me to him.

"You are trying to drive me insane, woman, admit it." His kisses had a fire in them I had not experienced before. They were everywhere, bruising my lips, burning my eyelids, and branding my neck. "You drive me mad with desire. Tell me you are trying to make me insane."

Waves of passion and love swelled within me, setting my skin alight and making my heart pound loudly.

"Griffin, please," I begged, returning his passionate embraces with a fervor I did not know possible. My fingers were buried in his hair as I pulled him to me, the hunger within me frightening in its intensity. "Please..."

"Please what?" he asked, kissing the answer off my lips.

"Please don't stop," I breathed, slipping my hands up the wonderful curves of his behind to his back.

"I was mad with worry," he growled as he nipped my earlobe, his hands cupping my breasts. The warmth of his palms seeped through the three layers of my clothing and scorched my flesh.

"So was I," I answered, desire overwhelming me as I tasted his mouth. The feel of his hard body crushed against mine sent my senses reeling. As I breathed in his masculine scent, shivers of sensual delight rippled down my back. The power of my desire was literally breathtaking, leaving me giddy and helpless against the ache that threatened to consume me. He was everywhere, everything to me. I felt him in my blood, heating me to a fever pitch. Deep, primitive urges cascaded until my head swam.

He looked deep into my eyes, his own a hot, burning brand of passion and need. "Tell me you want me, Cassandra. Tell me you need me."

"I do," I gasped as he lifted me up and pressed me back against the wall, pulling my legs up and wrapping them around his waist. "Touch me, Griffin. Hold me. Fill me. *Now!*"

The sound of cloth tearing was muted as he ripped my drawers off, and then he was there, hot and hard and surging into me with sure, strong strokes, filling me, *thrilling me* with his touch.

"You're so hot," he groaned against my mouth. "So hot and tight, I'll never have enough of you."

Words were meaningless sounds on my lips as I kissed him, kissed his jaw, curling my tongue into his ear as he pounded into me, my hips lifting to meet each thrust. I yanked his collar off, tearing at his tie until I bared his throat, that delicious strong throat, and scattered kisses along it as the familiar tension began to build within me.

"Ah, sweetheart, you're so good, you're everything I need," he moaned as I flexed my legs, nibbling that sweet spot beneath his ear. "I can't take it, I can't stand any more. Oh, God, Cassandra, tell me you're ready. Tell me you're with me."

"Always," I whispered against his lips, sinking within them to fire his frenzied emotions even higher. "I will never leave you."

He slammed me against the wall, his body moving in short, hard, fast strokes that matched our breath, his eyes wide with rapture as his muscles strained, my body answering by tightening around him as he sent us both flying to the stars.

He stood holding me for long minutes, the wood behind my back as hard as the man pressed against my front, our chests rising and falling in desperate attempts to get air, our hearts beating wildly. I let my legs slip from him, holding tight to him when they refused to bear my weight. He leaned against me, still struggling for breath, his voice low and deep, resonating deep within me.

"You infuriating woman."

I looked at him with surprise. This was not the lover's speech I was expecting. Instead, it had the hint of the lecture I had expected earlier.

"You exasperating, impossible...lovely woman."

I smiled at the last words, but it was a short-lived smile. Griffin quickly adjusted his trousers as I made what repairs I could to my drawers, halting when he wrapped his hands around my upper arms.

"Do you have any idea what hell I've gone through the last day?" He shook me slightly to emphasize his words. "Do you have any idea what you've done? Do you know," here he shook me very hard, "how worried I was?"

I tried to raise my hands, but my arms were pinned down tightly. The door to the library opened. "Are you all right, miss? I thought I heard—"

One look at Griffin's face was all it took. Mullin spun around and closed the door quietly behind him.

"I'm sorry—" I started, but was cut off.

"What were you thinking, woman?" he thundered at me. "You could have been seriously hurt! Helena could have been hurt! You could be in prison!" He stopped, let go of my arms, and sat down on the leather couch, one hand over his eyes. "You are the most maddening, unreasonable, delectable woman I have ever met."

I sat next to him, and placed my hand on his, pressing a little kiss to his ear. "I truly do appreciate the trouble you've gone to. I know my actions have caused you much grief, and I can assure you that in the future, I will do my best to keep Helena from any further participation—"

He snatched his hand away from mine and looked at me in horror. "Do you have the audacity to tell me—do you mean to say that you—that you can even *consider* further involvement with this group—" He choked to a stop.

"Of course I will consider further involvement. What happened today was a bizarre mischance. There's no reason I shouldn't participate in future events."

Scorched by the look on his face, I stood and walked over to the window with a nonchalance I was far from feeling. He followed, muttering oaths to himself as he took me by the shoulders and put his face very close to mine. "I forbid it! You will stop your association with that group immediately!"

"You forbid me?" My eyes narrowed in warning. I had not survived my father to have the first pig-headed man who caught my fancy to order me about. "What right do you have to forbid me from doing anything?"

"Good God!" he exclaimed, throwing his hands up in the air in a gesture of exasperation. "I give up! Will I never learn to get mixed up with independent, aggravating women?"

"I don't know, how many independent, aggravating women have you been mixed up with?" I asked curiously, aware that a sharp spike of jealousy accompanied the question.

"One too many," he said, pacing the length of the room.

He walked to the door and for a brief moment, I thought he was going to go out, but then he turned and paced back towards me. I watched him with concern, a vein in his temple bulging out in a most alarming manner, a fact he did not appreciate when pointed out.

"Damn my vein!" he shouted. He stopped pacing, and turned to me. "Do you not see," he began in a more reasonable tone, "that there are...*feelings*—"

I looked at him, confused by what he was trying to say. "We are lovers, so of course there are feelings. But, Griffin, that has nothing to do with my suffrage work. I am a New Woman, and you are a modern-thinking gentleman, and what we do in private can be of no concern to anyone else. If you are worried about my reputation, I can assure you, I don't mind."

"No, damn it woman, I'm not talking about that. Or maybe I am, I don't know, you have everything so twisted up, I can't tell what I'm thinking anymore."

He had to be worried that I would tell him I loved him, and demand the same in return. I knew men shied away from the softer emotions, and although I knew now that I loved Griffin with all my heart, until he felt the same way about me, I would not burden him with the truth. "Griffin, if you are worried about me putting demands on you because I asked you to be my lover, I can assure you that I won't. I understand that to a man, the act of lovemaking can give physical pleasure without emotional engagement."

"Damn it, woman, what I feel for you is not just lust!" he exploded. His hair, an unruly tangle, stood on end.

"Oh. I'm very happy to hear that. You, too, are more than just a lustful pleasure to me. " I chewed my lip, hesitating to put anything more into words.

"Cassandra," he growled again, pulling me to his chest, taking my chewed-upon lip into his mouth. I was just about to reciprocate when one of the library doors was flung open, two golden-haired girls romping into the room, accompanied by two large, reddish-brown dogs. The dogs leaped upon Griffin with a display of tongues and tails, while the girls threw themselves upon me.

"Auntie, Auntie, we're home!" they shrieked together, racing around me to chase the dogs.

"So I see," I said, looking with dismay at Griffin.

"Cassandra, my dear, we have had the most tedious journey. Amanda was seasick the entire way...." Mabel walked in and kissed me on the cheek, then stopped abruptly when she saw Griffin. She smiled and held out her hand to him. "How do you do? I am Mabel Garner, Cassandra's sister."

"I beg your pardon," I said. "Mabel, this is Mr. Griffin St. John. He is…a friend," I finished lamely, feeling Mabel wasn't quite ready for my New Womanhood just yet.

Griffin shook Mabel's hand politely, and sat down at her request.

"You have to forgive my daughters, Mr. St. John," she said, shooing them away. "We have been at sea for the last two weeks and they are a bit energetic. Oh, there you are, Joshua."

Two men stepped into the room, one of whom was Joshua, Mabel's husband. He was a round, short man with a pleasant countenance, and he held out his arms to me when he saw me.

"Cassandra, my dear! How long it's been since we've seen you!" I hugged him, kissing him on the cheek with great affection. He waved his hand toward his companion. "And you know Robert Hunter."

"Robert?" I said, turning to the second man. "Can it be? Robert?"

He stood behind Joshua, grinning at me. It *was* Robert! His skin was a dark tan, his blonde hair whitened by the sun, but his cornflower blue eyes were the same as when we were children. I squealed and threw myself into his arms, hugging him as tight as I could. He laughed and spun me around once before setting me back on the floor.

"Cassandra, you haven't changed a bit." He surveyed me from head to toe. "Well, I amend that statement—you have changed, and for the better."

I blushed and clung to his arm, gazing at him with admiration. Not a tall man, he was slight of build, but strong.

"You have changed, though, Robert." I touched the end of his golden mustache. "That's new."

"Cassandra!"

I turned to see why Mabel was outraged. Griffin stood awkwardly behind her.

"Oh, I'm so sorry," I said, and introduced Joshua to Griffin.

"And this," I grabbed Robert's arm and led him to Griffin, "is an old friend, Robert Hunter. Robert and I grew up together. Next to Emma, he's my oldest and dearest friend, and one whom I have not seen for many years."

The men shook hands, while I beamed at first at Robert, then at Griffin, delighted that the two men I loved most were together. Griffin was pleasant, but I noticed he watched Robert closely.

"I met Mabel and Mr. Garner in Jo'burg," Robert said, turning to hold my hands. "I was on my way back to England when they convinced me to delay my trip and travel with them."

"Now Robert, let's not have any more of that discussion. You will stay here with us as well," Mabel told him. She appealed to me. "He wants to stay at a hotel! Come, girls, I want you to get washed up. It was very nice meeting you, Mr. St. John. Will we have the pleasure of having you dine with us one night?"

Griffin bowed stiffly. "Thank you, I would enjoy that."

He excused himself, and started for the door.

"I will be back in a moment," I told Robert, and hurried after Griffin. I caught his arm at the front door, and stopped him.

"I am sorry about the interruption," I said with a wry smile. "I do want to thank you again for having me released. I will always be grateful to you for your kindness."

"No gratitude is necessary," he said coldly, not looking at me.

I gazed at him with dismay. One minute he was making love to me with a fire that would put hell to shame, the next he would not even look at me. Who could explain the minds of men?

He stepped forward to leave, then apparently thinking better of it, turned and looked towards the library door. In one swift, violent movement he gathered me into his arms and kissed the breath right out of my lungs. Releasing me just as quickly, he left.

I stood with one hand on the door, the other around my bruised ribs, out of breath and surprised.

"Will someone," I asked the empty hall, "explain to me what goes on in the mind of that man?"

The sound of my unanswered echo sent me running upstairs, where I had a quick wash and changed my dress.

CHAPTER FIFTEEN

Robert and I sat in the library after dinner, gossiping like two old women, fondly remembering the good times. It was from Robert that I received my first kiss, the day he sailed to South Africa to work on a farm owned by his older brother. I was sixteen at the time, and had thought myself in love with him.

When I recounted this, he looked sad and held my hand. "I didn't know. Why didn't you tell me?"

"Robert, I wasn't in love with you. I was bereft because I had lost a friend, not a lover. Mabel had married Joshua that spring, you remember, and Emma was away at school. I was alone with Father." I paused, remembering the anguish I had felt. "You and Emma were all I had. I was devastated when you left. I thought my heart would break, but later I realized I was just grieving for a very dear friend."

He looked at me curiously. "Do you...do you think you could love me now?"

"Oh, Robert! I *do* love you," I said with tears in my eyes, pressing his hand. I opened my mouth to tell him just what a dear friend he was to me when a blast of cold air swirled around my ankles.

Mullin was in the open doorway. Behind him, in shadow, Griffin stood with an impassive face. Our eyes met briefly. I gasped, feeling as if I had been struck when I saw the agony in his eyes. Suddenly, he was gone.

"Oh, blast!" I exclaimed, leaping to my feet. Pushing Mullin aside rudely, I grabbed Griffin's sleeve as he was going out the front door. "Griffin!"

He shook my hand off, and strode out the door. I paused for a minute on the doorstep, looked behind me to see Robert coming out of the library, then turn and ran down the steps. Griffin was mounted on Winston, urging him forward. Gathering my skirts, I leaped off the curb and grabbed onto his stirrup.

"Wait!" I gasped. "What you saw...it wasn't...Robert is an old friend—"

Griffin looked down on me, his face in shadow. "I quite understand. There's no need to explain." His voice was stiff and cold.

"No," I said. "You don't. If you will just give me a chance to tell you—"

"Let go of my stirrup. You do not owe me an explanation. You do not owe me anything."

"Of course I don't owe you anything, but I want to tell you—"

"Release my stirrup, woman!"

For a moment I had a picture of what a ridiculous scene we presented.

"Oh, this is stupid! I will not stand out here in the street begging you to listen to me as if we were two characters in a badly written novel. If you wish to deliberately misunderstand the situation, then do so. When you've returned to your senses, I will be happy to explain everything to you."

I turned on my heel and went back into the house. Stepping through the door I looked at Robert hovering ineffectually, and burst into tears. Robert, appalled at the scene, urged me back into the library where he offered me a handkerchief and brandy. I accepted the former, refused the latter, and indulged in a good cry.

"Is there anything I can do to make you feel better?" Robert sat next to me, concerned by my outburst.

"Nothing other than shaking some sense into that horrible man."

"St. John? Why is he horrible?"

"Because...he heard me say...oh, it's too complicated," I sniveled into his handkerchief, annoyed at myself for being so weak. "I will just say this: I had never been fond of those novels whose plots revolved around foolish misunderstandings between characters, but it's a thousand times more intolerable in real life."

"Ah, I begin to see." Robert sat back and watched me with a smile tugging at the edges of his mouth. "Could it be that your answer to my question was going to finish *but I love you like a brother?*"

"Yes. You know that, Robert, I do love you like a brother."

He grimaced, thought about it for a moment, then smiled. "I guess being loved like a brother is better than not being loved at all."

I sniffed.

"And St. John, he is the object of your affections?"

"Yes."

"Ah. So when he heard you say—"

"—that I loved you—"

"—he misinterpreted the statement." Robert smiled again. "This is a problem easily solved. I will go to him in the morning and explain everything."

"You will do nothing of the kind. I tried to explain the situation to him, but he is the most obstinate man I have ever met. When he is tired of playing the martyr, then I will tell him what I meant."

"Ah, Cassandra," he shook his head at me, "you are playing a dangerous game. It's best to clear up misunderstandings like this before they grow too big."

I thought about that for a few moments. "I suppose you are right. I could write him a letter explaining it."

He patted my hand. "There's no need. Since I was the unwitting stumbling block in your romance, I will go to the man and explain. Now, tell me about him."

I spent the rest of the evening talking to Robert about his life in South Africa, suffrage work, and Griffin. He was an excellent and compassionate listener, so it came as no surprise that by the time I retired I had agreed to let him call on Griffin. On my way up to bed, I encountered Joshua. He stood outside my room, fidgeting with the doorframe.

"Come in and sit down," I said, tired and annoyed with his nervousness.

He left the door open, and sat on the chair nearest it. "Cassandra, you know that your sister and I have the greatest affection for you."

"Why, yes, Joshua," I said surprised, "as you know I have for you both."

"Hmm. Yes. You know also that you will always have a home with us?"

"I do, and I thank you for that." I had a suspicion of where the conversation was heading.

"It has come to my attention that—ah—that you did not return home last night. I don't want you to think I am prying, but the servants were worried."

His round face was red with embarrassment at having to mention such a subject. I had wondered what the servants would tell him about the past evening, and the evening before, when I dragged Griffin into the library to have my wicked way with him. Joshua's household staff had the burden of being unusually conservative in their beliefs, but I believed they were genuinely fond of me, and wouldn't carry tales unnecessarily. I was pleased to find I was right. Mullin had only mentioned the one incident.

"Ah. Last night. Yes, well, I can explain that," I said, dreading what was to come. I disliked lying outright, but I did not see any harm in filtering the truth slightly. "I was unexpectedly required to be away from home."

Joshua looked at me blankly and waited for a further explanation.

"I was with a friend, who had been injured slightly, and I was…detained."

Enlightenment filled his eyes, and he nodded his head with sudden comprehension. "You were helping a sick friend. That is understandable and most admirable. I knew it must be something like that. I will inform your sister so she will not continue to worry."

"Thank you," I murmured.

He stopped at the door. "If you are called away again, please let us know if you will be gone during the night."

I hadn't been aware that Mabel was worried; she certainly had not said anything to me on the subject. I felt guilty about deceiving Joshua, but decided it was better for everyone's peace of mind if they were not exposed to the full truth.

Worry about Helena strengthened my resolve to speak with her and see how she was recovering from our experience. Knowing that any letter from me would never reach its recipient, I decided I would have to go through Griffin for that information.

"Griffin," I sighed, sitting on the bed and hugging my knees. I hadn't even questioned Griffin as to how he managed to get us released early, but however he had achieved this end, I was sure it must have been difficult. If only he weren't so pigheaded, I might be expressing my gratitude to him at this very moment in a very pleasing fashion.

"How on earth can a man be so warm, so loving, yet so obstinate and stubborn at the same time?" I asked my knees before crawling under the blanket and punching my pillow a few times.

We were in the drawing room after breakfast the next morning when Helena came to see me. Mabel was talking about South Africa, describing the many trials (as she called them) with which she had been forced to deal. I gave little notice to her chatter, paying attention only when she described some place of beauty. She had turned the discussion to my attendance at the evening's masquerade ball when Mullin announced Helena.

I jumped up at the sight of her unhappy face. "Helena! Whatever is the matter? Have you been crying?"

She looked with distress at Mabel. I introduced her, and Mabel, with a knowing glance, excused herself to look over the household accounts that I had so long neglected. I gave her a grateful smile as she left. Whatever else her faults, Mabel had a kind heart.

Helena gulped a few times, then grasped my hands in hers. "Oh, Cassandra, I've had the most awful row with Griffin. He had a terrible argument earlier with Harold about you—"

"About *me*?" I interrupted, astounded.

"Yes. Harold…oh, it was horrible, and Griffin said terrible things to him. I've never seen them so angry with one another."

"What were they arguing about?"

"Nothing! Everything! You, me…oh Cassandra, Griffin has forbidden me to participate in the candidate's meeting next week. He has forbidden me to attend any more of the Union's meetings, and—" She choked to a stop. "He has forbidden me to see you anymore! I had to tell them I was going to my costume fitting to come here now. What shall we do?"

She sobbed uncontrollably as I did my best to calm her. I sat her down and ordered strong coffee, feeling we could both use the stimulant.

"I have to say that I am not surprised, although dismayed with Griffin's attitude. If I may speak frankly, his arrogance in giving you orders as to your behavior is completely uncalled for. However, after the events of the past few days, well, I can hardly blame him for not wishing you to involve yourself with another protest. I think it would be best if you stayed away from the candidate's meeting at Exeter Hall."

She dabbed her eyes with a lovely and completely useless lace handkerchief. "You will be there, won't you?"

I hesitated, thinking of my family. "Yes, I will. I feel I must after our early release yesterday, if for no other reason than to show the Union that I support the cause whole-heartedly. But I don't recommend it for you because your family is so very opposed to your involvement, and further contact can only result in more strife at home."

"If you are attending the meeting, I will be there as well," she said firmly, and wiped her nose discreetly. "There is…something else I must tell you."

"Oh?" I looked at her warily.

"Griffin came home last night in a terrible temper. I've never seen him so angry, so cold. He frightened me. I couldn't find out what had happened, but oh, Cassandra, he's planning on leaving! He wants to sail in three days for Brazil. He even refused to go to the St. Alban's ball tonight after I told him you would be there."

"Oh, that stupid man," I said softly to myself. "That stupid, adorable man."

"Cassandra, you have to stop him. You're the only one he will listen to!"

"I think not," I said dryly. "At this moment, I fear I am *persona non grata* with him."

She looked at me curiously. "Why do you say that?"

"It's a long story—"

I stopped as the door opened. Robert stepped in, saw Helena, and apologized. Or rather, he started to. One look at Helena sitting in a canary chiffon day dress with ruffles at the neck and sleeves seemed to bewitch him. He stammered, and finally dragged his eyes off her to me.

"I was about to leave on that errand we discussed last night." His eyes went back to Helena. "Do you have any other instructions?"

I watched him with interest. "Only one—that you meet my very good friend Miss St. John. Helena, this is Robert Hunter, an old childhood friend who has come to stay with us."

Helena blushed prettily (a fact I noticed sourly—when I blush it clashes with my hair), and held out her hand.

"Helena is Griffin St. John's sister," I said meaningfully. Given the news Helena had brought, I was very anxious that Robert should be quickly on his way.

"How fascinating," he breathed, never once taking his eyes off of her.

"Yes, she is," I said, prodding Robert. "And I'm sure you'll have a chance to see Helena again, but right now you have a call to make."

Robert blinked at me. "I do? Oh yes, I have a call I must make."

"An urgent one."

He gazed longingly at Helena. "I hope to see you soon, Miss St. John."

I pushed Robert out of the room and turned to find Helena wearing the same dreamy expression. Sitting beside her, I asked, "Did Griffin say anything else to you last night?"

"Last night?" Her thoughts were evidently a million miles away.

"Yes, last night. The evening we most recently had. *That* last night."

"No," she sighed happily. "You've known Mr. Hunter for a long time? Does he...is he here with his family?"

"He has no family other than a brother in South Africa," I answered, watching happiness spread across her face.

I could see I was not to get any further information out of Helena today, so I gave her a brief summary of Robert's life, told her I would think of something with regards to Griffin, and sent her on her way. As she was leaving, a messenger delivered a letter for the family. It was an invitation from my aunt to dinner the following night, in honor of Joshua and Mabel's return.

An intimate family dinner, the invitation read, which could mean anything between four and forty people, depending on my aunt's whims. I gave the letter to Mabel, answered as many questions about Helena as I deemed necessary, and went out to meet Emma for the final fitting of my costume.

"I still think one of your simple Greek outfits would have been lovely," I told her an hour later.

"Yes, but just think how much more unique this will be," Emma said as I turned for the dressmaker. "There are always Greek women at a costume ball, but how many Scheherazades will there be?"

I had to admit that she had a point. After consultation with a scandalous version of the Arabian Nights, not to mention a good deal of money in the form of incentives to Madame Depui, the dressmaker, I had devised a costume made up of golden gauze embroidered with faux precious gems.

"I like the sashes," Emma said approvingly. "Green, blue, and purple—very dashing. But Cassandra, your midriff! Won't your aunt be scandalized?"

I looked down to the daring two inches of bare midriff peeking through the sashes that swept from my left shoulder to my right hip. "Madame Depui insists that it is perfectly suitable."

"Oui," Madame said, adjusting one of the veils that hung from a small, close-fitting cap. "It is perfect the way it is. Very catching to the eye."

"What jewelry will you wear?" Emma asked as I disrobed and began to get into my regular clothes.

"Nothing. I think jewelry would detract from it. Thank you, Madame. You will be sure to have the hem raised by this afternoon?"

"Yes, it is minor, the hem. I should have it done in time."

"Excellent." I tipped her generously, and invite Emma to take a walk with me in Hyde Park. "I have so many things to tell you. Robert is back from South Africa."

"Robert Hunter? How interesting."

"Yes, and you will have to come to tea to meet him. He's matured nicely, I think. And is a fair way to being smitten with Helena."

"Really." She looked interested, and pressed me for details. As we strolled to the park, I filled told her first about Robert and Helena, and then about my own troubles.

"It sounds to me like Mr. St. John is jealous," she said after a few minutes of silent thought.

She slid me a considering look. "Is there any reason he should be?"

"Emma! You know me better than that!"

"No, I meant that he wouldn't be jealous unless there was some sort of an emotional relationship."

"Oh. Well, as to that…" We had reached the park and had started across its expanse. I cleared my throat and paused a moment to admire the daffodils bobbing in the weak March sun. "You know it was my intention to offer Griffin the position of lover."

"Yes."

I glanced at her to see if she was laughing at me. Her face was averted as she leaned over to admire some crocuses.

"Well, I did offer him the job, and he accepted."

"I see." She turned to me, her smile knowing. "And I take it you approve of him in that role."

"I would have to be mad not to," I said, unable to keep from smiling myself at the memories that threatened to scorch my mind. "I just knew he would have the most outstanding derriere, but it has exceeded even my highest hopes."

She laughed and squeezed my arm. "So you have had your first lover's squabble, and now must find your way clear to making up."

"I would hardly call this our first squabble."

"Perhaps not, but this is the first one where your relationship has entered into the fray. Well, my dear, I have no advice for you other than to talk to him. I find that most things work themselves out if you just take the effort to talk."

"That's easier said than done." We had reached the edge of Rotten Row, and paused to admire the horses as they cantered past.

Just as we were turning away, I noticed I noticed a small man in a brown check suit standing at a little distance next to the railing. He turned, his eye meeting mine, whereupon he smiled, politely tipping his hat in greeting.

"The man with the gold tooth!" I gasped to Emma. "Or as I suspect, Mr. William Jones!"

"Who?"

"I'll tell you about it later." Emma followed as I hurried over to the man.

"Good day, miss," he said cheerfully, gold flashing as he spoke.

"It *was*. Would you tell me, please, who you are and exactly why you have taken to following me?"

"Me, miss? Follow you, miss?"

He did a credible job of appearing confused, but I was not misled. "Yes, you sir. There is no use in denying it, I know full well you have been following me. What I would like to know is why. I do not have a great deal of time; you will please make your explanation and apology succinct."

"I don't know what you're on about, miss. I haven't been following you, I'm just out for a stroll on a lovely morning." He smiled amiably.

"A likely story," Emma said scornfully.

I took a deep breath. "Very well, if you will not tell me, perhaps you will tell a policeman." I turned as if to go in search of one, expecting him to stop me, but he held his ground.

"By all means, if it makes you feel better."

Emma and I exchanged glances. There were no policemen about, only people strolling around the park, or those riding the Row. A group of young women on horseback, several carriages, and two men in military uniforms were approaching, but no bobby. I shrugged in imitation of defeat.

"Would you like me to beat him with my umbrella?" Emma asked, wielding that item as if it was a sword.

"That wouldn't be wise, miss, that surely wouldn't," the man said with another of his unpleasant smiles.

Emma took a step closer to me.

"It's tempting, but I don't believe it will be necessary," I told her. "I am sure I will obtain the information I seek by another means."

The group of giggling young women were a few feet away, followed closely by the two officers. I hated to use violence, but there are times when the needs must and all that. As the gigglers and their officers came into hearing range, I turned to Mr. Jones and slapped him on the cheek.

"You cad!" I shrieked, taking him and Emma by surprise. "You bounder! You brute! How dare you say such things to me! You, sir, are no gentleman!"

Englishmen to the tips of their toes, the two officers abandoned the pursuit of the young women and gallantly rode over to assist me. I clutched Emma's arm and leaned on her, my hand over my eyes as if sobbing.

"Ma'am," one of them dismounted and held his hat in hand, "may we be of assistance? Is this man bothering you two ladies?"

Mr. Jones threw one look at the two men, another at the grim determination on my face, and took off like a hare.

"He impugned my virtue," I cried, urging the officer after him.

"And mine!" Emma said, falling into the spirit.

"Never fear, ma'am, I'll get the bounder." The first soldier saluted, tossed his reins to his compatriot, leaped over the railing, and was off.

Fearing Mr. Jones was too wily to be caught by just one man, I grasped my skirt with one hand and ran after them, Emma on my heels.

"I'm sorry, ma'am, but he's done a bunk," the officer said, looking around in circles at the entrance to the street. "He's given me the slip."

"That's all right. You did the best you could. Thank you for your chivalrous actions."

He bowed, and offered to escort us somewhere, but we declined. After he left, I explained quickly to Emma why I sought him.

"We will cover more ground if we separate," Emma said, looking thoughtful. "You take this side of the block, and I'll do the opposite. Shall we meet up in about a quarter of an hour?"

"An excellent idea." I picked up my skirts and headed in the direction indicated, searching street after street without luck. Just as I was about to give up, I caught site of my quarry a block ahead, walking quickly around a corner. I ran after him, just in time to see him disappearing into a shop. I ran past a bookstore and Cook's office, stopping next to it at a gentleman's outfitter.

"There's nothing for it," I told myself, and plunged into the building. Blinded by the dimness of the shop after the bright day, I was startled when a voice spoke directly behind my right shoulder.

"May I...*serve* you in some way, madam?"

It was a shop clerk, looking more than a little astonished at my appearance.

"Thank you, no. I'm just browsing." I strolled nonchalantly over to a counter and prepared to interest myself in its contents. Once rid of the clerk's attention, I would casually work my way through the rest of the shop in search of my prey.

"Good heavens!" I cried, staring in horrified shock at the products of an intimate and thoroughly masculine nature held in the case. "Does that do what I think it's supposed to do?"

"Erm..." The clerk squirmed next to me.

I looked closer, reading the label with astonishment. "It does! It is suppose to increase the size of a gentleman's apparatus. Merciful heavens, who knew such things were in existence?"

"Ma'am—"

"Surely such a procedure must hurt," I exclaimed, peering closely at the item in question. "All that suction cannot be good for one. Have you ever tried it yourself?"

"Eh—"

"I can't imagine how it could be effective. Perhaps if I could just see it demonstrated. I would get one for my lover, but he is quite sufficient in that regards."

"Madam, please!" A second man joined the first, his face a picture of outraged indignation. He grabbed my arm and hustled me to the door. "Ladies are not allowed in the shop!"

"I don't see why not," I started to argue, but it was in vain. The door was closed rather firmly in my face.

I stood in thought, watching the shop. I could see the dim figures of the clerks move to the rear, and decided to partake of the opportunity. Casually I leaned against the glass, ignoring a display of men's intimate apparel, shading my eyes as I peered into the shop.

I am not a skittish creature, but the sudden blast of a raucous motorcar horn being blown in close proximity had me jumping. Unfortunately, I collided with a person as I did so, but was righted before I could fall. I turned to thank my benefactor, only to find myself face to face with Griffin.

I blushed. He scowled. We both looked at the motorcar, which was proceeding down the street making a horrible racket.

"Do you need assistance?" Griffin asked coldly.

"Thank you, no," I said with dignity, gesturing toward the shop. "I'm perfectly fine."

He glanced at the items displayed in the shop window and back at me. "Doing a little shopping?"

I colored deeper at the inference. "No, of course not. I was looking for a man."

"Just one?"

"Yes, just the one." I told myself to stop wanting to kiss him, and gathered up my things. "A man with a gold tooth, as a matter of fact. He has been following me for days now."

I left him with an expression of incredulity on his face, but my satisfaction was short-lived. Depression settled over me as I walked back to meet Emma. Helena's tale must be true if Griffin were at the Cook's office next to the gentleman's outfitter, no doubt obtaining his tickets for a journey abroad. I had no question in my mind as to the outcome of Robert's visit. Griffin obviously did not believe him.

Emma and I parted shortly thereafter, my spirits dampened and low when I returned home. Robert was in the library, staring moodily into the fire when I entered the room. He held my hands gently in his and looked at me with sad blue eyes. "Cassandra, I have failed you."

"What happened?" I asked resignedly.

"He refused to see me. I tried, but he refused."

"Blast the man." I sat down and pounded the armchair. "Why does he have to be so stubborn? This could all be cleared up if only he weren't so...so...so like a man!"

Robert sat opposite of me and tugged at his mustache. "Forgive me, but does it occur to you that...well...that you are also being the least bit stubborn?"

"Me, stubborn?" I was astounded by his suggestion, and was heatedly preparing to dispute it when I reconsidered. "Perhaps, if I am truthful, I could be more a very small bit more understanding in this situation. After all, Griffin did hear me telling you I loved him, and coming on the heels of the marvelous way he...er...well, that's not something I need to bore you with. I suppose if I were in his shoes I might feel the tiniest bit hurt."

Robert smiled. "I feel certain he would see you if you were to ask. Would you like me to fetch you writing paper? I would be happy to deliver a note for you."

I considered the cold reception I had received on the street. "No, I don't believe that he would come if I asked him to. I am going to have to make him listen some other way."

His face lit up. "Perhaps Miss St. John—?"

"Yes," I said, an idea dawning on me. "If we could pay a call on Helena...oh, but her sister-in-law would never allow me in the house." I chewed my bottom lip in thought. "Perhaps if we could arrange to call when Lord and Lady Sherringham were not home, but when Griffin and Helena were home—"

He jumped up. "I would be happy to deliver the note for you."

"Sit down, Robert," I said glumly, remembering Helena's conversation. "There is no way I can get a note to Helena. Both Griffin and the earl have forbidden contact with me. I will just have to try and see him some other way."

We puzzled over a number of possibilities without success. Depressed, I gave up and went to prepare for the ball.

CHAPTER SIXTEEN

Later, as I was dressing, I told Annie about my plan for her to have a cottage on my father's estate while she had her confinement. When she came back to work, as she professed she wanted to, the servants would know nothing of what happened.

"Are you sure you want to leave the child with your sister? I'm sure we could work out a way for you to keep the baby with you, although it would mean leaving Mabel's house."

"That's alright, miss. My sister said one more mouth wouldn't make that much difference, and I can visit whenever I like."

I thought the arrangement sounded sad, but Annie was happy, and I had confidence in her family. "What about Mr. Jones, Annie? Have you told him?"

"I've written to him, but he won't reply," she responded grimly.

I decided—for the present—not to push her further, but I was determined to see her happily settled. Mulling over a way to achieve this goal, I sat before the dressing table and braided my hair in preparation for donning a black wig purchased from the dressmaker. Certain that red hair was out of place on Scheherazade, I planned to wear the wig and the veils as my disguise, the thought of moving about in company completely unknown strangely thrilling.

Annie worked at twining faux pearls through the wig while I played with my braid and tried to work up enough nerve to bring out the item I had purchased earlier. I took a deep breath, opened a drawer, and nervously removed a small black object. Annie looked at me curiously, watching in the mirror. Consulting the (somewhat scandalous) Arabian Nights I borrowed from Joshua's library, I carefully outlined my eyes with the kohl stick.

"Oh, miss!" Annie gasped. "You look ever so foreign!"

I looked at my heavily ringed eyes. "I don't know about foreign—I certainly look as if I have been up a chimney."

"It's a lovely touch, miss, do leave it," she said as I made a move to wipe it off. "No one would recognize you with the black wig and the dark eyes."

Anonymity had its charms, so I left the kohl and finished dressing. I stood in front of the mirror, swathed from head to foot in floating veils, the embroidered jewels sparkling, and the long dark tresses of my wig reaching to my waist. I felt exotic and mysterious behind the veils, and relished the thought that no one would know who I was.

The walk downstairs to the library was a sensuous experience, the lightweight gauze swinging against my bare legs (Scheherazade did not wear stockings). I couldn't help but think of Griffin's kisses and touches as the material rippled around me, caressing my skin. Robert grinned as I came into the library, and let out a low, long whistle. Mabel fussed about the sheerness of the material, and almost had a fit when she saw my two inches of bare midriff. By the time Uncle Henry called at the front door Joshua had to physically restrain her from hustling me upstairs and into a sturdier ensemble.

Although his eyebrows went up an inch at my appearance, Henry had nothing but compliments for me as I donned my sapphire velvet coat. "You look charming, my dear, charming."

"Thank you. Are you not going to wear a costume?"

He pulled out an order from his inner pocket, and pinned it on his chest. "I shall go as a diplomat."

"And what a very good costume that is," I replied, smiling.

As I entered their carriage, my heart sank as I beheld the figure of Wellington, better known as Freddy.

"Mind my ruff, dear," Caroline said as I took my place next to her. She had worked wonders in the short time, and was dressed in an Elizabethan costume complete with a large, white ruff, and pearls down to her knees. "I'm supposed to be one of Henry's ancestors, since ours were not as prominent as his."

"Cousin, you are the epitome of beauty. I love you as a redhead, but as a brunette, you will break the heart of every man at the ball. Please promise me the first dance."

"If you like. Aunt Caroline, you look lovely, regardless of whose ancestor you are supposed to be. How on earth did you get the costume made so quickly? It has much more detail than my own, and I had to spend a fortune to have it made in time."

Uncle Henry coughed delicately. "It seems your aunt was planning to go to the ball all along, my dear. She thought it best to spring it on me suddenly, knowing my resistance to such social events."

"I ordered my costume from Messrs. Nathan," Freddy offered, referring to a popular theatrical supplier. "Do you like it? I think I make a particularly dashing Wellington."

"You are, as always, very handsome, Freddy."

We chatted about Mabel and Joshua on the way, and were soon at the St. Alban's townhouse. For a brief moment as we walked up the curved drive to the doors, I remembered a week past when I was on the outside of such a ball, trying to chain myself to a fence. "It's amazing what an impact one man can have in just a few days," I murmured to myself.

The house was brilliantly lit, the lights gleaming off of sparkling chandeliers and glittering jewels. Great vases of flowers filled the rooms with their heady perfumes, while distant strains of music promised dancing in the ballroom. A babble of conversation rose and fell as guests sauntered down the great marble staircase into the reception rooms below.

Aunt Caroline and I shed our coats and inspected our costumes in the ladies' withdrawing room while maids in black dresses ran to and fro, assisting guests, adjusting costumes, and bringing restorative cups of tea. The costumes themselves were almost overwhelming. Real jewels—not faux ones like I wore—clung to almost every surface, billowing waves of satins and silks accompanied each movement as women primped before several large mirrors. There were allegorical and historical figures ranging from queens to milkmaids, as well as fantastic creations which had their inspiration in the fertile imagination of their wearers.

Aunt Caroline and I, each on one of Uncle Henry's arms, walked slowly down the curved marble staircase with Freddy following behind. The crush of people was tremendous as we made our way down the reception line, but once we were finally released into the ballroom, I stood back and watched the parade of Society before me.

Freddy led me onto the floor for the first dance, his eyes as merry and concerned as ever, but it was another pair of eyes that consumed my thoughts. "You've been avoiding me, my sweet cousin."

"Not intentionally. I've just been busy."

"With more of those suffragette activities? My dear, if you must go to them, at least allow me to accompany you. I wish only to protect you and keep you from harm."

"I appreciate that, Freddy, but as you can see, I am perfectly well. I know you feel the demonstrations are fraught with peril, but I can assure you that even those such as the march to Parliament presented no real danger to me. So if you are about to offer for me again, please consider this a refusal."

His eyes glittered with a bright, strange emotion that left me feeling uneasy. "You scoff at me. You make light of my worries."

"No, I'm just assured of my own ability to keep myself safe."

"I can only hope nothing befalls you to shake that confidence, Cassandra." His eyes were hooded as he watched me, his gaze sending a small shiver skittering down my back. "Promise me that should you ever need me, should you ever find yourself in danger, you will seek my help."

I murmured a polite acceptance, and spent the rest of the dance chatting inanely about nothing. Freddy returned me to Caroline's side, and moved off. I searched the crowd again for Helena, watching everyone from over the top of my veils. Despite the disappointment that Griffin would not be in attendance, I very much looked forward to seeing Helena's reaction to my daring ensemble.

One of the ladies, also dressed as Queen Elizabeth, proceeded past me, followed by eight Yeoman of the Guard, all of who were handsomely clad in scarlet and gold tunics with white ruffs, and matching scarlet tights. As the group made its way to an improvised throne, the Yeoman disbanded. One of them, a tall man with light brown hair, came my way.

"Might I request the honor of a dance?" he asked.

I glanced over at my aunt who was holding court with her bevy of friends, and made a quick scan around the room, but saw no one who would fit Helena's description.

"I would be delighted," I told him, and accepted his hand.

"Lieutenant Angus Bell," he said, bowing as he led me onto the floor. "May I say, ma'am, how charming I find your costume?"

The dance was almost as pleasant as the lieutenant himself. He talked about his life in the army, asking me for another dance.

"Thank you, but I feel the need to keep an eye on my aunt."

He glanced at Caroline, clearly amused, but was polite enough to refrain from asking why. "Perhaps later in the evening."

I murmured something vague, and he went on his way. I spent the next hour alternately dancing and watching for Helena. It quickly became apparent to me why I had never sought invitations to such functions, for I had little in common with Society, and less tolerance for their airs and mindless chatter.

"Honestly, aunt," I told Caroline in a moment of privacy. "The men all talk about their hunting lodges, horses, or military careers. The women have even less of interest to discuss, and seem to focus on who was seen with whom, what they wore, what they were worth, and who their parents were."

"I'm sorry you're not enjoying yourself," she answered, nodding to a passing acquaintance.

I felt guilty at complaining since I had foisted myself on them. "Ignore me. I'm being out of sorts and petulant about nothing."

In an attempt to find diversion, I danced with a German princeling dressed as some character from a Wagnerian opera (I never did determine which one), who tried his best to impress me with tales of his bravery and courage. He found me a dull partner and returned me as soon as possible to my aunt. He bowed, clicked his heels, and kissed my hand, followed by the same niceties to Aunt Caroline's. As he stepped back, he bumped into an Arab sheikh who was approaching.

The Arab salaamed before me and asked in a thick accent for the next dance. Bored, I agreed, and watched idly as he strode off. My attention was caught by the way he walked. I took a few steps away from the wall so I could watch him better.

I knew that back. I knew those hips. I knew that deliciously curved behind. *Intimately.* There was no doubt about it, it was Griffin, disguised as a sheikh. "It can't be!"

"What can't be, my dear?"

Caroline moved over to me, calmly fanning herself as she smiled at people strolling past us.

"That man. The Arab. Did you see him?"

She looked where I indicated. "Not really. Why do you ask?"

"I think it's Griffin. Mr. St. John. But why would he make an appearance here?"

"Why shouldn't he?"

"He told his sister he wasn't coming. And what's more important..." I hesitated a minute, glancing at my aunt.

She smiled.

"You know, don't you?" I asked her.

"There's not much that escapes me, Henry always says."

I sighed and leaned against the wall. "Griffin and I had an argument over a silly misunderstanding. He was very cold the last time we met, which is why I'm so surprised he should be here now, asking me to dance. Unless...oh, aunt, do you think he didn't recognize me? Prince Heinrich didn't leave me off particularly close to you, did he?"

"Not particularly, no. But I am acquainted with Mr. St. John, and surely he would recognize me."

"But not me," I said thoughtfully. "Not in this wig, and with my face hidden behind the veil. He must not have known who I was."

"If you say so, my dear. But what does that matter? If he asked you to dance, he will soon learn the truth."

"You're right." I chewed on my lip as I considered the matter. "As soon as I speak he'll know me. What I need is an accent."

"Don't you think that's a little extreme?" Caroline asked.

"Not at all. He had one, he most definitely had an Arab accent when he asked me to dance. Therefore, it's only right I should have one. It's just that I only know one other language."

"I never did understand why your mother taught you Russian," Aunt Caroline mused.

"She hoped that someday Mabel and I would meet her relatives. Regardless, that will do just fine. Please don't be offended, but I'm going to move away from you now, just in case Griffin suspects something."

Her lips curved into a gentle smile as I distanced myself from her, surprising a variety of people whom I did not know as I casually chatted my way down the room.

As the music started for the next dance, Griffin came back to claim me, escorting me out to the dance floor. I was outraged that he would profess to have strong feelings for me, and yet be inviting a strange lady to dance. Just what were his intentions toward a mysterious dark-haired Russian clad only in a scanty, although highly attractive, Arabic costume?

I stared up through my eyelashes at his face as the music started, amazed at what change a huge, fierce mustache and dark coloring had done to his appearance. He wore a blue and white burnoose, a white blouse, and full, dark blue silk trousers tucked into long black boots. A scimitar was strapped to his waist by a length of red satin, and he had put some sort of stain on his hands and face to turn them a walnut color. Although his disguise could not fool me, I was glad for the anonymity of my veil and wig.

"You are Scheherazade?" he asked in a deep voice with a heavy accent.

I smiled to myself over the accent.

"You guessed that well. Yes, I am Scheherazade," I agreed in a close approximation of my cousin Katya's version of English.

His eyes narrowed. "A Scheherazade that is a long way from...Russia?"

"Yes. St. Petersburg. And you, you are a sheikh? Where is your harem?"

The large mustache quivered in a manner that indicated a smile, although I could not see his mouth beneath it.

He waved a hand toward the reception rooms. "I left them outside, where they would not be in the way."

He replaced his hand lower on my back and touched my bare skin. A jolt of electricity skimmed up my spine, setting my whole body alight. I frowned into his chest in an attempt to stop the strident clamoring of all my intimate parts, parts which very badly wanted to reacquaint themselves with his. "Indeed. Your harem must mean little to you if you keep them outside like animals."

"They are only women."

I looked up through my lashes into the lovely amber eyes that I would know anywhere, annoyed with his drawled words. "Is that the prevailing attitude towards women where you come from? Do they matter so little?"

"In Arabia, women do as their husbands tell them and don't question the men's wisdom."

"Which is probably why Arabia is sometimes viewed as being backwards," I retorted, fuming at his misguided perspective. "Any country with such an ancient history should have more sense than to allow a man to possess more than one wife. I have always felt the Arabs to be part of an intelligent, highly cultured society, but about this, I must admit they sadly fail to gain my admiration."

"Could it be, Scheherazade, you would like to have more than one husband?"

"Certainly not!" I replied indignantly.

The conversation was not going at all as I had planned. I found it difficult to flirt with him when he insisted on sticking to topics that irritated me.

"In *my* country," I continued with some heat, "women desire the love and respect of only one man. As long as they are treated as equals and respected for qualities other than the physical, they are happy."

The mustache twitched again.

"St. Petersburg must have changed since I last visited it. I don't remember its society being so liberal," he commented in Russian.

I smiled at his attempt to catch me out, and sent a thank you to my mother for having taught me her native tongue as I responded in the same language. "A good deal has changed, I am sure, since you last visited. Women are taking their rightful place in societies all over the world, not only in St. Petersburg."

He looked startled to hear Russian in reply, then the mustache twitched and the corners of his eyes crinkled in a smile.

We danced without speaking for a few minutes.

"What of the men in your country?" he asked finally, returning to English. "What role would you have them play? Jester to their queen, perhaps?"

The music ended. He put a hand on my elbow and we made our way through the crowd to the side of the room.

"Men play fools well enough without any help from women," I said lightly. The conversation was moving entirely too close to home for my comfort. I tried desperately to think of a way to change the subject, but was compelled to meet his gaze when he turned me to face him before releasing my arm.

"What would you have us do, Scheherazade? Stand by quietly and watch as you women trample on our hearts?"

I wondered if my disguise had been as successful as I had previously thought. Griffin watched me with an intensity that was almost intimate, waiting for me to answer a question that had not been asked.

I dropped my gaze at last, unsure of what he wanted from me. I didn't know whether he was making an advance to a strange woman, or whether he was asking *me* for my feelings. I was unwilling to answer until I knew which question he asked. When I looked up he was gone.

An enjoyable five minutes were spent a short time later in conversation with Helena, who was dressed as a French shepherdess complete with stuffed lamb. I recognized her at once, and waited until her sister-in-law, dressed as Mary, Queen of Scots, was engaged before I approached. "I can't talk to you long," she said nervously, looking over her shoulder at Lady Sherringham. "But I do want to meet with you. Would tomorrow morning suit you? I'm supposed to return books to the library at ten."

I agreed to meet her and asked casually if Griffin had changed his mind about attending the ball.

"Oh, no. He wouldn't even see me when we left. He locked himself in his study and refused to come out," she said sadly.

The better to paint himself as an Arab, I thought. I wondered if Helena would know him when she saw him...if he was still here. I had not seen the tall Arab sheikh since our dance.

"I see your cousin is here," she said with a giggle.

"Yes, unfortunately he is."

"I must run, but I will meet you tomorrow morning. Au revoir!"

A short while later, as I stood at my aunt's side, I noticed a flash of blue on the dance floor. Helena was dancing with Griffin and the look of delight on her face told me she had recognized him. I was possessed by the mad desire to know of what they were speaking, so swallowing my pride, I found Freddy and told him I would give him another dance.

"I live to please you, most beloved cousin," he said as he led me onto the floor. To my surprise, he did not once make a reference to either the Union or marriage, but instead chatted about commonplace topics. As we passed by Griffin and Helena, her gentle laugh reached my ears. I kept my face turned away, but watched out of the corner of my eye whenever possible. Griffin paused for a moment when he spied Freddy and me, but we were soon too far away to watch him any further. Freddy was difficult to lose after that but I made my escape by pleading a headache.

A long hall ran the length of the great house with doors to the various rooms opening off it. After attending to matters of a personal nature, I came down the stairs into the hall, aware of a man's voice floating up from below. Surprised by the name that was mentioned, I peered over the banister as I descended and noticed Freddy, tucked away behind a large palm, engaged in conversation with a man dressed as a giant white rabbit, complete with fancy waistcoat and pocket watch.

"Scheherazade? What's that, then?"

"It doesn't matter. Just don't botch things up again."

"Nothing will go wrong. Not this time. Not when I have this with me." The man in the rabbit suit pulled out an object—what, I could not identify—from his waistcoat and showed it to Freddy.

"Make sure it doesn't." Freddy moved off, leaving me with a distinct sense of unease. I hesitated for a second, then followed, but quickly lost them in the crowd.

The ballroom was even more crowded than earlier, with people clustered in small groups along the walls, talking, laughing, and watching those who were dancing. As I squeezed by a large women dressed as Catherine the Great, I came face to face with an American cowboy who was laughing with a tall, amber-eyed sheikh.

Abruptly the sheikh turned, and much to the surprise of the Columbine standing near him, whirled her into the dance. My chin up, I strolled past with only the briefest of indignant glares.

"Lieutenant Angus," I smiled, stopping as I spotted a familiar face, but unable to recall his surname, "are you enjoying the dancing?"

Excusing himself from a conversation with one of the other Yeomen, he replied to the affirmative. I batted my lashes and waited expectantly.

"Are you engaged for this dance?"

"Not in the least," I replied, my eye on the colorful Arab who was still dancing with the Columbine.

As we stepped into the dance, the music ended.

"Shall we wait for the next one?" Angus asked politely.

Far across the room two tall white rabbit ears bobbed and headed out a door which led to a courtyard. "I—I suddenly feel the need for a little fresh air," I replied, curious as to where Freddy's friend was going. I took hold of Angus' arm and tugged him toward the door. "Perhaps you would be so kind as to escort me outside for a moment or two?"

I really gave the poor man no choice, but he was nice enough to fall in with my wishes without complaint. Outside, stone steps led down to a pleasant shrub-lined path, running the length of the house. Large stone urns were interspersed between the tall shrubs, affording many choices should a person wish to avoid being seen.

One glance at Angus and I realized my mistake. He assumed I wanted to stroll outside for amorous purposes and moved closer in preparation. I considered my options and decided that an appeal to his sense of chivalry was the answer. Brushing aside my remorse at prevaricating, I spun a quick tale.

"Did you see the man in the giant white rabbit suit? No? Well, he came this way, and he has been…well, let us say, he has made himself objectionable to me. I wish to locate him to make sure he's not doing the same thing to another woman, and I had hoped you might help me confront him."

Angus, a typical example of his gender, puffed up importantly as I appealed to his masculinity. "Of course I will help you!"

I turned to face him as I spoke, simpering in a manner that I personally found repugnant, but which is so effective to those of the male persuasion. "I do so appreciate it, you see, there is no one else to whom I can turn."

As the words left my lips Griffin passed by, the Columbine clinging to his arm. His glare left little doubt in my mind that he had not only guessed my identity, but had also heard me utter the puerile drivel.

"Let's start down there," I pointed in the direction opposite to the one Griffin had gone, and started off towards a particularly dark corner. Annoyed with my draperies, I detached one side of the veils so I could search without encumbrances.

I instructed Angus to search along the far wall as I started down the side next to the house, examining behind and in each urn as I passed them, only to reach the far corner without success. A small metal gate led out to the street beyond. I looked out, shivering a little in the cold evening air, but could not see beyond the pavement directly in front of the gate.

"Well," I said, turning around to see why Angus had been so quiet, "I guess we will have to look at the other end."

"If you like," Griffin replied, his voice noncommittal.

I blinked at him for a moment before demanding, "What have you done with Angus?"

"The gentleman was needed elsewhere," he answered, frowning. He must have thought the horrified face I made was in response to his statement. "I realize he is *the only one you can turn to in a time of need*, but are you really that despondent at his departure?"

"Not in the least," I replied truthfully. "I am concerned about the man standing behind you pointing a pistol at your head."

Griffin spun around and would have lunged had not a voice from behind me ordered him to halt. Something cold and sharp pricked my jaw. I turned my head slightly and saw the open gate and the furry white suit of a giant rabbit behind me.

"One move towards my friend there, Mr. Sheikh, and the lady loses more than a veil."

Griffin turned back slowly, his face impassive. The short, stocky man behind him reached around and removed the scimitar, then nudged Griffin with the pistol and ordered him to walk. A hand gripped my shoulder painfully, forcing me to follow, the knife moving to press up against my shoulder blades. Anger rose within me as we passed through the gate and towards a closed carriage parked a short way down the street.

"This is ridiculous," I said as we were herded along. "Kidnapped in the middle of a masquerade ball. And by a giant white rabbit!"

Only the sight of the very real pistol held firmly against Griffin's back kept me from saying more. We stopped next to the carriage.

"Get in." The man with the gun pushed Griffin.

"No," he replied in a low voice.

I started forward as the thug shoved Griffin, slamming him with brutal force into the side of the carriage. The knife was back at my throat, digging in with a pain that cause me to gasp. Warmth trickled down my neck as the man in the rabbit suit pulled my head backwards, the wig loosening under his grip.

"Now, do you get in nicely or do we have to cut up the lady?" the rabbit asked Griffin, his voice striking a chord in my mind. I was sure I had heard it before.

Griffin glanced at me. His eyes focused on the trickle of blood creeping down my neck onto my bosom before they lifted to meet mine. A second later he leaped on the man with the gun, sending him flying backwards. I had enough wits about me to push backwards and down, slipping out of the rabbit's grip, leaving him staring in surprise his handful of long black wig and veils. Wishing I had my walking shoes on so I might impair him more effectively, I kicked him as hard as I could in an area that generally is known to disable gentlemen. It certainly did give the rabbit pause for thought.

"Cassandra, get out of here!" Griffin bawled as he lunged onto the rabbit man. I looked around for some sort of weapon, and spied the man with the pistol pulling himself up to his feet. Without even a thought of what I was doing, I threw myself on him, knocking my head against his as we tumbled to the ground. Gasping with pain, I sat up, shaking my head. The man beneath me groaned and tried to sit up as well.

I struck him as hard as I could directly on the temple and watched with satisfaction as his head snapped back and hit the curb.

"I am beginning to see the value of taking the offensive stance, rather than the defensive," I told the unconscious man.

Various oaths and strangled noises issued from the two men still locked in battle. Griffin had a hold of the knife, but the bunny-beclad thug was slowly turning it towards his face. Having successfully dealt with one man, I thought I'd assist Griffin with his. Sucking on a bleeding knuckle, I limped over to them and waved my fists at the attacker. Abruptly, the man released the knife, ducked down, and squirmed out of Griffin's grasp. Grabbing his semi-conscious partner, he leaped into the carriage, whipped the horses, and sped off into the darkness.

Griffin leaned against the wall, breathing heavily and holding his right shoulder.

"Well," I said, straightening my costume as best I could, feeling especially pleased at the villain's reaction to the threat I posed him, "there's another one for Caleb."

Griffin looked at me as if I was insane.

"Caleb was my father's stable boy. He taught me how to fight, and clearly that villainous rabbit saw that I knew what I was doing when I waved my fists at him," I explained.

"Despite your prowess in brawling," he replied grimly, peering under his hand, "I think the appearance of that bobby coming around the corner had more to do with them running than the terrifying thought of you attacking."

The sight of blood on his shoulder distracted me from a sharp retort. "Are you injured?"

I pushed his hand off and examined the wound. He had a long but shallow cut running across his shoulder.

"No more than you," he replied, straightening up to face the constable. I dabbed at his shoulder, then wiped off my own blood.

It took a good deal of explanation, but in the end we convinced the constable that we were not seriously hurt and couldn't identify our attackers. Griffin promised to report the incident fully in the morning.

"Will you stand still for one moment and let me tell you about Robert?" I asked as we limped back to the house.

"No," he snapped, and tugged me toward the stone stairs that led to the verandah.

"Of all the obstinate…fine, will you at least listen to my theory of the unwarranted attack upon us? I have a suspicion about the identity of the man in the white rabbit suit—"

"No," he said, just as shortly, and refused to say another word until he deposited me next to Caroline.

Despite our disheveled appearances, no one paid attention to our return. I had lost my veils and cap, and had to pull my braid around front to hide the dried remnants of blood. Griffin was dirty, but his costume fared better than mine. He escorted me to my aunt's side, then made a slight bow and excused himself. I was furious with him for refusing to speak on the subjects which weighed most on my mind.

"What a very dashing sheikh Mr. St. John makes. I take it from your frown that your disguise was not successful?" she asked.

"Not particularly, no," I replied, picking at a spot of blood on the delicate gauze as I fumed to myself.

She nodded. "Ah. Did you have a pleasant stroll with him?"

I looked at the well-meaning twinkle in her eye, and couldn't stop the words. "Not really. He still refuses to speak to me. Two men tried to abduct us, held a pistol to Griffin's head, and a knife to my throat. We escaped. I am a little sore and believe I will go home. If you don't mind me borrowing Geoffrey, I will wish you a good night."

My aunt is seldom surprised by anything I say, so the look of astonishment on her face was almost worth suffering the attack. I limped off to find my coat and Geoffrey, my uncle's coachman.

CHAPTER SEVENTEEN

I met Helena the next morning outside of Westminster Abbey, since the library was only a few streets away. After my success with the Scheherazade costume of the past evening, I was convinced I could manage to look like something less than a rag-picker next to her, so I wore a new white suit with a blue and white striped vest, and a white bolero jacket trimmed with blue braid.

I felt very proud of my smart new ensemble until I observed her in a pretty blazer suit of sky blue with rows of dark blue tubular braid.

My lips pursed as she drew close, causing her to burst into laughter at my jaded look.

"Well, really, Helena, it is too bad!" I said indignantly, circling her to get the full effect of the charming outfit. "Here I sit in my new white duck dress thinking that at last I can hold my own with you, and you insist on floating over to me looking like a rain-washed summer sky."

She raised her hand, still laughing. "I promise you, Cassandra, it is an old gown that I have had for two years."

"Hrmph." It was hard to be disgruntled with her when she looked so charming, so I gave her only a brief lecture as to the horrors of the feather industry with regards to her hat, and we settled down on a nearby bench to chat.

"I have so much to tell you," she said breathlessly, having giggled through most of the feather lecture. "Someone ransacked our house last night!"

I stared at her in amazement. "Good heavens!"

"They tore apart the study, stole my mother's gold candlesticks, and made a terrible mess of Griffin's room."

"How awful! Did the servants not hear anything?"

She peeled off her gloves and wadded them into a ball. "They weren't home, except for the under-kitchen maid. We were all gone, of course, to the ball, and the servants had been given the night off. Lucy, the kitchen maid, had a toothache and was upstairs in bed. She said she didn't hear a thing."

"Good heavens," I repeated, shocked that such a thing could happen.

"Griffin came home—did you know he was at the ball last night? Well, he came home early, and found two men ripping his study apart."

"That's terrible! What did he do?"

She worried her gloves. "He tried to stop them, but they were too strong for him, and one of them struck him on the head."

My stomach dropped into my boots as a wave of dizziness threatened to make me sick. I closed my eyes to stop the spinning.

"Cassandra, are you all right? You suddenly went pale. Do you feel well?"

"I am...it's just the sun in my eyes," I lied. "Is your brother badly hurt?"

She smiled, and I felt my stomach move back to its accustomed location. "He is in good health, thanks to Clairmore."

"Clairmore?"

"Our butler. He returned home early, and heard a commotion. When he went to the front of the house to see what it was, he found two men standing over Griffin, who was lying unconscious at the bottom of the stairs."

"But...you said he was in good health?"

"He is, don't fret. The concussion was a mild one, and he suffered no other injury, only a small cut to his shoulder. He had a slight headache this morning and no other bad effects."

I admit that I heaved a sigh of relief. It was hard work trying to hide the love I felt for that obstinate man. "I am horrified, Helena. Do you know the miscreants' motive for such an attack?"

She watched as a group of American tourists stroll by, reading aloud from their Baedeker. "Harold says they were out to rob us, but Griffin believes they were after something in particular."

I considered this. "He might have a point. How would common burglars know that your family would be gone for the evening unless someone told them? Did the police question your servants?"

"Harold wouldn't let us notify the police. He says it was just a random burglary, and that one of the servants must have told someone that the family was to be gone. Only..." She looked puzzled.

"Yes?" I prompted her.

"I would agree, except Griffin said he would be home that evening, so the servants couldn't have told anyone that the house would be empty."

A dreadful thought occurred to me, but I felt it best to keep it to myself. "Perhaps the burglars thought he would be asleep and out of the way," I suggested slowly.

"Yes, that would explain it! That must be what happened."

It seemed to me that the crime had been committed with one particular victim in mind, but I felt it wise not to share that opinion, and instead changed the subject. "Is your brother still planning on leaving soon?"

She sighed. "Yes, he is. I tried to talk him into staying a little while longer as I thought he might have a reason to—" This last she said pointedly to me, which I ignored. "—but he seems adamant about leaving in two days. Cassandra, isn't there anything you can do to keep him from leaving? I know he admires and respects you. Perhaps if you talked to him—"

I looked at the Abbey, the two magnificent spires, the colored windows, the warmth of the stones. It seemed so unmovable, so sturdy, so permanent. No doubt a great number of unhappy lovers had passed through its doors, and yet it had survived since Norman times.

"Your brother insists on perpetuating a misunderstanding, blowing it greatly out of proportion," I replied carefully. "When I tried to correct the error, he brushed me off in a very rude manner. Oh, Helena, I *have* tried to speak with him, but he refuses to listen."

She gazed at me forlornly, and I felt ashamed for my part in driving away her beloved brother. Miserably, I steered the conversation into what I hoped would be happier thoughts. "Did you enjoy the ball last night?"

"Oh, I did. Wasn't it wonderful? The dresses were so lovely, yours included. I must admit, I was jealous of your costume. It was so very daring! I didn't see you later, though. Were you not feeling well?"

"I was fine, just tired trying to dodge Freddy. He would insist on dancing with me at every opportunity."

"I thought he danced very nicely," she replied absently, picking at a piece of trim.

I looked at her with astonishment. "You don't mean to say that you danced with him as well?"

"Yes, I did. Shouldn't I have?"

"Well, no, I guess there is no reason. I am just surprised that you would want to."

"He was speaking with Harold and asked me if I would care to dance, and as he was your cousin..."

"Please, Helena, do not feel you must tolerate his attentions if you would rather not. He has become rather *intense* of late. It's beginning to worry me."

We were silent for a moment, watching as a couple strolled by.

"I would have never known who you were last night if you hadn't approached me. It seems you fooled many people last night."

"Indeed?"

She paused a moment, smoothing her gloves flat against her leg. "Griffin asked most particularly last night if you were going to be at the ball."

"Did he." I was oddly out of breath as I wondered at what point Griffin had determined who I was. Certainly he had seen through my disguise by the time he dismissed the amiable Angus, but what I badly wanted to know was to whom he believed he was speaking when we were dancing.

Helena made a noncommittal noise, and I was finally forced to look at her. She grinned as I demanded impatiently, "And did you tell him who I was?"

"No, I did not. I thought it was better that he found out for himself."

"Did he guess, do you know?"

Her smile faded a little. "He said later that he had seen you, but you were too busy with your many admirers."

"Many admirers," I repeated indignantly, remembering the Columbine. "That silly, misguided man. He knows full well that I—"

"Yes?" The curious expression on Helena's face made me reconsider.

"Never mind."

"Griffin was dressed as an Arabian sheikh. Did you see him?"

"Yes, I believe I did," I said slowly.

"It was a very good disguise as well."

We sat for some minutes and enjoyed the spring sun. A sudden thought intruded upon my moody contemplation of Griffin's character. "What on earth was Freddy doing speaking with Lord Sherringham?"

Helena shrugged, and pulled on her gloves. "I have no idea."

The more I thought about it, the more it bothered me. Something was definitely not as it should be on the Freddy front.

"I apologize for not being able to meet you at home, but the family…well, I thought it best if we met here, instead."

"Ah."

"The reason I wanted to see you this morning," Helena spoke slowly, "is because I have received a note from Maggie Greene. You have seen the newspapers, I am sure?"

"I have. Some of the Union members have not yet been released. To be truthful, I fear for the future of the Union with them in prison. What did Maggie want with you?"

"After my appalling behavior the other day, you must surely think me foolish to accept a letter from her, but she sounds so repentant that I cannot help but believe she has seen the error of her ways."

I looked at Helena with a weary eye. "You endow Maggie with attributes I fear she lacks. Has she asked for your support in a campaign to take over the Union?"

"Yes, how did you know?"

"I thought she might make a play for control after Mrs. Heywood and other officers were arrested. This means the end of the Union. The conservative members will never accept Maggie's leadership, while the militant faction will not accept otherwise. I wouldn't be surprised if they formed their own society."

Helena opened her bag and handed me a note written on cheap paper. It was from Maggie, asking for Helena's support, encouraging her to consider joining a new organization if the Union refused to endorse the militants.

I smiled grimly at Helena's astonishment and handed her back the note. "What will you do?"

"I'm not sure." She looked at her hands for a moment before glancing up and noticing my obvious disappointment. "Dearest friend, of course I will do whatever you think best. Please tell me what to do!"

"It's not for me to tell you what to do; you are a grown woman and must make your own choices. If you believe you can do some good by joining Maggie's forces, then you must do so. If you find you cannot wholly support her program, then you must tell her so."

We spent a long time debating the situation, and I believe she had convinced herself of Maggie's unsuitability to run the Union by the time Robert strolled up. It was Helena's turn to blush as she beheld my old friend.

"Ah, Robert, there you are. Helena, you remember Robert Hunter," I said mischievously.

She shook hands with him in a self-conscious manner. For his part, Robert was unable to take his eyes from Helena.

"I asked Robert to meet me here so he could accompany me later with some shopping," I explained, delighted with my foresight. "As you have a little time before you must go to the library, perhaps you will chat with Robert for a few minutes. I have the most overwhelming desire to visit the Abbey and see the crypt again."

"Certainly. I would be delighted," she answered, gaze cast down demurely.

"Excellent. I will be back shortly."

I strolled off to the Abbey and joined a throng of tourists. I spent as long as I could admiring the Lady Chapel, then went below to tour the crypt. Consulting my pocket watch, I made my way back outside to tear Robert away from Helena.

I hadn't the heart to separate the two. Robert insisted on escorting Helena to the library, fearing for her safety on such a hazardous mission, so I went about my shopping on my own. I returned home a few hours later to find Robert, the girls, and the hounds playing in the square across the street. I waved at them as I went in to dress for dinner.

In honor of my aunt and uncle, I wore a daring new Worth evening dress. It was made up of layer upon layer of gauzy dark green and cream chiffon, soft and flowing, with billowing sleeves. Although the bodice was boned, I was forced to wear a different corset from the Rational undergarment I normally don. When I looked at my reflection in my bedroom mirror, I almost gasped with pleasure. An embarrassing amount of flesh showed, but the gown floated about me in a most flattering manner.

"You look lovely, miss. Like a fairy princess."

"A very substantial fairy princess," I hugged Annie. "But thank you for the compliment. I feel...presentable." I looked at the reflection again. "Are you sure there is not too much of my bosom showing?"

"Oh no, miss, that's the fashion. You look lovely."

I went downstairs to sit in the library with Robert while we waited for Mabel.

"You look lovely, Cassandra."

"Thank you. It's the result of several hours of dedicated work by my maid. You look very handsome as well, although a trifle sad, I think."

He sighed. "I was thinking of Miss St. John."

"Ah." I watched him carefully, sure of what was to come.

"She...I...I have nothing, Cassandra, nothing which I could offer her. I spent all those years working for William on his coffee farm for nothing. He wouldn't even give me the parcel of land we agreed upon in exchange for my apprenticeship."

"Your brother has always been...well, we won't go into that now. Couldn't you raise the money to purchase a farm through some other means?"

He sighed again. "No. I did manage to raise a sum of money and purchase a small, inferior farm, but I lost it."

The poignant note in his voice made a lump come to my throat.

"How did you lose it?" I asked.

"William bought up the note." He stared gloomily into the fire. "When the first crop yield failed my expectations, I couldn't meet my obligations, and he foreclosed."

"There must be something we can do. I would be happy to loan you whatever sum you need."

He smiled and kissed my hand. "Dearest Cassandra, what a good heart you have. Thank you, but no. I will find a way by myself."

"But, surely a loan would solve all of our problems. I would be part owner, and you could marry someday, and take your bride to live on the coffee farm."

"What a fine husband I would make," he laughed bitterly, "borrowing money to be married then dragging my poor wife out to live in the wilds of Africa. No my dear, I will find my way without your generous offer of help, don't worry."

Joshua came in at that point and I said no more on the subject, although I resolved to have a chat with him later about Robert's situation.

As we rode over to my aunt's house, I listened alternately to Mabel making disparaging comments about the evils that befell women who went out in public dressed in an unseemly manner, and Joshua as he described the various merits of the motorcars he had tried out earlier. My thoughts were elsewhere, mostly concerned with the attacks on Griffin and myself.

Caroline's house was lit up when we arrived, bright electric lights shining from many of the windows. Although I approved of electric light for its qualities of brilliancy and efficiency, I missed the soft, romantic glow of gaslight for an evening party.

Robert handed me down and tucked my hand into his arm as we went in. As I gave my coat to Hargreaves, I asked him in a whisper how many people were expected.

"There are twelve for dinner, Miss Cassandra." That was a good sign, it meant my aunt had limited her guests to a manageable number. I have never been a fan of large parties where it is impossible to have a conversation with the majority of guests.

Hargreaves threw open the doors to the drawing room for Mabel and Joshua. I nudged Robert, who still wore a glum face. He held out his arm. I took it, and as we entered the room I tickled him under his chin.

"Cheer up," I whispered in his ear. "Try to enjoy yourself."

He smiled down at me.

I turned my head to greet my aunt and instead saw Griffin and Helena standing next to Mabel. I stopped, unable to go on, frozen with disbelief. Griffin's eyes were positively icy as they glared at me. My cheeks burn hot in response. Robert tugged me further into the room, looking at me with concern until a movement sent his attention to Helena. He dropped my hand and went to join her. Uncle Henry moved between Griffin and me, severing the mesmerizing gaze that trapped me. He greeted me, made complimentary comments about my dress, and turned toward Griffin.

"And here is a young man who will no doubt also appreciate the beauty of your gown. Mr. St. John, I think I can safely say that with the exception of the ladies present, there is no lovelier example of English womanhood. Wouldn't you agree?"

Griffin moved forward, the muscles in his jaw working. "I can't argue with you, Sir Henry. Miss Whitney is the epitome of beauty."

His voice was thick, but his eyes held only anger as a dull red flush crept over his face and neck.

Once released from his hypnotic stare, my spirits rose in response to his unspoken challenge. Because of *his* stupidity and obstinacy, I was to be cast into the role of a woman who had trifled with his affections. Unless I did something, he would go away and lick his wounds, a confirmed woman-hater.

"I would like to speak with you a moment, Mr. St. John," I said firmly, grabbing his hand and literally dragging him towards a secluded corner.

He followed stiffly, a frown on his face. My aunt and sister telegraphed disapproval by the means of eyebrow semaphore, but I ignored it.

"What do you mean by refusing to see Robert yesterday?" I demanded in a quiet, if terse, whisper.

Griffin stuffed his hands in his pockets. "I didn't care to see the gentleman. I believe I have that right."

"No, you don't, not he when went with the express purpose of speaking with you. He wanted to explain about the other evening."

He held up a hand. "I have told you, Miss Whitney, there is no need for explanations. Save your breath for one of your protest marches."

I glanced over at my aunt, who was greeting two guests. "Why are you being so obstinate?" I hissed between my teeth.

"I am trying to make myself clear. You have made your choice, and I am endeavoring," the vein in his temple throbbed as he struggled to keep his voice down, "to respect it."

I opened my mouth to inform him of the individual of my choice, when the door opened again and Lord and Lady Sherringham walked in.

I closed my eyes, unwilling to believe what I had seen. I opened them, but the Sherringhams were still there. I turned to Griffin, but he had walked over to stand beside Helena, glaring belligerently at Robert. I stood marooned on a small Persian rug and awaited my doom.

Uncle Henry introduced the Sherringhams to the guests who were unknown to them, and piloted Lord Sherringham my way. I stood still, hoping that if I didn't move I would escape notice.

"Of course, you know my niece Cassandra Whitney. You saw her the other night at the opera," Henry said in an even tone.

I lifted my head and met the outraged stare of Lord Sherringham.

"Good Gad, Benson! What is that woman doing here? I will have none of this! If she is dining with you, we will leave immediately. This...this *person* has been the cause of much family distress. She is unbalanced and dangerous. I tell you, if this woman stays I will leave!"

Everyone stared at me with varying degrees of abject horror on their faces. Griffin was the exception. He wasn't looking at me; he scowled at Robert, his hands clenched into fists.

Swallowing humiliation, I turned to my uncle, and said quietly, "I don't wish to be the cause of distress for one of your guests. If you will excuse me, I believe I will retire for the evening."

Stiffening my back, I walked across the room, opened the door, and shut it softly behind me. Too stunned to think clearly, I stood hesitantly in the hall. On the right, Hargreaves greeted new arrivals at the front door, while directly ahead two footmen advanced with trays of beverages. Unable to face anyone, I turned left and ran up the stairs to my aunt's boudoir, where I threw myself down upon her Black Watch chaise lounge, and sobbed in an embarrassingly uncontrolled manner into a Royal Stuart plaid silk pillow until I heard the front door slam below. I sat up clutching the pillow, then ran to the window to look out. Griffin had Robert in a firm grip as they looked up and down the street. "What the devil...oh, Griffin, you idiot," I muttered.

I stepped back quickly from the window and paced the room as I thought. "I need to leave the house. I can't take any more of Lord Sherringham, or of Mabel's distraught face, or of Griffin's cold eyes." The last couple words were spoken on a sob.

I felt like driven prey, forced from a safe haven out to where I could be attacked by anyone. Flight was the only answer. There were the back stairs, but the servants were sure to be there, great huge swarms of them. In my present mood, I could not face even them. As I paced towards the side window, I glanced out briefly, then stopped.

My uncle's house was a mellow golden-red brick, with ivy covering the front and sides. Uncle Henry claimed it reminded him of Boston, where he had lived for several years. Below, two floors down, there was a small side yard surrounded by a black railing. It was the tradesmen's entrance, and I knew the gate was not kept locked. If I could climb down the ivy, I could make my escape by the alley behind the house and no one would be the wiser.

"Oh, I am not sacrificing this lovely gown," I said, touching its delicate folds. "There has to be another way."

I crept quietly out of the boudoir to see if the front hall was clear. It wasn't. Henry was speaking to Hargreaves, and as I watched, Griffin and Robert had joined them.

"Just like men to be in the way." I made my way back to the boudoir, and with one last reluctant glance at my beautiful, delicate gown, opened the side window as quietly as I could.

The window squeaked in protest as it raised, but the masculine rumble of voices outside the door stirred me. I used to be very good climbing the ivy outside my bedroom window as a child, and I felt sure the technique was not one that I would forget. Taking a firm grip on the ivy, I swung my legs over, digging into the foliage with the toes of my delicate evening slippers.

I was about halfway down when I heard a noise above me. Henry leaned out of the window, looking down at me with disbelief. "Cassandra! What are you doing?"

His head disappeared suddenly, and Griffin's appeared. He roared something at me, causing me to lose my grip momentarily. I slid down the ivy some six feet before I could regain my hold and continue the climb down. I felt the ivy tremble, and looked back up. Griffin had swung himself over the windowsill and was starting down the wall.

"Oh, the fool!" I murmured to myself, and looked down.

It was about five feet to the ground, but a glance upward decided me. I hit the paving stones hard, but rose to my feet with only a few whispered oaths. Other than ripping my bodice, I was unhurt, and watched with interest as Griffin descended a few feet. Calculating the point at which the ivy would give way under his weight, I moved backwards. I didn't have to wait long—with a great ripping sound, the ivy separated from the wall, and both it and Griffin fell directly in front of me with a loud thump.

I bent over and peered into his face. "Are you hurt?" I asked solicitously.

"Yes," he groaned, his eyes closed.

"Good."

I walked out of the yard to the back alley. Noises issuing from the yard assured me that the household staff had been alerted, making it prudent for me to hurry. As I turned the corner, I ran into two men lounging in the shadows against the side of the building.

"Pardon me," I said, stepping back.

One of the men grabbed for me and brandished a dark object. My eyes widened as I beheld a black pistol.

"Well, if it isn't the lovely Miss Whitney." A gold tooth flashed as the speaker stepped forward into the lamplight.

"Mr. Jones!" I cried, irritation driving out the concern at being accosted in the street. "I knew you would show up again. Unpleasant things always have a way of reappearing when you least desire them. Now will you have the decency to inform me why you are harassing me in this manner? And why is this man waving a firearm at me?"

"Here, Percy, isn't this a piece of luck?" Mr. Jones ignored my demands and spoke to the man pointing the pistol at me.

"It is at that," Percy agreed with a leer.

"You're the man from last night!" I accused Percy, then paused, turning to the other man. "Which means you…I thought your voice sounded familiar."

"Oh, she's torn her gown, Percy." Mr. Jones took a step towards me.

"That's a shame, it is, a cryin' shame."

I moved back slowly, hoping they wouldn't notice.

"Yes, that it is. Torn right there—" He reached out to touch the fabric.

I slapped at his hand and turned, intending to run back down the alley, but his hand shot out and caught me in a cruel grip. I cried out as his fingers dug painfully into my shoulder, pulling me up until his head was close to mine, his breath soiling my neck as he spoke in a tone that filled me with foreboding. "Now, miss, there's no sense in being unfriendly. We're old friends, you and I—"

The thought passed through my mind that for a person who abhorred violence as much as I did, I was indulging in a great deal of it of late. I curled my fingers up into a fist, but Mr. Jones must have anticipated the blow I was about to land. By moving quickly he twisted my free arm up behind my back.

"None of that, or," he jerked my arm upwards, making me gasp in pain, "you'll have to be punished."

A whirlwind slammed into us and sent me flying headlong into a nearby lamp post. I shook my head groggily and wondered if there was some sort of lamp post conspiracy against me. As my eyes cleared, I stared openmouthed at an enraged Griffin. He rolled in the street with Mr. Jones in a violent embrace, while above them, Percy shouted something incoherent as he danced around the pair in an agitated way, waving his pistol, but clearly unable to take a shot without hitting them both. He finally abandoned the idea of shooting and threw himself into the fray.

I thought briefly of assisting Griffin with the duo, but clad in nothing but a delicate, and now sadly torn, evening gown without even an umbrella as a weapon, I felt there was little I could do. Besides that, I'd had ample opportunity in the past to admire Griffin's impressive physique up close, and I was certain that two men would be no match for him while I sought help.

"Oh, blast!" I swore, remembering the fall Griffin had just taken. I hesitated, unsure if I should run to my uncle's house, or go back and assist Griffin. There was only one clear choice.

I ran back to the scene and screamed as loudly as I could.

The effect was immediate and satisfying. Mr. Jones shot me a venomous look and ran off into the alley, while Percy struggled out of Griffin's grip and disappeared after his companion. I looked down on Griffin where he endeavored to sit up in the street, and shook my head sadly, saying, "I would have thought you could have taken both of them," before I turned and ran down the road.

Directly in front of me was one of London's smaller parks. Although it wasn't the cleverest idea to run through the park alone at night, the idea of being exposed to family and friends was unthinkable in my present agitated state of mind. A strange wheezing, roaring noise behind me indicated that Griffin was following, and since his were the eyes I wanted to avoid the most, I dashed into the park and towards a clump of trees, feeling my chances of evading him would be far greater there than on the streets.

Pausing to catch my breath, I heard the metal gate clang and knew Griffin had followed me in. The park was lined with trees and almost completely dark, only small patches of dappled light reaching the edges. I crept along between the iron fence and the trees, and was surprised to hear the gate close a second time.

I stopped. Had Griffin had left the park? Indecision gripped me as I tried to decide whether or not I could chance racing across the open expanse to the far gate. A bulky silhouette passed in front of me which, due to having spent time in the previously mentioned appreciation of his manly proportions, I easily identified as belonging to Griffin.

He moved with absolute silence, a task that certainly must not have been easy for so large a man. I put it down to his years of travel in dangerous places, and crept out to watch with curiosity as he skirted the front of the trees.

To be truthful, I was feeling more than a little ridiculous. The adrenaline that started my flight was wearing off, leaving me wondering what I was doing skulking around a park late at night, hiding from the one person I wanted so desperately to be with.

Griffin's cold eyes and the mortifying scene with Lord Sherringham flashed through my head and I felt a little less ridiculous.

"A weapon," I whispered soundlessly to myself. "What you need is a weapon in case you run into those two thugs again." I felt along the ground for a stick or fallen branch, but the groundskeepers had done a meticulous job, my search resulting in nothing but a handful of twigs. I hurried forward on the tips of my toes to a large fir tree slightly to the left, where I had spied a low branch. It was small in diameter, but considering the situation, I felt it would make an excellent weapon. I worked the branch back and forth quickly, trying to break it off.

With a soft snap, the branch severed. I clutched it and started off after Griffin. Although I had every confidence in Griffin's ability to handle two men by himself, I worried that the fall and tussle in the street might have drained his reserve strength. I wanted to be at the ready should he need me.

A woman's scream pierced the night and was quickly silenced. I froze next to a large shrub, wondering if I should take cover, or if I should go on ahead to assist whatever female the two thugs were now no doubt terrorizing. Angry voices shouting ahead decided me. Although I didn't recognize Griffin's bellow, I was sure he was in trouble. As I ran past a large cedar bush, an arm reached out and coiled around me, a hand clamping down over my mouth. I was pulled to the side, flailing my branch in what I thought was a menacing manner until a familiar voice hissed, "Stop swatting that thing around and be quiet."

Griffin let go of my face and crept forward. I leaned over quietly and put my mouth to his ear. "The man with the bowler is Mr. Jones. He's the one who has been following me."

"You mean someone really was following you?" His breath tickled my neck.

"Yes." I grabbed his ears and made him lean down long enough to kiss him. He pulled me tighter for a second kiss, then gently pushed me behind him.

"Stay here." He started to leave then turned back as I followed him out. "Stay *here!*"

"Absolutely not. Where are you going?"

"I have unfinished business with those two. For once, do as I say and stay here."

I was about to protest when he grabbed me by the shoulders.

"So help me God, woman—" he muttered and pulled me to him a third time. His kiss was hot and hard and quick, and stole all my breath. Before I could blink he dashed off in pursuit of Mr. Jones and Percy.

"Well!" I said to no one in particular, fanning myself with the branch, still feeling the imprint of his kisses. A few moments later, recollection of the embarrassment of the evening drove the many pleasurable thoughts from my mind. I had no intention of remaining where I was, and no desire to wait for Griffin in my present mood. I went after him.

A shot rang out, quickly followed by another. Suddenly I was running, racing down the line of trees, heedless of the noise I made. I flung myself out into the open area and flew at the man bending over a figure on the ground.

Being by nature a passive and peace-loving woman, not at all given to emotions of a turbulent nature, I have never had any violent thoughts before—at least, not before I met Griffin. However, the sight of my beloved lying dead on the ground, his life's blood flowing away while his murderer stood gloating overhead was too much for me. I hurled myself at the villain, catching him off guard, trying to get my hands around his neck as we crashed to the ground.

"If you've killed him—" I yelled, sprawled across the man's chest, my fingers digging into his neck.

The coward squawked in terror, obviously pleading for mercy, but I was not in a merciful mood. I dug my fingers in tighter around his Adam's apple. Suddenly his body twisted and I was on my back, pinned to the ground, his face looming over mine.

"Are you mad?" a hoarse voice breathed in my ear. I stopped struggling and flung my arms around his head, kissing every reachable spot.

"Are you all right? You're not hurt? I thought you had been shot!"

"So I gather."

I released his head and allowed him to move next to me, laying on the grass, breathing heavily and rubbing his neck. I sat up. "Then who were you standing over?"

We both looked. There was no one on the ground.

"Damnation! He's gone," Griffin snarled, and leaped up.

A quick search of the area turned up nothing but the pistol that Griffin had wrestled away from Percy. Griffin put the pistol in his pocket and turned to me, swearing softly to himself. One of his lovely eyes was swelling and starting to discolor, the other glared out at me balefully. I yearned take him in my arms, to comfort him, to kiss him—

"Good night," I said instead, and ran back the way I had come.

He bellowed my name but I ignored it, bolting across the lit area to where I could see the shadow of a gate. It took me a moment to orient myself, but I soon had my bearings and made my way home at a fast trot, slowing to a walk only when I encountered other people. I caught sight of myself in the bedroom mirror—my eyes were wild, my hair disheveled and full of twigs, the lovely dress torn, smears of dirt running down my cheeks, and somehow I had acquired a decorative clump of leaves in my bosom.

Later, I sat calmly combing my hair, wondering about the primitive compulsion for flight that had possessed me earlier, and waited for the knock that I knew would come at my door.

"Cassandra?" My sister's voice accompanied the knock. "Are you all right?"

"I'm fine," I answered. "I would rather be alone tonight, though."

Listening intently I heard the soft murmur of voices.

"Will you not let me in, dear?"

"No, thank you, Mabel. I just want to sleep."

More murmuring.

"All right. I will talk with you in the morning. Sleep well."

I sighed with relief as she left, picked up my once lovely Worth gown, and sat on the foot of my bed.

"Now what do I do?" I asked my reflection in the mirror. "I have disgraced my family and confirmed Griffin's worst fears as to my character."

The reflection had no answers. I crawled into bed, fully expecting to stay awake the entire night with my heartache and worries, but fate willed otherwise.

CHAPTER EIGHTEEN

I am usually at my best in the morning, cheerful and ready to tackle whatever obstacles the day may bring. This day was no different; I awoke feeling refreshed, and laid in bed mulling over my plans for the day.

Until something niggled at the back of my mind, something unpleasant. Suddenly, the full horror the previous evening swept over me.

"It's obvious that some apologies are in order," I told Annie as she brought me in a cup of morning coffee.

"If you say so, miss."

I had given her an abbreviated version of the evening's events, knowing I could trust her. "I shall have to make those first. And then there's Helena. Neither of her brothers deserves an apology, but surely I owe her some explanation for my sudden disappearance."

"That might be best," Annie agreed.

A glance at the clock set me into motion. Dressed in a navy and white checked day dress, I ran downstairs before any of the family was up. I wasn't quite early enough, however, for Helena.

"Oh, miss, you're up." Theodore looked surprised to see me downstairs so early, and held out a letter. "This just came for you."

It was a letter from Helena, pleading with me to let her visit, to apologize for both her brothers' bad behavior. She offered to come and see me at any hour, or begged me to visit her whenever I wished. I was welcome in her house anytime, she declared.

"I am quite certain that Lord Sherringham would never say that," I said as I tossed the letter into the fire. Helena's intentions were good, but I knew just how welcome I was at St. John House. I sent Theodore out to fetch a cab while I contemplated an apology to my aunt.

As luck would have it, my uncle is the one who received it, Caroline not having risen yet.

"My dear, you have nothing to apologize for," Henry replied comfortingly. "It is I who should beg your forgiveness for allowing the earl to speak to you in such a manner. You must accept *my* apology for including Lord Sherringham in the dinner party."

"Never mind, as long as we both forgive each other, all is well."

"Is it?" he asked, peering from under his bushy white eyebrows.

I felt uncomfortable under his knowing gaze. "I still have to explain myself to Mabel, but yes, other than that task, all is well."

"And what of Mr. St. John?"

I frowned and pulled back. "I see no reason to apologize or to explain myself to him. I own that I will speak with his sister on the matter, but I hardly feel it necessary to discuss the situation with a man who would stand idly by and allow his lov—a friend to be so mistreated by his own brother. No, Uncle, I cannot see that!"

"Are you so certain that St. John stood idly by?"

I looked at him with disbelief. "I was there! I heard no exclamation from Griffin. I saw no attempt by him to stop his brother. I heard no protestations against the slander, no defense of my innocence!"

"Perhaps, my dear, that is because you took us all by surprise in leaving so precipitously. I admit I was just as stunned by Sherringham's rudeness as anyone in that room, but you did not give me time to gather my wits before you left."

"I did not feel strong enough to take another blow," I said dryly. "I thought it an opportune moment to make my escape."

"No one would deny you the right to leave the room after having been so insulted," he agreed. "Because of that, you were not present to witness what happened after you had done so."

Well, that made me curious. "What happened after I left?"

"Your young man was an admirable sight to behold. It made me feel young again, watching him. There was a time when I was courting Caroline that she decided to test my devotion by amusing herself with a baronet...but I won't bore you with that ancient history now. No, my dear, your young man did you proud."

"What did he do, exactly?"

The white eyebrows beetled at me for a moment. "He made himself clear, in language that should not have been used in the presence of ladies, as to his opinion of his brother. Once that matter was finished, he turned his attention to Robert Hunter. I'm a little confused as to why he was under the impression that Hunter was engaged to you—he's not is he?"

I shook my head.

"I thought not. It was fairly apparent who the object of Hunter's attention was, to everyone but her brother, I should say. Regardless," he said, eying me speculatively, "St. John grabbed Hunter by the back of his collar and said something about finding you. He left the room with him in tow."

I said nothing, but chewed my bottom lip in thought.

"When they could not find you on the street, St. John almost knocked Hargreaves down trying to get the information from him that he had seen you run upstairs. The rest you probably know. All in all, I was most impressed with the behavior of your young man."

"I don't think he is my young man anymore," I said sadly.

"Really? I believe that will come as news to the gentleman. My dear," he leaned forward and put a hand on my knee, "a word from one who is much older and wiser than you: do not test the love of a man by games and deceit. All too often such plans end in sorrow."

I left shortly after that. Rather than go home and face my family, I cravenly chose to spend the morning at the hall devoted to my favorite charity. There I helped assemble clothing, books, and other donated items in boxes to be sent to needy women. It was a soothing task, and mindless enough to allow me to continue the interesting thoughts that had been generated by my conversation with Uncle Henry.

"Off home, are you?" one of the women asked as I was leaving the hall.

"I'm not sure…" I hesitated as I stood on the front steps, trying to decide what I should do next. "There is a meeting to discuss the leadership and future of the Union scheduled for noon. I suppose I should attend that, although…oh, I'm just being silly. I'll go."

There were a large number of women in the meeting hall when I arrived. Since I am tall, I sit in the back so as not to obstruct the view from behind me, although the current fashion in hats makes it difficult to see no matter where one sits. I found a few empty seats in the last row and took one behind a woman who was wearing a simple straw boater, and was congratulating myself on my choice of seats and looking through my pockets for my notebook, when a hand gripped my arm.

"Cassandra! My dearest friend—"

"Shhhhh!" the woman in the straw boater silenced Helena.

She looked at me pleadingly, and I rose and slipped out of the hall with her. Outside of the meeting room she turned and grasped me in a fierce hug. "Oh, my dearest Cassandra! Can you ever forgive us? Can you ever forgive *me* for having such a beast of a brother? What must you think of us?"

Fearful that she was working herself up to an embarrassing dramatic display, I walked her outside. A half-block away was a tiny square. I led her there and deposited her on a bench. She held a handkerchief to her eyes as she gazed at me with remorse.

"For heaven's sake, Helena!" I said in an exasperated tone, sure any kindness would result in more tears. "Collect yourself. I am fine."

"But—what you must think—"

"I think nothing unkind about *you*, I can assure you," I said fondly. "I don't blame you for your brother's rudeness."

"If you only knew how I feel about you. How *we* feel about you."

"Thank you, I know how your elder brother feels about me," I said with a smile. "I would rather not be forced to listen to any further expressions of his opinion."

She looked down at the gloves she had twisted off her hands. "I am thoroughly ashamed of Harold's behavior last night. I can only apologize to you for his rudeness. He is a proud man and sometimes seems a little irrational, unwilling to listen to reason. But Griffin and I—" She stopped, choked with emotion.

Despite my irritation with her dramatics, I felt tears gather in my eyes. She flung her arms around me and sobbed, "Oh, Cassandra, you are like a sister to me!"

I was touched by her sentiment, but embarrassed by the scene. I knew if she continued, I'd be in tears as well. I patted her in a comforting manner, and urged her to control herself.

"Is it true that you climbed down the ivy?" she asked when she had done so.

"Yes. It's not as difficult as you might think. I used to climb out my bedroom window as a child. I was quite good at it, as a matter of fact."

"But why did you run? That is, I understand why you ran from the drawing room—I cannot think of anyone who would want to stay in the same room after they had been so insulted—but why did you run from Griffin?"

I glanced at her, then looked away to watch a haughty elderly woman slowly promenade by with an equally elderly Scottish Terrier. I was torn between telling Helena the entire situation, and a reticence to embarrass myself further. "I had no other thought than to make my way home as quickly as possible. I was not running away from any *one* individual."

"But Griffin said you refused to see anyone last night. He and Robert spoke with your brother-in-law, and they all went to your house to see if you had gone there."

"I wasn't aware of that. It was kind of your brother to be so concerned on my behalf."

Helena stared at me with a variety of expressions, surprise and pity plainly visible, followed by a gentle, sympathetic look. "Cassandra, be kind to Griffin. I...he...I know you've only known each other for a short time, but he really cares for you very much. I don't worry that I am breaking a confidence. I'm sure you must know how he feels; it is very apparent when he looks at you. Please, I ask you as a sister who loves him, do not be too hasty in judging his faults."

Indignation filled me at her initial words, but soon gave way to a deep sadness. I watched her twist her gloves, and wondered how much money she spent each month in replacements. "I'm afraid whatever affectionate feelings Griffin held for me have been destroyed, due in part to his stubbornness and my inability to explain the situation."

"What do you mean?"

I looked around us. We were alone in a corner of the square, with no one but the elderly Scotty and owner. I felt I could speak freely. "Griffin heard me tell Robert that I loved him."

"Oh?"

I felt, rather than saw, Helena withdraw, and hastened to explain. "That is what he *thought* he heard, what he did not hear was me telling Robert in what manner I loved him. I have known Robert since I was a little girl, and have always loved him like a brother. In fact, he is dearer to me than any brother could be, because—well, someday he will make someone so very happy."

Helena let go of her breath suddenly, and beamed at me. "You love him as a brother. Yes, of course. A brother. That makes perfect sense."

"Griffin, being an adorable but extremely pigheaded man, heard only the first part of my speech, and left so quickly I could not explain the situation to him. Now he thinks he's being noble by not standing in the way of my happiness, when really—really—"

I couldn't help the tears from filling my eyes. Convinced that contact with Helena was making me prone to emotional scenes, I looked at her pitifully.

"—you are terribly unhappy," she finished with a sob. "Oh, my dear, can you ever forgive me for lecturing you! How could I tell you to be kind to Griffin when he has been so unkind to you?"

She sniffled into her useless lace handkerchief. I searched through my bag and pulled out two sensible linen ones. Dabbing at my own eyes, I handed her one. "I've taken to carrying an extra since I met you. Did Griffin tell you about the two men last night?"

"Two men?" A frown formed. "Why, no, he didn't. What two men?"

214

"A man attacked me as I left my aunt's house. I don't think they meant to attack *me*, you understand. I was just in the way. I suspect they were lying in wait for Griffin."

"No," she said faintly, her hand to her throat.

I thought what a shame it was that Helena would never be on the stage, and continued. "Later, when we were in the park—"

"You were in a park?"

"Yes. Helena, I am afraid someone *is* behind these accidents your brother has been having lately."

The color drained from her lovely face.

"Furthermore, I believe Griffin suspects that as well. It was my impression that the two thugs who followed him last night were the same two who attacked him in your house."

"Who could want to hurt Griffin?"

"I couldn't say. I suggest you ask him about it."

"Oh, yes, I will. He must take precautions. He must leave for his trip immediately!" She saw my face fall and tried to comfort me. "If he is out of the country, he will be out of harm's way."

"I hardly call travelling to far away, uncivilized locations out of harm's way. Besides, do you not agree that it would be safer for him to stay here, where he has the assistance of his family and friends, not to mention that of the police?"

"That's true. I hadn't thought of that—he must stay home. You must make him see that. But Cassandra! He's gone to see you this morning to apologize for Harold's unkind comments. You haven't seen him?"

"No. I left early to go to my aunt's house. He probably arrived after I left."

We stared at each other for a moment.

"Romantic misunderstandings, mysterious attackers, flights in the night…honestly, Helena, sometimes I think I'm caught up in one of those old gothic novels my grandmother used to read," I said, unable to keep from laughing.

She giggled with me, and after we collected ourselves, I rose. "As long as we are here, we shouldn't miss the meeting. They will be deciding about the future of the Union."

We did miss a good portion of the meeting, but managed to be present for Maggie's debate. A brilliant orator, she once again swept the audience up with her vision of women's suffrage, playing on our sense of duty, adventure, and outrage. I did my best to keep Helena's feet planted firmly on the ground, but I could not do the same for the other women in attendance.

The meeting ended in confusion, nothing having been decided although sides were clearly being drawn. The future of our protest at the upcoming election speeches at Exeter House was in question, with both sides claiming proprietorship.

We left the meeting hall still debating the merits of each side. As we arrived at my sister's house, Helena suddenly stopped her argument, and placed a hand on mine. "You will explain the misunderstanding to Griffin when he comes to you?"

"*If* he comes to see me, and *if* he gives me the opportunity, I shall certainly set him straight on the subject, have no fear."

"And you will talk him into staying home, where he can be safe?"

"I will try, but I doubt if my opinions carry much weight with him."

She waved good-bye, and I entered the house with some foreboding. Mabel pounced on me as soon as I took off my hat and coat. "Cassandra! Where have you been? I have been frantic with worry!" She frowned as we walked upstairs to the sitting room. "Mr. St. John came to see you. We were alarmed when we could not find you. And Cousin Freddy is here to see you. He is in the library with Joshua."

"I'm sorry, I had no idea anyone would be looking for me. I was at a meeting with Helena."

"Really, Cassandra, I think you might have a little more concern for us. We were worried about you ever since that horrible episode last night."

"I felt the need to apologize to Aunt Caroline."

She sat in a comfortable chair and picked up her needlework, a pinafore she was embroidering for one of the girls. "You might have left word that you were leaving. What Mr. St. John thought—he looked most hurt and distressed."

I hardly thought hurt and distressed would describe Griffin's feelings, but I endeavored to retain a charitable thought towards him.

"He came especially to see you. That brother of his! I've never seen such abominable behavior. Whatever you and Helena St. John might have done, I don't believe there was any cause for such an outburst, and in the middle of a dinner—"

This was a slight exaggeration, however, since I wanted to avoid seeing Freddy, I let Mabel chatter on.

"—I really do not know what he could have been thinking. But, Cassandra!" She put down the pinafore and looked at me steadily. "Whatever else you may say about him, Mr. St. John was very unhappy."

I listened to her lecture hoping that while it lasted Freddy would leave, but as luck would have it, he found me at last. Mabel gave me a pitying look and excused herself. I stood with my arms crossed and a stern, unyielding look on my face, hoping to intimidate my would-be swain.

"Dearest cousin," he said, taking my hands to kiss them. He was his usual handsome self, his eyes filled with warmth and concern that I suddenly found suspicious. "I heard about last night. Are you all right? Uncle Henry said something about you being escorted home by St. John, but I could not rest until I had seen for myself that you were not harmed."

"I'm fine, Freddy, thank you. It really was nothing, just a little contretemps, and then I took a silly notion to leave without anyone seeing me." His fingers tucked a loose curl behind my ear. I suppressed a grimace at the touch, and moved over to the couch. "I appreciate your visit, but I'm afraid it's must be a brief one. I have an engagement that I have to dress for—"

Freddy dropped to his knees. I sighed.

"Beloved Cassandra, most precious of all women, this time you cannot refuse me, not after last night."

"Freddy, please, not again."

He took my hand in his, his eyes glowing brightly. "You must see that you have no other choice. Without me at your side, you will continue to be vulnerable. I can offer you much, beloved one, not just my protection, but my heart, my devotion, my life if you wished it."

"I'm sorry, Freddy, I can't think of how to say no in a manner that you will accept, so I will simply say this: I have given my heart to another. I will never marry you."

His fingers tightened painfully around mine. I tried to pull my hand back, but his grip was too strong. "You would be wise to think twice about refusing me."

"Are you threatening me?" I asked, shocked.

"Of course not. I would never do such a thing," he said smoothly, his face earnest, but his eyes calculating.

"No, but you would talk to a man in a rabbit suit shortly before I was attacked," I said slowly.

"Rabbit suit?" He did a very good job of looking surprised. "Attacked?"

"Yes. At the St. Alban's ball the other night. I saw you speaking with the man who later attacked a friend and me. I heard you mention my costume to him before that."

"My dearest cousin, you do me grave injury," he protested. "As if I could do anything to harm you. I mentioned you to several people at the ball that night. Many of my friends had very complimentary things to say about your outfit. That is no doubt what you overheard."

It wasn't, and we both knew it, but I didn't feel in possession of enough facts to challenge him on the subject.

"I am appalled that you were attacked, but this does prove the validity of my concerns about you. You must see that to deny me any longer is the sheerest folly."

"I see nothing of the kind. I won't have you, Freddy, and that's final."

There was a curious flat expression in his eyes that sent a sudden chill of horror skimming down my back. I had seen that look before, usually just before my father inflicted some new form of punishment. "I have it in my power to make you a very happy woman—or one who will think back to your days with your father with longing. Heed me, Cassandra. You *will* be mine."

"Not in this or any other lifetime." I went to the door, threw it open, then marched out of the room and up the stairs. To my great relief, he did not follow, but gathered up his coat and hat and departed.

I hurried back down the stairs and poked my head into the library to inform Joshua and Mabel that it was safe to come out.

"Did he ask you?" Mabel inquired.

"For the umpteenth time, yes. And I refused him. Please don't let him wait for me again," I said, trying to calm my wildly beating heart. "He did not take my refusal well. I would rather not be alone with him."

The air in the house felt tainted by Freddy's anger, so I rounded up the two dogs and took them to the square across the street for a walk. We played in the park, chasing squirrels, leaves, and each other. Out of breath from the romp, I had to call them to me when a half-dozen indignant pugs invaded the square. After a brief scuffle with one of the more objectionable little pugs, I leashed the hounds and returned home.

A familiar motor was sitting in front of the house. I looked at it briefly, then turned toward the house and squared my shoulders. I would have to face the man at some time; it was better that it be in my sister's house and not in some public place.

After all, there were definite advantages to privacy.

I was attempting to remove the leashes from the dogs when the library door opened and out walked Joshua and Griffin.

"Ah, there she is," Joshua said happily.

The dogs, which had been racing around me in excited circles, succeeded in entangling me and throwing me off balance. One of the hounds, elated at the sight of Griffin, leaped up to kiss him. As I had one leg off the ground in an attempt to disentangle myself from the leash, the dog's sudden movement knocked me flat onto my back. My head hit the marble floor and I saw stars for the third time in a week.

"Ack!" I yelled incoherently, trying to push the dog back as it wiped its tongue on me. I kicked my legs in an attempt to free them from their bonds, but as the dogs were still attached to the leashes, I could not get my feet loose. The second dog, assuming I was desirous of more play, joined in the fun.

"Get off!" I bellowed in a very unladylike manner. The dogs jumped back, wagging happily as I struggled to a sitting position. Griffin leaned against the wall, doubled up with laughter. I glared at him and Joshua, who was trying very hard to not laugh and not succeeding in the least.

"Well, one of you might at least help me!" I said with as much dignity as I could muster.

The first dog, concerned by the tone in my voice, came up to show his affection by licking my face.

"Off!"

Finally, wiping tears from his eyes, Griffin unleashed the dogs. Joshua helped me to my feet and untangled the leashes from my limbs. With head held high I walked with a slight limp into the library. Griffin followed, still smiling, and after glancing at Joshua, closed the door behind him.

I lifted my chin in anticipation of a battle, but it was not a battle Griffin had on his mind as he scooped me into a fierce embrace. My knees buckled from the passion of his kisses. I was breathless, crushed to his chest, unable to move (not that I was complaining). His lips scorched mine, his mouth and hands and body starting a familiar burn deep within me. I was just about to return the affectionate greeting when he released me suddenly and scowled. "What the devil do you mean, scaring me like that?"

"Like what?" I gasped, clutching my ribs in an attempt to locate any broken bones.

"Last night," he growled. "When you demonstrated your acrobatic skills by climbing down the side of your uncle's house."

I wondered how a person would know if she had a cracked rib.

"Can you blame me for leaving the room?" I asked, still struggling to catch my breath. "After the things your brother had to say—"

"My brother is an idiot."

"I am hardly in a mood to argue with you there," I agreed pleasantly, finally convinced that my bones were intact. Now if only something could be done about the fire he started within me.

As I spoke, the door opened and Robert stepped in.

"Ah, Cassandra, my dear," he greeted me, then saw Griffin. "St. John, just the man I want to see."

Robert looked at me and winked.

I think it was the wink that did it; I suspect the familiarity pushed Griffin over the edge. He grabbed Robert by the shoulder and pushed him, with a good deal more force than was necessary, up against the wall. Leaning close, he growled, "I mean to have this out with you Hunter!"

Robert smiled at him, an act of bravery that I gave him much credit for, as an enraged Griffin was a terrifying sight to behold. "There's nothing to settle. You only heard part of a conversation the other night. The part you missed would have interested you more than what you heard." He looked thoughtfully at me, and added, "I'll let Cassandra tell it, she's much better than I am at this sort of thing."

Griffin released his stranglehold on Robert and watched him leave, then wheeled around to me and asked quietly, "What did I miss?"

I took a moment to lock the door against any further intruders.

"Quite a bit," I answered. "Why wouldn't you let me tell you what happened?"

"Because it was obvious what happened. I heard you express your affection for Hunter."

"You heard me telling Robert I loved him."

Griffin stood still, his eyes alight, watching me intently.

"What you didn't hear, and what you were too pigheaded to let me explain, was the continuation of that statement which ended *like a brother*."

"You love him like a brother?" His voice was flat and emotionless.

"Yes. As I believe I have had cause to mention, next to Emma he is my oldest friend, and I love him dearly. *As I would a brother.*"

"You have no other feelings for him?"

"On the contrary, I have quite a few, and I want to talk to you about them sometime, for they concern...well, they concern you, but right now I have other things on my mind."

"Such as?" Griffin relaxed as he took a step forward.

"I want to know why you followed after me last night."

"Why did you run from me?"

I raised my hand and ticked off each item. "The man I love ignores me, I am assaulted verbally by a peer of the realm, and am embarrassed before my entire family. Yes, I believe that accounts for the major items."

He looked intently into my eyes and said in a strangled voice, "The man you love?"

"Yes," I said, looking at him with wonder that he still did not understand, and reached up to touch the colorful tissue around his eye. "What happened when you met Percy in the park?"

"Nothing important. What about the man you love?"

"Hmmm." I chewed my lower lip in thought. "Percy must not have been hurt very seriously if he could take himself off while we were distracted. I assume they were the same men that attacked you in your house?"

"I think so," he grunted, then gave me a little shake. "You were saying something about the man you love?"

"Why would they want to attack—"

My words were cut off with a roar. "Cassandra!"

"What?"

His words came out slowly as if spoken with great control. "Who is the man you love?"

"You." I poked him in the ribs so he would get the point.

He peered into my eyes suspiciously.

"Do you honestly think I give you the job of lover if I didn't have strong feelings for you?"

He had the grace to look abashed. "You never mentioned that. All you said is that you were looking for a lover. And, I believe, a cigarette."

"Yes, well, I've given up on the latter, and as for the former...the position has been filled very nicely." I slid my arms around his neck, threading my fingers through the cool silk of his curls, tugging on them gently until his mouth was against mine. "And what about you, my gallant savior? Do you make a habit of dallying with women for whom you feel nothing but a mild interest, or are those feelings you mentioned the other day something I would appreciate?"

His lips did all the answering, but it was not with words.

"I locked the door," I breathed into his mouth.

His eyes were hot with sudden passion. "I am tiring of quick trysts, Cassandra. I want more. I want much more."

"As do I, but for the moment..."

We had our clothes removed in record time.

"Are you sure about this?" I asked Griffin as he pulled me over him. He was sitting in the middle of the couch, his arousal looking particularly large as I peered down onto it. "Are you supposed to be that imposing?"

"I am the same as I have always been, sweetheart. Now if you would just...oh, Lord...not...not...narrrng!"

I wrapped my hand around the long, hard length of him, amazed when he twitched, delighted with his gasps as I slid my fingers along the underside.

"Fascinating," I said, continuing my exploration. His head lolled back as I used both hands, adjusting my movements until I had him groaning almost non-stop. "This really is fascinating. I had no idea about all of this. Are you particularly sensitive here?"

He shot up off the couch, prying my hands off his nether bits. "Yes, yes, I am, and if you want me to see this through to the logical conclusion, you'll stop touching me there."

"Oh." We both looked down at the part I had been touching. It twitched. "What if I touch you here?"

His eyes crossed.

"This *has* been an informative afternoon. Now, if I do this, what exactly do you feel—Griffin!" He pulled me over him again, my legs splayed along his thighs, his arousal nudging my intimate self, which, true to form, was tingling madly. I looked him in the eye. "You expect me to impale myself on you?"

"Yes. Yes, I do. Right now. This instant. Earlier, if possible."

I squirmed around on the very tip of him. "I'm not sure about this Griffin. This seems rather an uncomfortaaaaaaaaaah!"

He gripped my hips and plunged upward into me, taking my scream of pleasure into his mouth. "Ah, sweetheart, if you knew what you did to me."

"Well, I know what you're doing to me," I answered as he showed me the rhythm that pleased us both. On top as I was I discovered I could control the depth and speed of my impalement, and quickly found that if I tightened all my muscles as I sank slowly down upon him, it made him buck and groan in the most satisfying manner.

"Cassan—oh, Lord, woman, don't stop. Move like that again."

I swirled my hips, enjoying my power, enjoying the fact that I had him babbling with mindless pleasure. Men were such simple creatures under all the sophisticated trappings, I thought to myself as I both tightened and swirled, which had the most amazing effect on Griffin. His hair stood on end and his eyes blazed.

"You're doing this on purpose, aren't you? You're trying to make me lose my mind with sheer, unadulterated ecstasy, aren't you? I know you are, I can see it in your face. Admit it!"

I smiled, rather smugly, I'm afraid, and tightened, twirled, and sucked his tongue into my mouth. "You were babbling just a moment ago, my love. I believe that settles the question of superiority of the sexes."

I paid for my smugness.

"I accept your challenge," he said just before he flipped me over so my back was to the couch while he covered me. My legs wrapped around him as he kissed my breasts, laving them, suckling and nipping and scraping his teeth gently along my nipples until I thought they were going to catch fire. "Now we will see who babbles. Now we will see which of us has more control."

I stroked my hands down his back, scraping a gentle line down his spine with my nails before letting my fingers fondle his so very delectable derriere. "If you...oh, Griffin!...if you think...just a little to the right, love...if you think you are going to make me babble...you...you...merciful heaven, Griffin, don't stop!"

"Never," he swore into my neck, his mouth hot on the tender flesh beneath my ear. His hands curved under to hold onto my behind, and if I wasn't enjoying myself so much, I might have been worried by the glint in his eye, but as it was, I didn't have any wits left with which to worry. He plunged, I thrust, we kissed and sucked and nibbled, our fingers lighting fires that burned bright as our bodies moved together in a dance of such sweet joy, tears streaking my cheeks when I sobbed his name into his shoulder, his voice echoing mine as he poured his life into me.

"I believe I would call that a draw," I said lazily some long minutes later as I gently kissed his neck. "However, in the interests of a rational, scientific examination of the subject of which of the sexes is superior, it behooves us to continue this particular activity until we are satisfied with the results."

Above me, Griffin's chest heaved into mine as he panted out his answer. "It will probably kill me, but I agree."

"I can't think of a better way to die. Griffin?" He lifted his head just enough to look into my eyes. I kissed his nose. "What are we going to do about this?"

"About what?" He nuzzled my neck.

"This." I freed an arm and waved it around the room. "You and me. Everything."

"Oh, that." He nibbled on my earlobe as I traced the long sweep of his damp back down to the wonderful contours of his behind. So firm, and yet so very soft. I let my fingers linger there.

"Really, Griffin, we can't go on doing this."

"Why not?" This was whispered into my hair as his lips caressed my forehead.

I tilted my head back and trailed kisses underneath his jaw. "What if we are out somewhere in public? With other people?"

"I don't see a problem."

Someone knocked at the door.

Griffin looked at me. I looked at him. "Caught!" I said in whispered exaggeration.

He pressed a gentle, gentle kiss to my lips, and disengaged himself from me. "With our trousers down."

"One moment," I called over his shoulder to the door as we scrambled back into our clothing.

"I do have a solution to the problem. Do you see my collar?"

"It's under my boot. Would your solution involve a house where no one is likely to interrupt us?"

"In a manner of speaking. It would involve your consenting to marry me."

"Forgive me," I said as I buttoned up my skirt. "I am a little lightheaded from our activities, especially that last bit. Lack of oxygen, no doubt. Did you say marry? You and me?"

"That's the idea. Here, I believe this is yours."

I took the undergarment offered. "But I don't wish to marry!"

"Why not?"

"I am a New Woman. We believe in lovers, not marriage. Well, not marriage right away. I would like to marry you some day, Griffin. But not yet. I wish to fully explore loverhood first."

"Your objection is ridiculous. We would do the same things as lovers as we would married."

"Possibly, although you can't deny there's a lovely sense of illicitness that makes everything that much more exciting."

"There's also the fact that we are limited to only having brief moments together."

"Yes." I sighed and buttoned up my skirt. "But if you were to come to my house in the country, we would have time together."

He gave me a look that let me know he didn't like that idea much. "We will marry."

"You don't approve of me!" I felt obligated to point out.

He stepped back and raked me with his eyes. I blushed at the look. "On the contrary, I very much approve of you."

I reached over to touch a curl lying against his ear. "That is, you do not approve of my political views any more than I approve of yours."

"That is easily arranged. You give up your participation in the suffrage movement, and I will give up my opposition to the subject of women's votes."

"Oh, that's a fine compromise! I forfeit all my rights and you lose nothing."

"I won't have a wife who gets thrown in prison for attacking policemen."

"And I won't have a husband who believes that it is his right to tell me how to live my life!" I stormed, buttoning up the last button on my shirtwaist. "And you know full well that was a false charge. I was doing nothing wrong. Ask Helena if you don't believe me."

He snorted. "I have asked her, and I get nothing but illogical diatribes about the abuse of women."

We stared at each other across the huge cavern of differences that separated us. I despaired of ever crossing it.

"It comes down to this every time," I said sadly, tears welling up behind my eyes. Why was he so maddening, so frustrating? Why couldn't he step over his pride and meet me halfway?

His face worked with emotion.

"Oh—damn!" I said, furiously, kicking the leg of an overstuffed chair. Griffin's eyebrows rose.

"Cassandra Jane Whitney," he said softly, "I'm shocked by such language. I never know what you will say next."

I looked at him, this man whom I loved with every part of my being, this man who sent me into raptures every time he touched me, this man who dominated my thoughts, and yet who made me so mad I wanted to do him bodily harm.

"I love you, Griffin St. John," I said simply as I went over to unlock the door. "And if you weren't so obstinate and stubborn, you would have the sense to see that. Now what, exactly, are you going to do about that?"

I didn't wait long to find out.

CHAPTER NINETEEN

When Robert returned home that evening from a visit to acquaintances in the city, Emma and I were in possession of Joshua's library while he had gone off to visit his sister. The two old friends exchanged greetings, and settled down for a long chat.

"Emma is going to Paris for a few days," I said conversationally. "I haven't been to Paris in years. Perhaps we can make a short trip there together, sometime soon."

"That would be delightful," he said glumly.

I exchanged a glance with Emma.

"Robert, I hope you don't mind, but Cassandra has told me something of your current situation," Emma said. "Naturally, I am distressed that your brother has treated you so callously. Have you had any luck in obtaining sponsorship?"

He stood with a hand on the mantelpiece, staring into the fire with a most forlorn look upon his face. He sighed. "No. My brother seems to have done his work thoroughly. I can't raise the capital it would take to buy another farm. So you see, my dear friends, it would be useless for me to make plans to go anywhere. Instead, I will begin preparations to remove myself from your sister's kind charity, Cassandra. I will find a job somewhere in town."

I gritted my teeth against the words that wanted to come out. Emma likewise bit her lip.

"There is always the military," he mused unhappily to himself. "Or I could hire myself out as a laborer."

It was an effort, but I continued to keep my silence. Emma opened her mouth to speak, shook her head, and closed it again.

Robert took our silence as agreement with his plans, and continued in a morose and extremely annoying tone. "I understand they are seeking men for work in the coal mines of Wales."

"Blast it, Robert! I cannot believe this is you I am listening to."

"Cassandra," Emma said, a warning in her voice as I stood up and shouted at him.

"No, Emma, I can't stand this no longer. Robert is our friend. I know you think we should let him work things out on his own, but I can't stand this any longer."

Robert looked at us both in surprise, watching with no little concern as I shook off Emma's restraining hand and grabbed him by the lapels of his jacket.

"I assure you I am not offended by your concern. I am humbled that my two oldest friends would stand by me," he started to explain.

I wouldn't let him finish. "Have you no dignity? Have you no pride? Have you no gumption?" I shook him with each word I spoke; he put up a hand to stop me, but I was too enraged.

"You are not the sort of man to take things lying down! If you love Helena, then you had better start acting like it!"

Robert looked to Emma for help. She gave a little shake of her head. "I'm sorry Robert. About this, I agree with Cassandra. No woman wants a suitor who sits around moping and bemoaning the fact that he is not worthy."

"We want a man who will bare his heart and soul!" I declared.

"Tell Helena of your feelings," Emma said. "Tell her of your situation. I'm sure she will understand."

"Yes, tell her, and then ask her to join you in a life that will be filled with love and fraught with difficulties, but for heaven's sake, stop mooning around and ask her!"

Robert looked stunned at our frank speech, but at least he stopped his insufferable wallow in self-pity. "But—but—"

"You must trust that we know of what we speak, Robert. We are not naïve young ladies; we are worldly New Women. I even have a lover!"

"You do?" He looked shocked down to his toenails.

"Yes. And both Emma and I know all about men, and what we want from them."

His gaze shot to Emma. "But surely you are—"

She raised a hand to stop him, making a wry face. "I think explanations about that would be best left for a time when Cassandra has a bit more experience being a New Woman."

"What explanations?" I asked her, distracted.

"Another time. Right now we are here to help and support Robert."

"Very well." I narrowed my gaze on Robert. "What's your decision?"

"What can my decision be? I have nothing—"

"Oh, for heaven's sake! We don't want to hear it. Either you have the decency to tell Helena of your feelings, or you will spend the rest of your life sniveling about what might have been."

It was probably the term "sniveling" that made the difference. I have found that gentlemen hate to be told they are snivelers. Robert looked at me coolly for a moment, then turned stiffly and marched out of the room. When Emma and I, exchanging small victorious smiles, followed him, we saw that he paused only long enough to gather his hat and coat before leaving the house.

"You don't think we've acted a trifle precipitously, do you?" I asked Emma as she collected her own coat and hat.

"Sending him into the lion's den with no protection, and his heart on his sleeve, you mean?" she asked with a little laugh.

"When you say it like that, it sounds so hopeless." I sighed. "I pray it will be enough."

"I'm sure it will." She paused for a moment at the door, giving me a long look. "I wonder if you and your Griffin would like to join me at the club for dinner next week. Tuesday is public night, and I would be happy to have you as my guests. There are a few things that I would like to explain, and I think it might be best if he were there to help."

"I'm sure he would be delighted, as would I, but what sorts of things are you talking about?"

She patted my cheek. "We'll leave that for then. Good luck with your campaign to rally Robert to brave new heights. I will send you a postcard from Paris."

A look at the clock reminded me of my promise to write a few words for inclusion in the next issue of the Union's publication *Sisters in Suffrage*. With my thoughts not entirely on the subject, I hastened to my typewriting machine to compose a brief article on a New Woman's duties regarding sexual freedom.

The article took me longer than I had planned; it was not until just before dinner time that I was able deliver it. The Union Hall was empty when I went in search of the editor, but as I passed down the side of the hallway I heard a familiar name being spoken. The door was open slightly and I would have stopped to listen had not the editor chosen that moment to come out.

"Ah, there you are, Miss Whitney. I was just leaving. Is that the article?"

I handed over my copy, and chatted with her for a moment about the latest political gossip. As we strolled back, we passed Maggie Greene standing in the door to one of the offices.

"You'll be sure to lock up, won't you Maggie?" asked my companion. "Everyone else is gone."

Maggie shot me an unfriendly look and agreed to secure the Hall. As we exited the building, I turned back in the doorway.

"I must have dropped a glove inside. I will just run back and fetch it."

Bidding the editor goodnight, I ran back into the Hall on the tips of my toes. Quietly, I listened at the doorway where I had seen Maggie.

"...otherwise we shall be voted down again. It's time we make our stand. If we do so now, the rest of the membership will have no choice but to follow. Cynthia Knox will not be able to rally the members against us, not while Heywood is still in prison."

"But St. John's brother is the leader of the opposition. Do you think it's wise to involve her in our plans? What if she tells him when and where we intend on striking?"

"She won't. I have thoroughly vetted her and she is an enthusiastic supporter. She has one of those weak minds that are easily led." Maggie laughed harshly. "I fancy she will do us a fair amount of good. Her name and her illustrious brother's stand will garner us a great deal of print and sympathy. I can almost read the headline: Peer's Suffragette Sister Imprisoned. Besides, I have a card or two up my sleeve. Our patron made it clear he wants the lovely Helena out of the way, and he won't pay up until we make sure she is. My plan is foolproof: we bring the Union to its knees, take control in the confusion, send the St. John woman to prison for several years, after which we collect a sizable donation to the cause."

"Who is the patron, Maggie?" an annoying, whining voice asked.

"My agreement with him prohibits me from revealing his name," Maggie said smoothly. "It's time to go. We shall start early tomorrow and rally the members. We will need their support, whether or not we decide to leave the Union intact."

There were noises of movement amid their laughter, sending me flying. Once outside, I hid in the space below the stone stairs, and waited to see to whom the other voices belonged. Voices drove me deeper into the shadows as Maggie Greene and five other women walked away to the entrance of the Underground. I did not know the other women, but I recognized them as being part of Maggie's corps.

I mulled over what to tell Helena about the militants. I sorely missed Griffin at that moment, not just his physical presence, but his emotional support. My head ached by the time I arrived home. I was almost to my bedroom when Robert stepped out of his room with a suitcase in each hand, his face haggard and worn. "You look as if you have pulled backwards through a fence, Robert. Where are you going?"

He set down the suitcases and took both of my hands in his. "Cassandra, my dear, I want to thank you for your love. You are a true friend, and one I will never forget."

"Robert!" I placed a hand against his cheek. "What has happened?"

He closed his eyes briefly and leaned into my hand. Sighing, he opened his eyes again. "I went to ask for Helena's hand."

"She has refused you?" I asked in disbelief.

"No, her guardian has refused to allow me to present my case."

"Her—oh, you mean Lord Sherringham?"

"Yes. I can't blame him, of course, I wouldn't want a penniless man with no future asking for my sister's hand. But I had believed...Helena is so...I had hoped..."

To my horror, I saw Robert was on the verge of tears.

"Oh, Robert!" I said, my own eyes filling. "Don't listen to Lord Sherringham. You should have spoken with Griffin, he likes you. He approves of you. He would be happy to see you married to Helena."

He shook his head. "It is to her guardian I must apply. He controls her—her—"

"Her fortune, yes, I know. I wondered if Helena would tell you about that. It would certainly allow you to marry and be coffee farmers, if that is what you wished."

He slumped into a chair next to the hall window. "Even if I wanted to be the kind of a man who lived off of his wife's money, I don't have the choice now. Sherringham has refused to allow me to call on Helena again."

"But, surely Helena does not care."

"No, Cassandra. It's one thing to ask a woman to support her husband if she has the ample means, but it's another to ask her to forsake her rightful inheritance to live a life of genteel poverty."

"Robert, you are being maudlin. There is no need for this. I am sure Griffin can help you—"

He stared at his suitcases, shaking his head. I had forgotten about them.

"Where do you think you are going?"

"To live with a friend in Chelsea." He stood and kissed me on the cheek. "Don't worry, I'll be fine. I will let you know my address later."

"There will be no need," I said with much firmness. "You are staying here."

"Cassandra—"

"I am not going to hear another word about you leaving."

"It's no use. I must go. I can intrude on Mabel and Joshua's kindness no longer."

I argued, I pleaded, and in the end, I finally badgered Robert into staying put. I felt that I had a better chance of helping him if I knew where to find him. Once I saw him safely returned to his room, I retreated to my bedroom to have a serious talk with myself.

"The truth is that you love Griffin, and although he has not actually said the words, you know he loves you," I told myself as I paced the width of my room. "The only thing holding you back from spending the rest of your lives together in happiness is your stubbornness."

The Cassandra who watched me in the mirror nodded and added, "In other words, until you are willing to compromise, you're going to be miserable and unhappy and can never live in peace with the man you love."

"Oh, what do you know, you're just a two dimensional image," I snapped at the reflection, and stared out the window at the darkened street for a few minutes before reluctantly admitting the truth of the statement.

A good portion of the stubbornness mentioned lay at my door. Griffin had repeatedly said that he did not want a wife who was arrested, but he said nothing about a wife who supported the cause in other manners. Recalling past conversations, I realized that his emphasis was on the dangerous aspect of my support, participation in the protests and demonstrations. I began to see a way clear to a compromise that would make Griffin happy and yet allow me to keep my self-worth and dignity. A glance at the clock on the mantle showed it was ten o'clock, too late to telephone or write him.

"As for the problem of Robert and Helena," I told my smug reflection as I donned my night wear, "I'm sure once I have told Griffin about my decision, I can persuade him to help them."

My reflection shook her head, but I ignored her, and fell asleep happy, wrapped in warm thoughts for a change.

CHAPTER TWENTY

I dressed carefully the next day, wanting to look my best as I informed Griffin of my newfound resolution.

"Oh, Annie!" I said, pounding my dressing table. "Why is it I spend an inordinate amount of time and money obtaining clothing, and yet when I want something to wear, it appears I don't have a single, solitary garment worthy of being seen outside the house?"

She smiled, and held out a mustard-colored dress. "How about this one, miss?"

"It makes me look sallow."

She pulled out one of the Reform walking dresses. "How about this blue one? You haven't worn it."

"It makes me look lumpy," I muttered. I was acting childishly, and I knew it. "Wait. I apologize, Annie. I'm out of temper this morning. Bring out the white lace blouse and the tan walking skirt. That will be good enough."

Before I went downstairs, I knocked on the door to Robert's room. He opened the door, tucking his shirt into his trousers. I pushed him back into his room, and ignored his shocked expression. "Can you be ready to go in five minutes?"

"Go? Go where?"

"I need to see Griffin."

He smiled.

"Stop smirking and just tell me whether you want to accompany me to see Helena."

His mustache drooped dejectedly. "What would be the good? I'm not worthy of her, and can never aspire to give her the things she is accustomed to."

It took a great deal of forbearance, but I managed to not strike him. "Robert, I am going to tell you something that will make your problem easy to solve. It took me a while to figure it out, but it is really very simple."

He looked at me with hope. "Yes? What is it?"

"This: either you can propose to Helena, and live happily ever after on a coffee ranch—"

"Farm," he said morosely.

"—farm, or you can mope around until someone else who knows what he wants comes along and marries her."

"She deserves someone like that."

"Robert, I could strangle you! She deserves *you*! She loves *you*! You are the one she wants, and by heaven, you are the one I mean to see her have!"

It took a little arguing, but eventually he saw the wisdom of my reasoning and agreed to meet me downstairs.

"Cheer up," I told him, leaving the room. "I have a feeling this is going to be a very good day."

I raced down the stairs and was heading into the library when Mullin stopped me. "Miss Cassandra, a cabby just brought this note. It is marked urgent."

Ignoring his look of curiosity, I took the note and read it on my way into the library. I stopped in the doorway, and turned back to the hall.

"Mullin!"

"Yes, miss?"

"Is the cabby still here?"

"He said he would wait out front for an answer, miss."

I thought for a minute, then gathered up my coat and bag. "Tell Mr. Hunter to wait for me. I shouldn't be too long."

I dashed out the door, gave the driver the address listed on the note, and leaped into the waiting cab. Smoothing the note, I read it again. *Cassandra: Come to this address as soon as you can. It is urgent and concerns a matter of grave importance. –G*

Obviously Griffin must have news of the two men who were so bent on harming him.

I was right, as I often am, only I had it twisted around, as, alas, I frequently do. When the cab pulled up at a decrepit looking house, it was Percy who opened the door for me. He had acquired another pistol, I noticed with dismay as he pushed it into my ribs.

"Now don't give me any trouble, and I won't have to use this," he said in a low, mean tone, pulling me inside before I could do so much as squawk.

We climbed a grimy and rotting staircase several flights to the top floor, stopping at a door blistered with age. I made a covert search for some sort of weapon that I might use to defend myself, but saw only refuse. The man with the gold tooth opened the door, rubbing his hands together gleefully at my appearance as Percy ushered me inside. "I've often said the best road is the straightest. You didn't have a problem with the lady, did you Percy?"

"None at all, Merlin."

"Merlin?" I asked, startled by his name. "I thought you were William?"

He laughed and took a step closer to me. "Mum had her fancies, she did. As do I—"

There was a note in his voice that was difficult to ignore, but I did my best. I raised my chin and reminded myself that I had triumphed over him on several occasions and although I was unarmed, I was not helpless. "Would you tell me why you have been following me? And why you have twice attacked Mr. St. John and myself? And why you have brought me, against my will, here now?"

I left out the solitary attacks on Griffin, feeling I had asked enough questions for the moment.

"Ah," Merlin said stepping even closer and running a finger along my ear. "Now that is a complicated story. It may take some time to tell, a very long time."

Pistol or no pistol, I was not going to tolerate being intimidated in such a manner. I reached out to slap him but he grabbed my arm and spun me around, my arm twisted painfully behind my back.

"Fun and games later," he hissed in my ear. "Right now I have a little business to take care of."

An entryway and several rooms led off the hallway, but Merlin ignored most of them as he marched me to the end and pushed me into a small, musty room with a warning not to try anything. He ignored my requests for information and demands to be set free with equal disdain, slamming the door and locking it quickly.

"I insist that you let me out!" I yelled, rattling the doorknob and pounding on the door, but it did no good. My hand went automatically to my head, only to remember I had left in such a hurry I was not wearing a hat.

"Damn." I pulled out a hairpin and looked at it critically. It would not do as a substitute lock pick. "Now what?"

I examined my prison. The furnishings consisted of a small iron bed with filthy bedding, a wooden chair that looked frail, and a chamber pot.

"Not a very inspiring collection," I mused, eyeing the skylight about ten feet above me. I had no ladder, unfortunately. "The first order of business obviously is to escape so I can warn Griffin."

I looked again at the skylight. If I could reach it, I could make my way along the roof and climb down the building. It was not a pleasing idea, but it was the only one that seemed remotely feasible. I was not about to try to force my way past two men, one of whom was armed.

Before I formulated a plan, footsteps echoed down the hallway toward my room. I snatched up the chamber pot and held it behind me, intent on using it as a weapon if the unsavory William/Merlin chose to attack.

The door opened. "Here's some water for you, miss. We wouldn't want you to croak before you've been claimed, now would we?"

"Claimed?" I asked, ignoring the dirty bowl of water that Percy thrust toward me. "Claimed by whom?"

"By your betrothed, of course," he cackled.

Still laughing, he closed the door, turning the key in the lock even before I could make it to the door.

I waited a few minutes to make sure he would not be back, using the time to contemplate his comments. "Now is not the time to waffle. Griffin has to be warned."

Half an hour later I perched on the end of the bed, upended onto its foot and secured to a nail in the wall with strips of the filthy bedding. I used a plank from the bed to balance myself, straightening up slowly to my full height. The bed creaked and wobbled, but the makeshift rope held. I reached up the remaining few feet to the skylight and opened it. I took as firm a grip as I could manage, breathed deeply, and hauled myself upward.

It took several tries, but eventually I hoisted myself up so that my upper half lay outside of the skylight while my legs flailed below. Bits of rock and debris ground painfully into my arms and torso as I pulled myself forward and sat panting next to the skylight. There was no way I could undo the makeshift ladder, so I closed the skylight as quietly as possible and surveyed the rooftop.

It was not very promising, but at least the section I was on was flat. The sides sloped down to a narrow ledge with windows leading into the floor I had just left. As I was assessing the situation, a cab rattled on the street, sending me over to the edge of the roof to peer down on the arrival. If it was Griffin, I would try yelling down a warning before the thugs had him in their grasp.

Although my position on the roof made it difficult to see who had arrived in the cab, I could tell it wasn't Griffin—this man was much thinner, and probably a few inches shorter. I was about to turn back to the door when I noticed an open window on the floor below.

"How very thoughtful of Mr. Jones," I muttered to myself as I avoided the pots and loose bricks until I stood directly above the window. I tried leaning over the edge as far as I could, but to no avail—I could not see in the window. A glance across the street relieved the worry that some concerned resident might come out to see why a woman was on the roof opposite. There were very few people on the street, and those present did not look up.

The beginnings of a plan formed in my head. Before leaving the building, I felt it prudent to ascertain what Merlin and his friend had in mind regarding Griffin. I went back to the skylight and paced off the length to the open window. It looked to be halfway down the hall from the room in which I had been placed.

"All well and fine, but if I can't get to it…" The words trailed off as I glanced down at the ledge. It was about six inches wide—

wide enough to walk along if I were very careful. I made my way down to the corner of the house and examined the drainpipe. It seemed to be somewhat loose, but I thought it would hold me long enough to get to the ledge. From there, it was only four windows down to the open one. I gnawed on my lip as I considered my options.

I don't recall the entire trip down the drainpipe to the floor below, although certain moments would reside in my memory with brilliant clarity for many years. Make it I did, however, and I have never been so glad to cling to the side of a building as I was then. With my back to the street four stories below, I shuffled my way down the ledge grasping whatever bits of the building I could find, peering intently into each blank window before I passed it. I approached the open window hesitantly, carefully looking in the dirty window before I slipped in. Like the other rooms, this one was unlit and empty, save for some broken furniture.

I knocked my shin against something wooden, and stifled an oath as I hobbled to the door. Opening the door slightly, I squinted through the crack. The hallway was empty, lit only by the single gas jet I had seen upon my arrival. Slipping out of the room, I tiptoed down the hallway toward the front door. Voices murmured ahead, causing me to hold my breath as I crept closer to the sound. The door to the sitting room was open, providing a perfect opportunity to eavesdrop. I hugged the wall and stopped just outside the door.

"I'm not showin' you anythin' 'til you show us the money."

That sounded like Percy speaking. I expected to hear Merlin in response to his statement, and almost had to bite my lip to keep my startled response from being spoken aloud.

"How do I know you haven't damaged her?" Freddy asked.

My stomach turned upon itself, fear fighting anger as I struggled to keep from throwing open the door and asking him what he thought he was doing. Only the thought of Griffin waiting to fall into this trap kept me silent.

"She's all right, although we had to give him a little tap on the head to keep him quiet."

"I don't care about him so long as he's out of the way. I just want to make sure there's nothing apparently wrong with the girl when the clergyman comes."

Girl? Clergyman? Freddy's words had me concerned, but I ignored them to worry over Merlin's reference to a man. Could it be that Griffin—

"She'll be right as rain. Locked up safe she is, with no way out," said Merlin, interrupting my unpleasant musing.

Except the roof, I thought to myself with no little smugness.

"You have the stuff?" Percy asked.

"What stuff? Oh, the laudanum? Yes, I have it here."

"Give it over. I want to give the gent another dose in case 'e wakes up. It took all we 'ad to get 'im up here."

"You can have it later, after I'm done with the girl." Freddy sounded annoyed.

A horrible picture formed in my mind as I listened. The mention of the opiate, myself, and a clergyman settled into a nauseating scene in which I was doped just enough to be married to Freddy, apparently with my full consent. If Freddy had a clergyman in his pocket—and Percy and Merlin as witnesses—it would be difficult for me to deny my willingness in the ceremony.

I had to find out if Griffin was the man they were talking about. I crept forward silently and peered into the room. The men were sitting around a fireplace that ran perpendicular to the door. Percy was in a high-backed chair with his back to me, and Merlin was stretched out on a couch that faced the door, but he watched closely as Freddy gazed out of the window. Next to the door was a battered sideboard.

My spirits picked up at the sight of it, for on the top lay a ring with three keys. I knelt on the floor behind Percy's chair and inched my way forward, keeping one eye out for Freddy and Merlin. My hand snaked up the side of the furniture, touched metal, and closed over the keys with painstaking slowness. I held my breath, hoping the keys wouldn't clank together.

Freddy turned his head to speak with Merlin and I froze, not wanting any movement to catch his peripheral vision.

"Blast the man. When did you say he would be here? It's already half past and I don't have all day to wait around. If I don't get to Roget's by mid-day, I might as well leave the country."

Merlin laughed unpleasantly. "I've heard that old Roget employs men who know how to break bones without leaving a mark."

Freddy shuddered, then asked petulantly, "Are you sure the girl's all right? She has to look feasible, you know."

"I'm sure, I'm sure. If you like we can check, although you aren't getting her until we are paid."

Freddy made an annoyed noise and turned his head back towards the window. Merlin tipped his head up to blow a smoke ring. With the keys grasped firmly in my fist, I crawled quietly out of the room into the hallway.

Down the hallway I went, trying the doors gently. There were only two locked—mine, and the one across the hall from it. I turned the key in the lock and slipped into the room.

There were wooden slats across the window, but enough light filtered in for me to recognize the still form lying on the floor. I rushed to Griffin's side and examined his head carefully. He had a lump on his temple and a small trickle of blood, but no bones gave under the anxious pressure of my fingers.

I sighed with relief and hurried back to the door to look out into the hallway. No one was in sight, so I closed the door quietly and locked it from the inside. Tucking the keys into my bodice, I went back to Griffin and tried to bring him around.

CHAPTER TWENTY-ONE

Kisses and endearments didn't do Griffin any good, but it made me feel quite a bit better, although worry about the amount of laudanum he received soon had me gravely concerned. I'd seen people under the influence of that opiate, but never had I seen someone so completely unconscious.

"Forgive me, darling," I whispered as I smacked Griffin soundly on the cheek. He stirred briefly, then fell back into a stupor.

I slapped him again. His eyelids flickered, but no more. I looked around the room for some water, but there was nothing. I returned to slapping him, trying desperately for ten minutes to rouse him. At the end of that time I sat back on my heels and let a tear trickle down my cheek. I could not wake him for more than a few seconds at a time. I tried sitting him up, thinking I could half carry him out of the room, but he was too heavy for me in his drugged state.

A door banged down the hall and I jumped up, terrified. I ran to the door and listened, but heard nothing. Cautiously, and with a glance back at my recumbent prince, I slipped out, locked his door, and dashed across the hallway to my own room. The key turned in the lock with a squeak, but I managed to make it in and lock the door from the inside before I heard approaching footsteps.

I stood with my ear pressed against the door.

"'Ow do I know where the blasted keys went? I'm not the one as was in charge of them. That's Merlin's job."

The doorknob to my room rattled and there was a sharp knock. "You in there, miss?"

I moved back from the door, and said in my most arrogant voice, "Yes, I am, and I am getting tired of being held in here. I demand that you let me out!"

"Not yet, miss. Your time will come soon enough."

"What about the other door?" I heard Merlin ask.

"It's locked too."

"Well, come on then, don't just stand there like you have all day, let's find those damned keys."

Their voices rumbled back down the hallway and I heaved a sigh of relief. I had been worried that they might have a duplicate set, but was heartened by their response. I just hoped they would not think of a skeleton key before I could get Griffin out.

I had to wait some time before I could go back to Griffin's room; Percy and Merlin were all over the top floor of the building searching for the missing keys. Judging by the acrimonious comments that were being bandied about by Freddy, no one had yet thought of a skeleton key. Taking my chance at a rare quiet period, I left my room, locked it from the outside lest they decided to check on me, and dashed into Griffin's room, locking the door again from the inside.

I managed to rouse him by resorting to several sharp slaps, and had him in a sitting position with his head between his knees when I heard voices outside the door. After unnecessarily cautioning the barely conscious Griffin to be quiet, I crept to the door and listened. What I heard turned my blood to ice.

"Well, someone must have a pass key! Go downstairs and check, you idiots."

"Now then, Mister Black, there's no reason to be calling us names. I'll just send Percy downstairs to the manager, like, and ask politely for a key. She likes you, doesn't she, mate?"

Percy sniggered.

"Good. Fine. Just do it! I'm already an hour late for my appointment, and Mr. Hope won't wait around here forever."

I assumed Freddy was talking about the clergyman. Crawling back to Griffin, I found him with his head sunk down on his chest, sleeping.

"Griffin, you must pull yourself together," I hissed, smacking him on the cheek.

"Huh? What? Cassandra?"

"Yes, my love, it's me. You have to stay awake and concentrate."

He blinked at me groggily, and I slapped him again. His head snapped back, his eyes opened wide but unfocused. I reached out to slap him again, but his hand shot up and caught mine.

"Listen to me, Griffin, this is very important." I spoke with my face close to his, peering intently into his beautiful, clouded amber eyes. "We are being held prisoner. We have to get out, now. Do you understand?"

He blinked at me a few times, then said thickly, "Prisoner. I understand."

I helped him to his feet, which were none too steady, and unlocked the door. There was no one in the hallway, and only occasional sounds from the sitting room. I put both hands on Griffin's head and shook it until he started to protest.

"Be very quiet. The men are in that room, and they are armed. We have to go past them without them seeing us. Can you do that?"

His eyes were still confused and clouded, but he nodded his head. I grasped his hand and started to lead him from the room, but stopped when someone pounded on the door to the flat. Pushing Griffin back into his room, I held the door open a fraction and watched as Merlin emerged from the sitting room to answer the door. I expected to see Percy—my jaw dropped when I saw a familiar face.

"William Jones, I want to speak with you!"

It was Annie, *my* Annie, come to confront her paramour.

"Why haven't you answered my letters?" she demanded, shaking her fist and unleashing a torrent of angry comments.

Merlin backed up, his hands outstretched, obviously trying to defend himself against the tongue-lashing Annie was giving him. He held up a hand, said something too quiet for me to hear, and went into the sitting room, closing the door behind him.

I didn't have time to dither. "Annie," I hissed, poking my head out of the door.

She looked up, her hands on her hips, the very picture of a righteous, indignant woman. Surprise flooded her face as she saw me.

"Shhhhh!" I cautioned. "Don't tell him you know I'm here, but I need you to help me."

The sitting room door opened and Merlin appeared, his back to me as he carefully closed the door behind him. I peeked out carefully.

"Now Annie, my love," Merlin started to say in a placatory tone.

"Don't you 'Annie my love' me," she warned. "You have me in the family way! Why haven't you answered my letters?"

"Letters? I didn't receive your letters, my sweet—"

"Not much, you didn't! Oh! Oh!" She suddenly grasped her chest.

"What's wrong, Annie?" Merlin seemed more concerned in watching the door to the sitting room than with Annie.

"It's my heart. The doctor said I should rest when it acts up."

"You go home and have a good rest then, love."

"I can't—" she panted, clutching her chest harder. "The doctor says I have to lay down right away when I have these spells. It might be fatal!"

If Annie ever chose to go on the stage, I would be happy to support her endeavor by any means required. I had no idea she was such a natural-born actress, but the performance she gave Merlin was outstanding. Unsure if she understood the urgency of my message, I was half worried that she really *was* suffering from some sort of heart ailment.

Merlin settled her in one of the free rooms. "I'll look in on you in a few minutes," he said, returning to the sitting room. He didn't even glance toward our room.

A soft tap on the door alerted me to Annie's presence. "What are you doing here, miss—oh, isn't that—"

"Annie," I spoke in a low voice but with an urgency that was hard to mistake. "Your friend Mr. Jones has kidnapped us. Mr. St. John and me, that is. He's drugged Griffin, and I don't think I can get him out by myself. You have to help us."

"William did? *My* William?"

"Your William. Will you help us?"

Her face set in a grim expression. "Tell me what you want me to do, miss, and I'll do it."

I hugged her. "I'm just worried that Percy will return from sweet-talking the manager before I can get Griffin out. I need you to cause a distraction that will focus the attention of the men away from the door so I can get him past it without being seen. Can you do that?"

"I'll make a scene that William won't forget in a long time," she promised. "It will be a pleasure to tell him what I think of his ways!"

She slipped out and closed the door. I turned back to Griffin and alternately shook and slapped him into semi-consciousness. He staggered against me drunkenly as I tried to keep him awake and moving.

I could hear the raised voices even through the door. Opening it quietly, I gave Griffin one last shake and, putting my shoulder under his arm, led him down the hall. We came to the open door of the sitting room where I leaned him against the wall and hissed to stand still. I peeked around the corner of the door and saw Annie in action. She ranted, she yelled, she threw bits of crockery at the men. Bless her heart, she had all three men crouched in the far corner as she aimed a large jug at them. Whirling around, she slammed shut the door to the sitting room. A loud crash indicated the jug had fulfilled its destiny.

I grabbed Griffin and dragged him towards the door. He stumbled and fell against me heavily, but we managed to get out of the flat before the door to the sitting room opened. I didn't stop to sigh with relief at our escape, knowing that Percy would be on his way up any moment. We started down the stairs cautiously, Griffin leaning on me and stumbling because his legs weren't working as they should. I worried that Annie might have put herself in danger by helping us, and was relieved when I heard her voice echo down the stairwell.

"That's the last you'll see of me, William Jones," she shouted.

Griffin and I made it down two floors when I heard someone starting up the stairs. Annie was above, clattering her way noisily downward, muttering as she descended.

Panicked, I hurried down the passageway, pulling Griffin into the deepest shadows I could find. His head lolled sleepily, but he was still standing.

I roused him quickly. "Griffin, put your arms around me."

"Mmmm?"

I lifted one of his arms onto my shoulders just as Percy paused on the landing.

"Oooh, Basil, stop that!" I squealed with a high pitched giggle, and rubbed my hands through Griffin's hair. Poor man, he lifted his head and tried to focus his eyes on me, but failed. I peeked over his shoulder as Percy looked hesitantly toward us.

"Some people don't have nothing better to do than watch them that are enjoying themselves. Get on with you and let those two have some privacy," Annie sniffed in a disgusted tone as she passed him on her way down.

Percy, wilting under her comments, continued up the stairs.

With Annie's help, we stumbled our way down the remaining two flights and out the front door. Angry shouts and oaths from above informed us that the pass key had been used and our escape was known.

"Blast," I swore as Griffin tripped over the debris and rubbish that littered the street. He was leaning heavily on me as we stumbled along. "I'm not going to be able to last for any great distance, Annie."

"What do you want me to do?"

I looked around frantically for a spot to hide. We half-dragged Griffin around the corner where I spied a side yard, similar to the one at my aunt's house, although this one was full of trash bins.

"An excellent hiding place. You go look for a cab, while I hide Griffin."

Annie took off at a smart trot while I hauled Griffin down into the side yard, and tucked him away behind two bins, pillowing his head with my coat. After covering his legs with the cleanest debris

I could find, I was satisfied that no one could see him from the street.

With no place for me to hide, and shouts from the street indicating the nearness of the thugs, I had no choice but to set up a false trail to keep them from discovering Griffin. I dashed across the street just ahead of Merlin, who had rounded the corner at a run. He spotted me, yelled, and the chase was on.

I have no doubt that Merlin, under ordinary circumstances, could out-run me any day, but the desperate need to keep him away from the side yard that held Griffin gave me a speed I have not yet duplicated. I picked up my skirts and raced down the sidewalk and around to the next street, Merlin in close pursuit. A man and woman walked towards me. I skidded to a halt before the man and begged him for help.

"I'm being chased—a man has killed my mother and now he's coming after me."

Merlin rounded the corner, slowing to a walk at the sight of other people.

"There he is," I screamed, pointing.

The woman clutched her man and tried to pull him away.

"There's a reward for his capture!" I yelled, pushing the hapless man at my pursuer. He looked hesitant, but started towards Merlin. I turned and ran in the other direction, taking the next left. Running straight at me was Percy. I spun around and jetted across the street, narrowly missing a dray loaded with fish. Percy pounded after me as I desperately looked for any refuge. At the next intersection Merlin leaped out. He narrowly missed me, and collided with Percy, sending the pair of them down in a tangle of legs. I raced down the street, spun around the next corner and saw the shadow of an open door. Racing through it, I closed it quickly and leaned against it, breathless and gasping for air.

The door was too solid to hear through, but I gave Percy and Merlin enough time to check the street and move on before I opened it.

"Here, what's all this?" A man with a butcher's apron emerged from a room behind me.

"My apologies, wrong house," I said, slipping out the door.

I peered around the corner and, seeing no one familiar, ran down the street the way I had just come. I hoped Annie had found a cab by now, not sure how much longer I could keep up the dog and hare performance.

One street away from where I had left Griffin a cab moved slowly.

"Thank heavens," I panted to myself and dashed up to it, ready to heap praise on Annie's head.

"Why, cousin—" a familiar voice drawled.

"You!" I gasped, snatching my hand back from the door.

"You look distraught," Freddy said, all charm and concern as he opened the cab's door. "Let me help you in."

He stepped out of the cab, his arm extended to me. I grabbed the cravat around his neck and yanked him forward, throwing him off balance. Blessing my decision to wear my stout walking boots, I stamped on Freddy's foot and kicked him hard on the knee, then harder in another, more vulnerable spot.

"Here, now, miss," the cabby cautioned as Freddy screamed, clutching his groin as he toppled to the ground.

"This man is a criminal," I cried, kicking Freddy in the ribs. "You must help me, he attempted to abduct another man and myself."

"Well—" the cabby hesitated, watching as Freddy writhed on the ground.

"I'll pay you twice the standard fare."

"Get in," the cabby said.

I showed him the yard where I had Griffin hidden.

"But ma'am, there's no one there," he pointed out as I scrambled out of the cab. "Just some trash."

I peeled the refuse off of Griffin's legs and moved one of the bins.

"Why, bless me, there is a man there."

I hated to do it, knowing his cheeks would be bruised in the morning, but I slapped Griffin a few more times. His eyes flew opened but they were still out of focus. I shook his head until he

251

protested, then the cabby and I got him on his feet. Once we had Griffin settled in the cab, I told him to drive around the area.

"But that gentleman—" He pointed down the street to where Freddy was crawling toward us.

"He can take care of himself. I'm looking for my maid. She went to find us a cab and I cannot leave without her."

"No cabs around here, ma'am. If she's looking for one she'll have to go up to the Crescent."

We set off for the Crescent. I watched fearfully out of the window, but only saw Merlin and Percy once, from the distance of a block. I doubted if they could see into the cab, but ordered the cabby to pick up the pace.

We found Annie about ten blocks away. She was exhausted and on her way back to help me, having been unable to find a cab.

"I think we did it," I said, sinking back against the ratty seat, finally able to relax. Griffin's head lolled over onto my shoulder. I stroked it and smiled to myself at his soft murmurs. Annie sat on the other side and watched us with just a hint of her dimples.

The debate about where to take him raged within me as we drove away from the slums. I was torn between tending to him myself, and letting his family, who must surely be worried about him by now, take care of him. "I suppose it's only right to take him to his home," I said after much internal debate, and gave the cabby Griffin's address.

"I can take you there, ma'am, but it's quite a ways away. More than two shillings. I'll have to ask you to show me that you have the fare," the cabby said apologetically.

"Oh, money," I sighed. Percy had taken my bag and I had nothing in my skirt pockets.

"Annie?"

She shook her head. "Just a few coppers."

We both looked at Griffin. I searched his pockets until I found a collection of coins that satisfied the cabby; what he must have thought of us, I shudder to think. I was disheveled, hot, and dirty from my experience on the roof and running around the streets.

Griffin looked disreputable with a bloodied head and drunken appearance. Annie alone was presentable.

The Sherringham's footman flinched when he saw me standing on the steps with my tangled hair and a torn, dirty dress, but responded to my question. "Lady Helena and Lady Sherringham are out, but Lord Sherringham is in, Miss Whitney."

I looked at the semi-reclined figure of my hero in the cab, and my heart revolted at leaving him in the care of his brother. "Tell Miss Helena that Mr. St. John has been taken ill, and is recovering at the home of Mr. Joshua Garner."

"Yes, miss," he said haughtily, sniffing in disgust.

I gave the cabby the address, and in a relatively short time we were home. Mullin had the door opened before I could step down from the cab.

"Miss Cassandra! The family has been most distressed about your absence," he said with a look of strong disapproval at my appearance.

"It's a long story, Mullin, and not one I want to tell on the street. Is Theodore about? I need help. Mr. St. John is ill, and Annie and I are exhausted."

In the end, it took more than Theodore and Mullin to get Griffin in the house and into a guest room. The laudanum was starting to wear off and it left him antagonistic, causing him to fight groggily, but with great strength. I did the best I could to calm him, but by the time we settled him in a bedroom, Theodore had a black eye, Mullin had a loose tooth, and Robert walked with a pronounced limp.

We propped him up on pillows, and while we waited for the doctor to come, I sat on the edge of the bed and tried to pour coffee into him. More coffee ended up *on* him than *in* him, but we made a valiant effort.

Dr. Melrose, a darling round man who was my sister's physician, came at once. After eyeing the available footmen, he ordered everyone but Robert out of the room, saying he might need Robert's assistance to conduct a thorough examination.

I dashed to my own room and had a perfunctory wash, then spent the rest of the time pacing the hallway. Periodic sounds of crashing and harsh yelling emitted from Griffin's room, sending me more than once to knock on the door and ask if my help was needed. Joshua did his best to calm my fears, but Mabel insisted on knowing exactly what had happened after I ran out so early, and why Annie accompanied us home.

"That doesn't matter right now," I snapped. "Not until I know—until I know—oh, damn!" I kicked at a chair that insisted on getting in my way.

"Cassandra Jane! I will not have such language in my house," Mabel started to lecture, but she was cut short when Joshua gently guided her downstairs.

Loud voices in the hall drew my attention, and with a reluctant glance at the door to Griffin's room, I went to the head of the stairs. Standing in an arrogant posture before Joshua, Lord Sherringham was bellowing at the top of his lungs.

"I won't have it! You have no right to hold my brother against his will. I demand that you hand him over immediately!"

The tone of his voice grated on my already sensitive nerves, but it took me no longer than a second to commit myself to action. I marched down the stairs, my jaw tight, my eyes narrowed, and my fists clenched.

"Lord Sherringham," I said in a firm but frigid voice, "your brother is currently receiving the attentions of a doctor. You will kindly lower your voice."

He spun around at my words and turned a hideous shade of purple. "You—you—" he sputtered incoherently.

"Yes, it is me, and I am in no mood for one of your arguments. Until the doctor informs us it is safe to move him, Griffin will remain where he is. We will keep you notified of any changes in his physical status."

"How dare you speak to me that way, you harlot! You are to blame for my brother's attack! How dare you stand there and pretend to protect him. I am removing him this instant to my own home, where I can be sure he will be looked after properly. Move out of my way before I take my whip to you." He raised his riding crop in a threatening manner.

There are a few moments in my life about which I feel an overwhelming sense of pride; this was not one of the brightest, but it was one of the most satisfying. I took two steps forward, snatched the crop out of his hand, and snapped it over the banister.

"If you dare to lift one finger towards Griffin," I threatened, "*one finger*, it will be the last thing you do."

Joshua told me later that at that moment he was afraid—afraid that I would attack Lord Sherringham on the spot and that he would be unable to stop me. Joshua's description comes fairly close to the emotion I was feeling at the time.

Although he continued to bluster and demand, the steam had gone out Lord Sherringham's engine and he left after threatening to consult his solicitor. Taking the stairs two at a time, I ignored the protests of my shaking body and continued to pace the hallway outside Griffin's room until the doctor emerged at last. He was rather disheveled, but looked optimistic.

"His head—" I faltered.

"Ah, Miss Whitney. The patient is fine, nothing more than a mild concussion and an extreme case of laudanum overdose. After he sleeps it off he should be fit as a fiddle."

"Thank heavens. Is there something we should be doing? More coffee or other stimulants?"

"No, you've done just what I would have suggested. It's a good thing you got him moving when you did, though. The amount of laudanum he seems to have consumed, combined with the concussion, might have done him harm had he been left in a stupor."

My stomach lurched at the thought of my Griffin left to Merlin's mercy.

"What he needs most is to be allowed to rest. He's a little bit hostile right now, so you must be careful. For some reason he seems to think he must escape the house."

I thanked him and hurried into the room. Robert and Doctor Melrose had managed to undress Griffin and get him into bed with only minor damage to the various articles in the room. Robert was stooped down collecting bits of a broken jug.

"Don't worry about that, the maid will pick it up," I told him as I stopped at the bed. "Have you had the doctor look at your leg?"

Griffin lay with his eyes closed, a furrow between his brows. I tried to smooth it out, but his hand shot up and grabbed my wrist with a strength that was almost painful. His eyes opened at my gasp of pain. I was happy to see his lovely amber eyes were once again in focus, although it took a few minutes before he recognized me.

Robert slipped out of the room, saying he would get a compress for his knee, and I was left to sit with my fallen hero. I brushed back the hair from his temples and laid a hand alongside his cheek. "How do you feel?"

He looked at me for a few moments while the words filtered through his fogged brain. "Feel tired."

"I know, my poor darling. You lay there and rest. You're safe now."

I murmured endearments as he dropped into a restless sleep. After I was sure he was resting as comfortably as I could expect, I went downstairs to face the familial equivalent to the Spanish Inquisition.

Conversation stopped when I entered the sitting room, faces turning to me with ill-concealed expectation. I smiled wanly, refused a cup of tea, asked for one of coffee, and sank exhaustedly into a chair. Mabel glared at me, evidently still annoyed at my rudeness earlier. Joshua watched me patiently while Robert stood gazing forlornly out the window.

"We were kidnapped," I said in answer to the unspoken question.

The response was more heated than I had expected, and I closed my eyes until the exclamations were finished.

"Would you like to wait to tell us, my dear?"

"Thank you, Joshua, but I think I would rather tell you now. Griffin may need me later."

"Doctor Melrose said he would be fine in a day or two," offered Mabel, her anger apparently forgotten. "I don't think you have anything to worry about. Now, tell us about this kidnapping."

I went over the entire amazing episode, leaving out only the part concerning Freddy. I would deal with him later.

"My one concern now is whether or not we should contact the police," I finished wearily.

Joshua asked, "Can you identify the men who kidnapped you?"

"I know their first names, and I would recognize them again if I saw them."

"Hmm. How about the place you were held?"

"Probably not. It was near the river, I know that. But the exact street? No. The note I received was taken away from me, and I cannot remember the address."

"Well then," Joshua said, standing in front of a welcome afternoon fire, "I don't see what good the police will do. You can't identify the men, you can't identify the house in which you were held, and you don't even have the note that sent you on the journey."

Robert turned from the window, and agreed. "Even if you could identify the building, the kidnappers will be long gone."

I clutched the chair tightly, my head swimming. Robert's words seemed to be coming from a very long way away. An inky, dark pool loomed up before me.

"Delayed reaction," I heard someone say, and thought I heard Helena's voice just before my head went under the dark water.

CHAPTER TWENTY-TWO

"You startled me, you know. I've never had anyone swoon just because I entered a room." It *was* Helena I heard before I fainted. "You didn't say anything, either. You just toppled quietly to the floor, clutching a cup of coffee."

I summoned up a smile for her, although I was sure it wasn't a very brilliant specimen.

"Are you sure he's going to be all right?"

Helena was almost panic-stricken with concern about the state of her brother's health until we trouped upstairs together. Side-by-side we stood, watching him sleep.

"The doctor says he just needs to sleep. There's no real damage." A thought struck me, causing me to giggle under my breath. Helena looked askance at me, horrified that I could laugh in the face of her brother's brush with death. "Can you imagine what Griffin would have to say if he knew we were standing here watching him sleep?"

A smile stole across Helena's lips, and after she delivered a final kiss to his forehead, and I one to his adorable lips, we went downstairs.

Several hours later, the library was the scene of a domestic storm.

"No! I will not have it, Cassandra! You might be betrothed to the man, but it is beyond improper that you should spend the night in the same room with him."

I glanced at Joshua, hating to make a scene, but resolute. "I'm sorry to give you grief, Mabel, but that is not acceptable. Griffin has been severely drugged. I will not be able to sleep knowing he might have some sort of the reaction."

"The doctor said he would be fine."

"I don't care. I'm spending the night with him." I started to rise from the sofa.

"I will *not* have it!" Mabel yelled, startling Joshua. "No sister of mine will behave with such impropriety!"

"For heaven's sake, Mabel—the man was drugged almost to death!"

"I don't care! I refuse to allow you to shame us with such scandalous behavior. What if it got out? How would we hold up our heads?" she shouted.

"There is nothing we could do that we haven't already done," I yelled back.

Mabel gasped, and things pretty much went downhill after that, dissolving into one of our rare arguments that ended in hurtful accusations and slammed doors. I stormed up to my room and waited until she went to rail at Joshua for having such an unreasonable sister before slipping into Griffin's room, where I crawled into bed with him, my hand on his chest just because it made me feel better to have it there.

Griffin slept through the night and late into the morning. It wasn't until noon that I found him sitting up in bed, rubbing a hand over his stubbly cheeks.

"Ah, sleeping beauty awakens," I joked as I entered, turning to hail Annie as she left my room. "Send up some coffee, please. Lots of it."

"I thought I was dreaming," Griffin said, yawning, looking around the room. "What am I doing here?"

I sat carefully on the bed and ignored, as best I could, the large expanse of hairy chest in front of me. I reminded myself sternly that he was recovering from a head wound and overdose of opiate, and although he might enjoy the expressions of affection that I was so desirous of showing him, it would be better to wait until he had fully recovered.

"Do you remember anything about yesterday?" I asked, keeping my eyes fixed firmly on his face.

He frowned and rubbed his head, grimacing when he touched the injured spot. "Not much. I remember you, and a fat man who tried to take my clothes off." He looked down at himself, then pulled the blankets up modestly as a housemaid came in with coffee.

"Do you remember anything about being drugged, or hit on the head?" I asked as I poured him a cup.

"No. Just a bad dream about stairs."

I told him briefly what had happened. My narrative was interrupted frequently and punctuated with several outraged comments and scattered oaths throughout.

"Very well, I will promise that I will never again—"

"—under any circumstances—"

"I will never again under any circumstances climb out of a skylight, frolic on a roof, scramble down a drainpipe, or walk along six-inch ledges."

"And?" Griffin asked, glowering at me.

"Oh, nor will I use myself as bait of any sort. Are you happy now?"

"No. But tell me again what you said to Sherry."

I repeated it. His scowl faded and a little smile curled his lips. "I wish I had been there. He must be furious. I can't wait to see him."

Our eyes met and the smiles left both our faces. I placed my hand gently on his cheek. We sat like that for a moment, then he pulled me forward and onto his chest.

"I owe you my life," he whispered, kissing me gently.

"It wasn't quite as dramatic as that." My hands moved to his bare chest as his mouth claimed possession of mine, a moan of pleasure slipping from my lips as his tongue stirred the embers of a fire than never completely extinguished. Carefully, gently, slowly I pulled myself away from him. "You're not supposed to overextend yourself. The doctor said you must not make any quick or strenuous actions, lest it cause your head to hurt."

He protested, but I left him to get dressed by himself. Ten minutes after he came downstairs to the sitting room, Mullin entered, murmuring, "Lady Helena St. John...er..."

"It's all right, Mullin," I said, climbing off from Griffin's lap. I straightened my dress and tried to look like Griffin hadn't been in the middle of a detailed examination of my mouth, simultaneous with a tactile mapping of my upper person. "Helena! Here is the brave hero, all in one piece, as you can see."

"Yes, I can see he's feeling much better," she said with a smile as she kissed his cheek. Robert, who was behind her, grinned.

"Much," Griffin said, sliding me a glance that instantly set my heart beating faster.

I cleared my throat and tried to not think of how close we had come to being discovered in a far more embarrassing position. "Mabel and Joshua have taken the girls to the zoo. You'll stay for luncheon, I hope."

All three agreed, and before long, we were sitting at the dining table, a cold repast before us.

"The time has come for all of us to be completely honest," I told them as I passed around cold chicken.

"Honest? I've always been honest with you," Helena said.

"Of course you have; I never doubted that. My comment was aimed primarily at your brother. It's time he tells us what he suspects."

Griffin grumbled a bit at that, but in the end agreed. "I will, but only after you explain what you think has been happening."

"Very well. I shall begin by telling you all about my cousin's role in this."

"Your cousin?" Helena asked. Griffin scowled at me.

I quickly explained Freddy's part in the kidnapping. "I am fairly confident that his plan was to marry me after he had drugged me just enough to make me not quite lucid."

Griffin muttered a few choice phrases that I thought best to ignore.

"But that's illegal," Helena protested.

"Of course it is, but I now realize I have been shockingly misled as to Freddy's true nature. But there is more to it than that—I'm convinced that he has some connection with Lord Sherringham."

Helena laid down her fork, shocked at my comments. "My dear Cassandra, just because I saw your cousin speaking with Harold, it doesn't follow that he had a part in your kidnapping!"

"I'm lost—what does the earl have to do with you two being kidnapped?" asked Robert.

We all looked at Griffin.

"There isn't any proof," Griffin said to me, acknowledging the suspicion in my mind.

"No, but the connection is there. Helena saw them talking at that costume ball." I smiled at the recollection. "You made a charming Arab, you know."

He grinned in return. "I thought we made quite a pair."

"Oh, come now, you didn't know who I was until Helena told you."

"I didn't tell him," Helena reminded me. Robert looked confused.

"I knew you as soon as I saw you. There are not too many women with brilliant green eyes, and yours, sweetheart, are unmistakable."

I smiled at his compliment and continued with a more sober train of thought. "To answer your question Robert, it has been my belief for some time that someone means to…well, to be blunt, to kill Griffin."

Helena gasped in horror, but took the news better than I had expected. "I knew it! But, why? Why would anyone want to harm you?"

"The most common reasons are for gain, love, or revenge," I mumbled as I fought with a tough piece of chicken. I looked up and saw I had the attention of the table. Turning to Griffin, I set down my fork and knife and asked, "Who would benefit by your death?"

"Helena mostly, and probably Harold."

"Do you have a will?"

"No. I've been meaning to make one, but just haven't found the opportunity."

"If you were to die in your current state, your estate would likely be divided equally between Helena and your brother; at worst it would go to Lord Sherringham in its entirety."

"Possibly." He frowned.

"Helena, you told me once that you inherited from your mother. Who controls your money until you are of age?"

"Harold does. Oh, and there is another trustee, Oliver Hope."

"And if you marry, is your fortune settled on you?"

She blushed and only just refrained from glancing at Robert.

"No. I won't have it until I'm twenty-five."

Something niggled in the back of my mind, but I couldn't pinpoint it.

"I don't understand the purpose of your questions, Cassandra. What are you trying to say?" Robert asked.

I ignored it and turned back to Griffin. "Why would he want you dead? He's got everything, a title, an ancestral home, respect, position, a house in town—"

"Debts up to his knees," Griffin interrupted. "There is no money from Rosewood, and he has run through what little money Letitia brought to the marriage. The house in town is mine, not Sherry's. I bought it when his creditors forced him to sell it."

"The house is yours? Does your brother have a house?"

Their heads swinging in unison between Griffin and me as if they were at a tennis match, Helena and Robert watched us in stunned silence.

"He had Rosewood, but that was destroyed, and all that's left is three hundred acres of land leased for the next forty years."

"If the house had not burned," I said absently, "it might have kept him from coveting your income."

He looked at me oddly, his mouth twitching. "You should know the worst if you're going to marry into the family. I don't have any proof, but I've always believed that Sherry burned the house down himself."

"Griffin!" cried Helena, clearly unable to comprehend what her brother was saying.

"I'm sorry Helena, but it's time you know the truth, too. Sherry always was a little different, and he loathed having to share Rosewood with us. My father specified in his will that Rosewood always be our home as well as Sherry's, Cassandra. He hated that. It wasn't too bad when I was at school, but when I came home—"

"I can't believe it. Do you know what you are saying?" Helena asked.

"He knows, Helena," I said sadly, wishing I could shield her from this heartbreak. "But you must admit, it fits. Lord Sherringham is an important person in the House of Lords but has no means and no house, living in his brother's home; I can only imagine what that would do to a man of his immense pride."

Helena had tears in her eyes. "But to kill Griffin—our own brother—he couldn't do that!"

"No, I agree with you there. That's why he had to find someone to do the job for him. With Griffin out of the way, he would inherit...a sizable fortune?" I looked the question at Griffin, who nodded wearily. I forestalled the urge to kiss him silly. "I have a suspicion your brother has been less than honest with your inheritance, as well, Helena. When was the last time you had an accounting?"

"I—I don't pay attention to those things," she mumbled miserably to her plate.

"What about the other trustee? Wouldn't he notice if Helena's brother were embezzling funds?" Robert asked.

"I hardly ever see him," Helena answered.

"Hrmph. I think it's time someone had a look at your trust, Helena. I'll speak to Hope about it in the morning."

She smiled gratefully at Griffin. We talked the situation over for a while longer, but didn't come to any conclusions. Robert and Griffin were all for immediately confronting Lord Sherringham, but Helena and I cautioned them against doing so.

"After all, we don't have any proof," I pointed out. "Nothing but a few suppositions and coincidences. As Joshua mentioned earlier, we don't know anything other than the first names of the thugs, or where they took us. The police would laugh at such an unsubstantial accusation, especially when it targets an important person like Lord Sherringham."

Everyone agreed with that.

"What we need is evidence," Griffin said, frowning at the orange he held in his hands. "I think I can get that."

"How?" Helena and I asked together.

"I've been thinking about it, and I believe I know the reason you were kidnapped as well as me. Yesterday, no, it was the day before yesterday, I told Sherry we were engaged."

"Engaged?" Helena gasped, leaping up to hug me. "Now I shall truly have you for a sister. Oh, I am so happy!"

I stared at Griffin, astonishment uppermost in my mind as Robert congratulated us both, and Helena kissed her brother. I decided to keep to myself the observation that I hadn't actually agreed to marriage, feeling it was best to deal with the threats hanging over us first.

"I take it Lord Sherringham was not pleased with this news?" I asked Griffin when Helena and Robert sat down again.

"You could say that. He was enraged and tried to forbid me marrying you, but I told him to mind his own business."

"So, he would want to get rid of Cassandra as well as you? Why?" Robert asked.

"Because he knew one of the first things I would do would be to make my home ready for my bride. That would mean he and Letitia would have to leave, since they would refuse to tolerate Cassandra's presence. I'm sorry, sweetheart. I didn't mean that to sound so harsh."

I smiled at the look of concern in his beautiful eyes. "I understand. You are quite right, they would see me as a threat, a thorn in Lord Sherringham's side that he could not possibly tolerate."

"But why did they need to kidnap you?" Helena asked.

"I'm not absolutely certain your brother is guilty of that particular crime. My cousin Freddy is deeply in debt. He has been proposing to me almost on a daily basis." I interrupted myself and turned to Griffin. "What or who is Roget's?"

"Hmm? Roget's? Moneylenders."

"That would make sense. If Freddy was being pressed to make good his debts, he would be desperate to find an easy way out. I've always been fond of him, and can only assume that he thought I would be happy to accept him on the basis of that affection. Once we were married, he would have access to my money and be able to pay off his debts."

"How terrible!" Helena shuddered.

I looked into Griffin's endlessly deep eyes. "Yes, it would be terrible."

His frown deepened. "That means both your cousin and Sherry have employed the same men—a situation that's far too unlikely to be coincidental. There must be a connection between Merlin Black and Sherry."

Everyone looked at me expectantly. I hated to disappoint them but had to admit I didn't have the slightest idea of an answer. "I agree, there has to be something there, something the two have in common, but what it is…well, your guess is as good as mine."

"We just need to reason it out." Griffin rubbed his eyes. "You overheard your cousin talking to the two men who attacked us twice—three times if you count the assault on me at home—"

"Possibly a fourth and fifth time, as well," I interrupted, looking at Helena.

"Oh?"

"There was the bag snatching episode," I reminded him.

"And the white slavers," Helena added. "Don't forget about them."

"White slavers?" Griffin asked, looking incredulous.

"Er…it seemed a plausible theory at the time," I said, clearing my throat and ignoring his and Robert's laughter.

"All right, so now we have five attacks. Two on you and Helena, one on me alone, and two on you and me together. It doesn't make sense. Either that or I was hit harder than I thought."

"No," I agreed slowly. "I think it's clear now that there were two distinct campaigns of violence against us, one targeting you with a very serious intent, and one focused on Helena and me that is really nothing more than a mild annoyance. But who is behind the latter? Surely Freddy has nothing to gain by frightening us…" The words froze on my lips as my eyes met Griffin's. He nodded.

"Oh! He wouldn't dare!"

"It looks like he did."

"Did what?" Helena asked.

My lips thinned. "He tried to scare me into marrying him. That rotter! Well, that explains a great deal."

"But not the connection between him and Sherry," Griffin said wearily.

He was looking decidedly tired, so after making him promise he would, under no circumstances, confront his brother or otherwise endanger his life, the St. Johns went home; Helena to fret, and Griffin to do a covert search of his brother's papers for proof of his nefarious activities.

I decided my time should be spent in a productive manner.

I sat in the library and worried.

CHAPTER TWENTY-THREE

The following day I received a note from Mrs. Heywood informing me that she had been released from prison, and asking if I could stop by and see her the next morning, as she had something of importance to discuss with me.

The day passed slowly, the hours dragging by at an interminable pace. I was unsettled, and paced aimlessly around the sitting room, unable to stay in one spot for more than a few minutes.

"Cassandra, for heaven's sake, you are making me nervous! Sit down," Mabel complained, craning her neck as I passed her for the tenth time.

I sat down and watched her work on her embroidery.

"And don't stare at me, that makes me even more nervous." She looked up from the pinafore. "What's wrong with you? You're not normally restless like this."

I stood, too fretful to sit any longer, and went to the window to look out at the overcast morning. "I feel like something is hanging over my head, like I am waiting for something to happen. I feel...unsettled."

She went back to her work. "Go pay a call. Or read a book."

I stared out the window, uneasy.

"Perhaps you could invite Mr. St. John for lunch?"

"He's busy today, writing an article for the Royal Geographic Society. I plan to visit Helena later, but she is gone this morning."

"With Robert?"

"Yes, they have gone riding."

I soon grew tired of answering Mabel's questions and listening to her talk about the trials of motherhood. In an attempt to shake myself free from the unpleasant feeling, I spent a few hours at the headquarters of a charity devoted to providing convict's wives with employment.

Much to my regret, Robert was still out when I returned home. Uneasy ennui settled over me again, leaving me almost desperate to be out and doing something. I walked the dogs, played with the twins, wrote letters to distant friends, and sat in the library until Joshua asked if I would kindly take myself elsewhere as my restless lurking made him nervous.

I had just decided to go upstairs and weed through my wardrobe again with an eye to giving away the outcasts, when Robert returned.

"There you are," I cried, happy to see a cheerful face. "I wondered where you had been. Did you enjoy your morning?"

Robert, adopting the expression worn by smitten men everywhere, was busy detailing Helena's many charms when I cut him short.

"Is Helena home now?" I asked.

"She was when I left," he said, still walking on the cloud of oblivion that love had created.

"Ah. Good. I want to speak with her." I chewed my lip as I tried to decide whether to telephone, or go in person. The desire to do something, and particularly the urge to see how Griffin was doing, made the decision an easy one.

"I believe I will pay her a call," I said, gathering up my coat and hat.

Robert was in the process of wandering into the library when I spoke. He spun around and marched over to me and held my coat.

"I will go with you," he offered happily.

I thought of teasing him about another visit so soon to his lady-love, but decided to leave him alone. Once in the cab, however, I could not help but broach a topic that had been on my mind for some time.

"This is none of my business, Robert, except that you are an old and dear friend, and I think of Helena as I would a sister. Have you told her how you feel?"

The color washed out of his face as he looked at me with something akin to grief. "I have no means, Cassandra. I have nothing to offer her but my undying devotion and love. How can I tell her my feelings? I cannot hope to marry her."

"We have been through this before, Robert. If you refuse to believe me when I tell you that it will not matter to Helena, ask the lady herself. You may be surprised to find out what she considers to be important in a suitor."

He looked so doubtful and miserable that I bit back the rest of the lecture I wanted badly to give him, and instead contemplated a visit with Griffin.

The footman showed us into a small, dark, seldom used parlor while he ascertained the whereabouts of Griffin and Helena. I looked around with pleasure until I noticed that Robert seemed to be in the grip of some nervous complaint. His leg twitched spastically, and he was perspiring freely about the forehead. I was about to ask him if he was ill when the door opened. I turned with a smile on my lips to greet Griffin, and came face to face with Lord Sherringham. My smiled faded when the little man puffed up indignantly as he transferred his glare from Robert to me.

"You!" he bellowed at me in a good imitation of Griffin at his loudest. "How dare you step foot in this house? How dare you show your face here? You will leave at once! That goes for you, sir, as well!"

I thought briefly of running, but my recent experience with the earl gave me courage. My chin went up. "I am here to see your brother, Lord Sherringham, not you."

"You will not see him, madam. You will not see *anyone* in this house. Don't think I am not aware of your insidious plans—I am!"

"What plan would that be?" I asked cautiously, thinking of the Union plans.

Robert, to the left of me, gripped the chair. I was pleased to see he showed no signs of intimidation, and instead looked as if he would welcome a battle himself.

"Your plans to ingratiate your way with my brother. You will find that I am not oblivious as to the reason you have attempted to ensnare him. Can you deny that you are guilty of trying to get hold of his fortune?"

I found it curious that the only reason Lord Sherringham could imagine a woman wanting to marry his brother was for money, and had that on the tip of my tongue when the door opened and Griffin strolled in. He had a smear of ink on the bridge of his nose, and a corresponding blotch on his hand. He looked so adorable I was hard put to refrain from kissing him in front of Robert and Lord Sherringham.

I looked back at the earl. "I do not deny that I am guilty of an attachment to your brother, Lord Sherringham. But my motives in desiring him do not include greed."

I looked pointedly past him as I spoke, hoping he would take the hint, and would have said more had Helena not entered the room. She looked cool and lovely in a pale pink morning dress, her cheeks bright with matching color. "Is anything the matter? Why is Harold shouting? Robert?"

Griffin stepped forward, lifted my chin with one of his strong hands, and kissed me gently, his lips lingering on mine, starting a slow burn inside of me. I sighed into his mouth as he pulled away.

"Nothing is the matter, Helena," he said, his eyes smoldering with desire. I smoldered back at him. Lord Sherringham started to sputter, but Griffin turned on him. "Sherry, you will apologize to Miss Whitney for your rude behavior."

"I will do no such thing."

Griffin took a step towards him. Although he made no move to threaten his brother, his anger was almost palpable, his voice dropping to a low, nearly inaudible tone. "Apologize to her."

Helena and I glanced at one another. We both recognized that growl. Lord Sherringham, still sputtering, looked at his younger brother hesitantly. Evidently he recognized it too, for he turned an even darker shade of red, then choked out, "I apologize for my comments."

"Consider them forgotten," I said softly.

Griffin as held the door for his brother. Lord Sherringham glared at each one of us, then, muttering what sounded like a string of oaths, stomped out of the room. I heaved a sigh of relief and turned to Helena with a feeble smile. She grabbed my hands in hers, and kissed me on the cheek.

"I'm so sorry for whatever Harold said to you." Her eyes wandered to Robert, quickly clouding with worry. I was astonished to see Robert looking pale and wan, as if he would be sick.

"Robert? Are you ill?" I inquired solicitously.

He swayed slightly, cleared his throat, and looked even worse, if that were possible. Griffin, standing next me, grinned. I frowned at him, ashamed that he should be so insensitive to Robert's illness.

"Robert, if you are in need of medical attention, I'm sure we can locate Doctor Melrose. Or perhaps you should sit down with your head between your knees. Griffin, would you get him some water?"

I started over to help Robert to a chair but was stopped by Griffin's hold on my arm. He spun me around towards the door, and shooed me out of it. "Helena, go show Cassandra—oh, show her the conservatory."

"Griffin!" I was puzzled by his behavior. "I believe I can do more good here with Robert."

"I doubt that," he said, closing the door in our faces.

"Well!" I said, looking at Helena in amazement. "What was that about?"

She looked as puzzled as I felt as we walked down the hall to the conservatory. "I don't know. Did Harold say anything to Robert?"

"No. He confined his anger to me. But I am glad to have this chance to speak to you." I sat down on a rattan chair next to a hideous molting macaw in a large iron cage. "I wanted to talk to you about a problem in the Union...er...what on earth does it have?"

She looked at the cage. "Oh, that's his book. Raphael likes to chew on the paper."

I watched the bird for a moment as he carefully peeled a sheet of paper out of the book, gnawed on it for a moment, then dropped it.

"I want to tell you about something unpleasant. I am sure you won't like to hear it, but I believe it will do you good to know just what is going on."

"Oh!" She grasped the ruffles at her throat. "What is it? Tell me quickly!"

"It's about Maggie Greene," I began, watching the bird out of the corner of my eye. "I happened to overhear a conversation among her and some of her supporters. Helena, I hate to tell you this, but they are using you."

"Using me? How can they use me?"

"They plan for you to be a scapegoat," I explained, then paused, fascinated as the bird peeled off another page. "What is he reading?"

"Dante's *Inferno*."

"Ah. Suitable."

A frown crossed her face as I related the conversation I had heard at the Hall, leaving nothing out. When I was done, she was pale, but had a fire in her eye that delighted me. "Thank you for telling me about this, Cassandra. I shall know what to say to Miss Greene when she next telephones."

"Has she been telephoning you?"

"Sometimes. I know how you feel about the militants, but even you must agree that no price is too much to pay to further the cause."

"I certainly do not feel that way. Helena, I am as devoted to women's rights as much as any other Union member, but I believe there is a line we must draw. Arson, attacking police, breaking windows—they are all examples of actions that have gone too far. Why, I read in *The Times* that there are women in the east who have made it a policy to ram their hatpins into the flanks of police horses!"

She gasped in horror.

"Yes! Can you possibly condone such atrocious acts of cruelty?"

"No, of course I can't." She wiped at a misty eye. "But you are so devoted to the cause. Was it not you that said to compromise on any part of suffrage was to lose the battle?"

I moved in my chair uncomfortably. "Well, yes. I want to talk to you about that as well. I have decided—you know that Griffin and I—"

She smiled gently. "I know about you and Griffin."

"No, not that. Or yes, that. Helena, I have decided that after the next protest, I will no longer participate in any other demonstrations." I watched with fascination as the bird sat on the bottom of the cage, wadding up the paper into little brown balls. "I would not even attend that protest, but after our promise to Mrs. Heywood that we would support her at the candidate's meeting, I can hardly refuse to join in that one, last protest."

"I shall miss you in the fight for our rights, dearest sister. Without your charming spirit, your happy countenance—"

"Spare me the flattery, Helena," I said abruptly. "I had hoped you would join me in the decision to end our protest careers."

"I will no longer support Maggie Greene, of course, after her treachery, but that does not mean I shall leave the cause as you will do."

"I have no intention of leaving the cause," I said firmly. "I feel strongly that Griffin will have no objection to my supporting the issue in a less active manner. I shall continue to do my part in every way except the actual demonstrations and protests."

She cheered up at that thought. "What an excellent idea. There are hundreds of ways we could make ourselves useful, and still make our—" Her gaze dropped.

"Husbands happy?" I finished with a smile.

"Perhaps. Certainly your husband will be happy with our decision. Very well, Cassandra, I agree. I will stand by your side for the candidate's meeting, and will make it my last demonstration as well. Are you sure, though? Have you considered your decision fully? I would hate for us to compromise our beliefs in such a manner that will prohibit our involvement in any form."

"I understand your reticence. I know you enjoyed the idea of demonstrating, but I honestly believe that this is a solution that will allow us to live in harmony with our husbands and still retain our self-respect and satisfy our needs to see justice done. Mrs. Heywood herself has said that not every woman is required to go into battle; warriors can be found in many guises."

She blushed at my frank speech, and picked at the embroidering on her sleeve. "You may speak for yourself, of course, you're so happy with Griffin, but I don't believe I shall ever marry."

Another lovesick sweetheart, I sighed to myself as I watched the bird assemble a collection of small paper pellets. "Helena, not twenty minutes ago I had a conversation with Robert about you."

She looked up, her eyes thick with tears. "About me?"

"Yes. Although I am breaking his confidence, I can assure you that he feels towards you as you feel about him."

"Are you sure? You spoke with him? He loves me?"

I could not help but smile. Things were working out so well. "Yes to all of your questions. So, wipe your eyes and keep your spirits up. I have a feeling you will soon be as happy as I am." A thought struck me. "In fact, unless I am mistaken, your happiness is the very reason Robert wished to speak with Griffin."

"Oh," Helena said happily.

My eyes were drawn to the bird. "What does he do with the paper pellets?"

She looked at me blankly for a minute, then frowned at the macaw. "He ejects them at the servants. He's Letitia's bird."

"That would explain a great deal."

"Cassandra, why is Robert speaking with Griffin? Why isn't he speaking with Harold? It is Harold who has control over my fortune."

"He has spoken with Lord Sherringham," I spoke softly, watching her carefully.

"He has?" The color faded from her face as she put a hand to her mouth. I expected her to swoon, but she surprised me. "It doesn't matter. I am old enough to marry whom I please. I will have control over my fortune in four years, and then it won't matter what Harold thinks."

Her face was flushed now, and she had a peculiar light in her eyes. I was happy to see that she, at least, would fight for the one she loved.

If only Griffin has done his job, I thought to myself, and given Robert the assistance he needs. We did not have a long wait to see if he had; the door opened and both men walked in. Robert was flushed, but looked cheerful. Griffin was no longer grinning, although I detected a certain twitching about the corners of his mouth that was suspicious. He held out his hand for me. I glanced at Helena. She looked as if she would faint.

"Helena?" I asked, rising to go to her, concerned about her waxen appearance. Griffin grabbed my hand, and pulled me toward him.

"Come, my dear. I want to talk to you."

"Griffin, now Helena is ill."

"No she's not. Come with me." He pulled me out the door, and led me to a small room off the hall. It was filled from floor to ceiling with books. I turned to face him.

"What can you be thinking? First Robert, and now Helena—" I paused. It occurred to me that Helena might not really be suffering.

Griffin nodded.

"Thank heavens. Now I can stop being a confidante of the lovelorn. It has been a rather frustrating job."

He frowned for a moment, then spun around and left the room. "Stay here. I'll be back in a minute."

276

CHAPTER TWENTY-FOUR

Griffin's study gave an interesting insight into the man—it was untidy, but fascinating. I had just settled down with a book containing engrossing descriptions and illustrations of the natives of Borneo when he returned.

"I wanted to make sure Sherry didn't interrupt them, but I couldn't find him." He frowned at the Borneo book. "That's not suitable reading for a lady."

"Oh, don't be such an old maid. I am a New Woman. I have a lover. Penis sheaths and virgin sacrifices are nothing to me." I looked up to where he stood. "Were you aware that there is a tribe in Borneo that has a ritual of manhood consisting of three young men and one nubile—"

He snatched the book from my hands and put it in a drawer, leaning against it. I smiled and stood up to kiss him. "The book also had some interesting things to say about mating rites. I believe I would like you to explain them in greater detail."

He wrapped his arms around me and nuzzled my neck. I twined my fingers through his curls and kissed a line along his jaw. "I will be happy to do so at a later date."

"Mmm. I'll hold you to that. Did you give Robert the push he needed?"

"I gave him a whiskey and the benefit of my advice," he murmured as he sucked my earlobe into his mouth. "The rest he'll have to do himself."

"I should ask how you are feeling today," I breathed, running my hands over his hard-muscled torso. As much as I liked touching him, I couldn't help but wish it was his bare flesh my fingers were skimming over. "The doctor would expect me to check you out."

"Perhaps a physical examination is in order," he answered, his hands tugging and pulling until they slipped under my shirtwaist, the warm heat of his palms cupping breasts that had been clamoring for just very touch.

"I don't believe we have time for that," I pointed out, unable to keep from wriggling against him. He was aroused, and would, I believe have settled for a quick examination if I hadn't remembered something I needed to do. I slid out from his embrace, circling behind a tall armchair. "I have something to say to you."

Griffin put a hand on the chair and took a step forward. "What would that be?"

"It is about us."

"I'm always happy to discuss that subject." He took another step forward and I found myself in the circle of his arms again.

I put my hands on his chest and pushed out of the embrace. "No, none of that."

"Why not?"

"I need to talk to you, and it is impossible for me to talk any sense when you…you know."

"When I do what?" he asked, moving closer. His lovely amber eyes mesmerized me, deep, endless pools of amber that I could gaze into for an eternity. He pulled me tighter. "Perhaps you mean this?"

With a quick, heated kiss he picked me up and set me down on the desk, spreading my legs and pushing my skirt and petticoat up over my thighs.

"Griffin, we don't have time—"

"We have time for this. I've wanted to do this since that first night when you gave yourself to me," he answered, tugging at the ribbon to release my drawers. A moment later that garment went flying as Griffin pulled me forward to the edge of his desk, my legs resting on his shoulders as he knelt before me.

"Griffin?" I asked as the dark curls brushed my thighs. "*Griffin?*"

His mouth was warm on my flesh as he kissed a path up my thighs to that spot that had recently been making strident demands regarding him. "*GRIFFIN!*"

His lips were a brand burning into my tender flesh as he his tongue did things I had no idea a tongue could do. He kissed, he sucked, he licked and nibbled and caressed, touching me in ways that made my heart pound and my breath stop in my throat. I tensed as he eased a finger into me, the familiar tightness of the winding coil inside me promising bliss. A second finger joined the first and suddenly I was there, blazing a trail into the heavens like a fiery comet. I clutched his head to me and cried out his name, almost sobbing with the pleasure of his selfless homage to our love.

He held me until I recovered myself enough to speak.

"Was that, by any chance, in the book of the Borneo natives?"

He chuckled and kissed me. "No."

I licked my lips. "Hmm. That's...different. Is it...can I...do men enjoy reciprocal treatment?"

He kissed me again. "Very much so."

"Hmm. I will make a note of that, but before I can explore the idea further, I want you to go back around to the desk. There's a subject upon which I need to speak, and I can't do it when you are doing that."

He withdrew his hand, grinned, then handed me my drawers and leaned against the desk, watching as I put them on. "You have my undivided attention."

I shook out my skirts and took a deep breath. "About the next suffrage protest—"

He scowled. Before he could interrupt me, I explained about the planned appearance at the candidate's meeting. "I know you are against my attending, and I appreciate your concern, but I have decided to fulfill my promise even though it is against your wishes, and the wishes of my family. I have spent a good deal of time thinking about you lately, thinking about us. It did not take me long to realize that no matter how strongly I feel about assisting the cause of women's emancipation, I feel stronger about you."

He started toward me. I held my hands out to keep him back. "Let me finish, please. I can't imagine life without you. For that reason I have decided that, after the next event, I will give up my active involvement in women's suffrage."

He looked at me in wonder, and I gazed back at him, happy with my decision, knowing it was right, sniffling just a little at the tears that had somehow slipped from my eyes.

Griffin set down the pipe he had been holding, then came to me, taking my face in his hands and kissing away the tears. I tugged on his hair until his lips claimed mine, and told him in every way I could just how much I loved him.

I don't expect you to give up your work. If it's that important to you, I can live with it. All I want is to keep you from being hurt."

Love for this wonderful, understanding man flooded me. It was what I had been hoping for all my adult years—a man who could respect me as well as love me. I placed my hand on his cheek. "As long as I have you, nothing can hurt me. Helena and I have decided that we will be content supporting the cause without endangering ourselves in the protests themselves."

He started unbuttoning my shirtwaist, kissing each bit of exposed flesh. "An excellent solution," he agreed, and slipped a few more buttons through the holes.

A sudden loud noise from outside the room disrupted him. We both turned toward the door as it was flung open. Griffin's grip on my waist tightened as he beheld his brother, red with fury and sputtering incoherently. I quickly redid my buttons, peering over Griffin's shoulder at the earl.

"Griffin," Lord Sherringham roared, "What have you done! How dare you tell that—that—" he glared at me, evidently for inspiration, "—that young scoundrel that he may marry Helena? I found him now, in the conservatory, proposing to her. He had the audacity to say you had given him permission."

I sank into the chair behind me, watching Griffin closely. He turned slowly. "I have given my permission, since you will not."

"How dare you! Have you considered who he is? His expectations? His means?"

"He loves her and she loves him. He is a good man, and will make her happy. What else should I consider?"

"I forbid this marriage. I cannot forbid you your own mistake," he waved a pudgy hand toward me, "but, by God, I can halt another disaster in this family."

"You can't stop Helena from marrying, and I would hope that you have the decency to give her an ample allowance until she is in control of her own fortune," Griffin said, his hands fisted.

"I will do no such thing!" Lord Sherringham seemed to be calming down, but I did not care for the look in his eye. "Very well, as you point out, she is free to marry whomever she chooses. But I am free to dispense her money as I see fit, and I will not see her wasting any of it on that fortune hunter."

I expected Griffin to argue the point, although I knew it would do no good. He didn't, however, he simply jammed his hands in his pockets, and said mildly, "It doesn't matter how tight you hold on, Sherry. She will have her money in four years and until then—" He shrugged.

A wave of love swept over me as I watched him. I knew then he would arrange to help Robert back onto his feet in a manner that even the sensitive Robert would accept. Helena would have Robert, Griffin and I would have each other, and everyone would be happy. I gazed at the love of my life, my eyes brimming with admiration and love.

"I'm sure you will be turning us out now, so that you might welcome *that woman*. I will tell Letitia. Mark my words, Griffin," Lord Sherringham spat out the words, "you will regret the day you made this decision."

He spun around and slammed the door behind him as he left.

Griffin scowled at the door until I placed a hand on his arm. The muscles beneath my fingers were tense and taut.

"I shouldn't have come today. I'm sorry that I've caused so much trouble." I looked into the amber eyes I loved so much, dark now with anger, and placed a finger on his temple. "Did you know that your vein is bulging again?"

He stared at me for a minute, then threw back his head and laughed. Grasping me in another bone crushing embrace, he said, "My darling Cassandra. What man could resist such lover's talk?"

Shortly after that we went in search of Helena and Robert. We found them were we had left them, although not in the same state. Helena was weeping on Robert's shoulder, and he was flushed and red with anger.

"Ah. I see the traces of a visit from Sherry," Griffin said dryly. He handed his sister a handkerchief. "Helena, stop crying."

Helena took the offered item, and attempted to wipe her tears. "But, Griffin! Harold said we could not marry, and he was *rude* to Robert!"

Griffin pulled Robert to one side, and spoke with him in a low voice. I went to Helena, and put my arm around her. "Don't worry, my dear, Griffin will see to everything. He has already seen Lord Sherringham, and—" I sighed with happiness. "—he was magnificent."

Her expression lightened. "I'm so happy you're not fighting with Griffin anymore. He loves you so very much."

"I think we have worked things out," I said, my eyes wandering to his admirable profile.

Griffin took us home a short while later in his motorcar. I had a few minutes to ask him if he'd had any luck finding incriminating evidence against Lord Sherringham, but he had not found anything.

"You forbade me to confront him," he reminded me. "If I could just get him alone, I could make him tell me what he's been up to."

"Be patient, my darling. He will reveal his hand in some way or another." I started into the house, then stopped. "And for heaven's sake, be careful!"

I was at Mrs. Heywood's door early the next morning, consumed with curiosity about the subject of her note. Her butler escorted me into the morning room, where I sat drumming my fingers on a lovely walnut table for a quarter of an hour. Mrs. Heywood arrived, apologizing for her tardiness, received my congratulations at her release from prison, and settled down to business.

"We have decided to move up the date for the candidate's meeting protest to one held tomorrow evening. Due to problems within the Union the officers have decided to disseminate details about the protest to only those people who will participate. As both you and Miss St. John have committed yourselves to the protest, I thought it best to tell you in person about our arrangements."

I listened with eagerness as she detailed the plan for the local candidate's meeting, at which the general public was encouraged to ask questions of the various candidates. The National Women's Suffrage Union would send a delegation of five members: one would act as speaker to ask each of the candidates whether or not they would support women's rights, the other four would stand in solidarity behind her.

"I have been asked to be the speaker, but feel it a task beyond my strength," she smiled wanly. "Mrs. Knox has kindly offered to stand in for me, and will ask the questions of the representatives."

We were interrupted by her butler, summoning her to a telephone call. "I must take this call, my dear, so I will let you be on your way. I do want to caution you about giving out this information to anyone other than Miss St. John. As you know, we suspect that a certain member might use the information to cause a scene that would be detrimental to the cause."

"I won't say a word to anyone but Helena," I promised.

As I left her house, I decided it would be beneficial to my bemused brain if I walked home rather than took the cab. I paid off the cabby, and started toward Mayfair. The air was heavy, but the sight of new green buds on the empty tree branches gave hope of brighter days. My spirits lifted despite the gray clouds.

Passing a nearby church, I paused to watch a wedding procession. The bride was lovely in white satin and orange blossoms, sending my thoughts inexorably spinning towards Griffin. The young couple stepped into an open carriage and drove off to the cheers of their friends. As I started forward I spied a clergyman in traditional black garb.

The sight of the man in profile flooded me with memories of three men cowering in the corner of a small room as Annie yelled and threw crockery. Mr. Hope, Freddy had called him. Chills ran down my spine as I remembered Helena's faltering voice saying that, along with her brother, Oliver Hope was her trustee.

"Mr. Hope!" If it was the same man, it would be a tangible connection between Merlin, Percy, Freddy, and Lord Sherringham, the very proof that we sought. With these thoughts chasing around my mind, I immediately hailed a cab.

An overturned dray near Griffin's house had me setting off on foot for the last block. As I approached the house, a cab arrived from the other direction, and a figure alighted. Thinking it was Helena, I raised my hand in greeting. The woman who walked up to the door did not see me, but I quickly saw from her short stature that she was not Helena. She wore a hooded coat and dark dress, and something about her sent a chill of premonition down my spine. I walked a little faster, thinking she looked familiar.

Griffin's butler opened the door and accepted a letter from the woman, who then turned and, without looking to either side, stepped back into the cab. A brief gust of wind blew back her hood as she entered the cab.

There was no mistaking the features of Maggie Greene.

Lost in thought as I watched the cab pull away, I stood next to the stone steps leading up to the front door. Maggie Greene and Lord Sherringham? What would they have in common? Certainly they did not share the same political beliefs, and yet, the suffrage movement was the one tie that bound them.

The butler did not even raise an eyebrow at my request to speak with his master, but informed me that he was out. I admit that at that news I wrung my hands.

"Lady Helena is in, miss, if you would like to speak with her."

"Helena! Yes! She would know if her Mr. Hope is a clergyman or not. At least I could get that point cleared up. I will see her, please."

I was shown into the dark parlor to await her. As I passed a half-moon marble table that stood next to the front door, I noticed the silver salver waiting with a stack of letters for their recipients to claim them. I paced the floor of the parlor anxiously, trying to piece my terrible thoughts together. The sight of the letter in Maggie's hand tormented me. I had to know if it was addressed to Lord Sherringham or to Helena.

With exquisite care I opened the parlor door and looked out. The hall was empty. I tip-toed to the marble table and stared with a growing sense of horror at the letter on top.

It was addressed to Lord Sherringham and marked urgent.

There is no excuse for my action except one: I was trying to prevent the further attacks upon the man I loved. I snatched the letter off the stack and raced back to the parlor. The letter was sealed with wax and bore no clue as to the sender. I could not in all conscience open the letter myself, but I hoped Griffin would not feel bound by similar morals.

"Dearest Cassandra," Helena cried as she entered the parlor and hugged me.

I held the letter behind my back, embarrassed by the theft. "Griffin—do you know where he is?"

Her smile faded at the urgent note in my voice. "Why, yes. He has gone to consult his solicitor. He told Harold he was having a will drawn up. He should be home soon, if you would like to wait for him. Robert went with him to see about some other matter."

"He told—" Fear struck me with an almost palpable blow. I had a hard time swallowing the lump that suddenly appeared in my throat. "And what did Lord Sherringham say to that?"

"He smiled. It...it wasn't a very pleasant smile, but he said nothing..." Her voice trailed off.

I felt almost lightheaded with fear as I brought out the letter and held it wordlessly before Helena.

"I don't understand, why do you have a letter addressed to Harold?"

"It was delivered by hand. That is, I saw it delivered just a few minutes ago...by Maggie Greene."

Helena's eyes opened wide in disbelief. "Maggie? What would Maggie have to say to Harold?"

I paced the length of the room, barely able to get the words out. "Helena, I must see Griffin. I can't open this letter, but he could. We have to know what Maggie is communicating to your brother, we have to know if he—if he is planning—"

A horrified expression stole across her face as she clutched my arm in a fierce grip. "Cassandra, you can't mean that Harold has something to do with what you told me about Maggie's plans?"

I nodded miserably.

"It can't be!" As I believe I have had opportunity to mention, there is a streak of steel running through Helena that is not apparent from a casual glance. It was evident now. "We must confront Harold with this!"

"We can't! If we wait for Griffin—"

"No. Harold is at home now, I just left him in the library. He was speaking with a business acquaintance, but as soon as Mr. Jones leaves, I will—"

"Mr. Jones?" I all but shrieked, horrified at the name. "Mr. William—or Merlin—Jones?"

She paused. "I believe his name was William. Do you know him?"

I crumpled into a chair, my knees no longer able to hold me. "Helena, you must tell me, did Mr. Jones have a gold tooth?"

"Why, yes, he did. Cassandra, are you ill? Shall I fetch someone?" She ran to me as I moaned, my hands clutching my head.

"Everything revolves around your brother, everything comes back to him. Maggie, Freddy, Merlin—it all comes back to one person."

She was on her knees before me, holding me as I rocked back and forth trying to deny the terrible truths that finally fell into place.

"You are distraught, my dear. I will fetch you some smelling salts."

I clutched her hand as a blinding flash of light lit up my brain. "You said you just left them—your brother and Mr. Jones—are they still here? Helena, I must hear what they are saying. That would be the proof we need!"

"Yes, I'm sure they're still in the library, but proof of what? What is it you suspect? I fear from your countenance that it is something terrible. Oh Cassandra, what do you think is happening?"

I thought furiously. The library. I hadn't been in Griffin's library, only his study. "Is there another door to the library other than the one to the hall? Somewhere we can listen to their conversation?"

"No, only the one door. Although there is the alcove."

"The alcove? Could one hear a discussion in the library from the alcove?"

"Yes, it's a small opening on the first floor that overlooks the library. But Cassandra, you haven't answered—"

And I didn't answer her questions. Instead I leaped up and grasped her hand, dragging her with me as I ran out into the hallway and up the stairs. "Where is it? Where is the alcove?"

She showed me down a narrow hall to a small round room with windows on one side, and a curved bench following a dark wooden railing. I peered over the edge and looked down into the library. The room was long and shaped like an L with the alcove on the wrong side of the short end. To the left, a paneled wall of some five feet blocked my view into the rest of the library. I held my breath and heard the soft murmur of voices.

"Is there no other way to hear?" I whispered.

"No."

"Then I shall just have to lean out and do my best. Hold onto my skirt."

I stepped onto the couch and stretched forward, bracing one hand against the paneling, the other holding tight to the railing. Helena clutched at my belt to keep me from falling.

It wasn't enough. I still could not understand what the men were saying. "Let go of my belt," I whispered back at Helena. "Hold onto the hem of my skirt."

I stretched further forward as she released her hold and was gratified when a man's arm came into view. The words were louder, and almost intelligible. With both hands flat against the paneling and my feet wrapped around the bench railing, I stretched a last few inches.

"—will do it tonight, if you can make sure he's unconscious." The pleasantly bland voice was that of Mr. Jones.

"It shall be done," Lord Sherringham replied.

I see now that my mistake was in trusting the strength of my feet and ankles. Helena held on for dear life when I suddenly slipped down the paneling as my feet cramped and lost their grip on the railing, but she could not hold me up as I tumbled down onto the (thankfully) carpeted floor of the library below.

I lay stunned for a moment, unsure of what happened, then slowly my vision returned. I looked up. Mr. Jones smiled down on me, his hands tucked into his waistcoat. Lord Sherringham stood behind him, sputtering and turning a dangerous shade of red. His eyes held a glazed, thoroughly unstable look.

"You!" the earl snarled, the unhealthy gleam in his eye growing stronger. Spittle collected in the corners of his mouth. "You are the cause of all my misery! I have you to thank for being turned out of my home! I have you to thank for the engagement of my sister to a fortune hunter! I have you to thank for the alienation of my brother!"

I glanced up to where Helena stood clutching at her throat, staring down at the incredible scene. Lord Sherringham followed my look and gave a great roar of madness, for mad he clearly was. The look in his eye and his incoherent comments made it evident that he had been pushed over the edge.

"Helena," he screamed, rattling the windows.

Helena stood frozen with horror, unable to move.

"Run, Helena, run out of the house! Find Griffin—find Robert—*run now!*" The panic in my voice must have reached her, for she suddenly spun around and was gone. Merlin glanced at Lord Sherringham, then dashed out of the room. I hoped Helena would have enough sense to not run straight down the stairs into Merlin's waiting arms.

Lord Sherringham, his hands clenched into fists, his eyes ablaze, walked forward toward me. I rose hastily to my feet and looked for escape. There was none.

"Is there any reason I should not place my hands around your neck and squeeze the life out of you?" he asked in a high-pitched, deranged voice.

I took a step backwards.

"A great many reasons," I said, admittedly with a false bravado, my heart beating wildly. I was no stranger to facing down a madman, I just had never thought I'd have to do it again. "For one thing, I am not the true cause of your troubles, it just appears that way. Your sister was bound to fall in love at some point, just as some day she will take possession of her inheritance and then your abuse of her funds will be known."

He stopped briefly as a look of fury spasmed across his face, then took another step toward me. "It was you who introduced her to Hunter. If she hadn't have met you, she would still be under my control."

I didn't see the blow coming. I would have thought that years living with my father would have honed my senses to anticipate a blow, but the earl's hand whipped out and struck my face with enough force to send me reeling back into a chair. My cheek throbbed and stung as tears sprang to my eyes. I turned back to face Lord Sherringham, determined to make him admit his crimes.

"And then there's your brother's alienation. Don't you think your many attempts on his life might have something to do with that?" I asked.

A growl issued from his mouth as flecks of spittle dotted his dark waistcoat. The look in his eye was definitely not one of a sane man. "You don't know what you're talking about. You told him to throw us out, it's because of you that we will be shamed, disgraced, and dishonored before everyone. He was given everything by his doting mama! All I was given were debts!"

He slapped me again. This time I saw it coming and ducked as he lashed out, but he caught the edge of my jaw painfully. I calculated my chances of either launching an attack or escaping the room, but neither was good. Although he was not a large man, his was the strength of madness, and I was not feeling my best after having fallen from the alcove.

"I could see why you hired Merlin and Percy to do the dirty work for you, but what about the accidents Griffin had in the house? Was it you who loosened the stair rod and poisoned his food, or was it Lady Sherringham?"

A high-pitched giggled escaped his lips. "My dear Letitia is the most helpful of wives."

"And as for your being turned out of your home, perhaps it was not the best idea to burn down Rosewood." That last was a guess based on Griffin's comments, but it hit home.

"Rosewood!" His voice was almost a scream. "He made me do it. The old man wouldn't let me have it to myself, *he* was to have it as well."

I was slightly confused by his use of pronouns, but gathered that he was referring to the fact that the old earl had wanted Rosewood to be a home for Helena and Griffin.

"And now this," I said, pulling out the envelope I had filched from the hall table. "It seems your cohort has something to tell you. Perhaps Maggie Greene wants to tell you about the latest suffrage protest—" I spoke louder as the door behind him opened. "—or maybe she has a question about your role ensuring the suffragettes are arrested."

Lord Sherringham was directly in front of me, his hands outstretched and almost touching my throat. I looked over his shoulder and delivered the coup de grace. "Or could it be that Maggie wants to talk about how much money you promised to give her when she arranges for Helena to be sent to prison?"

He screamed and lunged at me, digging his thumbs into my throat, sending me sliding toward a long, inky pool.

CHAPTER TWENTY-FIVE

"Can you ever forgive me?"

"Of course. You saved my life."

"Only by the slimmest of margins," Griffin said, nuzzling my throat.

"Ahem," I said, nodding toward Helena and Robert, who were fussing with a tea tray. "You can make amends by telling me what happened."

Griffin released me, and allowed me to sit without his support on a brocade sofa. "I didn't know what to think when we came in to see that bastard Black dragging Helena toward the library. It took us a few minutes to get her free and him disabled, and then she wasn't in a state to do anything but say the word 'library' over and over again."

"It was horrible," Helena said, handing me a cup of tea. "I thought Harold would kill you."

"He might have if Griffin hadn't broken his jaw," Robert said, sitting next to Helena on a loveseat.

"You broke his jaw?" I asked, looking at the love of my life.

"It was the only way I could get him to release you," he said in a raw voice.

We contemplated the recent events in silence for a few minutes, silence made all the more stark by the recent insane screams of Lord Sherringham as he was taken away, struggling, to the local asylum in a straight-waistcoat.

As a woman's voice sounded in the hall, Griffin rose and excused himself.

"I still can't believe Harold did that to you," Helena said as she moved over to sit next to me. "It all seems like a nightmare."

Our heads turned in unison as a horrible scream rent the air.

"That would be your sister-in-law hearing the news," I said in answer to her shocked face.

Helena was on the verge of tears, and I was about to ask Robert to take her elsewhere when Lady Sherringham appeared in the doorway, her eyes burning and hands outstretched like talons.

"You have ruined everything," she screeched, flying at me. Spitting curses, she tried to claw my face. Robert leaped forward and pulled her off before she had a chance to reach me. The countess struggled briefly, then suddenly went limp, sobbing hysterically.

Griffin arrived, mopping blood from his face where she had clearly attacked him. Waving me back to the couch from which I had risen, he took the countess firmly by the arm and escorted her from the room.

Helena sat with her face in her hands, weeping. Realizing that perhaps Robert could comfort her better than I could, I slipped out of the room and waited in the hall for Griffin.

Later, when a pale and furious Lady Sherringham had left for the comfort of a sister's home, we gathered in the sitting room and I recounted the disturbing conversation with the earl.

"Harold truly did plan to have me imprisoned simply in order to steal my fortune," Helena said, as if speaking the words out loud would make them less painful.

"I'm sorry, Helena," I said miserably from where I was curled up next to Griffin, cuddled into his side, my fingers twined through his. "I believe it would be kindest to think that the madness had taken over, leaving his mind unbalanced and not at all that of a brother you loved."

"Yes, that is true." She leaned into Robert for comfort. "And the madness would explain his attacks on Griffin, as well."

"He all but admitted the two accidents you experienced at home were the work of your sister-in-law," I told Griffin. "I assume they were done at the earl's behest."

"I thought Sherry was acting a little odd when I came home after this last trip," he answered, rubbing his chin meditatively. "He seemed to be angry all of the time."

"To think he would go so far as to kill you." Helena glanced at the bruises blossoming on my neck. "Both of you!"

"I don't understand why he wanted to have Helena arrested," Robert complained, shifting so that Helena was at his side.

I sipped my tea and let Griffin explain it to him.

"I don't know for sure, but I'll wager an examination of Helena's inheritance will show that she was being systematically robbed by Sherry. When you appeared on the scene, Sherry saw at once that Helena was—ahem—fond of you. He knew that even though she could not touch the money held in trust until she was twenty-five, a husband might take more of an interest in her fortune and would demand an accounting."

"Lord Sherringham would never have been able to carry off the embezzlement of Helena's inheritance if it were not for his partner in crime, Mr. Hope," I added.

I turned to Helena. "You must know—your trustee, Mr. Hope, is he in the church?"

"Yes," she replied wearily, leaning heavily against Robert's shoulder. "He was the vicar in the parish at Rosewood for years, then he left his post."

I turned to back to Griffin.

"You wouldn't remember because you were drugged at the time, but it was Mr. Hope that Freddy intended to marry us. Freddy and me, that is," I added, blushing at Griffin's scowl. "I didn't see much of his face, but I have little doubt that the Mr. Hope, clergyman, who was so obliging to Freddy is the same Mr. Hope, clergyman, who was Lord Sherringham's friend and co-trustee to Helena. I assume the earl decided to help Freddy in his underhanded scheme after Griffin made known his intentions towards me. I suppose we'll never know until we talk to Freddy."

I sat back, pleased with my bit of reasoning.

"But how did your cousin know Lord Sherringham?" Robert asked.

"As I see it, Merlin Jones was the link between the two men. Perhaps not the only one since I caught Freddy with my Union notebook in his hand, so he may well have seen the potential to raise a little capital, and who better to approach than the man who was leading the opposition to the Cause. Freddy has been mentioning, with increasing vigor, the dangerous aspects of a woman involved in suffrage. He obviously tried to play on my fears by hiring Mr. Jones to conduct worrisome, but not really frightening attacks upon me. It just so happened that each time one was arranged, Helena was with me."

"Helena saw him talking to Sherry, which means he probably passed on Jones' name as a thug willing to be hired for any number of plans," Griffin said.

I nodded. "Plans such as kidnapping you from the masquerade ball, attacking you in your study, and so forth. Yes, I'm quite certain you are right."

"And Maggie Greene? How did she meet Lord Sherringham? And why would she want to have Helena jailed?" Robert's voice was distinctly puzzled.

"I'm sure she met the earl indirectly through Helena. According to the note she left, which Griffin so obligingly opened, she was passing along information about upcoming Union events to him."

Helena looked as puzzled as Robert. "But why would she want to sabotage the Union, Cassandra? I know you don't support the militants, but surely you can't believe they want the Union to fail?"

"I think in a way, they do. Maggie probably realizes that there were just too many moderate suffragettes, and that she will never be able to take over the Union. Her plan was to divide and conquer—bring the Union down by giving sensitive information to the police, thereby insuring that the leaders and most active members would be arrested and jailed. Later, when the opposition was silenced, she would pick up the dregs and form a new organization with herself at the helm and a militant policy in force. She may still do it, too," I mused.

"Well, at least Helena's safe," Robert said, gazing at Helena with a silly grin of bliss. She smiled giddily back at him.

"Yes, I think everything has turned out rather well, all in all," I said, watching Griffin with concern. He had been quiet too long, and I was worried that he was overly tired by the recent day's events.

His lovely eyes met mine and I'm afraid that, for a time, we all looked silly.

Helena and Griffin came to dinner that night, and we explained to my family what had happened earlier, as well as what we had pieced together. Mabel was shocked, Joshua concerned, and Mullin delighted with the exciting goings-on of the family.

After dinner, I had a moment to speak to Helena alone and told her about the protest at the candidate's meeting the following evening. "Mrs. Heywood asked specifically that we attend. She has hand-picked the members, and is placing a great deal of trust in us with this assignment."

Helena had recovered from the trauma of the day extremely well, due in a large part, I suspected, to the support and love of Robert. She gazed at him now as he stood talking to Griffin next to the fire, and when she spoke, her voice throbbed with emotion. "I would be proud to accompany you tomorrow. It will be our last demonstration, and is only suitable that it should be an important one."

"Yes, well—" I cast my own eyes towards the two men. "We have yet to inform them of our plans. I have a feeling we shall meet with a fair amount of opposition. Are you prepared to defy your beloved's wishes?"

She answered my smile with one of her own. "I should never think of going against Robert's wishes in any manner," she said with unconvincing demureness, her eyes twinkling.

"The trouble with you, Helena, is that you avoid confrontation. I used to do the same, but now I realize that there is nothing wrong with a healthy discussion of the issues. In fact, with the right person, such discussions can be very stimulating. Allow me to demonstrate."

I walked over to Griffin and whispered in his ear, "The Union has moved forward our attendance at the candidate's meeting. It will be held tomorrow evening, and Helena and I have promised to attend."

I stepped back and watched the results with great satisfaction. We spent a good half-hour arguing the point, Helena and me against Griffin, Robert, Mabel, and Joshua. We went round and round, until finally Griffin held up his hand and roared for silence.

"This arguing is useless," he said in a conversational tone of voice, his eyes meeting mine. "They will go to the meeting."

I had my mouth opened to make a retort to a particularly unkind remark from Mabel, but shut it in surprise at Griffin's statement.

"They will?" Robert asked him in disbelief.

"Yes. Cassandra has agreed that this will be her last demonstration. I assume Helena has made a similar promise?"

She nodded, a smile hovering on her lips.

"Then it is settled. They will make this last demonstration with the understanding that they will *in no way endanger themselves*." He glared at me to make sure I noted the emphasis.

"But, is it safe?" Mabel asked him.

"With Sherry put away, I think it is. Even if Miss Greene found out about the demonstration, and Cassandra tells me no one but the five women who will attend are being told about it, she has no one to give the information to. I can't see her going to the police; that information would become public too quickly. I think they will be safe."

He placed a hand on my shoulder, and looked down at me, his amber eyes warm and fathomless. I beamed at him, ecstatically happy that, at last, our future looked bright. We spent a little time discussing the plan, and decided that we were to meet the following day outside of the labor hall hosting the meeting. Griffin and Robert agreed to escort us there and back, but would not interfere.

"Unless we see you in danger of being attacked," Griffin growled. I considered protesting his arrogant attitude, but decided the protective urge in a male can have its charms. I smiled at him instead.

Robert and I were early the next day, and stood talking outside the hall while we waited for Griffin to bring Helena. Robert told me about a possible job managing a coffee farm in British East Africa. His eyes shined with happiness as he detailed the life he hoped to make with Helena, and how much he would enjoy being in Africa again.

"And what of you? What of the fair Cassandra?" he asked, turning suddenly to me.

"That will depend a great deal on Griffin. We might travel—I have always longed to travel, and Griffin has mentioned several exciting places he wants to visit—he wants *us* to visit," I said happily.

We fell silent, thinking about our promising futures. Small groups of people started to arrive, chatting and calling to one another merrily. The audience was made up of mostly low to middle class citizens, a fact I kept in mind when dressing for the event. Rather than wear an afternoon dress or even a suit, I had dressed in a conservative gray skirt and pale blue shirtwaist with a simple straw boater and matching blue ribbon. Recent news stories had hinted that suffragettes were made up of women from the idle class who had nothing better to do with their time, hence my particular pains to appear in a neat but simple costume. I hoped Helena had a similar insight.

Mrs. Knox arrived looking calm and cool. She motioned me over to her, and spoke in a quiet tone. "Have you explained the situation to Miss St. John?"

"I have. I must tell you, this will be our last demonstration."

She raised her eyebrows.

"Neither of us wishes to leave the Union," I hastened to explain. "We both would like to support the cause in a less...*physical* manner."

"I quite understand, my dear. We have many members who support our efforts without stepping foot in a march or holding a single banner. You need not risk imprisonment in order to be of benefit to the cause." She glanced meaningfully at Robert, standing nearby. "I can understand your decision."

I flushed, and was going to correct the false impression, when she continued. "I also wished to tell you that the Union also does not hold it against members if they choose to not serve their sentence in prison. I was happy to see that you and Miss St. John were released early."

I shuffled my feet uncomfortably at the subject.

"Helena's brother had us released," I said nervously. "We were prepared to serve our time, but he had us released instead."

"There is no shame in obtaining a release, my dear." Dark circles under her eyes emphasized her fatigue. I was sure Maggie's destructive plans were the primary cause for her weariness. "No woman is meant for every role."

I spotted familiar figures strolling towards us, so thanked her and turned to watch Griffin and Helena approach. My heart performed its usual contractions and physical jerks when I saw Griffin. I wondered idly how long it would take before I no longer received a thrill upon seeing him.

"A very long time, I hope," I said out loud as Griffin greeted Robert, then sighed when I took a closer look at Helena. Rather than dressing down to fit in the crowd, she had outdone herself with a rich plum-colored afternoon dress with pink silk inserts. Her hat was large and extravagant, bristling with ostrich feathers. I dragged my eyes from the horror of her hat to her brother. Griffin was taller than most men around him, and presented an impressive picture of physical strength. I was meditating on his many masculine charms—best seen when he was unclothed—when he approached, an endearing grin upon his face. I believe he would have embraced me if I had not stopped him.

"Cassandra, can it be you no longer enjoy those kisses I thought pleased you so much?" he teased as I held him back with a firm hand.

"On the contrary, I enjoy them too much. In addition to which, I know you, Griffin. You would not be content with a polite greeting."

His grin deepened. "There can be no embarrassment in two engaged persons showing their mutual affection."

"There is when that affection is displayed in a public place. And as we are on the subject, I don't believe we *are* engaged."

"We are!" he rumbled, trying to draw me closer.

I eluded his grasp. "No, I think not. For an engagement to take place, there must first be a proposal, and I do not recall having received one."

"Whether or not you remember it, you did." His jaw took on a familiar stubborn appearance. "I asked you that day at your sister's house."

I blushed at the memory of our activities on that day. "As I recall, you suggested marriage as a solution to a problem. I hardly think that can be classified as a proposal."

"Hrmph." He frowned, eyeing me speculatively. "But we have already announced our intentions, so we *are* engaged."

"*You* announced an engagement," I corrected, enjoying every minute of his discomfort. "I believe I was most adamant about waiting several years before I marry."

Griffin glared at me while I smiled sweetly at him. That was how Robert and Helena found us, Helena pointing out that the other suffragettes had gathered, and that we were wanted.

I glanced at the gathering and a spike of fear gripped me as I saw a face I recognized—one of Maggie Greene's captains was included in the entourage. She stood with the other three women, waiting expectantly for Mrs. Knox to give the word to go in. I turned back to Griffin as Helena went to join the group. I wanted to tell him, but one look at his calm, unconcerned face made me bite back the urge. I resolved instead to keep a firm grip upon Helena, and make sure she was not anywhere near the militant woman.

Griffin took my hand, instantly easing my worry. "You remember your promise?"

"Yes, Griffin, I have already told you I will stay behind the speakers and not interfere. Helena will be behind me. We will not in any way obstruct or attack the audience or other speakers. We will not participate in any—what was your phrase?"

"Scrummage."

"—scrummages. We will not chant slogans or wave signs lest we should inadvertently strike someone. Do you mind terribly if we breathe?"

"Only if you have to."

His lovely amber eyes were full of trust, love, and even—I might have been mistaken—pride. I grabbed him by the sleeve and pulled him towards me, kissing him quickly, then turned and ran after Helena.

Three women were clustered around Mrs. Knox, waiting to receive final instructions. As she handed out the *Votes For Women* sashes, she reminded us that our duty was to stand quietly and make ourselves visible but not vocal or physical. I watched the militant from the corner of my eye, and frowned at her smug look.

I felt sick then, for I knew her presence meant trouble. Caught in a trap of my own making, I grabbed Helena by her plum-colored sleeve, and held her back until everyone had passed.

The meeting was typical of its type: working class men and a few women who came to hear their favorite candidates. The rhetoric from the stand was as it usually was, promises that would never be kept, derision against a faulty government that would be corrected under the candidate's office, benefits and good times ahead. In the middle of the speeches, a sudden movement to the right caught my eye. I glanced down the row and saw to my horror that Maggie Greene and two other militants were seated on the other side.

"Damnation," I muttered to myself, worry filling me at the sight of her. I knew the militants were present solely to cause trouble, and I was at a loss as to how to prevent it. Mrs. Knox was clearly out of her element; although she leaned sideways and held a brief conversation with Maggie, it was with an unhappy and concerned face that she sat back.

Question time came, and several members of the audience rose and asked the standard questions. We sat for thirty minutes or so before the designated speaker from our party rose and made her way to the questioner's podium. Maggie was among the group, and although I tried, I was not able to keep Helena at a distance from her. Eight of us stood behind Mrs. Knox, on the surface a solid supportive line, but below, a group divided. I was desperately worried and shot several meaningful glances at Maggie.

"Mr. Chester," Mrs. Knox called out in a loud, clear voice, "if you are elected, will you do your best to make Women's Suffrage a government measure?"

A roar went up from the crowd, and several stewards moved in towards Mrs. Knox. They spoke to her in a low tone. She shook her head, and repeated her question, louder than before.

I watched the stewards nervously, aware of the four militants standing directly behind them. The candidate consulted with a short man in an appallingly loud checked suit and derby hat.

"Answer the question, please, Mr. Chester," Mrs. Knox said.

"I am afraid," Chester said finally, "that I am unable to answer that question at this time. It is a matter for some thought, and not one which I have had sufficient time—"

"You are afraid to answer the question!" Maggie shoved Mrs. Knox aside and took over the questioner's spot. "You are the same as every other man here, afraid to let women have any power! You would do well to be afraid!"

I missed the initial assault upon the candidate because I was simultaneously pulling Helena away from where she stood near the militants, and watching Mrs. Knox in hurried consultation with the other moderate member. I heard the horrified gasp from the crowd, however, and saw the results.

Mr. Chester lay on his back, blood streaming from his head. As I stared in shock, the four militants removed large rocks from their skirts and threw them at the remaining candidates. Two of the stewards grabbed for the women, initiating a brawl that seemed to spread instantly to everyone in the area. Helena struggled against me, trying to reach the women.

Suddenly, the room was full of police constables, seeming to stream in from everywhere, racing down the aisles, and up from the speaker's platform. The audience, in a panic, began to push their way toward the doors. I was rudely shoved aside by a large man making a hasty exit, and lost my grip on Helena. Stewards and policemen dragged the militants through the crowds, towards the back of the hall. I struggled to work my way to Helena, who was now pushed into the far aisle. The number of people attempting to rush down the narrow aisles caused a dense backup of bodies, all fighting frantically to reach the two exits.

As I slipped out of the hold of a constable, I saw Griffin to my left, trying to fight the crowd and make his way down the aisle. He was being pushed backwards by the sheer volume of people, and although I saw him bodily lift people out of his path, I lost sight of him when I was suddenly snatched from behind by a constable. Helena was ahead of me, struggling to help Mrs. Knox. In front of me, one woman was knocked down and trampled by the crowd. I tried to avoid stepping on her as the constable dragged me towards the back of the hall.

Unlike my prior arrest, this time I fought, but was only rewarded by having my thumb bent backwards until I thought it would break. My arms were wrenched behind me and, blinded with pain, I was dragged down the aisle toward the back entrance. I was stepped on and kicked in the process; the front of my shirtwaist was ripped almost exposing my undergarments.

As I was being dragged down the aisle, I saw a policeman beating one of the Suffragettes on the breasts. I kicked out toward him, and had the satisfaction of making contact with an extremely vulnerable spot. I could not see Helena anywhere, leaving me with the hope she had made an escape. Our *Votes For Women* sashes had served as a target for the police who were obviously lying in wait, for only members of our group were being attacked. The thought crossed my mind that the militants had wanted this result, and I felt certain it was Maggie and her group who had tipped off the police to our presence. Just how Maggie had finagled one of her captains into the delegation was a matter for later conjecture.

I was dragged out to an alley and tossed into a waiting Black Maria. My head hit the side of the van and I saw stars for a few minutes. Shaking my head to clear them, I could feel someone's leg underneath me. I tried to rise, and was knocked down as another woman was flung into the van.

The ride to the police station was unthinkably miserable. Not only were we all nursing injuries, I had lost Helena and had no way of knowing what happened to her. Worse, I was sure the militants had sealed our fates—we would be arrested and charged according to their plan. Griffin would have a hard time obtaining a release for Helena and me once we had been convicted of assault for a second time.

In a repeat of the earlier scene in the police station, we were herded into a small, bare room, then interviewed briefly. When asked whom I would like to notify, I declined to offer any name. I would not have Mabel and Joshua involved, and I knew Griffin would find me somehow.

We spent the night in cells alone, a torment made worse because I had no knowledge of Helena's fate. I had inquired of the police, but they either did not know or refused to tell me. I asked the two other Union members, but no one had remembered seeing Helena after the police had swarmed. I did not see Maggie Greene, a fact for which I was eternally grateful.

I spent the night alternately weeping and pacing the cell in desperation. By morning, I was near frantic with worry.

"Come along, it's time for you to go before the magistrate," the wardress told me.

"How many members of the Union were arrested, can you tell me?" I asked her on the way there.

"Couldn't say, but there were several people arrested last night as a result of the riot."

That gave me a minuscule ray of hope that public opinion was beginning to turn in our favor, but it did not answer my question of what had happened to Helena.

I made a pitiful picture for the magistrate with my skirt and shirtwaist torn and dirty. I had lost my hat, had a bruise on my jaw in addition to the ones Lord Sherringham had left on my neck, my hand was swollen and stiff, and I walked with a pronounced limp. I was, however, defiant, and refused to admit my guilt. This time I was not given the option of paying a fine, instead I was charged with assault upon a policeman and several other individuals, and sentenced to nine months in prison.

"Nine...*months*?" I gasped, stunned at the sentence.

I had assumed I would be asked to pay a fine and would be released upon the payment. Instead, in a nightmarish scene that I will remember for many years, I was driven immediately to Strangeways prison with Mrs. Knox and one other member.

Our clothes were taken from us, and we were given horrible prison dresses made of coarse material, a flannel singlet and calico chemise, stockings but no garters or drawers, and shoes of different sizes. Both of mine were too small.

I was led to a dark cell that contained only a chamber pot and a bed. The bed was merely a wooden plank with a raised object at the head, presumably a pillow. I was afraid to get near it, since it looked as if it crawled with vermin, and ended up kicking it into a corner of the cell. I was cold, my knee and hand hurt, and I was numb with shock and fear as I sat in the near-dark on the hard wooden plank.

The prison doctor came later to my cell to evaluate my wounds. After a superficial exam, he dismissed them.

"Nothing serious. The swelling will go down in time," he said, handing his nurse his bag. "I assume you are on a hunger strike?"

"I am," I answered with as much dignity as I could muster. I knew it was a badge of pride amongst imprisoned suffragettes not to take any food until they were released.

He made a notation on a chart. "You have three days to change your mind. After that we'll be forced to give you hospital treatment."

I had no idea what he meant, but I was so depressed that I did not give it much attention. I refused the evening meal, and lay on my bed, cold, hungry, and sick with worry. That I had only myself to blame for the situation did not make me feel better.

"Once again, you have created a situation that would try a saint's patience," I told myself. "Only this time you've involved Helena."

Guilt over her mingled with my misery, both weighing heavily on me. I sat on the hard wooden cot, heart-sore and sick of myself, until I fell into an uneasy sleep.

The next morning the prison matron visited me. A short, gray-haired woman with a long face, she explained the rules, and asked if I wish to eat some fruit.

"Thank you, no. I will continue the hunger strike."

She had brought me some water to drink. That I accepted.

"Do you have any questions?" she asked kindly. I had expected the prison matron to be a cold and harsh woman, and was surprised by her warmth.

"I have two, if you would be so kind as to answer them. Can you tell me if a friend of mine who is also a suffragette was arrested? Her name is Helena St. John."

She thought for a moment, and said, "Yes, she is three doors down. She was injured in the arrest, but is doing better."

My heart fell into my stomach. I had promised Griffin I would not allow harm to come to Helena, and I had failed him. He would never forgive me, of that I was sure.

"How many women were arrested, do you know?"

"I know that seven were charged, including you. Was that your second question, my dear?"

"No, my second question was about something the doctor said. He called it *hospital treatment*, and said I would undergo it in three days. What is this treatment?"

"Oh, dear. I hate to tell you, but you should know—this is why I urge you to start eating. If you will not eat in three days, the doctor will subject you to forcible feedings."

"Forcible feedings?" I questioned suspiciously. I had heard whispers of force feedings, but had always assumed the horror of them was greatly exaggerated. "How can he make me eat if I don't wish to?"

She told me in detail how the feedings were done. The very description made me sick, and after advising me again to think about the hunger strike, she left. I sat hunched on my bed, my feet tucked under me in an attempt to warm them outside of the binding shoes, and considered my new life. Force-feedings! Prison! The thought of Helena lying injured just a few doors down was maddening; I wanted to comfort her, but was unable to leave my cell.

The day passed slowly, with no interruptions except the wardresses coming at each meal to ask me if I would eat. I refused all food.

I thought I had reached the depths of my depression that day, but I was wrong. The following morning I was told I had a visitor. My spirits rose at the thought of Griffin, but it was Mrs. Prince, one of the Union's head officers, who stood outside my door and talked to me through the grill.

"Is there anything I can do for you? Anyone you would like contacted?"

"Yes, I would like to see Miss St. John, who has also been imprisoned. She is in the cell a few doors down, and has been injured. She is very delicate, and should be released for medical reasons. Can you arrange it that I might see her? Or can you contact her brother, Griffin St. John, and alert him to her condition?"

"I have spoken with Miss St. John's sister-in-law, Lady Sherringham already. Regrettably, she has washed her hands of the affair, and will do nothing to assist her."

"But her brother—Mr. St. John—will he not help?"

"I am not aware of a brother."

The room swam briefly. I sat down and put my head between my knees until I could think straight. Lady Sherringham? Why was she contacted instead of Griffin? Of course she would not lift a finger to help Helena, no doubt her sense of revenge was strong. But Griffin, where was he? Why was he not moving heaven and earth to get Helena and me out? The despair must have shown on my face as I turned back to the door.

"I will try and contact this brother. Do your best not to worry. Until I can find him, I will speak with the prison doctor about Miss St. John's situation. I have not seen her yet, but I will do so next."

"Could you please let me know how she is doing? Could you not ask the matron if I might share a cell with her?"

"I will ask, but I don't wish to raise any false hopes."

I closed my eyes, so great was my pain. I had failed Griffin, Helena, Robert, my sister—it was entirely due to my own obstinate ways that innocent Helena was to suffer. Although I hated it, although I dreaded what was to happen to me, the thought that I might have removed Helena from that blasted meeting hall before the trouble started haunted me throughout my waking moments.

"I am also trying to have your status raised to that of a political prisoner, rather than a criminal one." She sighed heavily. "I don't hold out much hope for that either, but I will try."

She left, and I sank back onto my plank and curled up into a ball. I was crying quietly to myself when I heard voices outside my cell. I went to the door in time to see the prison doctor and four wardresses march down the hall. They stopped at the cell opposite mine where a suffragette had been transferred from another cell. I was shaking with fear, although I did not know why the sight of them should fill me with such loathing.

I soon understood the matron's plea with me to eat some fruit. The hospital treatment was being inflicted upon the poor woman across from me. No matter how long I live, I will never forget the sounds of that horrible torture. When they left the cell, a voice from another cell banged on the door and yelled, "No surrender!"

A weak but defiant, "No surrender!" answered from the victim's cell. The governors had ordered this inhuman treatment so the prisoners would not die martyrs. I sank to the floor, faint with terror, and wondered how I was to survive it.

The following day was the third and final day of my hunger strike. I had not heard from Mrs. Prince, but the prison matron had stopped long enough to tell me that Helena was recovering, although she too was on a hunger strike. She had refused my request to share a cell, but promised to keep me informed as to Helena's well-being.

The days had quickly settled into a routine; I awoke from a nightmare into a waking hell. I was not allowed to leave the cell, nor had I any visitors other than the officials and Mrs. Prince. What my family must have thought I could only imagine. Griffin had warned me that he would not be able to secure our release again, and despite my conviction that he would do everything humanly possible to have us released, I feared we were beyond his help.

"No surrender!" rang out down the hallway in tormented voices as the doctor made his rounds. The screams of anguish, sounds of retching, and other torturous noises only stiffened my resolve. I had wanted to be a part of this great campaign, I had wanted to devote my body and soul to a cause, and I was solely responsible for placing Helena and myself in this position—I would take my punishment and continue my hunger strike.

I was weak with lack of sleep and food when they came for me the next day. I lifted my head from the plank as they stopped outside of my door. Dread and terror knotted up my stomach until I thought I would fall into an oblivion of darkness. The doctor and four wardresses entered the room. He asked me if I would take food. Unable to speak, I shook my head.

What followed next haunts me still. Two wardresses moved into position by taking hold of my arms. I shrank back into the pallet as one held my head, the other my feet. The doctor sat on my knees, and leaned across my chest to get at my mouth. I gritted my teeth together in an attempt to keep my mouth closed, but he had some sort of steel tool that he used to pry into my mouth.

I held my mouth closed as long as I could, but at last I could no longer bear the pain. As soon as my mouth opened, he stuffed a gap into it, turning the screw and widening it until my jaws were held wide open. I thought they would break, but the worst was yet to come.

With a brutal move, he shoved a thick tube down my throat. It was too wide and very long, and I gagged the second it hit my throat. He poured the food into the tube quickly; and yanked the tube out. As soon as it was out, I retched the food up all over him. He slapped me, and shoved the tube down again, pouring more food in it. This time I held it down until he had the gag out; as soon as it was removed, I retched all over the floor.

Exhausted and stunned with pain, I lay half on the bed, and sent a blasphemous wish that I should die.

"No surrender!" The cell door across mine clanged.

I looked up, wiping the bile from my mouth. I had survived, I had not given in to my fears. Never again would I worry that I could not triumph over adversity.

I raised my chin and as loudly and defiantly as I could, croaked, "No surrender!"

As much as I dreaded and hated the force-feeding, what came next made me crazed almost to the point of insanity. I heard the doctor working his way down the cells, and knew Helena must be facing him soon. I wept for her then, and wracked my brain feverishly as to a way I could save her from this fate. I found no answers.

The matron came to see me that evening. I was lying on my bed, shaking with cold and shock, my mouth still bleeding from the metal implement the doctor had used to pry my jaws open, my throat shredded by the large tube. I sat up when she handed me a jug of water.

"I won't ask you how you are, because I can see that for myself," she said. "I promised to tell you about Miss St. John, as I knew you must be worried about her. She is as well as can be expected, but I am worried that she has a fever. I have asked the doctor to see her. He said he will do so in the morning."

I stared at her dully, not comprehending what she said. It was hard for me to concentrate, but I made an effort and focused on each word she spoke.

"Please, please have him release her." My voice came out cracked and hoarse. "She is too fragile to withstand this treatment."

"I will do what I can. Try to get some sleep now."

Left to my own private nightmare, I sank into an exhausted sleep in which there was no rest, only horror.

Time ceased to exist for me. I know it must have been the following day when I heard the doctor making his rounds again, but I had no feeling of time passing. There was no distinction between what was real and what was imagined. I could hear the screams, the sounds of the struggle, and the defiant, "No surrender!" follow the doctor as he came down the corridor. A rattle at my door indicated he had arrived. I gritted my teeth, and looked up to see a wardress beckoning at me.

"Get up and come with me. The Governor wants to see you."

She had to repeat the message before I could comprehend it. My legs were so weak I stumbled into the door as I left my cell. Taking a deep breath, I lifted my chin, stood up straight, and walked slowly and deliberately after her. I had to concentrate on taking one step after another, but at last I made it to the Governor's offices. I was left sitting in an outer chamber, the door locked behind me. I sat with my head between my knees to keep from swooning, sure they had brought me in to tell me Helena had died. I wondered how long I could stand the treatment, certain now that I would not be released. Did I have the strength to last the entire nine months of my sentence?

There were no tears left for me to shed as I waited endless, grievous hours, dreading every passing footstep in case it should bring me news of Helena's demise. Unused to the lights and relatively fresh air, I stood up and walked around the room to regain the use of my legs. The door opened behind me, but when I tried to turn quickly, I stumbled and would have fallen had not strong arms caught me.

"Cassandra, my beautiful, brave Cassandra," a voice murmured in my ears, a familiar voice that accompanied kisses pressed to my forehead. "Tell me you're all right, sweetheart. Tell me you haven't been hurt."

I lifted my head and Griffin's beloved face swam before me. Reaching a hand up to touch it, I asked, "Where on earth did you get another black eye?" just before I fainted.

310

CHAPTER TWENTY-SIX

"Helena!"

I wept tears of sheer joy when, five minutes after Griffin and the wardress brought me around, Helena staggered into the room.

"Cassandra? Griffin?" She collapsed into Griffin's arms, weeping hoarsely. I made my way over to them, hugging them both, feeling my own happy tears mingle with hers.

"You look much better than I imagined," I told her, although I noted her eyes had a feverish brightness to them.

"I am just so happy to see you both," she said, letting Griffin ease her into a chair.

"I have brought you some tea," the wardress said as I took the seat next to Helena.

We looked at each other, then at the wardress. She made an annoyed sound and added, "You can drink it, you've been officially released. The charges against you were dropped."

I have had many beverages in my life, but none that tasted of such ambrosia as did that hot, sweet tea. As we were sipping it gratefully, Robert raced into the room and flung himself at Helena's feet. Griffin had been hovering between Helena and me, but with the arrival of Robert, he sat next to me, pulling me to his side with a protective arm.

"Robert? Oh, my dear, darling Robert!" Helena murmured, stroking his head. When he looked up, I was shocked by his face— he had a torn lip, an oddly shaped nose, and two discolored eyes.

I turned to Griffin, who was scowling at the wardress as she fussed with the tea things. "What happened to Robert? Did he break his nose? And why do you both have black eyes?"

He pulled me closer. "I'll tell you once we're out of this damned place."

Helena had to be carried out of the prison. I made it on my own feet, although I was glad for Griffin's strong arm. I admit that I collapsed into his embrace on the way home, but I didn't feel that

Robert and Helena would care. I was a little puzzled as to why we were taking Joshua's carriage home, but leaning against Griffin's shoulder with his arm around me, I didn't feel like inquiring. I did ask how he had secured our release.

"I saw some people," he said grimly. "Letitia helped."

"Letitia?" Tucked as I was against him, I could not see his face, but watched his Adam's apple fondly as he spoke. "I thought she refused to help Helena?"

"She did, until it became worth her while to do so."

I wanted to ask what Griffin did to make it worth her while, but a suspicion took hold and was confirmed when we stopped in front of my sister's house.

Mabel and Joshua were on the doorstep to greet us, as was Doctor Melrose. Robert carried Helena up the stairs to the guest room, the doctor following closely behind.

"Shall I take you to bed as well?" Griffin asked.

I tried to summon up a smile. "Is that an improper suggestion, Mr. St. John, or do you just wish to be rid of me?"

Griffin kissed me gently in response, and helped me into the library. I sat on the leather couch with my feet up, wrapped in a rug, and sipped the brandy Griffin ordered me to drink. He sat on the floor next to me, close enough so I could twine my fingers through his hair in between sips.

"All right," I said, putting the brandy snifter down, pulling the hand he was kissing free. "Enough, my head is swimming. Would you please tell me what has been happening? How did you get us out?"

"Letitia put me in touch with some of Sherry's friends. I showed them a few letters she gave me which detailed his plan to destroy the suffrage movement, you, Helena, me…and incidentally, a number of members of the House of Lords who did not see eye-to-eye with Sherry. They agreed to help me in order to cover up what would be an otherwise ugly scandal involving a peer and the House. When the police were presented with the testimony of two impeccable witnesses who stated that you and Helena were unjustly arrested, the charges were dropped and you were freed."

I ran my finger lightly along his jaw. He took my hand again and kissed my fingers. Little sparks of fire ran down my arms to start a thrumming deep inside me.

"What did you have to do to make Lady Sherringham help you?"

He looked at my fingertips. "I gave her something she had wanted for a long time."

I put a hand on his cheek and turned his face toward mine. "You gave her your house?"

"Yes. How did you know?"

I smiled at his handsome face. "A guess. They always seemed to be lord and lady of the manor there, I assumed they felt the house was rightfully theirs even though your brother lost it. With her husband locked away, what else does she have?"

Mabel accompanied a maid laden with a tea tray. "You will be happy to know that Doctor Melrose says Helena is not suffering from any illness, just exhaustion and malnutrition."

'Thank God," I murmured gratefully.

She poured me a large cup of tea, and loaded a plate with food. "You drink that tea first, then eat."

I looked askance at the food. "Mabel, there is no way I could eat half of that."

Griffin took the plate and said quietly to my sister, "I'll see that she eats."

Mabel beamed at him, looked at me fondly, and bustled out. I took a few sips at the tea, and sighed as it slid down my sore throat. "Oh, that is heaven."

Griffin sat next to me on the couch, kissing my throat in a most distracting way.

"What have you done with Mabel?" I asked, having gathered enough wits together to remember how to speak. "I expected to receive a tongue-lashing like none I have received before."

"I'm sure you will hear from her about the subject," he said with amusement, transferring his kisses to my jaw. "I think just now she is simply grateful you are back."

I turned my head until he gave me what I wanted. His mouth was warm and caressing, not demanding and aggressive as it usually was, but soft and teasing, gently stroking away the horror of the last few days and replacing the pain with pleasure.

I pulled away from the hot lure of his mouth and touched his second bruised eye. "Now, tell me about that."

He sighed, and made himself comfortable, which meant I was made extremely comfortable half-draped across his chest. "Hunter and I were in the balcony of that blasted hall, watching over you."

I made a sound of protest, but he stopped it with his mouth.

"I won't tell you unless you drink that tea," he said, pulling away and nodding toward the cup. "And no interruptions."

I hurriedly picked up the tea. "Continue."

"We had a feeling that there was going to be trouble, so we decided to watch over you two from the balcony. When the police sprang out from their hiding places, we knew you were in a dangerous situation. We tried to get down to you but the entire crowd panicked, and we were caught on the stairs, pinned and unable to go anywhere. By the time we did make it downstairs and onto the main floor, the police had most of the women rounded up. We went to free you and ended up fighting the police." He touched his eye gingerly. "I got this as a souvenir. We were charged with assaulting a policeman, and thrown into jail for three days. I tried to reach everyone I knew who had some pull, but had no luck."

I put down my tea, touched that he had risked his own life for ours.

"When we were released, I went home and found that Letitia had refused to help Helena. I knew your family did not have the contacts to help you, so I persuaded Letitia to give me Sherry's journal and the letters that detailed his plans."

I thought for a few moments. "And now you are homeless?"

"Yes," he grimaced. "Your brother-in-law has kindly offered to shelter Helena until I can set up a new house."

"And Robert? Have you promised to help Robert so he can marry Helena?"

"Ah, Robert. Oddly enough, I have an acquaintance in East Africa who is looking for someone to manage his sizable coffee farm while he is away."

"Really?" I asked suspiciously.

He gave me an enigmatic smile. "Hunter thinks it will be ideal for him. I have a feeling that in time, my friend will be willing to sell him the farm. I think Helena will like Africa."

"There's Freddy to be taken care of yet. I dislike the thought of him being allowed to escape without repercussion of his foul actions."

"Your cousin will be taken care of," Griffin said with a grim note of promise in his voice that I decided I would not investigate. Whatever Freddy suffered, he had coming to him.

"I see," I said gravely. "And what about us, do you think I would marry a man who cannot even provide me with a home?"

He looked at me, his amber eyes glowing with an incandescent light. We stared deeply into each other's eyes, then he grinned that charming, irresistible, boyish grin.

"Won't you?" he asked, pulling onto his lap, his hand sliding under my skirt, up the length of my bare leg.

"Well," I said softly as I nibbled his ear, "as you are asking, I suppose I will."

ABOUT THE AUTHOR

For as long as she can remember, Katie MacAlister has loved reading. Growing up in a family where a weekly visit to the library was a given, Katie spent much of her time with her nose buried in a book. Despite her love for novels, she didn't think of writing them until she was contracted to write a non-fiction book about software. Since her editor refused to allow her to include either witty dialogue or love scenes in the software book, Katie swiftly resolved to switch to fiction, where she could indulge in world building, tormenting characters, and falling madly in love with all her heroes.

Two years after she started writing novels, Katie sold her first romance, Noble Intentions. More than thirty books later, her novels have been translated into numerous languages, been recorded as audiobooks, received several awards, and are regulars on the *New York Times*, *USA Today*, and *Publishers Weekly* bestseller lists. She also writes for the young adult audience as Katie Maxwell.

Katie lives in the Pacific Northwest with her husband and dogs, and can often be found lurking around online. You can visit her at www.katiemacalister.com or www.dragonsepts.com

CPSIA information can be obtained at www.ICGtesting.com
Printed in the USA
LVOW10s1731220316

480284LV00012B/189/P